Mary Lee watched him make himself a cup of instant coffee and begin sipping it black. "Curtiss, you're saying the West's major profit centers are being bought out from under us. That organized crime will be the universal boss of us all."

"Not right away, Mary Lee."

"Then when?"

"Maybe never."

He took the rest of the cracker from her and began munching it. "The way I see it, the mob could have started doing this long ago. They have had a billion-plus in cash flow ever since, say, the 1960s. It's all laundered and untraceable."

Curtiss picked up his cup. There was no sound except a glass chip pinging out of the window. A round hole opened. The cup in Curtiss's hand exploded. . . .

GAMEPLAN

GAMEPLAN

Leslie Waller

BANTAM BOOKS
TORONTO · NEW YORK · LONDON · SYDNEY

*This low-priced Bantam Book
has been completely reset in a type face
designed for easy reading, and was printed
from new plates. It contains the complete
text of the original hard-cover edition.*
NOT ONE WORD HAS BEEN OMITTED.

GAMEPLAN
A Bantam Book

PRINTING HISTORY

*First published in Great Britain by Granada Publishing 1983
Bantam edition / May 1984*

ISBN 0-553-24244-X

Published simultaneously in the United States and Canada

*Bantam Books are published by Bantam Books, Inc. Its trade-
mark, consisting of the words "Bantam Books" and the por-
trayal of a rooster, is Registered in U.S. Patent and Trademark
Office and in other countries. Marca Registrada. Bantam
Books, Inc., 666 Fifth Avenue, New York, New York 10103.*

PRINTED IN THE UNITED STATES OF AMERICA

H   0 9 8 7 6 5 4 3 2 1

PART ONE

·

The Siege of the Cité Odiot

1

At Snowfire, eleven thousand feet high among the awesome peaks of the Sangre de Cristos, the main lodge and cottages were designed by a disciple of Frank Lloyd Wright from nearby Taliesin West. But the private home that dominates the peak, higher than anything else, is only a series of anonymous prefab cubes, flown in by helicopter and joined together in a careless sprawl, as if a child had thrown down its nursery blocks in the keen, thin, noiseless air.

Although it has its own funicular, the scatter of connected cubes is usually reached by helicopter. Locals say the owner pilots himself. Although they have little to do with him, they can fairly accurately describe him as young, tall, spare of frame, handsome in an intense, dark-eyed way.

One of the cube modules is double-pane glass, a kind of solarium twenty feet square. Locals arriving by copter have seen the owner in the glass room, reading, napping, eating snack meals. In fact, he usually sleeps here in the intense silence once the sun disappears behind the range to the west. The rest of the time he spends elsewhere in the congeries of cubes.

He can usually be found in the terminal room, which remains in permanent night. His eyes require a minute or two to adjust to the change from the brilliant sun of the solarium. Then the video and high-speed printers are easily operated. He can patch into a satellite link he rents by the year. The segment is blind below the equator but covers places important to him: London, Paris, Basel, Milan, Frankfurt, Vienna, Singapore, Hong Kong and Tokyo.

This week the weather over Snowfire had been particularly clear and constant. As the sky lightened at about six a.m., a perfect bowl of bright blue began to stretch from east to west over the solarium cube. The tall young man awoke at once, checked his wristwatch and moved into the eternal darkness of the terminal room.

Without waiting for his irises to adjust he punched up the cathode projector array and let it get warm. It cast across the far wall a television image test pattern the size of a bedsheet. He shifted the projector to a memory program and tapped out instructions on a nearby computer console.

Instantly a broad chart glowed in fervid color on the far wall. Across the top, starting at the left, were four pairs of dates: 1814–1819, 1861–1871, 1920–1929 and 1974–198?.

Below these dates a thick black graph line rose and fell like a series of ragged incisor teeth in the muzzle of some gigantic mastiff or hound. The line peaked abruptly at the first of each pair of dates. Then it dropped slightly. It peaked again, a little lower, at the second of each pair. Across the top of this chart, in brilliant crimson, ran the legend:

KONDRATIEV PROJECTION 55-YR K-WAVE

The tall young man squinted through the half-dark at what was a statistical picture of world economies for almost the past two centuries. He touched the keyboard and the image on the wall zoomed in on the last double peak, 1974–198?. He tapped in a new command. The computer changed 55 to 65 and began regressing a year at a time.

The man who had summoned all this up sat watching the due-date of the next major world depression. It shifted slowly back from 1995 to 1985. One had one's choice. The interlocked economies of the West would tumble, crash and self-destruct on any of ten dates, depending on the mathematical model used.

He who had caused this ultimate in bad news to be spread across the entire far wall now stared gloomily at his handiwork. The computer retraced its steps and repeated its slow countdown to oblivion like the tolling of a great funeral bell.

In the hectic light of the great wall projection, the man's face showed concern, but not the kind one would expect if this were the fever chart of a human being dear to him. He looked, instead, something like a crack surgeon checking life signs before cutting in.

At last he snapped off the display, patched into his leased

circuit and tapped out 011–41–61, access code for Basel. He added six more digits for a private number.

"*Salü?*" a man's voice said.

"Urs," the dark young man began, "that impact analysis." The Basler switched to English. "I have it."

"Give it to me on loony tunes."

He punched up an image on the nearest video screen. The picture that snapped into view was hash, dots, splinters and blobs. He coded in two more numbers and the scrambled image appeared quite legibly. It read:

SEP 12 GAMEPLAN INPUT. CLIENT DISCOUNTING PARIS SOURCE. GRADE 2 SURVEILLANCE ONLY. IF SOURCE REOPENED ESCALATE TO GRADE 1 SECURITY. TERMINATE PARIS SOURCE AT ONCE.

"OK for a go, Urs. You distribute simulfax scrambled."

"Right, Ben. *Wiedersehen.*" The line to Basel went dead and so did the image on the video screen.

Methodically, the young man in the terminal room shut down all systems. He sat there in the darkness, thinking about the need to commit such an incriminating directive to video, even scrambled video.

But the people for whom the order was destined were the kind who treated written matter with greater care and accuracy. Oral directives could be misunderstood, especially since they often needed translation into other languages.

It didn't pay, this late in Gameplan, to overlook such matters. It didn't pay to let an avoidable error jeopardize ten years of hard work, especially an error in a directive as important as killing a man.

2

Turning north off the Champs-Élysées into the rue Washington, one quickly reaches an archway on the right that leads out of the noisy heart of Paris along a short tunnel and into a parklike garden ringed by small apartment houses. It is the Cité Odiot, very private, very discreet, an ideal place for Curtiss to live.

He likes everything looking natural, ordinary. His apartment is also his office. If one mounts the stairs to the second floor and enters Curtiss's rather large flat, one finds few rooms, all big. The smallest of the four is the office, proximity wired with heat, sound and air-turbulence sensors.

But, again, natural and discreet. The alarms are silent. They activate low-light-enhancement television cameras. There is nothing much to steal in Curtiss's apartment-office, but he is always interested in watching a videotape of someone who might try to crack his safe. (There is nothing much in the safe, either, another of Curtiss's typical ploys.) If one were looking for the few papers he needs to keep on hand, they would be found folded into the pages of the *International Herald-Tribune* lying carelessly in his magazine rack. Curtiss, like Edgar Allan Poe in *The Purloined Letter*, relies on the most fundamental, the simplest strategies.

Like a lot of Parisians, Curtiss comes home for lunch. In his case it is not to take a nap but because his main office opens at nine a.m. in New York and his boss, Bill Elston, likes to get on the phone then, which is three in the Paris afternoon.

It was, as a matter of fact, only two p.m. when Elston's call came through on that cold, dark, drizzling October afternoon in 1980. Curtiss had finished a small home-made lunch, no more than cheese, bread and soup.

"*Allo, oui?*" he responded.

The telephone gave a chirrup, as of a fat cricket in the hot sun. Curtiss frowned and placed the receiver in a foam-rubber padded cradle. He glanced at the wall calendar in his office. The scrambler code was simple if one had the date correct. October was the tenth month. Today was Tuesday, second day of the business week. Two into ten made five. Curtiss set the scrambler to Number 5, sat down and picked up the machine's own telephone.

"Good morning, Bill."

Elston coughed for a moment. "Morning, Curtiss. Sorry for the scrambler voodoo but this bears the AA label."

"So the only people to know will be you, me and the Sûreté, once they decode the scrambler."

"Sûreté wouldn't be interested in this." He coughed again. "Who said anything good about autumn in New York?" he asked nobody in particular. "Lousy, polluted, humid, germ-laden." He stopped himself. "Does the name Mary Lee Hunter mean anything to you?"

Curtiss sat back in the chair and glanced out of the office window at a day easily as miserable as the one Elston had described. "She from that Delaware banking family?"

"That's the one."

"Just signed on as an exec. vee-pee at Jet-Tech?"

"Executive Vice-President, Financial," Elston amended. "She's Jet-Tech's liaison with us, their lead bank. I don't have to tell you, if Jet-Tech asks for something, we kind of stir our ass getting it."

"What is Miz Mar'lee askin' fer?" Curtiss drawled.

"She's just a li'l ole country girl from the horsy part of Maryland. All she has is her MBA from Stanford and six years with the Federal Reserve, doing games-theory planning and making computers sit up and beg. But she's still innocent enough to think that somewhere out there exist real answers."

"To what questions?"

"Nothing immense. Little things like, uh, what's going to happen to the human race? Small stuff."

"And she's dumb enough to ask a bank?"

"Not *a* bank, Curtiss." Elston's voice got mock-huffy, except that, as Curtiss knew, he really meant it. "*The* bank. *The* largest commercial bank in the world, United Bank and Trust Company, NA. The one that pays your vast salary and mendacious expense account." He coughed loudly and long.

Curtiss sat waiting for Elston to climb back down from what was, for him, an emotional outburst. UBCO kept only one security man in Europe. It had hundreds of uniformed guards at dozens of offices from London to Vienna. But only Curtiss handled delicate security matters, absconding vice-presidents, swindlers who had conned New York into lending on stolen bonds, borrowers who had gone bad and taken to the tall timber, the occasional corrupt government hoping to weasel out of its UBCO loans by fomenting a fake revolution, the occasional real revolution bankrupting an otherwise creditworthy regime.

"Anyway, Curtiss, I am telefaxing you her stuff, scrambled, at 1600 hours your time today. Give it top priority."

"I'm trying to find Bulic."

"Bulic will have to wait. You thought he might be suicided by now."

"Until I know that, I have to assume he's alive and still in possession of those bearer bonds."

"Put Bulic on the back burner. Dream up some crystal ball stuff for Miss Hunter. Grade A Bumpf. Make it look like you know what you're talking about. Fax it back to me by tomorrow. Bulic can wait till then."

He couldn't. Curtiss found him in a small weekly rental flat on the Île de la Cité the next evening. Bulic had stuffed the windows and turned on the gas. They don't always forget the pilot light, Curtiss noted, but in this case Bulic had. The stone front of the building had blown around dinner time, spoiling many people's appetites and ruining Bulic's for all eternity. Although it was possible that the explosion had also blown the bearer notes to the next world, Curtiss doubted it. Somewhere in the crowd that gathered quickly around the ruined house, some neighbor was even now wondering what to do with the bits of paper he had surreptitiously pocketed.

So an otherwise unmemorable week in October 1980 had passed with only one highlight to its account. Later, when Curtiss had cause to remember the start of Operation Gameplan, the week in which he wrote that memo to Mary Lee Hunter was easy for him to recall. It was the week Bulic had blown himself up.

He still retained a copy of her original questionnaire, headed "Gameplan Survey: Main business trends of the 1980s." Her questions had ranged from what the respondent thought would happen to lending rates all the way to his forecast of political trends. Curtiss assumed she had polled political scientists far cannier than he on such matters. His notions of interest rates wouldn't be likely to thrill her much, either. So he had bypassed most of the stuff and gone right to the "Other" section.

"Other" was the name of Curtiss's game. "Other" covered his field of expertise. The often ludicrous, often nasty, always fascinating traits of other human nature that didn't fall into neat columns under economics or politics, these were what Curtiss knew best.

He could tell, for example, where a fifty-year-old vice-president of UBCO would go, having abstracted himself half a million dollars of bank funds. It wasn't that Curtiss was an expert on male menopause, being still in his thirties, but more that he understood what a colorless bank officer would feel he *deserved* from life after thirty drab years working his way only partly up the UBCO tree.

That was one reason he kept his office in Paris. With the Côte d'Azur of Southern France and the Costa Brava of Spain, these were the three tired, tatty targets of lost opportunity an absconding vice-president would head for. It often took Curtiss as long as forty-eight hours to pick him up, get the money and pack him off to his wife and kids in Scarsdale, New York. The rest was up to Bill Elston.

It was the side of the human heart that turns wild and criminal which Curtiss knew best. He had a kind of innate empathy with those who go bad. In his early days as a scrounging travel writer, dining like a king one week as the guest of some hotel chain and starving the next, he had had his first frightened peep into the dark heart of crime that we all carry in our breast.

Curtiss still kept his travel-writer cover. "Travels with Curtiss" continued to be syndicated in a few newspapers, enough to give him at least a low grade of journalistic credential. It was enough for his work, which in a way resembled that of a journalist: moving around, asking questions, trying to make sense of the answers.

He hoped Mary Lee Hunter would make some sense of his, even though she'd have one hell of a time coding it into a computer projection. He had heard nothing back on the questionnaire, either from her or from Bill Elston, so he supposed it had slipped by without much notice or remark.

He was quite wrong. Although Curtiss took pride in his work, he had very little sense of his own unique abilities. If asked, he would never describe himself in any but an ordinary manner, something like his apartment or the way he dressed, jeans, sports jackets, striped shirts under sweaters, no tie, the whole effect self-effacing in an American ambience but a bit distinctive in Paris.

He had no idea, for example, that the things put into his response for Jet-Tech were that much different from what others were thinking. Nor could he have dreamed that it so upset his boss, Bill Elston, that he almost refused to pass it along to the client. Instead, he had leaked it privately over a lunch with Mary Lee Hunter, sounding her out to see if she wanted her carefully programmed projections warped and skewed by the input of, as he called Curtiss, "a loon, a maverick, our best man."

That was why Curtiss was so totally unprepared for what happened the next year, 1981.

As a lot of leading people at Jet-Tech had remarked about Mary Lee Hunter, she was definitely not what one expected in the way of a top financial executive or any other kind of female manager. Too tall to be cute, she was an attractive young woman who had learned something not taught at Wharton or Stanford, how to dress.

She was certainly not what Dave Grissom had expected when they'd bypassed him and replaced his former boss with Mary Lee. Grissom had not been bitter, not openly and, like many another financial man, he'd learned the value of patience. His father had inculcated it. He'd given Dave a silver dollar bearing the year of his birth, 1950, on each of his thirty-one birthdays. The value of this collection now stood at about thirty-one dollars. Ah, but at some future moment, Dave sincerely believed, their value would soar out of sight.

Although this story wasn't widely known around Jet-Tech, Mary Lee learned of it her first week. "Why, Dave," she'd enthused, "would you believe my Daddy did exactly the same thing for me?"

Grissom tried not to return her friendly grin, but he lost. "So the two of us," he kidded, "are going to be rich some day, right?"

"You, maybe." Mary Lee's smile had brightened her pretty face. "Me, I cashed them on my twenty-fifth birthday and started buying into a Sausalito building and loan. The twenty-five bucks are worth about two thousand by now."

It was no wonder Grissom detested her, but he was quite alone at Jet-Tech, particularly in the upper management echelons where Mary Lee's forecasts were devastatingly accurate and, thus, profitable. To have included a report like the one UBCO had sent from its man in Paris would have upset everything. Curtiss's ideas ranked 10 on Mary Lee's Richter scale, the trembling uptick of a major quake in what seemed to be the firm foundation underlying Jet-Tech and, indeed the profit centers of capitalism. Or else Curtiss was some kind of kook.

Then came the Consolidated Welding flap. The small firm handled so much of Jet-Tech's subcontracting that the big company wanted to buy it. When more money didn't seem to do the trick, Mary Lee asked Dave Grissom for a report. A week later he'd come up empty. A telex to Dun and Bradstreet—an elementary procedure which Grissom should have known—produced the information that Consolidated was controlled by an anonymous syndicate operating through Bank Rup in Basel. In other words, Jet-Tech was bidding against organized crime in one of its faceless incarnations.

"But this is what that UBCO character warned us about," Mary Lee Hunter told her board that day. "One of these days, as soon as I can shake loose, I'm going to Paris to pick brain."

Her board chairman, a man in his early fifties called Lederer, made a pained face. "Not till we finish this damned—"

"I know," Mary Lee cut in. She shuffled through taupe colored folders. "It never rains but it pours, my mother says," she quoted deliberately, having observed that a few ladlefuls of folk wisdom usually reassured her board and, in particular, Lederer, that she was older and more prudent than she looked.

"Here." She distributed stapled packets of financial sheets from a folder labeled "New Issue." The eight men sitting around the table grunted noncommittally as they paged through the report.

"It's not a new concept, the zero percent debenture," Mary Lee began. She waited for someone to ask for an explanation, but men never did. How would it look to admit they didn't understand what the one woman did? "At the risk of oversimplifying," she went on as if asked, "it's a bond issue that pays no interest on redemption. But it's sold at a large up-front discount. This assures the buyer of a return he can count on, whatever the interest rates will be in ten years. And it assures us that everyone holds onto our paper for the full ten years. Then we redeem it at face value, meaning we can budget for it with total accuracy."

Lederer shifted uneasily in his chair. "I don't know," he muttered, which was his way of asking what the others felt before committing himself.

Mary Lee Hunter looked from one face to the next, ready with whatever answers were required. Someone on the board would be sure to ask how much of a discount they would have to give away to attract investors. For this she had no answer as yet. It would be a matter of intense and bloody bargaining

with the East Coast brokerages handling the issue,
bargaining that would not come to a head for some time yet,
fortunately.

As she looked around, she had the same feeling she always
did in these board meetings, of being caged in with hostile
animals. Not tigers, not this bunch. But certainly jackals.
This was a *male* place, Mary Lee Hunter knew. Male things
went on here and often there wasn't time to clean up the
carcasses between acts.

It seemed only fair to Mary Lee—and once she'd explained
it, to Curtiss, too—that their business needn't be transacted
in the mingy little room Curtiss occasionally used at UBCO's
branch behind the Ritz. The thing needed more air, in Mary
Lee's opinion, which was why she conducted their first
interview over a dinner in a Champs-Élysées restaurant that
would end up costing Jet-Tech the equivalent of several
hundred dollars, before deductions.

"So," Curtiss said, exhaling with pleasure, "is this how it
goes in the States these days?"

Mary Lee watched their waiter pour a third bottle of wine.
"God, no. We only drink California stuff." His face went
foggy. "You mean doing business over a big-ticket meal?" she
went on. "The corporate mode in my age bracket is New
Austerity. Jogging, Perrier and alfalfa sprouts. I happen to
like indigestibly rich food and wine." She poured more into
each of their glasses, bringing the level near the brim.

"They hate people to do that," Curtiss said, grinning
broadly.

She frowned with some authority. "It's not red. Doesn't
need air in the glass." She sipped the sweet dessert Sauterne.
"Okay. Business."

Curtiss glanced around the restaurant. "This place is designed to keep the cares of the world at bay. My flat's only a
few blocks away. We can have after-dinner liqueurs in—"

"—peace and quiet," Mary Lee finished for him.

Curtiss assured himself he had no ulterior motive. But
when she agreed he felt something expand under his heart.
Then a moment of uneasiness: she'd seemed too intelligent
for such an old ploy. Then he forgot any such qualms. After
all, it hadn't been a ploy.

3

Most of Mary Lee Hunter's encounters with men had proceeded along the usual two lines. There were the men who had picked her because she was tall and thus something of an achievement to knock down. Or there were those who had chosen her because she was extremely bright and, when defeated mentally, constituted a living monument to their— the men's—intelligence.

This Ping-Pong kind of relationship to the opposite sex had begun quite early with Mary Lee, in childhood as a matter of fact, amid three brothers who regularly punched, toppled, tramped on and mentally vanquished each other a dozen times a day. If there were a Hunter family slogan it was the gleeful expletive "Gotcha!" yelped at a moment of triumph.

She had grown up to be a very competitive young woman who was in the process, now in her early thirties, of tramping on and vanquishing her brothers, all of whom worked in the family bank. Mary Lee had chosen the financial-life career too, but in the business world. She expected by the time she retired—somewhere in her early forties—to have left her brothers light-years behind.

It was thus something of a tactical reverse for her when Curtiss took her back to his apartment and proceeded to talk finance.

Three wines or not, Mary Lee had already sensed stirrings in Curtiss's libido. A woman who couldn't pick up those signals in her antennae would never have got as far in life as Mary Lee. But in his odd, even strange apartment in the Cité Odiot it was as if he had suddenly remembered she and Jet-Tech were clients of UBCO and had to be treated that way.

Sipping a sweet wine called Lillet, Mary Lee glanced around the living room and saw that Curtiss had stripped one long wall back to the bricks and caused to be fastened into it immense timbers, four-by-tens as long as the room. These giant's shelves were filled with ashtrays, small pictures in

13

easel frames, a sandstone statue four inches high, books, magazines, an inlaid box that looked as if it might play music, not much more than that.

The rest of the room was bare, except for an end table, a Moroccan rug across the parquetry and two easy chairs.

She tried to picture his life here, this lone sentinel of American banking expertise, this guardian of UBCO's internal security. Obviously he had his guests one at a time. Or none at any time. Yet it hadn't seemed difficult for him to invite her here.

She contrasted this bachelor pad with her own, in a high-rise condominium-cum-swimming-pool community near Redlands, California, where Jet-Tech's home offices spread out over many acres amid orange groves and lettuce farms.

She, too, had a big living room, but its outer wall was glass, leading to a sun terrace. Where Curtiss had a bedroom and an office, she had precisely the same layout, minus the burglar-proofing she had noticed but not mentioned when he showed her the place. But, try as she might, Mary Lee had never achieved this stripped-down, monastic-cell look. Resist as she might, she could never *not* put up the new painting or add the new whatnot to the glass étagère. She was an accumulator. Curtiss was either a thrower-away or a non-buyer.

". . . especially at this moment in financial history," he was saying.

Mary Lee almost blinked, but it would have been too easy a clue to a detective mind like Curtiss's that she hadn't been paying attention. "Why this moment?" she managed to ask.

"The great leveling is about to begin," he said. He sipped his Lillet. "For the past fifty years, two-thirds of the world has gone down and the third we live in has gone up. I am not arguing that this was deliberate, that we pushed down the Third World to aggrandize our own lives. I am merely making the simple observation."

"But you said a leveling would begin?"

"Our world, which we call the West for some silly reason, is about to sink beneath the waves. The rest of the world is not going to rise. It's going to be as famished and disease-ridden as ever. But now we of the West are going to be right down there in the mud and lice with them."

Mary Lee put her glass down on a curved plywood end table. "Curtiss, I didn't come four thousand miles to hear this kind of gloom-and-doom scenario. I am an upbeat chick. I am a real Chamber of Commerce go-getter. Us Jet-Tech execs think positive."

"When you think at all," Curtiss amended. He remembered to smile.

She noted with slight satisfaction that he definitely wasn't giving her the client-kid-gloves treatment. Perhaps there was hope for him.

"Where does the Mafia fit into it, then?" she persisted.

"Stop thinking Mafia." He got up and began pacing, something she felt he did a lot of in this monk's cell of his. "There is a Mafia in every major industrial or community center of the West. But it's only a core, around which all elements of crime collect. In some places the organization doesn't even have many Italians or Sicilians in it. In some places it does. Much better to call it a syndicate. Or a conglomerate."

"Whatever you like to call it," she told him, "where does it come into this crummy scenario?"

"The report of mine last year," he responded. "It simply said that organized crime had a way of secretly buying control of major corporations. My point was that where there's a way, it will be taken. It's a form of Murphy's Law. If it can happen, it will. The syndicate's cash flow, just from the U.S. alone, is many billions a year. These megabucks go to Swiss numbered accounts for laundering. They come back to the States as buy orders on blue chip stock, or loans on construction, or merger tenders or what-have-you."

"I know. We learned that one the hard way."

"But if you were running this syndicate operation, and you suddenly got the notion—the obsession—that you wanted to buy up every major profit center of the West from British Petroleum and Siemens to General Motors and Kodak, it still wouldn't be possible."

Mary Lee heaved a mock sigh of relief. "Can I have some more of this junk?"

He filled her glass. "Icky sweet, huh?"

"I'm working on liking it."

He topped off his own glass and sat down in the chair opposite hers. "It still wouldn't be possible because even the mob's immense cash flow is not nearly enough to grab a controlling share of Western capitalism. But."

Mary Lee made a face. "I don't like the sound of your but."

He grinned at her. "But at the moment the whole West is

expecting a major financial contraction. In Europe, we're looking at what may be worse than a recession. In the States some economists are predicting a deep depression, especially the people who follow Kondratiev theories."

She nodded and said nothing. Jet-Tech had already laid off a third of its workforce worldwide, doing it in dribs and drabs to avoid publicity. So had other space-technology industries. Every company was cutting back, but calling it a process of "streamlining." She glanced at Curtiss, who was watching her intently, like Ruts, a wirehair terrier she once had, when she went anywhere near his leash and he sensed he might be taken for a walk. For a moment, watching his intent look, the memory of Ruts flooded over her.

Her view of him suddenly misted over. "Is something wrong?" he asked.

Mary Lee shook her head. "Keep talking, Curtiss." She sniffed mightily.

"What was I—? Oh, yeah. Brink of world depression. Okay. I was saying that especially at this moment in history, a syndicate strategist might see a way to achieve his magnificent obsession. Because in a downturn lie many, many bargains."

He hunched forward on his chair now, intent on finishing his explanation. "Let's say a few years back, maybe five, this underworld genius began buying lots of stock. Some corporations are so widely held that you can control them through a percentage of ownership as narrow as 10 or 12. Some are so closely held you have to buy up 30 or more percent. It's a long process because if you move too fast you alarm the corporation and give away your hand."

Mary Lee nodded. Why did he have to resemble Ruts, she asked herself. That was pretty sneaky of fate, wasn't it? She tried to focus on what he was saying.

"So the years go by and you're establishing a very solid secret position. The stuff you're buying is all what you believe to be depression-proof. That means basic industries, foodstuffs, but nothing in services or housing or autos. Our mythical Mafia manager is buying into oil companies and the like. But his eye is on the drop."

"Meaning what?" She sniffed again. The tears were gone. Damn this Lillet. It must be stronger than it tasted.

"Once the markets crash all over the world, once lines of credit crumble and banks close and millions are out of work and companies are facing bankruptcy, there are an awful lot of bargains to be picked up. Stock prices plummet. A company that would have taken you five years and a hundred million to control you can now have in five minutes for ten million. It's just that crude."

She nodded vigorously, to show that she was following his line of thought. "You scavenge," she said. "But why isn't your own cash flow as pinched down as everybody else's?"

He was silent for a moment. "People will always need drugs and stolen goods. They will always need to gamble and watch pornography. They will always want something that's illegal that only their friendly neighborhood mobster can promise them because he's got the local law in his pocket. And, even in depressions, there are still rich people. They need a speeding violation removed from their driver's license. They need a strike broken. They need a strategic material when there's a shortage of it. They need a murder hushed up. They need the industrial secrets of their competitor. They need two girls who will do anything they ask for the next twenty-four hours. They need a senator removed and a friendlier one elected. They need a tax indictment quashed. They need laundered cash. They need personal cash sequestered in secret accounts. They need an inconvenient wife removed. They need an island republic overthrown. Dear God, what don't they need that organized crime is not ready and able to provide? For a price. So please, Mary Lee, don't worry about the syndicate's cash flow during bad times."

She started to sip her wine but ended up draining the glass. This guy was tough going, wasn't he? He didn't seem to want to topple her or best her in a mental contest, he simply wanted to depress her enough so she cut her throat.

"Curtiss," she said. There was a long pause. "Curtiss?" He waited. "Curtiss, do you actually believe all that?"

He nodded. "I believe that if it was ever possible, it gets even more so when we head into a depression. I think now's the time. I think our mythical genius thinks so too."

"I mean all that stuff about the rich. You think they're that corrupt? That amoral? That immoral?"

"Is that a nerve ending you don't want pressed?"

She laughed softly. "Is that a question I have to answer? You are looking at Miss Overachiever, Curtiss. I have gone far and fast. It's not that I'm a hungry kid from the slums. I could always eat, Curtiss. But I've been programmed somehow, by my own brothers I suspect, to get as high as I can where the real power is. And now you tell me it's hazardous to human life at that level."

"Yes. I did say that, implicitly. I think the West has always been a hazardous place, for the life of the planet and its inhabitants. And you goddamned well know precisely what I mean," he added vehemently.

Mary Lee was silent, mulling over this sudden note of passion. "Sure," she said at last. "But as you said, it's a nerve ending that hurts too much when somebody presses it."

"More Lillet?"

"Less Lillet. Is there a place I can throw up?"

"Seriously? That terrific dinner and all?"

He came across the room and stood looking down at her. She glanced up for a moment, then lowered her eyes to the floor. The fact that he was attractive to her seemed to make everything that much worse. It was not the resemblance to Ruts, although that helped. It was . . .

God knew it was not his mind. Mary Lee had run into men as intelligent as her, although not very often. Her best friend's husband, Bennett Brown, was such a man. But in Curtiss, the intelligence seemed to go deeper, too much deeper. The smart men she knew applied it to affairs of the moment, mainly making money. Curtiss seemed beyond that. It wasn't part of his job to look into the future. There was something perverse and anarchic about doing that. Nobody ought to know what lay ahead, especially if it was something catastrophic.

He knelt beside her and lifted her chin so as to look into her face. "You're a little green. The john is—"

"Never mind," she interrupted. "I'm not going to be sick. That was a m-m . . . a m-metaphor."

He looked stricken. "You mean I was making you sick?"

She lifted her glance and tried to search his face for clues. Why was she so damned attracted to him? She didn't need to take to her bosom this kind of asp. "Oh, Curtiss," she moaned.

"Come on." He was trying to get her on her feet. His hands felt firm on her ribs. He was much stronger than he looked. That was *it*! Deceptive. Underneath that sandy hair and innocuous Mr. American face lay chaos.

"Chaos," she muttered.

His eyes widened unhappily. "Can you stand up?" When

she didn't reply, he seemed to grow more anxious. "Mary Lee. Speak to me."

"I didn't come all the way to Paris," she began uneasily, "to have a man I hardly know." She paused and tried to breathe more steadily. "Open a door and show me." She could feel herself slumping back into her chair. He held her firmly. "Chaos."

"I didn't mean to do that. I had no idea it would hit you that way."

"Insensitive bastard. I *am* going to be sick."

"Stay on your feet. The john is right over—"

"Stop leading me to the john, Curtiss. It's your fault, anyway."

"I'm sorry. Christ, I'm sorry."

The stricken look made him even more appealing, she noted. It was an utterly dismal prospect, falling in love with this harbinger of doom. Why couldn't he simply hit and run? Why did he have to trigger off his bomb and then hang around while she shattered to pieces? Still, being put back together by him was not entirely a grim prospect.

"Oh, Curtiss." The moan seemed to come up from her toes.

She let her head fall forward on his shoulder. Tears welled up. They coursed down her face and into his blue-striped shirt. "Oh, Curtiss," she whispered.

Now she was sobbing. "I t-take these th-things big," she managed to say, her lips pressed sideways into his shoulder. "My whole w-world . . ." Her body seemed to convulse. He tightened his hold on her as if to cushion the shock.

"Easy," he was saying. It seemed to come from far away.

It came to her, also from far away, that she could rely on this man to reassemble the pieces. In his hands she could fall apart without fear. He had the key that opened the door to chaos. It had hit her so hard because she had always known there was such a door and such a key. She knew he was right about what lay beyond the door. She admired him for knowing and hated him for showing it to her. They were all dancing on a crust. Beneath it lay primordial holocaust, disease, death, destruction, but as long as it held, keep dancing. Isn't that right? The fires of hell could be ignored as long as the music kept playing. Not hell. The planet was cooling. Icy death. A global tomb of ice hurtling through dead, airless space . . .

Look, she told herself, he might resemble Ruts a lot, but weren't terriers the most reliable breed? Dogged. She began to laugh as she sobbed. Dogged Ruts.

She was going to break apart now. She was standing in the center of a newly frozen lake and listening to the hissing rupture of thin ice radiating out from her feet. As she went down into icy hell Ruts would grab her collar and slide her over the ice to dry land.

"Could you do that for me?" she asked Curtiss.

He was holding her tightly to him. When she sobbed, both their bodies convulsed in unison. "Sure," he promised.

"Okay," she murmured. "It's a deal."

4

Julian, slightly out of breath, strode up the Rittergasse, the street that runs along a cliff in Basel overlooking the Rhine. A tall, lean man in his fifties, Julian Sykes-Maulby had great hopes of one day being knighted, more or less for the same reason an earlier Queen Elizabeth had knighted the buccaneer Drake. Julian fancied himself something of a modern privateer sailing under letters of marque that gave him the right to grapple, board and slaughter any non-British corporation for the greater glory of the mother country.

Here in Basel, however, he had concluded the sinking of a small English company in the electronics field, a deed he hoped the Queen would never hear about. He had scuttled the company in conference at the Schweitzer Kreditanstalt's home office, a huge glass-walled building down the street from the Kunstmuseum, by explaining precisely why the loan they were arranging for the English company would never be repaid.

When it came to pressing the right buttons protruding from the backs of Swiss bankers, Julian had no peer in any realm. Satisfied that he had sent the small firm to the bottom, he was now pacing uphill along the Rittergasse towards the Bank Rup, there to discuss his victory with his own private banker, Urs Rup.

On a street of fifteenth-century houses, carefully tended

and modernized during the intervening years, the Bank Rup
was a slightly shabby outcast. The ornate oak door needed
revarnishing. The brass knocker hung green in places. Julian
surveyed this scruffy building with a smile of great satisfaction, pressed the buzzer and was admitted.

He went directly to Urs Rup's office, not neglecting to
waggle his considerable eyebrows at Margit, Urs's private
secretary, who rather fancied Julian. Women did. It wasn't
that he was handsome, in a cadaverous, long-nosed way, or
that he knew how to dress, or even that he was rich. In
addition to all these, there were vibrations. They could, in
fact, light up a room full of secretaries if he chose. But he had
already decided, if Urs didn't object, to focus on Margit
today.

Sitting across from the banker, he began a slow, up-and-
down nod of his head. "Did 'em down, my boy," he said. "A
stout stick to the backside, let me tell you. Now we'll offer
'em the carrot. I'm buying out their shares at, um, six pounds
thirty. Low, but interesting."

Rup made a note on his desk pad. Still in his thirties, the
son of the owner and soon to inherit the entire private bank,
Urs Rup went out of his way to look like what he was, the
banker of choice for many of the world's nerviest financial
pirates. His blond hair grew quite long. He wore pale suits in
hues from beige to pistachio and *café au lait*, offered handrolled
joints to clients he knew well and a snort of white to those he
knew best. Considering the flamboyance of some of his
clients, Urs might have been better advised to dress in dark
grey but he fancied himself a buccaneer, too. In the end, his
style only endeared him more firmly to his customers.

His private telephone line rang and he ignored it. When
Margit came to the door and made a helpless he-must-talk-to-
you gesture, Urs excused himself. While he talked, Julian
and Margit compared notes about where they would dine
tonight.

"Donati's, my dear?" he suggested. "Those white truffles
are back."

"Hello Ben," Urs said. "I might have guessed it was you.
Margit wouldn't break in for anybody else."

"Sorry to bother you," the American voice said across five
thousand miles of crackles and bleeps. "Gameplan's heated
up. She's *in* Paris. I think we go to Grade 1 security. There's
only one reason she'd go to Paris, do you agree?"

"Ben, you know her better than I." Urs frowned, trying to overhear Julian and Margit. He didn't like her dating clients of the bank unless Urs arranged it.

". . . do one a really noble steak right in my hotel," the Englishman was purring.

"At the *Drei Königen?*" she asked, "But it's heaven."

"The problem," his American caller was saying, "is that we can't afford to activate termination while she's there. And we can't afford not to."

"I see. Quite a problem. Unless. . ." Urs stopped for a moment. "Unless you have an objection to a double exit."

"I goddamned well do."

"Then you're tying your own hands," the Swiss told him.

"I want him eliminated. I want her left out of it."

"Be serious. That kind of precision isn't possible," Urs Rup said.

"Did you hear what I said?"

There was a long pause. The banker glanced at Julian, who seemed not to have heard a word of this highly perilous conversation. "Very well," Urs said at last. "I'll reprogram the thing and get it into distribution at once."

"Right."

"But don't expect some of these birdbrains to understand the kind of refinement you're asking for."

"Save one, kill one? It's really quite simple," the voice at the other end told him.

They both hung up simultaneously. The banker eyed the Englishman again. By neither a look nor a gesture did he seem to have paid any attention except to the luscious Margit. The two of them were deeply involved in an eye-to-eye flirtation in which peculiar half-conversations meant nothing.

Margit had her uses, Urs reflected. She could distract the normally overastute Julian. She could divert Urs in his spare time. Although he had never told her what he and Julian and Bennett Brown were doing, she was far too intelligent not to suspect. And far too discreet to ask.

She had her uses, he repeated silently. Chief among them being to keep him from going mad.

Julian Sykes-Maulby stood at the window of his hotel suite, looking down at the fast-flowing Rhine. At this time of night only a few lighters were moving swiftly from right to left on their way through Basel into Germany or France only a few miles away.

His long, lean body, hairless and knobby-muscled, looked very much at ease. He glanced at his travel clock and saw that it was not yet midnight. And the champagne in the ice bucket, still chilled, had hardly been touched. He poured himself a tulip glass of it and was pleased to see it had lost none of its fizz. He poured another and carried it to the bed.

"Margit, sweet one."

She had not been asleep, merely lying there wondering if she would spend the night or go home to the rather attractive apartment she kept in the old town half way up the tortuous Alley of the Ten Thousand Virgins. As Urs Rup's official mistress, she got the heavy down payment for the place from him. As a solid Swiss citizen, however, she expected to keep up the payments on the mortgage herself, although in truth it was the lowest-rate mortgage Bank Rup had ever written.

She smiled lazily and accepted the champagne. "To us," Julian said, raising his glass. "Old friends are the best, eh?"

She let the smile broaden to a grin and patted the bed beside her. Sex with Julian was quite unlike sex with Urs Rup. First of all, with Urs she was usually in a fog of pot smoke, or high with cocaine. She could never be sure afterwards whether what had happened had happened.

With Julian and his ever-present Veuve Clicquot, one was never in doubt. He liked quickies and he liked several of them, having the recuperative power of a teenage boy. Now, putting his glass aside, he was busily at work on her clitoris, teasing, tweaking, nibbling. None of this was her fantasy, Margit reminded herself. It was, as the girls in the computer room would say, a real-time fuck.

When by her moans she signaled that she was past ready, Julian consummated the event at once, entering with not much gentleness. You were never in any doubt, Margit reflected. Then she stopped reflecting and let him finish both of them off with long, forceful strokes, his face gleaming over her, as poised and free of perspiration as if he were merely taking her temperature with a probe.

Later, lying beside her under the down comforter, Julian sipped champagne and sighed contentedly. "Old friends are very much the best," he said again. "That's why I'm concerned about Urs."

"He's perfectly fine."

"That phone call he took today. Didn't like the sound of it one bit. Dodgy."

"Only business."

"With an American." He shook his head. "Don't bother to deny it, sweet girl. Urs's English changes accent depending on whether he talks to an American or an Englishman. You wouldn't be expected to notice it, but to an English-speaker it's very apparent. And he called him Ben. Which means I know who he is."

"Dear Julian, my favorite master spy."

"I distinctly did not like the sound of it, precious girl." He waited to hear more from her. Then, realizing that Swiss banking secrecy was even pervasive enough to extend to this very bed, Julian gave up. "Never mind. He'll come through alive, or not."

Margit frowned. "You think there is danger?"

"Weren't you eavesdropping, darling one? Something about a double exit?"

"Surely he must have been talking to his architect," Margit lied. "Perhaps the entrance for the remodeled bank. You do agree it's time Bank Rup had a facelift."

Julian laughed softly and for some time. "Charming girl, how I wish I had an assistant like you, with such a fanciful and imaginative and pretty head on her shoulders."

She snuggled up to him and began pinching his nipples. He groaned happily. She could feel his erection begin.

"'Once more into the breach, dear friends,'" Julian quoted in a high honking stage voice. "'We'll stop the gap with English dead!'"

5

This year, for reasons of economy, the annual meeting of RCA was being held in its own Studio 8-H, where one of its subsidiaries, NBC, broadcast television programs. Studio 8-H was part of the Radio City complex of which the RCA Building forms a section. This studio is not big by modern standards, since it was designed originally in the days of radio to provide room both for an audience and for the actors and sound-effects men who performed the program on a small raised stage. But the corporate officers of RCA judged that it would certainly be large enough for the few hundred stockholders expected to attend the meeting.

The corporate secretary, in fact, wondered if there would be even that many. There had been a marked lack of interest in this year's elections to the board. The slate proposed by RCA had been virtually unopposed, unless one counted a proposal from several large midwest stockholders on behalf of four names, most of them unknown in Eastern seaboard financial circles.

The names had been duly entered into the running before proxies were sent out to shareholders of record. But the secretary had noted an unusual lethargy this year among those thousands of people who owned RCA stock. They simply weren't responding by mailing in their proxies. True, many of them never did. But certainly a great many more normally mailed the votes in than this year.

Based on this reading of the issues, the secretary felt the meeting, too, would be ill-attended.

He was right. As he noted in an undertone to the chief executive officer just before he opened the meeting: "I don't even make it two hundred. This is going to be a short one."

"Shorter the better," grunted the CEO. He gaveled the dais lectern. "Ladies and gentlemen, friends and shareholders. I declare this annual meeting open. Mr. Secretary, will you read the..."

The meeting droned on through reports on the financial situation of the parent company, RCA, and its chief divisions, including those that produced hardware for the space program and the defense effort, the consumer products division that produced and sold television sets and the newly developed videodisc recorders that were proving so hard to sell, the separate concerns that sold carpeting or did various kinds of financing, the Hertz section that rented cars, trucks and equipment, and the National Broadcasting Company subsidiary which, this year was able to show some profitable rises in Neilson ratings and overall sponsorship fees.

The election of board members for the coming year came as the seventh item on the agenda. The secretary took back the microphone and shuffled the papers in front of him.

"Of the more than half a million votes recorded, I can report that to date four hundred and ten thousand yeas have been registered for the eight-name slate presented to the shareholders. Seventy thousand votes have been cast for the four-name slate of opposition candidates. Therefore—"

"Mr. Secretary," a young man from the audience said. He stood up. An usher moved towards him, carrying a microphone on a pole. He extended the microphone until the young man could speak into it.

"Mr. Secretary. My name is Alfred J. Marston. I represent the brokerage firm of Brown, Brown, Pierce, Finch and Cohen."

"Yes, Mr. Marston?"

"I am also the holder of record of one thousand shares of RCA common."

"Yes, Mr. Marston."

The young man, skinny and tall, mopped his high forehead. Perspiration glistened there at the start of his receding hairline. "I am also empowered, in a non-fiduciary relationship, to represent here today approximately four hundred thousand proxies tendered to my firm by various shareholders both here and abroad."

"Did I understand you to say four hundred thousand?"

On the dais, corporate officers began to confer in hurried whispers. "The figure," Marston said, referring to a spiral-bound notebook, "is four hundred and five thousand, eight hundred and twelve."

Now Studio 8-H was humming, perhaps with the sound of two hundred people trying to add up votes announced by the secretary and by the tall young man.

"Would you be good enough, Mr. Marston," the secretary said after a ferocious interchange of whispers with the CEO, "to advance to the podium and tender your various authorizations and other documents?"

"Certainly, sir."

Marston wiggled his fingers at one of the doors to Studio 8-H. As he started forward to the podium, the doors swung open slowly and two young men advanced into the room pushing two huge wheeled canvas postal dollies, each about a yard square, each near to overflowing with envelopes.

All three young men seemed to move with a certain pomp and sense of high circumstance towards the corporate secretary. Although he put on a bravely bland face, he had the sudden fantasy feeling that this was some kind of religious ritual, not a wedding or a funeral but...

"It was the queerest feeling," he told his wife later that night after she'd made him a third vodka martini. "It was like one of those, um, Aztec things."

"Aztec?"

"Mayan. You know, one of those sacrifices where they ripped the heart out of a living victim."

"My God, Edgar."

Later, in New Mexico, the morning sky stretched like a seamless canvas of brilliant blue from one mountainous horizon to the other. High in the east the perfect disc of the sun warmed the craggy bare rock of the Sangre de Cristo peaks, jutting up out of their permanent mantle of snow.

Bennett Brown stood naked and alone in the solarium cube at Snowfire and did Canadian Air Force exercises, jumping up and down, swinging his arms, his deep, dark eyes fixed as if in a trance on the eastern horizon. Then he draped a towel around him and stumbled inside the congeries of cube-rooms. He flopped into a chair and breathed deeply. In an instant he was asleep.

This terminal room at Snowfire, in permanent semidarkness, now seemed to be deserted. But the tall, dark-eyed young man who slumped over the terminal keyboard was only catching a catnap and waiting for his New York man to come through on a secure line.

Alfred J. Marston, a certified public accountant and a member of the New York State Bar Association, had his own offices in the financial district. But after the RCA coup he had asked for and got a tiny office on the 49th floor of Radio City's RCA Building, 30 Rockefeller Plaza. Neither had telephone lines that were secure.

A thin, bodiless bleep sounded near the sleeping Bennett Brown. He came awake at once, his dark eyes searching the various keyboards and panels for a blinking light. When he found one and patched into it, he activated the voice amp. "Freddie?"

"It's me, Ben," Alfred J. Marston announced. "I am calling from a pay phone in Saks." He repeated the number and hung up.

Bennett Brown rearranged his circuits and made the return call. "So tell me," Marston began without preamble, "what's so vital I have to be standing here in Saks at ten a.m.

watching a collection of the fattest, most overdressed broads in Manhattan filing past?"

"You have to hustle up the RCA dismantling, Freddie."

"I can't understand the rush. If it was a good enough conglomerate to latch onto, it's good enough to keep in one piece."

"Wrong." Bennett Brown tapped the keyboard and a series of tables of organization, boxes connected by lines, flashed on the CRT. He frowned at the image. "The manufacturing lines are fine," he told Marston. "I want you to double-check the new men we put on the RCA board. Make sure you tighten the clamps on them. Make sure they understand the strategy and the daily tactics."

"No problems, Ben."

Brown made a face. "Don't give me that 'no-problems' shit," he warned Marston. "These new board guys are just ordinary local businessmen. Who the hell were they before we put them on the board? One of them runs an electrical company. Another paves streets. One owns a five-state supermarket chain. That's who they *are*. But only you and I know *why* they obey us. The electrical guy likes twelve-year-old girls. The pavement specialist happens to be three-quarters of a million in debt to the Chicago families. The supermarket guy is one of ours that we slowly shoved up the chain of command, teaching him how to read and write along the way. These are low-end product, Freddie. Never forget that."

"All the more reason they do what we tell them."

"Following orders is one thing. We're now asking them to operate on their own, without detailed, daily contact. I believe all of them have enough intelligence to do it, or enough fear. But somebody has got to fill them in very carefully, painstakingly. That's you, Freddie. You have to explain the official line."

"Naturally."

"And my job is to give the line to you. Understand?"

"Don't get so upset, Ben. It's not good for your heart."

Bennett Brown's tight face relaxed slowly. "You're right, you bum." He inhaled calmly several times. "Now let's get back to the dismantling. We hold the manufacturing in place. That's clear. But as soon as possible we start peeling off the service subsidiaries."

"You crazy, Ben? You're talking CIT. You're talking Hertz."

"I'm talking soft spots in the underbelly of the economy."

There was a long pause. "Christ, I'm standing here wondering what you think is a hard place."

"Freddie, shape up. CIT has to get its money at the same high rates as any other financing operation. As for Hertz, the trend is away from even buying cars, much less renting them. The whole rental idea is a victim of the oil scam. People are going to hang onto their old clunker till it dies on the street."

"Ben, you are one rough baby."

"So scrape CIT off the plate," the dark young man continued. "Unload it on something that can afford the money. Unload it on UBCO, maybe. Dangle it and see if UBCO starts sniffing."

"What about Hertz?"

"Haven't figured it out yet. There's one angle of rental that still might have appeal. Equipment leases. It's off-the-balance sheet cost, with all the maintenance and depreciation writeoffs. It might appeal to some schmucky corporation somewhere."

Alfred J. Marston stood in the Saks phone booth and watched a particularly attractive young woman saunter past. "Ben, I take that back about fat broads. Something just walked by h—"

"Okay, Freddie, whack off on your own time." The line went dead as Bennett Brown switched off all circuits.

6

The smell of coffee woke Curtiss at about ten a.m. He glanced around his bedroom, noted that she had carefully folded her clothing over two chairbacks—something neither of them had bothered about last night—and was now making noises in Curtiss's kitchen.

In the bathroom, peeing, he saw that she must be wearing his wool robe. Donning the lightweight one, he padded on bare feet into the kitchen. Her back to him, she was carefully breaking an egg into a coffee cup, smelling it and adding it to a bowl in which three yolks already waited.

She was about Curtiss's own height, five-ten, he now estimated. They had last night lain head to toe, horizontal equals. In heels, she had been a bit taller than he, which didn't disturb Curtiss. But she was far thinner than he was, with very long legs, a small, boyish ass and what could be described as modest breasts.

"If you're expecting to smell a bad one, forget it," he told her. She swung around. "I get those hand-delivered by a little old man, a veteran of two world wars, who guarantees that he takes them each morning from his own hens."

"That a fact?" She gave him a sweet smile. "Tell me why two of them have these little white tails. It's the sure sign of a storage egg."

He returned her smile. He hadn't fully realized she was a woman after his own heart—cynical and dangerously bright—but he did know he was in the presence of something special.

Curtiss tended to be shy about women. Two failed marriages had left him with the realization that he never would ever understand women, not in a million years, so he tended to tread softly around them.

Mary Lee Hunter put down the coffee cup and advanced on him for a tight hug and a brief kiss on the lips. "You look like you just dropped off a rattler from Butte, full of white alky and red ants."

He burst out laughing. "Jesus H. Christ," he said, "I ain't heard no proper 'Merican talk fer nigh onto ten years."

She began beating the eggs with a wire whisk. "Set a spell and coffee up," she told him. "And let's give the dialect a rest. I came here to pick your brain, Curtiss."

"Is *that* what happened last night." He poured some coffee and tasted it, black, hot, strong. "I thought we covered all the ground, uh, is it Mary or Mary Lee?"

"Mary Lee." She had heated his omelette pan and now dropped a large slab of butter into it. Still whipping the eggs, she added salt, pepper and water from the tap. Just as the melted butter began to smoke, she poured in the eggs. A terrifying hiss filled the room. Amid the steam, she poked and lifted with a spatula. Instants later she dished the omelette onto two plates and sat down beside Curtiss at the plain pine table. She patted his hand. "Toast?"

He shook his head. "Mary Lee," he said then, "I don't eat breakfast."

"You'll eat this one," she responded in an ominous tone. "Eggs are two dollars a dozen in this crazy town. How does UBCO afford having a man here?"

"I told you. I don't eat breakfast. That saves them a big

bundle right there." He tasted the omelette and kept on eating it.

As they ate he watched her face. She had one of those wide jaws, not pointed at the corners, but with enough chin to make you hesitate fighting her, and a small nose between wide-set china blue eyes. She looked a bit like Curtiss, whose jaw showed a lot less determination, that kind of all-purpose, all-nationality American look almost never seen in movie stars, a bit plain, very regular, not too memorable. It was an ideal face for Curtiss. He could get lost in a crowd, even a European one. For Mary Lee, he surmised, it would have to be enhanced by makeup and hairstyle before it could look really pretty. It would never look gorgeous but it looked terrific at the moment, minus makeup *or* hairstyle.

"You're cute," he told her. "You always carry on this way?"

"Hardly ever," she assured him. "I had no idea what you looked like. All I got out of Bill Elston was that you were a one-off loner. So when you showed up at the restaurant last night I wasn't prepared for you being My Type." She grinned. "Is it important that I be chaste?"

"Not when you meet Your Type."

"I was prepared for some sort of thug. I mean, Curtiss, your inside knowledge of the underworld is too much. When I read your report I said to myself, this guy is either a liar or a reformed Mafia hitman. I deliberately left it out of our 1980 projection because I had no programming category for it. Then the mob took over Consolidated Welding and I said to myself, 'Hey, wait, that crazy man in Paris, he predicted this.' We had a hell of a time combing the boys out of Consolidated because they had 18 percent of the common and Jet-Tech only held 19. So I had to come here and see Curtiss for myself."

Curtiss pushed his empty plate away. "The mob has been taking over small companies for years, local ones. It's ancient history. They have to invest their cash in something, so they buy a company or scam it. Either way they own it and operate it for profit or let it go bankrupt to give them tax losses. That's not what I was talking about in that report of mine last year."

She sat there silently, watching his mouth. When it stopped moving she touched his lips gently. "Is this Saturday or Sunday?"

He frowned, momentarily at a loss. "Uh . . . Saturday."

"Good. Back to bed."

"What if I'd said Sunday?"

"Sunday I have to fly to New York."

"Shit."

She got up from the table. "Can you come back home with me tomorrow?"

He shook his head. "I'm due in Rome. The Minister of Industry in the new government is setting us up for a fall. He wants to renege on an UBCO loan the size of the Ritz."

She took his hand and led him back into the bedroom. "So we've only got today and tonight and tomorrow morning."

She had slipped out of his wool robe and was standing naked in the center of the room. Weak sunlight filtered in from behind the closed curtains, giving her body the shadowless look of museum-lit sculpture. He could see her nipples grow hard. When she turned away from him he wondered why he had thought her ass boyish. It was small, but it had that heart-stopping inner curve to each cheek and the three dimples over it. He half fell on, half tackled her, spilling her face down on the bed as he began softly biting her buttocks.

They woke again around noon. Curtiss went to the front door and retrieved the Saturday–Sunday *Trib* as well as the Saturday London *Times*. They sat up in bed reading bits to each other. Scattering newspapers wildly, she climbed on board Curtiss. In this position, he vaguely noted, her modest breasts looked no bigger, but it really was no longer anything to think about. Both of them stopped thinking for a long time.

When they woke again it was after two and, although he was starving, Curtiss felt it would be rude—and fatal to their mood—to suggest they get dressed and find a local eating place before everything shut down till dinner. Eyes closed, he was hazily mulling over words to introduce such an idea when her voice came to him from somewhere in the vicinity of his navel.

"I am really no good," she muttered, her mouth pressed against the line of hair that ran up from his pubic area. "I have a million questions to ask you and all I want to do is fool around." She sighed. "Curtiss, why did you have to be My Type? I was doing fine before yesterday. B. J. and I had made it as far up as two girls from the Wharton School and Stanford could ever hope. She was controller of Piper and Farr and I was leaving the Fed for Jet-Tech."

"B. J. who?"

"Brown, now. Married name. B. J. and I were college roomies. She would've made it big in the corporate ratrace but she let a man con her out of it. And look what's happening to me!"

Curtiss turned her head so he could stare down into her pale blue eyes. "Mary Lee, I have no interest in wooing you away from the ratrace. I like you just as you are, sexy and making two hundred grand a year."

She bit his flesh. "Plus options," she added. "You see, Bennett Brown was B. J.'s *type*: tall, dark, gorgeous. You are mine: short, sandy and feisty, like a wirehair I once had. He made her hormones bubble. You stir mine to the core. Hormones and business never mix. There's a moral there." She sighed and began nibbling her way southward. "I just know there is."

7

B. J. Brown, clad only in the bottom half of a bikini, rolled over from her stomach to her back. The California sun is not that hot in March, but the Brown compound along the coast south of Newport Beach was hedged in by a living barricade of eucalyptus, force-raised in only five years to a height of twenty feet.

Privacy B. J. had, and also an almost total absence of breeze. She could feel trickles of perspiration form on her distended belly and breasts as the sun poured down on them. The books on pregnancy described a host of nasty symptoms B. J. had yet to experience; none of them mentioned feeling like a kipper in a frying pan, oozing oil.

How smart Mary Lee was, B. J. thought. Where was it written that powerful attractions had to be sealed by marriage writ? Come to think of it, marriage had been Ben's idea. And the reason was now taking its time developing in her belly.

She hauled herself to her feet and slung a terry robe around her. The relief was instant, a cool-down of body heat. Shoving her fingers through her long, dark brown hair, B. J. glanced at the surf a hundred yards from her, firmly turned her back on it and marched inside the curious home Ben had built for her, a kind of pile-up of children's blocks, immense cubic modules stuck together at odd places.

Inside one walked up and down short flights of steps from room to room. It was impossible to keep servants more than a week. But the place had been designed, like the one in Snowfire, for easy maintenance. Even pregnant, B. J. found she could keep the place moderately neat. As for cooking, the freezer was filled with gourmet stuff and the microwave oven did the rest. She, in fact, had time on her hands, time to regret her decision to quit a career, time to fret over the two years of tension and angst in which she had tried to become pregnant, time to worry about how she soon would take to motherhood. Too much time.

"Ben?"

"In here."

She moved noiselessly on bare feet to the flight of steps that led down into the terminal room. The national brokerage firm of Brown, Brown, Pierce, Finch and Cohen was billing half a billion a year in commissions and fees. It was a small, labor-intensive firm with offices in five cities and a nation-wide staff of no more than two hundred. But most of its work, and certainly all of its planning, took place right here, beneath the tight-cropped black hair that covered Bennett Brown's skull.

"Hungry?" she asked.

He looked up from the video screen. He seemed to think for an extraordinarily long time, as if news from his stomach was taking forever to reach his brain. B. J. watched his long, oval face with the high cheekbones, sharp as knives, and the small discreet mouth. He had eyes like ripe olives, jet black, no distinction between pupil and iris. In the dark or the sunlight, his eyes seemed always to remain the same, grave, with a kind of inner regard, as if they were seeing in both directions, inward and outward, at the same time.

It was unnerving to be regarded so fixedly by Bennett Brown's eyes, even if one loved him deeply and was bearing his child. "Lunch?" B. J. asked.

Back in the days when both she and Mary Lee had dated Ben, in the pre-marriage period that seemed aeons ago, they had discussed him, not often but thoroughly. He had not seemed intense enough then. He had seemed to both of them to be "on hold," not yet ready, too cool for Mary Lee, at any rate.

"I like cool," she had explained. "But too cool approaches disinterest. It gives you a Mr. Unattainable feeling. This man is no man. This man is a voyager from a distant planet. In his veins runs green *crème de menthe*. If you marry him you will give birth to an infantoid replica cunningly constructed of titanium mesh embedded in linear polyvinyl chloride."

They had giggled a lot about Ben's desire to get married and have children, something neither B. J. nor Mary Lee was about to do, if ever. But then, after a while, something old-fashioned and "hot" seemed to emerge beneath the cool. At least B. J. saw it. Mary Lee obviously never did, although she kept quiet about it once the marriage happened.

Close as the two women had always been since childhood, there was nevertheless a difference in the way they perceived Ben. "He's obviously your type," Mary Lee told B. J. "You dig 'em long and lean anyway, always have. *And* dark *and* mysterious *and* just a tiny bit disinterested. I think it's the disinterest hat turns you on."

"How can you say that? He's very interested in me, as a vessel of motherhood, if nothing else."

"It's like the fact that you dig cats and I like dogs."

"What is that supposed to mean?"

"Cats go their own way. You might be able to train one into being a close personal friend, but I doubt it. They are them and they treat you as another species, which you damned well are. That makes them standoffish a little. You dig that, B. J. That's why you dig Ben."

Remembering, B. J. tried to stare back into the deep, dark eyes of her husband now, willing him to speak, to respond. God, she thought, Mary Lee was right. He is the cat that walks by himself.

In two years of marriage she had come to love him a great deal more than when she'd rushed through a quick Las Vegas weekend wedding. It hadn't seemed real. The justice of the peace had been a hennaed old lady in a magenta-and-white robe. The honeymoon had been spent at the blackjack and roulette tables. She had begun to loathe the man who'd married her in haste.

"Look," he'd said on the flight back to Los Angeles, "I don't feel any more married than you. Let's do it right, in a church or something."

So they'd got married again, this time back east in Maryland in the bosom of Mary Lee Hunter's family and her own.

Before an Episcopal priest. And she had begun to love him intensely from that moment. He had hit on something deep inside both of them, something old-fashioned and traditional. The cat that walked by himself wanted to do it in tandem. She was being let inside his private world. He was showing her a side of him no one else knew about. He was letting her peer deeper into those bottomless eyes of his, to where someone lived who, it seemed to B. J., was very like herself conservative about things like marriage and love and babies.

"Ben," she told him now, "you must know how that look melts my insides. But it doesn't tell me if you want lunch."

When he spoke, she was unprepared. "What do you hear from Mary Lee?" he said.

B. J. made a thoughtful face. "Nothing in a week. Why?"

"I mean, how's she doing at Jet-Tech?"

"They love her, far's I know."

"Love her how?"

B. J. shrugged. "She's there less than a year. But last week they upped her option plan and gave her a 20 percent raise. I say it's love." She frowned. "Is this your way of telling me you're not hungry?"

That small, careful mouth distorted in a slight smile. "It's my way of finding out how a dear friend is doing, that's all."

"Just fine. She told me her new financing plan is already costing them less, with better protection against currency fluctuation."

"I could use some of that." He glanced at the video, thought for a moment and closed it down with a few taps on the keyboard. "I'm hungry."

The microwave oven yielded two steaming portions of Coquille St. Jacques which they ate on the terrace overlooking the beach. Ben opened a cold bottle of Muscadet. He touched his glass to B. J.'s. He ran his other hand firmly, possessively, over her swollen belly.

"To him," he said.

"To it," she responded.

"And to Mary Lee," he added unexpectedly. "May she continue in good health."

B. J. watched him sip his wine. What a peculiar toast, she thought. Still, one could hardly complain about it. "Did she tell you where she was going this weekend?" B. J. asked then.

"Me?" Those deep, bottomless black eyes regarded her gravely. "I have no idea where she might be this weekend. Or with whom."

B. J. frowned at her husband. "If I didn't know you better," she said in a thoughtful tone, "I'd call that a jealous remark."

"The wife," Ben said in a cool voice, "is always the last to know."

8

Some kind of sharp temperature change was taking place in the parklike grounds of the Cité Odiot. Curtiss stared out past the slit in his gauzy window curtains at the gathering nimbus around each street lamp. It was only six in the evening, but a mist was already forming low to the ground. Above it, at the roof level, the jagged skyline of chimneys, roof angles, dormers and ventilator vanes stood clear against a sky of deep indigo.

In his bed, Mary Lee slept. Curtiss had spent romantic weekends with other women, but none of such concentrated fervor. They made love each time as if it had never happened to them before, nor would again.

He watched a couple walking past his window to the apartment house next door. As they turned up the steps, a shadow shifted behind one of the broad chestnut trees. Curtiss started to open the curtain slit wider, then froze. The shadowy figure was moving to keep the tree's shield between him and the passing couple.

This was an ancient tree, more trouble than it was worth, Curtiss had often noted, a yard thick at its base, with branches and leaves higher than the buildings, choking off what sunlight Paris offered, keeping any grass from growing beneath its boughs. It made a poor hiding place.

As if he had communicated this thought as a warning to the watcher, the shadow moved back through the low-clinging mist and disappeared behind a line of shrubbery. Curtiss's eye caught movement at the other end of the garden area. Someone had come in through the tunnel to the rue Washington, paused a moment, then eased into another patch of bushes.

One of the few drawbacks this apartment had, in Curtiss's view, was its single exposure. It faced only to the front.

Another tenant, seeking security, might have felt this an
advantage, since it gave predators only one way in. To
Curtiss, however, it suggested the opposite, only one way
out. He would have welcomed some rear-facing windows, but
there were none.

He got a pair of night binoculars. Taking a stance well back
from the gauze curtains, he shifted sideways until he could
focus past the slit at each shadowy watcher in turn. Even with
the binoculars, there was little to see. The mist was too thick.
Curtiss wondered if it were merely evening ground mist,
which could be expected to disperse soon enough, or one of
those Paris chokers that engulfed the city for days. In any
event, he told himself now, the mist was as bad for both
watchers and watched. As long as he and Mary Lee kept the
lights off, if they were being watched, it was a standoff. He
wondered if he ought to tell her straight out, or wait till he
was forced to by circumstances. As always, he took the
second choice. If Curtiss had a style about his work it was one
of waiting for someone else to make a move. First.

A third shadowy figure was inching his way around from
the right, towards the shadow in the shrubbery behind the
chestnut tree. Three men. Curtiss put away the binoculars.
He moved across the cold parquet floor into the bedroom.
Mary Lee lay in absolute, deep sleep. Even her eyes remained
motionless behind closed lids. She lay mostly uncovered.
Curtiss drew the sheet up over her and began to dress
quickly in track suit and tennis sneakers. The light in the
downstairs entrance hall had burned out two weeks ago. The
handyman had yet to replace it. With any luck Curtiss might
reconnoiter the Cité Odiot, relying on the mist to hide him.

He scribbled a note and put it next to her on the pillow,
then let himself out of the apartment by the rear door, the
one through which garbage was collected. The handyman
used a rickety flight of iron stairs, much like an American fire
escape, for his work. Curtiss felt in his pocket for the apartment keys, reassured himself, and firmly closed the rear door
behind him.

He moved silently down the iron stairs and landings to a
small service courtyard, gritty with cinders. The door to the
cellar was always unlocked. He moved quietly along a
whitewashed stone hallway and came out at the stair landing
below the front entrance.

Curtiss paused, holding his breath. If anyone were in the

front stairway that led up to his apartment, they were keeping very quiet. He tiptoed up the stairs to the entrance hallway. Light flooded the area. The damned bulb had been replaced.

Over his head a board creaked.

He backed down to the cellar, let himself out into the service courtyard and slowly climbed the iron catwalks and stairs, thinking all the while.

Four men. Minimum. Not a cop stakeout. Paris police didn't work that way. Besides, he had friends among them who could be counted on for a warning. Four men concentrated on him. Meaning they knew he was in his flat. If they weren't sure of that they wouldn't have wasted all four men on the job.

He let himself in the rear door, locked it behind him and stood in the middle of his kitchen, still thinking. Had the men been there earlier? He and Mary Lee had arrived here before midnight last night. Neither of them had been especially wary or watchful. And since that moment some eighteen hours ago, neither had been a reliable witness for anything except each other.

Wait. Before noon he'd opened the door to take in his newspapers. The man who normally delivered them had come and gone without event. Was there a way of telephoning him to find out? Did he have a name?

Thinking of the telephone, Curtiss had a new idea. In his office he stared at the silent instrument for a long while. Then he switched on a small, black Bakelite-fronted box on which several knobs and a volt-meter were displayed. He picked up his telephone and started to tap a number on it. After the first digit, the meter's needle swung over to the left past an area of black numbers into a quadrant shaded red.

Curtiss continued with the call until he got the talking clock recording which gave him the correct time and was about to repeat it when he depressed the telephone shutoff. The meter needle dropped back to zero. He released the shutoff and got a dial tone. The needle flickered upward slightly. But when he touched a new number, it swung into the red.

Curtiss hung up the phone and went back into the bedroom. He took his unread note from the pillow, crumpled it and cupped his hand over Mary Lee's shoulder. "Mary Lee?"

"Mm." She rolled over on her left and came awake. "Morning," she said almost cheerfully. "You dressed already?"

"It's evening. Listen."

They were silent for a long moment. "I don't hear anything."

"No, I mean, listen to me," he explained.

"But you aren't talking," she pointed out with the clarity of the well-rested. "Is this something you're finding hard to tell me?"

"Yes."

She sat bolt upright in bed. "Curtiss, that look on your face."

"Mary Lee, when you take off for Europe, who handles your travel plans? I mean, your secretary, someone else in the company, a travel agent?"

"This is a personal weekend. I booked myself. But my secretary knew I was planning to get over here the first chance I got. So she could reach my hotel, if need be."

"How long has she known you were coming over?"

Mary Lee got out of bed and stood naked, staring down at her toes. Then she put on Curtiss's shirt. "Stop creeping up on it, Curtiss. What's happened?"

"There are three guys out there in the shadows," he said, pointing in the direction of the living room, "and one on the stairs breathing shallowly through his mouth. I am not normally paranoid. Three guys could be watching some other apartment, not mine. But a mouthbreather on my stairs tends to narrow it down. This mini-army may be watching my downstairs neighbor, the widow of a grocer. She's in her early eighties, Madame Boneuil. Or my upstairs neighbor, who's been in Australia since Christmas and isn't expected back until May. Or me."

"And me." She sat down on the edge of the bed and resumed her examination of her long, narrow toes, faintly tipped with a silvery polish. Curtiss could see the rumple of blond hair at the top of her head, where normally it was combed in an almost mathematically neat sunburst.

When she looked up, her china blue eyes were luminous in the dim light. "Somebody in Jet-Tech, who did nothing when your original report came in a year ago—did nothing because *I* did nothing—now realizes I have gone to see the author of the report. The minute *I* do something, *he* does something."

"Does he have a name, this guy?"

She shook her head. "Fascinating, in a slimy way. As long

as I was underwhelmed by your report, they just sat there, waiting. They didn't go after you then. Why not? How did they know you weren't shooting your face off to other UBCO clients with this horrible forecast of yours?"

Curtiss was silent for a while. "Maybe because they have ears in other companies. Or ears in UBCO."

Mary Lee made a disgusted face. "That's disheartening, that is. So, somehow or other, they know you're not wandering the earth preaching your philosophy to anybody but Mary Lee Hunter. But the patience of them, Curtiss. Like a spider at the center of her web. No unnecessary moves. Not even a twitch. Old Mary Lee thinks nothing of it, we cool it. We sit and wait and watch. If she still thinks nothing of it, that's cool, too. But—" She paused, thinking.

"But the moment Old Mary Lee gets to Paris," Curtiss finished for her, "they call out the wrecking gang. Because if she gets the whole, full, unabridged, vellum-bound version of it from Old Curtiss, she is going to steam back to the States and start tearing up the pea patch. And they can't have that."

"So they set up business here, waiting to make their move."

He sighed. "Up to something, for sure."

"Something lousy for us."

"That's how I read it."

"But what kind of something?" she went on thinking out loud. "How long have they been there? What are they waiting for?"

"They're waiting for us to go out for a meal."

"Why?"

"To get us away from our natural protection, this apartment."

"Why?" she persisted. "What makes this place impregnable?"

"They'd expect me to start shooting, sound an alarm. They'd figure the place is wired and I'm heavily armed."

"Which you are."

He shook his head. "I don't own a gun. Never use one."

"Don't they know that?"

"It depends who's sent them." Curtiss thought for a moment. "Yes, you're right, they might know I was unarmed. But they couldn't be sure about the alarms. They have the phone tapped in case I want to holler for help that way."

Her generous mouth set in a flat line. "Tell me what *we've* got going for us."

· "Not much. The fact that they don't know they've been spotted."

"Nothing else?"

He hesitated. "They may have orders to leave you alone. It's only a guess. That's something, though."

"Figuring I would let them grab you and keep my mouth shut?" she asked. "They don't know me well, do they? Let them kidnap my Number One Boyfriend?"

He laughed. "You're strange, Mary Lee. I do admire you an awful lot."

"Well, you haven't had much experience bedding executive vice-presidents. And you haven't been back to the States in ten years, I think you said. Women are growing up different these days, Curtiss." She was silent for a while, watching him with the faint grin. Then: "So what's our next move?"

"Holler for help."

"Out the window?"

He shook his head. "I'm making a tricky call. If it works we get help. Otherwise . . ."

He went to the office, picked up the phone and tapped out a number on it. The VU-meter needle flickered busily in the red quadrant. After five rings he was about to hang up when a deep, gruff, sleepy voice answered the call. *"Alors, dites-moi."*

"What the hell are you doing asleep?" Curtiss demanded.

"Oh, *merde*, it's you." The French voice slipped into an American-accented English. "How goes it?"

"Wonderful. She's fantastic."

"Toujours, la même chose. You are a lucky fuck, Curtiss."

"I just called to brag, but now she's out of bed walking around. So, *à bientôt*, Jean-Paul." He hung up.

Curtiss turned to look directly into Mary Lee's eyes, at the same level as his. "That was a cry for help?"

"It's the home phone of a friend of mine, high up in the Frog *gendarmerie*, a guy named Louch."

"Jean-Paul Louch."

"No. His name happens to be Raymond."

9

"Very rare, Don B," his visitor said, picking a ripe, dewy kernel of red flesh from the heart of the pomegranate and letting it release a squirt of tart sweetness between his teeth as he crushed it. "To find the fruit so ripe this early in the year is unheard of."

The elderly man who accepted this compliment sat upright in a cane-backed armchair, very alert, perhaps not as thin as he once was, but with those deep-set dark eyes that seemed to see into everything. He made a disparaging gesture.

"A little trick of my own, Don Gino," he replied in the same Calabrese dialect they both spoke. "It's from my own hothouse. I watch over these beauties as if they were small children."

Both men smiled. Business associates for many decades in America, they had both retired, Don Gino to his native town on the Ionic Coast of Calabria, that part of the Italian "boot" under the toe and in the arch. Don B had elected to return here, in the Conca D'Oro, among Sicilians of the Palermo district, rather than his own *paisani*.

He had not liked the way events had developed in Calabria, where the local organization went by the name of Ndrangheta and was filled with hungry youngsters with no respect. They would as soon kidnap and hold him for ransom as an outsider without status in the honored society.

So Don B had retired to Sicily. There is no love lost between the inhabitants of these two southernmost regions of Italy, perhaps because they are so alike, the Siciliani and the Calabrese, a racial mixture of Greek and Saracen, Norman and Spaniard, equally oppressed over the centuries by foreign despots, equally at home with brutality, intrigue, treachery and the steady day-in-day-out deceit of a people racked by suspicion and doubt.

Equally, too, they understood fear, these two people. Although they could never become close, they could fear each other. Fear, Don B knew, was the precondition for respect.

Here the Palermitani respected him. They had no choice. Had he not stood steadfast in America all those years, the pivot around which all the other families swung? Had he not faced down the McClellan and Kefauver Committees, the Strike Forces? Had he not engineered the forty-year standoff with J. Edgar Hoover which left the families free to grow and flourish?

The architect of all this great work, close associate of the financial genius Lansky and the tacticians Gambino and Genovese, godfather of Luciano and Magaddino, of Trafficante and Bruno, personal adviser of the puppet Battista, major contributor to the finances of Nixon, co-conspirator with Marcello and Giancana in both the Hoffa affair and the Kennedy double exit, confidante of the CIA, patriot, businessman, churchgoer, father and soon to be a grandfather... the Siciliani had no choice but to pay this man respect.

A half century of history rode on Don B's narrow, aristocratic shoulders. Decades of deals, dates, names and amounts lived behind those dark eyes, nestled in papery cushions of wrinkled flesh.

He picked at his own pomegranate and chewed the kernel of juice. "I prefer them a bit less ripe," he told Don Gino. "We Calabrese, we like things really tart, *non è vero?*"

His guest smiled neatly, a compact movement of lips and eyes. "Tell me, *onorevole*, I had expected to see my boy Turi. He is away from Palermo?"

Don B nodded and made one of those complicated hand gestures, a kind of touching of thumb and forefinger in a shaking motion, as if flicking off water or wine. "Salvatore is too valuable to sit around here watching an old man die," he said. "I have him in Paris at the moment. An important problem. He is my first choice to handle it."

Don Gino's smile broadened with pride. "I am pleased you feel that way about Turi, my friend. He is not the most intelligent boy in the world, but he is loyal and brave."

And unbelievably stupid, Don B added silently. If I had only put someone else in charge of it, he thought, his face immobile, the whole matter would now be solved, neatly and forever. But this *cretino* of Don Gino's didn't have the brains to squash a louse if you put his heel on it.

His fingers probed a pocket of his waistcoat and removed a slim gold watch which he consulted gravely. He cleared his throat. "Can you join me for dinner, Don Gino? I have some of the 1980 *vendemmia*. The white is ready for drinking."

"With great pleasure, Don B," his guest responded.

"Then refresh yourself and excuse me to make a telephone call." Don B got to his feet, a slight man, jockey-sized, erect as a lad. Indicating the guest bathroom that adjoined this open-air patio, he hurried inside his villa and went directly to the telephone, punched a number and waited. When someone answered he spoke in the same Calabrese dialect, but this time with the special vocabulary of his home town which, in this year of 1981, perhaps only five hundred people in the whole world could speak.

"Turi, tell me."

"Nothing yet, godfather."

"Greetings from your own father. He is with me. Can I tell him my faith in you is confirmed and truly vindicated?"

"Soon, honored one, very soon."

"Let me speak to the tall one."

A new voice came on the line. "Command me," it said.

"Respond with yes or no, nothing more."

"Yes."

"Does he understand? One, not both?"

"Yes."

"The changed order came through to you from Switzerland?"

"Yes."

"Only the man. Not the woman."

"Yes."

"If it goes well, I must know. At once."

"Yes."

"If it goes badly, he must be removed. At once."

"Yes."

The dinner table was set up under the fine-shaded trellis at the far end of the patio, overlooking the Mediterranean. Don B lifted his glass of white wine to his guest. "To Turi, your loyal son."

"To Turi, *onorevole*, my first born."

"May he live forever," Don B added sentimentally.

10

By nine o'clock that night it was evident to Curtiss that Louch had not adequately understood his rather cryptic message. Calling him by a wrong first name could have indicated a number of things to the French cop: that Curtiss was kidding, or drunk or forgetful. Or signaling for help. In any event, none came.

Easing open the back door to the iron landing, Curtiss thought he could see, in the almost total blackness, that the stairway and the courtyard were still devoid of watchers. He asked Mary Lee to take a look and she confirmed his guess, but unwillingly. "Couldn't you get some sort of light turned on down there?"

"The concierge is off on her dinner break. When she gets back to her little kiosk, I could phone her."

"Please." She watched him pacing the darkened apartment. "I'm so sorry about this, Curtiss."

"Not your fault."

"Of course it is. I brought them with me, so to speak." She thought for a moment. "If I hadn't wanted to know more about your theories, none of this would've happened."

He chuckled bitterly. "What more do you have to know?"

She sat down at the kitchen table and nibbled a cracker. "You never did name names. I mean the idea that in the 1980s the Mafia could take over blue chip firms like Kodak or Jet-Tech or British Petroleum without any of us knowing... that was expressed more or less theoretically."

He filled an electric kettle with water and plugged it in. "You have to stop calling them the Mafia. That's just one piece. In many places *mafiosi* are the backbone of the operation, but they have affiliates and allies and subsidiaries and whatnots that you'd never believe had a mob connection."

"Let's not get stuck over nomenclature," she said in a dry tone. "You experts kill me. Four thugs have us pinned down and you're arguing what to call them."

"As for me having expressed it theoretically, there's no theory about it. It's being done every day."

"Every day the mob is buying up shares of blue chip common stock?"

"Why not?"

"And what about Regulation 13-D?"

"I explained that. The SEC regulation says when you buy 5 percent of a company's shares you have to identify yourself. But the mob buys through nameless Swiss accounts. So when they've bought 4.9 percent of, say, DuPont, they seal off that account. It buys no more DuPont. They then open a new numbered account that starts buying 4.9 percent more of DuPont. And nobody, not even the Swiss banks, knows that each 4.9 is really owned by the same principal. Clear?"

She watched him make himself a cup of instant coffee and begin sipping it black. "Curtiss, you're saying the West's major profit centers are being bought out from under us. That we soon won't control any of it. That organized crime will be the universal boss of us all."

"Not right away, Mary Lee."

"Then when?"

"Maybe never." He took the rest of the cracker from her and began munching it. "The way I see it, the mob could have started doing this long ago. They have had a billion-plus a year in cash flow ever since, say, the 1960s. It's all laundered and untraceable. They could have started buying up Unilever or IBM or Fiat long ago. Instead they concentrated on small banks, regional businesses like supermarket chains, trucking companies, construction firms, vending machines, always local in scope."

"I understand that," she said. "A mob family is regional. It makes sense to keep the investments local."

"That's half the answer. The rest is that no family ever truly trusts another family, not on something involving billions. Suspicion is genetically encoded in these people. And since every mob family is a lot like the next, they know what treacherous bastards the other can be."

She looked sad. "Make me a cup?"

He prepared a second coffee. "Who's outside the house now," he told her as he handed her the cup, "I don't know. But what I'm afraid is that they represent the one thing that hasn't happened before."

"That the mobs have finally got together."

"That someone has the respect and clout to make them all toe the line, kick in to a consortium and let it be managed for them."

"The other worry," she mused, "is how long ago this miracle-worker began undermining the big corporations. This year? Last?"

Curtiss shrugged. "Five years ago? Who knows?" He picked up his cup. "Come on. Maybe the mist's lifted."

They moved into the darkened living room. Curtiss stared through the curtain slit. "Visibility's better, don't you think?"

Mary Lee sipped her coffee, staring out of a different slit towards the far end of the parklike area below. "You may be ri—"

There was no sound except a glass chip pinging out of the window. A round hole opened. The cup in Curtiss's hand exploded. Coffee splashed over the parquet floor. He dropped to his knees. Mary Lee hit the floor and rolled sideways from the window.

"Son of a bitch," Curtiss murmured, his knees soaked with hot liquid. "Son of a bitch. Silencer. Small caliber. Sniperscope sight. Bastard can see in the dark. Infrared radiation. Zeroes in on the hot coffee cup."

"My God, baby." He could hear her teeth chattering. "What if you'd been holding it against your chest? My God!"

"Keep low. The angle's against them. If we keep low they can't get a bead on us."

She crawled over to him. "You all right?"

He nodded. She had her arms around him now, shaking with her own fright and trying to rub his body as if to warm him. He held her for a long while until they both stopped shaking.

"Do you think we can get out of here down the back stairs?"

He shook his head. "It only leads to the cellar. I'm going to try to raise the concierge. Or call Louch again."

They crawled across the smooth wood floor to the office. The moment Curtiss, kneeling beside the desk, picked up the phone, he could hear it was dead. The needle of the meter remained at rest. There was no dial tone. When he blew into the microphone he got no "side tone" through the earphone. "Cut," he said.

Mary Lee was silent for a long moment. "Then what's their next move? They still aren't sure if you're armed or not."

"But we know something about them. The two of us have been moving back and forth. They could have taken a shot at us any time. They chose to try for me. That tells me they don't want you."

"You're not being logical."

"By their logic I am." He sighed unhappily. "The way you winkle us out of this place is really *not* by trying to sharpshoot with an infrared scope. That's superchancy. If you want to do the job right the first time you put a grenade launcher on your rifle and you lob something highly destructive into this room when you know we're walking around in it. Shrapnel will do the rest. Follow me?"

"Yeah."

He rubbed his damp knees. The smell of coffee permeated the air. "Okay, you don't do that. Instead you take your least favorable option. You try to pick me off. It doesn't work. Now what?"

"Yes, I see."

"But if I'm right, they *can't* use the grenade because that would get both of us. It's only me they want."

Their glances locked in the darkness, their pupils wide and black. "I don't know," she said. "I wouldn't mind dying next to you."

"Mary Lee, stop being romantic."

"Romantic? We're both overage for Romeo or Juliet." She watched him closely. "But this is beginning to shape up like a final scene, isn't it?"

"Not necessarily. Grenades are noisy. So far they've been using silencers."

"A grenade might rouse the whole neighborhood?" she asked.

He nodded. "But neither of us would get much comfort out of it," he added grimly, "if the guy's aim was any good."

11

"*Sentite*," the tall man hissed in the shadows behind the shrubbery. The guttural clicks and stops of the dialect came in a singsong whine, as of a bitter complaint. "What are you doing, Turi?"

"You see?" The other man had clicked a long, fat cigarlike grenade to the launcher attached to the barrel of the rifle. "Do I have to explain?"

"But this will kill both of them."

"What they deserve," Turi muttered, dropping to one knee and cradling the rifle.

"Remember the orders, Turi."

"I am not a slave." He sighted through the thick monocular of the Sniperscope.

"Turi, the man, not the woman."

"Fortunes of war." He steadied himself. The grenade launcher moved slightly upward as he zeroed in on a window in Curtiss's apartment across the gardenlike lawn.

"It cannot be, Turi."

"You will spoil my aim, coward."

"The orders must be obeyed."

When he saw that Turi was ignoring him, the tall man quickly reviewed what options he had. Almost none. Don B's orders had been quite clear. He stared down at Turi with a peculiar look, penetrating and thoughtful, but with no hint of human linkage, as of one person to another.

Spoiled Calabrese princeling, the tall man thought. These southerners were all alike, as he himself should know, having come from that same region of Italy. Perhaps the tall man had avoided this kind of spoiling because his mother had turned him loose on the streets when he was five. Not for him the coddling of the sons of the rich.

And make no mistake about it, Don Gino, who had sired this rebellious, disobedient princeling of a Turi, was rich. Living in his mountain village in Calabria, a tiny hill town called Sabbia D'Oro, Don Gino seemed on the surface more of a peasant than the meanest *contadino*. But that was camouflage. And he had thoroughly spoiled this Turi until he was useless in the kind of work to which Don B had assigned him.

Turi's mother, or aunt or grandmother or cousin or nurse, had spoon-fed him through childhood, cut up his meat on his plate until he was eight or nine years of age, denied him nothing, allowed him to run free, screaming, as a blatant annoyance to the world, no discipline, no punishment, no consequences. The sons of the southern rich.

But tonight, right at this moment, faced with following orders or behaving like a petulant child, Turi was pushing far beyond the bounds of his ability and the respect that should be shown him. He was isolating himself from his own power base and didn't seem to realize it.

"Obey, Turi," the tall man rasped. "Obey orders."

"From a skinny old man a thousand miles away. For shame, coward."

"Turi, I beg of you."

"Shut up. Let a man work."

The blade, well-honed, began with a thin two-edged point but widened into a thick chunk of steel with grooves that let air into the wound. It sank four inches up to its hilt in the space between Turi's neck and shoulder where the artery runs. His eyes rolled up into his head. The tall man let the knife remain in Turi as a plug, stopping the jet of hot arterial crimson blood that would spout. He lowered Turi to the ground and picked up the rifle.

"*Maladetta testadura!*" he groaned under his breath.

"All right," Louch said in French, shoving a Walther PPK in his gut. "Drop the cannon, *paisano*."

The tall man's eyes narrowed as he obeyed. "How long have you been watching?"

The tall, heavy-set cop in plainclothes shrugged carelessly. He disarmed the gun and frisked the tall man for another weapon. Finding none, he whistled softly, twice. Scuffles broke out here and there around the mist-shrouded perimeter of the Cité Odiot.

"Ever since you cut the phone line, stupid man," Louch said then. "When I could not call him back, I knew what was up."

He yanked the tall man's arms behind him and clicked them together with handcuffs. "Now for the citizen on the stairwell inside."

"He will never surrender," the tall man boasted.

Louch crossed the bare ground where the high chestnut tree made grass impossible to grow. He opened the front door of Curtiss's building. "*Paisano*," he called up the stairs, "we have the other three. Drop the gun and come down the stairs with your hands over your head. *Capische?*"

Silence. Louch turned back for a moment to watch the strong white teeth of the tall man bared in a triumphant smile of pride. The strongest discipline in the world, Louch reminded himself.

From the stairs above he heard a thud. Slowly, hands above his head, a short, squat young man came cautiously down the stairs, eyes wide with fear. Louch kept the Walther aimed at his stomach. "Outside," he said quietly. He watched as one of his men came up, frisked the newcomer and handcuffed him.

"There's a stiff in the bushes," Louch said. "Get all of them into the patrol wagon. I'll be with you in a moment. And be careful with the stiff. Leave the knife where it is."

He continued up the steps, pocketed the Browning .9 on the landing and knocked discreetly on Curtiss's door. He waited, slouching as if tired, but this was a pose he often took. "Curtiss," he called through the door. "Don't force me to shout. I do not want to alarm the grocer's widow downstairs."

The door swung open and Curtiss stood there, still in his sneakers and track suit. "Going for a run?" Louch pushed past him into the room. "What the hell *is* all this?"

"I would tell you if I knew, Louch. But all I can do is thank you. You saved my life."

Louch looked at his damp knees, then at the remains of the coffee cup on the floor. His glance also took in another coffee cup on the floor, unbroken but spilled. His glance returned to rest heavily on Curtiss. "You'll have to come back to the station with me. I need a statement."

"Certainly. Now?"

"Certainly now," Louch said in a no-nonsense tone. He stared at the unbroken cup. "You have no explanation at all?"

"None."

"No suggestion?" Louch didn't wait for an answer. "I can hold them a while. After all, one of them knifed his pal. But there is nothing to explain why he chose the Cité Odiot in which to do it. Perhaps they will be more talkative than you." He paused and grimaced. "Anyone would be. Let's go."

At one a.m. Curtiss wearily climbed the stairs. He had done the best he could with Louch, who obviously thought he was lying to save someone else. Which he was.

For the time being, Jet-Tech and Mary Lee Hunter's connection with all this would remain hidden. She had had plenty of time to leave the Cité Odiot unnoticed, return to her hotel and book herself out on one of the early morning flights to New York. As her UBCO adviser, Curtiss had done what was expected of him, protect the client.

He let himself into the flat and sank down in an armchair in the living room. She had removed the broken bits of cup and cleaned up the spilled coffee before she left. He let out a low sigh. Something strong about now. Scotch and ice and very little soda.

She was right about bringing them with her. The minute they knew she was going to see him in Paris, they knew they had a job on their hands. And it wasn't finished.

"Here," Mary Lee said, standing in the doorway with two glasses of Scotch. "I read minds."

"I expected you to have gone."

"My flight doesn't leave till noon. We have tons of time. How much do the police know?" She sat down on the floor and hugged his knees.

"I managed to deflect Louch for a while, but he knows someone else was in here with me. He's not pursuing it because he's not sure it has any bearing on the case. He probably thinks I'm playing Sir Galahad for a lady fair."

"And she appreciates it, baby." She hugged him tighter. "Drink your drink."

"Drink yours."

"Can't. Too upset. This isn't over, Curtiss."

"No. It's only beginning. What's happened is what I was afraid would happen. The big scam is under way. Someone *has* got it all together. He does have complete mob loyalty. And he can't have either of us blowing the whistle on him."

He stopped talking. "No," he said again, helpless to stop himself, "it's only the beginning."

PART TWO

•

A Tale to Chill Your Flesh

12

The two men resembled each other physically. They had stretched out in two deck chairs rented from the attendant in Green Park. Beyond the iron fence Piccadilly traffic roared by in the hot sun. Tall red buses, trucks of all sizes, cars and motorcycles spewed a pale blue haze above the pavement. But here, two hundred yards away, the roar dwindled to a murmur and the air smelled sweetly of newly mown grass.

Julian, who claimed to have not yet reached the age of fifty, was the more formally dressed of the two, in grey trousers, a dark blue double-breasted blazer with gold buttons, blue striped shirt and school tie.

The other, who was in his late fifties, had been playing tennis in Cadogan Place and was still dressed in shorts, a V-neck white shirt and sneakers. His long legs looked firm and his face, except for the deep hollows under his cheekbones, seemed hale enough. In fact, unless one knew Woods Palmer, Jr. rather well, one would have thought him perhaps younger than Julian. Only his racket, the oversized Prince type, gave away the fact that in middle age his eyes needed help.

"Lovely, isn't she?" Julian was saying as both men followed the progress of a young woman barely in her twenties. She had made for a chair and was now removing her blouse and skirt to reveal a bikini swim suit. Other people were exposing themselves to the June sun of London, but no one had done as thorough a job of it as this young woman.

"A quid says she doffs the top," the Englishman wagered.

Palmer laughed. "I never bet with artful coves on their home turf."

"She may turn on to her tummy to avoid exposing the peerless globes," Julian added. "But free them she will."

"And with you on hand," Palmer put in, "the globes will not remain peerless for long."

Julian studied this remark a while. He was not unfamiliar with American humor, but trod carefully in its presence. Palmer had lived abroad for many years, holed up on a mountain top in Switzerland with his mistress, a smashing woman named, uh, Helen? Ellen? So perhaps his humor had become more European. Still, "peerless."

Julian produced a polite laugh.

"My dear Palmer," he continued, "you do my heart good. Just seeing you glowing with the old piss and vinegar makes me hope for my own middle years."

Palmer's smile curdled slightly at the edges. "My spies tell me you and I were born the same year, Julian."

The Englishman made a face of horror. "Wot, Vintage of 1923?" He fell silent. Then he seemed to perk up slightly. "Still we're both fairly well preserved, you with your tennis, I with pious fucking."

He glanced sideways at Palmer to gauge the effect of this remark. He found Palmer eyeing him in the same shifty fashion. They both broke out laughing. At which point the young woman bared her breasts and slowly turned over on her tummy.

"But never that young," Julian continued almost without pause. "I have a weakness for the mid-thirties, the early forties. Women are really at their best then. Do you know the Bank Rup?"

Palmer nodded. "And I know Urs's secretary."

"Gad, what a spy system you do maintain, old man."

"It's just me. And a friend in Paris."

Palmer sat back and thought about Curtiss without mentioning his name to Julian. Although Palmer had long retired as chief executive officer of UBCO, he and Curtiss remained friends. Something of a mentor-disciple relationship persisted. Curtiss was good at what he did, but he had never been a banker and would never really understand the mystique as Palmer did. A banker's son, Palmer had done nothing else in his life but banking, except for a period in Intelligence during World War II when Major Palmer of the U.S. Army had found himself working with Capt. Julian Sykes-Maulby on a precarious project in Sicily before and during its invasion by Allied troops.

They had become friends then and still were, but in that peculiar Anglo-American manner, often not seeing each other for a year at a time but always able to pick up strong threads

of intimacy within moments after meeting again. Their encounters were never planned, always as accidental as this
one, when Julian, tiptoeing out of a lady's flat on Sloane
Street at eight this morning, had spotted Palmer playing
tennis across the street. Pure accident.

"How amazing to run into you," the Englishman said once
more as they sat in their canvas chairs. He studied the bare
curve of the young woman's back, then put it aside. "Fortu-
itous coincidence. Your name came up only last week. Some
chap asked if I knew where to get hold of you. Can I tell him
you're in London?"

"What chap?"

"One of my directors, Jack Heddon. He's with Nat Ken,"
he added using the nickname of one of Britain's bigger
national banks.

"What's he doing as part of your pirate crew?"

"I do crave respectability on my board, old man. Yearn for
and desire it beyond rubies. Directors like Jack give it me."

"And a knighthood? Not yet?"

"Not bloody yet," Sykes-Maulby admitted. "I'm too little
known to the general public for there to be any deafening
demand."

"Thank God for that, eh?"

"No jokes, Woods. I do bleed."

Both men were silent for a while. Palmer had begun to get
that feeling most good bankers have, certainly those who had
done four years in Army Intelligence, the feeling that he was
being set up. Julian just happening to see him on the court at
eight a.m.? Julian, who could never stir himself out of a bunk
before ten in the morning, even as a young man, even under
aerial attack by Stukas? Palmer's nose twitched. The quid
Julian had wanted to bet on the breasts? He'd be willing to
wager a fiver there was nothing at all accidental about being
accosted in Cadogan Place this morning.

"Well," Julian was saying. "It wasn't really Jack Heddon
alone. I cannot tell a lie to an old comrade, Palmer. We all
longed to talk to you and when our spies reported you were
on that bloody court every bloody morning at bloody eight
a.m., well..."

Palmer nodded. Much better. Julian's technique, always
smooth, constantly improved. A banker can stand anything
but being lied to. He turned to face Julian more directly.
Both men were squinting into the hot sun.

"What are you longing to talk to me about?"

"Advice," Sykes-Maulby snapped. "My group does a bit of financing through UBCO. But we're not—"

"I have no connection with UBCO any more."

"—the only ones who have noticed this," Julian sailed on blithely through the interruption. "Many other investment groups have seen the same thing. So have the British banks. UBCO is not being managed well, Palmer. There's the truth of it. The present top men are passive. They have neither fire in the belly nor blood in the veins. Their favorite word is 'no.' But they aren't candid enough to utter it. Instead they tergiversate, procrastinate, committeeize, and generally bury every request under a mound of memoranda until we go elsewhere, having wasted up to a year of our time."

He took a long breath and patted his forehead with a florid handkerchief. Then, stuffing it with artistic carelessness back in his breast pocket, he turned to Palmer. "And don't tell me this is the first time you've heard such a complaint."

"I can't tell you that," Palmer admitted, "because you're not the only one who thinks I still have some influence over UBCO. I don't. Yes, I am a stockholder. But I know no more than what I read in the printed annual report."

"A major stockholder."

"Yes. All right."

Julian patted Palmer's arm as it lay on the wooden side of the deck chair. "Don't sound so defensive, old man. It's not your stock that makes us long for you. It's the thought that—" He stopped and was silent for a long moment. "It's the fact," he went on more slowly, "that UBCO was never better managed than under you. That once you left, despite its vast size, it turned into a helpless giant ministered to by lackeys, not leaders."

When he failed to go on, Palmer realized he was expected to know the next step, which he didn't. "Are you cooking up some sort of palace revolution in New York?" he asked. "Is there a proxy battle? Do you want my shares voting your way?"

Sykes-Maulby's head was shaking gravely from side to side. "No, no, a thousand times no, old man. It is not your shares we covet. It is your body."

"Beg pardon?"

"Back at the helm. In the saddle. Whatever the appropriate American slang is. We want to replace the top men with a real leader. We want you out of retirement running UBCO.

And you will have the knowledge that when you are gathered to your Maker, you will go with the heartfelt blessings and undiluted loyalty of every financial bloke in Christendom."

Palmer was grinning. "What an incentive. The thanks of every international moneyman, con-artist, embezzler, loan-kiter, assets-raider, conglomerator, Ponzi swindler, syndicator, market manipulator, shares inflator, Eurobond discounter, factor, currency speculator, commodities faker and arbitrageur from London to Vienna and from Singapore to Hong Kong?"

Julian decided this was definitely humor. He laughed free-ly, noting along the way that Palmer had already ticked off more than a few lines of activity the Sykes-Maulby group occasionally indulged in.

"Then the answer's yes?" he asked brightly.

"Julian, you never let up, do you?"

"Not when you're this close to agreeing."

Palmer shook his head in wonderment. "You've met Eleanora? Yes, two years ago when you visited me in Morcote. You remember the good life we lead? And you have the mindless temerity to ask me to give it up for the New York ulcer-mill?"

"For the excitement, old man. The sense of achievement. In Morcote you are in aspic. There is no movement. Yes, your Eleanora is a lovely companion. I remember her as being highly intelligent as well. A most attractive companion for one's old age. But you are not yet old, Palmer. Nothing you do in that vegetable life you lead in Morcote has damped the fire in *your* belly."

"Nonsense. When it's dull we go to Paris or London. Or New York. We see what life has become in the big-time world and return to Morcote as fast as we can. Suddenly it isn't dull. It's healing."

"I grant you that," Julian retorted. "But man does not live by rest-cure alone. *Homo faber.* Man, the maker. Not eternal-ly at rest. Plenty of time for that after the funeral."

Palmer sat without speaking for a long time. "Very well put," he said then in a somewhat faraway voice. The girl with the bare breasts turned on her back. No one was watching. Along Piccadilly an open-topped sightseeing doubledecker bus had paused in traffic. After a moment it disappeared beyond the Ritz.

"I used to feel that way, Julian," Palmer said at last. "Almost precisely that way. Life was short. We were here to make our mark. But then I began to examine the kind of mark we were making. I decided the world would be much better off if we—we bankers in my case—stopped making our goddamned marks."

"You jest, old man."

"Dead earnest."

A fly settled on Palmer's bare knee. He watched it for a moment. It preened its wings, glistening blue-green in the sunlight, then flew up, circled, flew away.

"The banks have a lot to answer for," Palmer said in a low tone of voice. "Or, rather, our credit policies have. Right after the war we broke out into unlimited credit. It was what people wanted. It's so common now people think debt is a form of savings. We've completely stood logic on its head."

"Another public service of the banking fraternity."

"Don't make black jokes." Palmer stared up at the cloudless sky. The hollows under his cheeks disappeared momentarily. "But the anxiety of hundreds of millions of private debtors is nothing to what we have done to stimulate corporate debt. Government debt. Everything now is borrowed, even I am sure next week's salary for that bobby giving directions over there to the three German backpackers."

"You may be certain of it, old man."

"Our world moans about inflation," Palmer went on, still in a quiet voice. "But the main reason prices keep rising is the amount of debt service hiding inside everything. Everything. There's no more money to be made in industry, either by the industrialist or his workers. They're both on the same debt spiral. Both look to government to end inflation. But government's the biggest debtor of all. Why should your government, or mine, cut inflation—assuming it could—when it means paying back at some future date in cheaper currency? Deferring payment a few years almost cuts the cost of repaying in half."

"Spare me, Palmer. I live in this world, too."

"Sorry. Carried away."

"No offense, old man."

"But you do see," Palmer persisted with more emphasis than before, "why I am no longer interested in being *homo faber* if what I make is more debt."

"Dear, dear," Julian muttered. "Touch of the dread male menopause, I do believe."

Palmer grinned. "I've *had* that, thank you. Eleanora is the result. A mistress twenty years younger does wonders for the middle-age blues."

"Not that part of menopause," the Englishman demurred. "The part where one gazes fixedly on one's past and labels it shit. Terrifying. But temporary, old man, I promise you. A man with your feel for things at the helm of UBCO again? The greatest medicine in the world for you."

"It's my mental health you're catering to?"

"I have ulterior motives, of course." Sykes-Maulby gestured airily. "One always does. But surely one needs no clearer motive than to bolster the acumen and profitability of a great bank. That I am a comrade of its once and future leader is all to the good. But I would be interested in the health of any major international bank. Weakness anywhere leads to weakness everywhere."

Palmer frowned slightly. "It's when you go all patriotic and altruistic that you worry me, Julian. Just tell me what deals you have cooking that need a pal at the UBCO. Just be Julian."

The Englishman glanced around him quickly, but casually, as if checking the possibility of eavesdroppers. Overhead a white Pan Am 747 gained altitude slowly, almost unheard in the medley of London sound.

Julian glanced upward at the plane as if suspecting long-range listening devices. Then he sat forward in his chair and listed sharply to his left, bringing his lips within a few inches of Palmer's right ear.

"I would," he muttered, "unfold a tale to chill your flesh, old man. I only have a piece of it. But before I do, tell me something. Am I dreaming or did you once have a run-in with the Sicilian allies of our youth? Hadn't some of them breached the UBCO hull and begun boring from within?"

"You are not dreaming."

"And you beat them off with a stout stick?"

"Something like that."

"So I thought. So I told Jack Heddon after an abysmal fiasco involving UBCO. I said, dear me, they are at it again. Or words to that effect. Didn't Woods Palmer fumigate 'em some years back? And Jack's eyes lit up. 'Palmer!' he cried aloud. 'The very man!' Which is where today's grisly fandango began, old man, sending poor Sykes-Maulby out into the cold at eight a.m. and onto a park chair watching twenty-year-old titties. At my age."

"Go ahead. Chill my flesh."

"Well," Julian began, warming slowly to his tale, "it begins with a bit of a flyer my group was taking in oil leases out Bahrein way. The details are superfluous, of course. Suffice it to say we had our local Wog with his half of the dib, royal family, all the latest mod cons, Harvard business school, rarely wears a tablecloth on his head, fornicates woman rather than boy. All in all a likely local partner."

He leaned back in his canvas sling and took a long breath. "Abdullah, as he will be known in these chronicles, awaited our half of the dib. We looked among a very select group of sources for as few primary leaders as necessary. We were yearning, in fact, to do half through UBCO, which has a reputation of expertise in matters oily. Once secured, their loan would bring in the rest at a velocity approaching the four-minute mile, stumbling all over each other to get a piece of our action. Right?"

He sighed heavily. "Right. Meanwhile those sods at UBCO simply couldn't pull out the finger. They sat on the request, bucked it from committee to committee and in general gave us a diddling none of us enjoyed. And Abdullah got wind of it, we know not how."

He yanked out his decorative handkerchief and patted his forehead again. "In respect of my reputation with wine and women I was deputized to Concorde myself out to sheik land and keep Abdullah happy. One night in the midst of a truly Lucullan Arabian Nights festivity I had laid on at crushing expense—dancing girls, laughing girls, fucking girls, a bloody operetta—enters a lackey with a phone on a long cord. 'California,' he says, handing the instrument to Abdullah."

Julian stuffed the handkerchief back into his breast pocket. He stared moodily at the girl's bared breasts for a moment. Then: "Too lushed to realize I could hear every word, Abdullah talks for five minutes with a broker named Ben who is offering him—listen hard, old man—not the 50 percent we offered him, but—" His voice soared upward in anguish. "Two fucking thirds! Before I could gulp or choke, the deals were consummated."

He glanced around him again to make sure no one had taken notice of his outburst. "You can imagine what my group had to tell me when I reported this contretemps. Pipped at the post by—and this was what hurt—not another group or another bank. A lowly brokerage firm, rank newcomers. But there was yet a deeper profundity to which our sorrow was forced to sink. A brokerage, old man, with primary financing from—wait for it—UBCO!"

Palmer turned slowly to him. "Rotten luck."

"Luck had nothing to do with it." He pulled for a moment on his long, aquiline nose. "Name Bennett Brown mean anything to you? Brown, Brown, Pierce, Finch and Cohen?"

"You're making that up." Palmer's mind sifted. "Brown. Bruno. Benedetto Bruno." He was silent a moment. "Don B."

"The father. Bennett Brown, the son. Harvard School of Business Administration, class of Abdullah. Class of Urs Rup as well."

Palmer sighed and turned away. "I can't tell you how I loathe what you just told me," he said in a low tone. "This is what I was talking about before. All I want to do is fly back to Morcote and forget I ever heard what you said."

"You're free to, old man."

Palmer hesitated. Julian, for all his deviousness, had been quite frank. Things had been hidden, of course, but Palmer expected it. There were always hidden things. Palmer, for instance, was going to hide from the Englishman the facts Curtiss had reported to him from Paris last night, just as Curtiss, Palmer felt sure, had not given him all the details.

Details were not needed. It was clear enough. Elements of organized crime had established a beachhead at the top of UBCO. It might be as high as the board itself. It might be simply one of the executive vice-presidents. The disturbing thing was not so much that it might be true, as that Bill Elston hadn't caught on yet. It was his job, among others, to stop such attempts.

Two stories, Julian's and Curtiss's, both quite different. But one thing they had in common which neither man realized. Only Palmer could have spotted the connection.

The name Brown.

13

Giggling, two naked young women disappeared inside the cubelike beach house surrounded at the edges of the compound by tall, shaggy eucalyptus trees. The sun was bright and hot. A faintly menthol-like smell was given out by the leaves and scaly bark of the trees.

Both women were tall and in their mid-thirties. One was pregnant. She led the way down three steps in the cool half-dark of the house. In the kitchen cube she opened the top of an immense freezer box the size of a baby grand piano. Both women stared down into its frosty depths, chill air streaming around their bare bodies.

"Veal parmigiana," B. J. called out, "veal piccata, veal scaloppini, veal peperoncini, veal cacciatore. Totally nude veal without a damned thing on it."

"Jesus, B. J., don't you ever make anything from scratch?"

"What's scratch?"

They broke into giggles again. Then Mary Lee shivered. "Pick something before I freeze to death."

"Hey, here's a real gourmet treat," B. J. removed two wrapped cheeseburgers and a packet of French fries. While these heated in the microwave oven, she poured two cans of Coke into tall glasses choked with ice. "Talk about American grub. Ketchup on the fries?"

"Oh, wow."

Waiting for the oven's telltale bleep, they wandered here and there through the up-and-down levels of the house. In the living room cube they found themselves facing a wall of plate-glass mirror. The sight of the two tall, not unattractive bodies arrested them. They gazed, fascinated.

"Your muff is positively luxuriant."

"It's just darker than yours," B. J. explained. "Will you look at that belly? Will you? That's not a baby, it's a great white whale."

"Twins?"

"Scan says no."

Mary Lee examined their reflections. "Should I have one? Curtiss seems capable of doing the job. It's safe enough. He doesn't want to get married any more than I do." She fell silent, smoothing down her flat belly. "How does it feel?"

"Not my favorite condition in the whole world," B. J. admitted. "Have you watched me try to pick up something I just dropped in front of me? And what is all this dark grungy skin building up around my nipples?"

"I guess it's supposed to thicken up like that."

"You guess. I guess. Obstetrics, the leisure avocation of the whole world. I have a doctor. Now and then he takes time off from tennis and surfing and hang gliding to deliver a baby. Keep his hand in, so to speak."

Mary Lee hooted. "As long as you can—"

"—make jokes," B. J. finished for her. "Mary Lee, don't get knocked up."

Her words, half blurted, turned them both melancholy. Faces grave, they gazed questioningly at the two naked women in the mirror. "The continuation of the human race," Mary Lee said at last. "Who asked for the responsibility?"

"The continuation of who?" B. J. picked up in a low, faraway tone. "It gives me the creeps to know I have a stranger in there, half of whose forebears are a mystery to me. I know Ben. But I've never even had one of his kinsfolk pointed out to me across a crowded room. As far as I can tell he sprang full blown from the brow of Zeus."

"That's not the creepy part," Mary Lee assured her. "What about the soon-to-be paternal granny and grampaw? Where are they, les Browns? Your folks drop in and buzz around like a pair of fruit flies. Where are Ben's folks?"

"Ever tried to force Ben to talk? Those black eyes? Ever had them on you in dead silence for anything longer than a minute?"

B. J. stroked her belly with a circular, brushing motion as if currying a horse. "You see what I mean about not getting knocked up? Mary Lee, if he makes the hormones fizz, love him just the way he izz. Where is it written that Mr. Right makes either a good husband or a good father? Keep taking that pill, Mary Lee."

Mary Lee stared at her friend's face in the huge mirror. "Hey," she said at last, "something sour between you and Ben? I won't have that, B. J. I look around and see a lot of couples breaking up because they're miserable with each other and I tell myself, forget it. B. J. and Ben still love each other. That means the dream still holds. So I can ignore the reality."

B. J. took her time answering. "The reality is I love him. Maybe worse than ever."

"That's a great way to put it."

B. J. nodded in agreement. "He still does something to me. And I know I'm not alone. I see the way women react to him at parties." She paused. "Used to react. We haven't been out at a party for some time now."

"Why not?"

"No idea. I think Ben has some notion that staying up late and drinking booze is bad for fetuses. And, automatically, it becomes a no-no."

"Still playing the pregnant father."

A rather heavy sigh escaped B. J. "That's what attracted me to him, you know. He had this obsessively old-fashioned feeling of family. I suppose it's because he has hardly any himself. Things work like that, don't they? So he desperately craves a family of his own and, by God, pretty soon you're sharing the obsession with him and you want to give him the biggest damned family in the history of gestation."

"That," Mary Lee said slowly, "is love."

"Well, what else would it be?" B. J. demanded. "I see these guys free-floating around California. Ben used to seem like the rest of them, cool. But he isn't that at all. Inside there is this very warm, family-oriented, intensely personal man. Being private doesn't mean being disinterested."

Mary Lee smiled into the mirror. "You don't have to promote Ben with me, baby."

"I know. You love him, too." B. J. made a face at her naked figure. "I just didn't want you to confuse advice I was giving you with my feelings about being married to Ben and having his child. The advice still goes. The fact that I have taken another route doesn't invalidate anything I said."

"Nor does it mean that if you were single again, you'd spurn Mr. Right," Mary Lee suggested perhaps too smoothly.

B. J. laughed. "There is only one Ben."

"The fatal feeling." Mary Lee massaged her forehead with her fingertips. "I had this hallucination in Paris. The ice was cracking under me and I was breaking up with it. Underneath, chaos. And I said to myself: Curtiss will handle it. He'll get me back together. It won't matter because I can trust him. He's unique. There is only one Curtiss."

"Danger signals."

"But not for you," Mary Lee countered.

"Leave logic out of it, will you? We're talking about witchcraft. Magic. Ben wove a spell around me. I'm quite happy inside it. Which doesn't mean . . ." B. J. stopped talking. "Look at those two loonies," she said then, to the mirror.

As they stared at their bodies, B. J. slowly turned sideways. She pulled in her abdomen but it made no difference in her profile. At the same time, Mary Lee slumped to emphasize hers. Her attempt at equalizing the difference, a failure, went unremarked.

"If we could step through the mirror," Mary Lee said softly, mooning at their reflections. "On the other side, like Alice."

"On the other side," B. J. picked up in a voice full of fake confidence, "you find your world in which men carry the babies. Yes, ladies. Women slither around like snakes fucking anything that stands still. But your average male has a rough time if he wants to get laid. And, ladies, you will hardly believe the schemes and strategems he uses to avoid the dread pregnancy. Pills, crazy thingies stuffed up his penis, foams squirting, little rubber catcher's mitts. Not a moment of peace. And if he lets down even one night, bingo. A baby starts growing in his penis. Right, ladies? And the poor male has to either have it or kill it. A lot of men can't handle that, being sentimental softies. Can you imagine, ladies, what it does to their careers? How can they possibly function effectively? Why, it's hard to see how any of them hold onto a job, except by putting out for the boss."

"And later in life," Mary Lee picked up, using the same salesman's tone of voice, "what happens if they get their bit of fibroid or cyst or whatever? What do the leading women doctors tell their male gynecological patients? Well, ladies, whip-snip, off it comes, balls and all. Now here is where I get to the part about lumps on their shallow male breasts."

"Not ready for it."

A long silence, gazing into the mirror. Finally Mary Lee sighed. "You do miss your job, don't you, B. J.?"

Another long silence. "I had achieved something. It took a lot of doing. Now I've traded it for something even a feeble-minded teenager can pull just by lying still and shutting up." She patted her belly. "Hi-ho."

The microwave oven bleeped cheerily in the other cube.

When they carried the piping hot food out onto the terrace, a group of young men in bare minimum bikini bottoms were playing volleyball on the beach below them. Mary Lee reached for her robe to try to cover up. "Not necessary," B. J. told her as they watched the players grabbing each other and administering friendly little gooses as the ball flew back and forth overhead. "They're gay."

The naked lunch progressed swiftly for a few minutes, then slowed down as the weight of the sun and the leaden sogginess of cheeseburgers prepared in this manner seemed to smother both women in lethargy. Even the stomach-stopping chill of the Cokes failed to rouse them.

"Eat anywhere nice in Paris?" B. J. pushed away her plate.

"I ate only one meal in three days. Not counting an omelette I whipped up at his apartment."

B. J. shrieked on a rising note: "You spent the whole weekend with him? I thought it was an evening. You really blew your cool."

"Blew more than that." Giggles swamped them. "B. J., this was my first."

"Come on, first what?"

"First time I didn't get up and leave. You know me: one night and I'm on my way." She watched the young men cavorting and the surf breaking behind them. "Of course, Curtiss had help."

"Mary Lee! Two guys?"

"Nothing that bizarre. Just a very hairy situation. You know," she turned to her oldest and best friend, "maybe the two of us have been together too long. We kind of keep the juvenile alive in both of us. I like that, B. J., don't get me wrong. But outside the world you and I have, there is a very dark, unpleasant place. We don't support each other there. We can't. Giggles don't help there. It's a *male* place. They made it and they understand it, the murderous bastards."

The two young women sat in silence, contemplating the inedible food. As if at a signal, they each pushed it out of sight and watched the volleyball game.

"Maybe Ben can give you some advice," B. J. said at last.

"You think he could help?"

"He'll be home late tonight. And you know Ben. If he can help you, he will."

14

London's charm is partly its ability to hide away quiet villages within a few yards of roaring metropolitan thoroughfares. One such enclave of privacy is Kinnerton Street.

It lies off Knightsbridge's deafening glut of top-heavy

buses, rumbling dreadnoughts, taxis, cars and motorbikes. Down Wilton Place past a hotel so expensive it bears no name, a sharp turn-off leads to Kinnerton Street.

Along this mews of two-story homes five lanes lead back into protected courtyards. At its far end, near Motcomb Street, the street explodes into high-rise apartment houses. Whatever strategy one chooses for hiding—anonymous mews house or featureless flat—Kinnerton Street seems peculiarly adapted for privacy.

One particular house that stands at the courtyard end of a narrow lane bears a secret of its own. In its basement two other routes lead to escape, a handy way of confusing idle onlookers, neighborhood gossips and hired observers. One can come out either through the lane one entered, or a second nearby or, through the rear via William Mews, to Lowndes Square.

It is perhaps not surprising that this house of many exits is owned by Julian Sykes-Maulby.

A few of his favored female companions know about the lanes leading back into Kinnerton Street. But only one woman in Julian's busy life knows the exit to Lowndes Square and he has never bedded her. Nor ever will.

Miranda Smith, née Lamb, now in her early thirties, is well married to a medium-level Foreign Office Secretary. Their two children combine family lines far more illustrious than the royal one. Their mother Miranda is one of those chic, self-possessed women whose presence on a charity committee automatically signals upward-striving folk to say: "Ah, well, then, we'd best join at once."

Her husband, Giles Smith, has a schizoid distaste for these charitable galas but, for Miranda, the events are occasions at which she can openly engage in light-hearted banter with the man whose mistress she has been for some time, the exalted person Julian refers to as Himself.

It was Sykes-Maulby who first introduced them after Himself had asked that such an encounter be created. This discreet house off Kinnerton Street was the place in which their romance blossomed. Himself came and went, with his guards, via Kinnerton Street. Miranda departed by the Lowndes Square route.

It was not Julian's idea of a fulfilling relationship since its moments were snatched from Himself's intense schedule of public events and travels. In any case, Sykes-Maulby saw himself as a gatekeeper in his own home, living on the first floor and keeping the ground-floor flat in a condition of permanent readiness.

Only a handful of close friends even suspected his role in the affair. Of the affair itself, rather more than a handful knew but kept it quiet. No onus attached to Julian. No one called him an unkind name like pimp, nor did a business rival sneer at the potential profit to be made. Quite the contrary. Among those who knew, Sykes-Maulby enjoyed tremendous respect. Even envy.

Tonight, it being well after dinner, Julian could relax. He would have the house to himself, no lurking guards, no tormenting visions of what the luscious Miranda and Himself might be up to, often quite audibly, on the floor below.

Julian had installed himself on a chaise-longue with a glass of the old Veuve Clicquot and that morning's *Financial Times*. He had yet to scan its pink pages, being one of those money-wallahs, as he put it, who made the news others only read about. But as Bennett Brown was due to ask for his suggestions next week, Julian had to study share price listings and other entrails of the financial beast.

When the unlisted phone rang at nine-thirty, a voice he knew to be a security aide of Himself asked the key question: "All clear?"

"No one's here, old boy, but me."

"Quite." The line went dead.

Sykes-Maulby put away his paper. Miranda he knew to be in Scotland, so it was obviously to be a business chat between himself and Himself. Julian checked his supply of port and removed from the small fridge a round of blue-veined Stilton cheese in its scabby brown skin. He hoped it would warm up in time.

There were long-standing links other than Miranda between Julian and Himself. Ten years before, the financier had been conveyed a substantial amount of sterling with instructions to invest it discreetly but at high return. As if, Julian sniffed, such a thing were possible. Only his newly formed trust seemed to suit the purpose. Although someone as much in the public gaze as Himself had few opportunities to put together secret cash for investment—and Sykes-Maulby specified cash—over the years a rather large sum had accrued. In bad years Julian's trust portfolio only ticked over at ten to twelve percent. But twice it had doubled its principal in a year. Nothing in Himself's highly public life had panned out half as well as Miranda *and* the trust. He was devoted to both.

Julian had made a wealthy young man—who would be waiting decades for his full patrimony—into a downright rich young fella *right now*. Himself belonged to a generation for which instant gratification was important.

"All well and good," he'd once told Sykes-Maulby, "to get it all one day. One day, indeed. It's *right now* that counts."

"Quite, sir."

"And I can hardly put any of Miranda's whacking great bills on public expense, can I?"

"Just so, sir."

"So keep building the secret exchequer, like a dear man, won't you?"

To be fair to Julian, he had not arranged all this because Himself would one day become one of the most powerful men in the world. At that point, sadly, he would have grown beyond reach. Even more sadly, his liaison with Miranda Smith might have to end. But *right now* Himself moved in many circles, picked up innumerable bits of information and saw nothing wrong in gossiping about them with his financial advisor.

The financier had just reknotted his foulard when he heard a car stop downstairs. He saw young men alighting from a Daimler. They began their usual security check-out, shadowing Himself fore and aft until he entered Julian's house and mounted the stairs to the first floor. A security aide preceded him into the apartment. Sykes-Maulby bowed from the waist.

"Your Highness," he said, as they shook hands.

15

Don B's villa, on the outskirts of Palermo, commanded only a small area of land—half an *ettaro*, about an acre—but guarded it extremely well.

A high stone fence, topped by broken glass set in cement, had formed the borders of the land when he bought it some years before. But this had not been enough for Don B, who added cyclone fencing, barbed wire and high voltage to a height of twenty feet. Visitors came and went by only one gate, with a 24-hour guard on duty.

At ten in the morning a black Mercedes 600 arrived at the gate. The driver, in an ordinary suit, used the horn for some time until the presence in the rear seats of Don Gino and one of his associates was reported to the gateman and telephoned to the villa.

Don B, sipping fresh-squeezed orange juice, had heard the horn and had already guessed the identity of the visitors. "Yes," he told his aide in a weary voice, "let him in."

He had been expecting this all morning. The news that Don Gino's son, Turi, had died in Paris would have reached him late last night. Don B glanced at the blood-red juice, as red as that of tomatoes, and made a face. He preferred *biondi di Calabria* oranges that gave a strong yellow juice, not these Sicilian blood-oranges. So thinking, he felt a shiver across his shoulders. He nodded gravely, recognizing the premonition for what it was, a warning of his own death.

He heard footsteps in his patio, composed his face in the lineaments of grief, and went out to meet his visitors, arms outstretched. Silently, rocking back and forth, the two old men embraced. They patted each other's backs in almost the same place that the blade had been shoved into Turi at Don B's orders.

"What a sin. So young."

"So strong and full of life."

"Poor Turi. A fine son."

"May his murderers rot in hell."

"May their mothers watch them hang from the gibbet."

The litany of grief moved almost mechanically back and forth in measured antiphony. Then, dry-eyed, both men stepped back from each other. Don Gino's lieutenant came from their home town on the Ionic, a killer named Frangipani, a first cousin. Don B's own aide hovered at the same discreet distance from the epicenter of grief established by the elderly men.

"They say," Don Gino began, "that the French police tortured him before they killed him."

"Such a man as Turi," Don B responded, "even under brutality would produce no information."

"They say others were captured with him."

"Are they dead yet?" Don B asked blandly.

"Only Turi."

"And the rest?"

"Released."

Don B produced an instant look of shock. "No! Can it be?"

Don Gino eyed him coldly. "So they say."

Don B's arms went out and up. Christlike, he mutely testified to his innocence of such shameful intrigue. "But how is this possible in a civilized country?" he demanded of all of them. "How can the French be so stupid?"

"So corrupt," Don Gino amended in a heavy voice. He glanced sideways at his cousin Frangipani. "Someone paid well," he added.

As if this had been a signal, two more of Don B's men appeared behind Frangipani, not obtrusively, but in a manner that made their presence known. Don Gino drew himself up to his full, bulky height of five and a half feet.

"Here in your Sicilian villa," he told Don B, "surrounded by your hired people," his voice stressed the word "hired," "you lead a secure life."

"It is true," Don B admitted.

"Outside these walls," his visitor added somberly, "life proceeds in other ways."

"That is wisdom."

"May you have the good fortune always to remain within your own protection," Don Gino said in a flat tone of voice, as if pronouncing a ritual benediction or curse.

He and Frangipani left quickly and the gate was shut behind them. A few moments later, in Don B's office, all his guards had gathered.

"You heard?" their employer asked. "He was speaking the dialect of our village, but you understand he holds me responsible for the death of his son? You understand?"

An uneasy, muffled chorus responded, "Sí, *padrone*."

"Extra vigilance, then. Back to your posts."

He watched them leave, some trotting along to impress him with their devotion to duty. But Don Gino had put his finger on the sore spot. These were hirelings, while Don Gino was supported by true family. And in a vendetta, only family could be relied upon.

For make no mistake, this was the start of a vendetta.

16

At night the Carlton Tower Hotel at the head of Cadogan Place seems quiet enough. This part of London, by day, is thick with shopping traffic along Sloane Street and Knightsbridge, heading to or from Harrods and a dozen other stores. But the Carlton's double-glazed windows take care of daytime noise. And being a guest gives one entry to the two tennis courts in the park below.

Palmer stood at the broad picture window of his suite at nine o'clock in the evening and tried to make out the courts down below, beyond Pont Street in the south half of the park. The trees made the courts impossible to see, even in early summer moonlight.

"Relax, Woods, please."

Eleanora Gregorius spoke from the long couch, where she was reading a magazine. She watched the back of Palmer's body, tense, poised. He had asked Curtiss to get here as soon as he could from Paris and now he was impatient with the delay.

"Woods, it takes hours to get here. Even by plane."

"Especially by plane," he responded without relaxing his vigil at the window.

"Let's eat then. Leave word where we are in case he arrives."

"The food here is impossible. American roast beef. I don't live in Europe because I pine for American food."

He turned to her. Although they had been together now for seven or eight years, he still enjoyed looking at her and she still seemed the same young, exciting woman as when he'd met her first. She had been assigned to him as an interpreter on a trip he'd made to Europe for UBCO. In those days he'd been married—just—with children below high school age. Now all of them, Woody, Tom and Geraldine, were out of college. His first wife, Edith, had remarried. The only constant through it all had been Eleanora who sometimes, because of her age, seemed closer to his children than to him. Certainly when they visited him in what Gerri called "this tacky eyrie of yours" they spent more time with Eleanora than with him.

Palmer supposed he was to blame. He really could no longer converse with young people. Curtiss and Eleanora were the exceptions because they put themselves out to make communication easier. But none of his thoroughly American children let him off the hook that way, catering to his interests. They had their own. Pop had to fit in or drop by the wayside.

"Are you really hungry?" he asked Eleanora.

"You have started me salivating with the talk of American roast beef." She smiled at him. "You Americans take it too much for granted."

"Then let's eat downstairs. I can always find something on the menu."

"Let's have it brought up." She reached for the telephone and dialed Room Service.

Palmer turned back to stare out at the night. Behind him he could hear Eleanora, in her smooth, only faintly accented English, ordering herself a slice of rare rib roast and, for him, poached salmon and *pommes vapeur.* After she had hung up she said:

"It's almost bedtime in Koblenz. I'm going to call Tanya."

Palmer nodded. Her daughter visited them about as infrequently as his children did. It was almost as if around their "tacky eyrie" over the Lake of Lugano, they had posted too many "No Trespassing" signs. Perhaps it had been true once, in the early years of their relationship, that they had avoided visitors. But soon enough, it seemed, nobody visited them at all, except after repeated invitations. It was not an easy part of Switzerland to get to. One had to fly to Milan and rent a car. Still . . .

Palmer found himself wondering why in his middle years he was suddenly feeling the need for family around him, his own three and Tanya. But neither he nor Eleanora had any other living relatives.

He could hear her speaking in her soft German, which he only minimally understood. In the war he had learned the language for Intelligence work without having had much chance to use it. Eleanora, of course, spoke all the major languages of Europe. German was her native tongue, though she had spent her childhood in Holland.

"*. . .und schlaf fest, liebchen.*" She hung up. Immediately the telephone rang. Palmer turned to her.

"It's Room Service," he suggested, "telling us the salmon has run out."

"Hello?" She frowned. "*For* Mr. Curtiss? He hasn't arrived yet." She glanced up at Palmer. "Yes. But he isn't— Hello? I did tell the operator he isn't here yet. Can he call you back, Miss . . . ?" She paused. "One moment, please."

She handed Palmer the phone. "She sounds hysterical. Perhaps you can get a message out of her?"

"Who *is* this?" an American female voice demanded.

"We expect Curtiss soon. Would you like to have me give him a—"

"He's not in Paris," she cut in. "He left this number on his answering service."

"If you're calling from P—"

"No, California." The woman paused and seemed to pull herself together. "I was fine till now," she said then. "All I wanted to do was to talk to him. But when his answering service said he was gone I began to worry a lot. Do you happen—? Can you tell me—? Are you an associate of his?"

"Yes. Woods Palmer. And your name?"

"Mary Lee Hun—"

"Here's what you do," Palmer cut in fast, glancing at his watch. "When it's 3 p.m. your time, call this number collect. From a phone booth. Is everything all right at your end?"

"Why, uh . . . I guess so. I just wanted to know how he was."

"Everything seems quiet here. He'll tell you more when you call back. From a public phone booth."

"Yes," she said rather drily, "I did get that part."

Palmer hung up and made a cheek-puffing face, as if blowing out air. "And that lunatic Julian wants me back in New York. The moment we leave Morcote, we're hip deep in sewage."

"What was all that *nuschel-muschel* about phone booths?" Eleanor asked.

"That's what I mean. The woman is calling from where? On whose line? It's bad enough she's calling through a hotel switchboard on this end. We can't help that, but at least we can cut down exposure on her end."

"Does this have to do with that story Curtiss told you? The Sicilians with the grenade launcher?"

"This is the girl who was with him."

Eleanora made a what-do-you-know face. "I had no idea Curtiss was a ladies' man."

"He's been married twice." Palmer grinned. "Whatever that means."

"No children?" Palmer shook his head. "Smart man," she went on. "He's learned a lesson you and I figured out too late."

"Too late for the kids. Not for us." He sat down beside her, his arm around her shoulder. "Did you invite Tanya to visit?"

"Her semester ends soon. We are getting two generous weeks of her time before she goes back-packing with—significant pause—her friend Pavel."

"We've never met the boy. Doesn't that worry you?"

"Tanya's eighteen. At that age I was already pregnant with her." She paused and looked at him a bit as if apologizing in advance for what she was going to say. "Woods, would it matter if we knew the boy well? Suppose we did and he was an awful person."

"Then at least you could tell Tanya to get rid—" Palmer stopped. He laughed without mirth. "Listen to me. I can't even give advice to my own children, much as I itch to. It doesn't do anything. They don't pay any attention to it. Or they do the opposite."

"The world has shifted," Eleanora said. "Perhaps too much."

"It's a shift they asked for," Palmer responded almost defensively. "It's a shift they will end up paying for with their own disappointment."

"Because they didn't rely on your experience?" she asked him. "What would you have told Curtiss last night? Don't get caught in your apartment with a client when somebody's trying to kill you? Would that be the instructions? How do you protect people against life? We have a saying in German." She thought for a moment, obviously translating it into English. "It's a riddle. When do children put beans up their nose? Answer: when you warn them not to put beans up their nose."

"Curtiss," he said gruffly, "is not my child."

"Then why have you summoned him back to your side?"

"Because," Palmer said, "he's in big trouble and so is UBCO."

17

Atop Snowfire, winds of gale force whipped the leftover drifts of last winter's snow in horizontal ponytails, streaming out to lengths of several yards. The wind cried mournfully as it split against the angles of the cubes, sharp edges cleaving the air like a logger's axe.

Bennett Brown stood in the glassed-in solarium and stared across at his helipad, where the small Sikorski was roped down but tugging at its ties, as if eager to take off. The wind had been like this all night. Taos Weather had predicted it would end at any moment. But they'd been calling it that way for a long time.

He saw a bulb light up red on the doorway and heard a thin, cricket-like chirp. Turning away from the scene outside the glass, he half shut his eyes to start acclimatizing them to the dark of the terminal room. He moved surefootedly down a half flight of stairs and picked up a phone in the dimly lit room.

"Yes?"

"Ben, it's B. J. You okay, honey?"

"It's still blowing up a gale. I was due at a meeting in L.A. twenty minutes ago."

"You were due here with me last night."

"I'm sorry, honey. How's the boy doing?"

"The fetus is fine. Mary Lee is disappointed she couldn't see you. She wanted to talk to you."

He opened his eyes wide in the darkness. "About what?"

"Won't say."

"Well, tell her I really will get home tonight."

"She can't stay that long."

He hunched forward, frowning. "What the hell? Try to keep her there."

"She's due in Washington tomorrow."

"Tell her I will personally hand-carry her to Washington on time if she stays over with us tonight."

"How can you do that, Ben?"

"I have ways."

"That's nonsense, honey. It can't be done."

"B. J.," he said brusquely, "I don't ask a hell of a lot of you. Now I'm asking you to make her stay."

"And if I can't?"

"I'm *telling* you: keep her there." He slammed down the phone. Fucking nothing was going right. His mistake had been to think you could expect a nosy woman like Mary Lee to let this alone. But who could have dreamed she'd fall for the guy?

As he thought, he was tapping out telephone numbers to Palermo. When Don B's villa answered he asked in a high, unnatural voice:

"*Serafina c'è?*"

The man at the other end encoded the scrambler setting and in a moment he was talking directly to his father. "I am disgusted," the old man began without preamble. "It is so far a total disaster."

"I know," Ben admitted. "But we'll finish it off in the next few hours, for sure."

"And your wife's friend?"

"I tell you, it's not necessary. I told you that when she was in Paris."

"But, because you stayed my hand with her, I now have a blood enemy."

Ben was silent for a while, thinking. Don Gino by himself was no great threat in a vendetta, even with the death of his son as an incentive. But a lot of suspicion still surrounded Don B for not returning to his homeland of Calabria, for preferring Sicily. If any of that suspicion somehow got back to the U.S., it would jeopardize their plans much more than the kind of doubts and questions a man like Curtiss had.

"What are you thinking?" his father demanded gruffly.

"I'm thinking Don Gino could make much more trouble for us than anyone else."

"And who do I thank for that?" his father asked with thick sarcasm.

"Sorry. My responsibility."

Overhead, gale winds howled around the corners of his giant collection of cubes. If he couldn't copter off Snowfire in such a wind, he'd take the funicular down, drive to Taos and charter a jet.

"And begin by making sure of the woman," his father told him.

"I *am* sure of her."

"There is only one way to be sure," Don B told him.

Ben closed his eyes in desperation. God, these old-timers had only one solution for everything. You distrusted someone? Kill. It was like saying you could only trust a corpse. "What did we agree?" he asked his father now. "This is my show. When I need help, you provide it. But you don't *run* my show."

Now it was his father who fell silent, thinking. Ben had a good idea of his thoughts. Without Don B's influence, without the respect he had earned over the decades, what his son hoped to do now would have no chance of success. He was like the guarantor on a loan: without him, nothing. But he didn't pretend to have the expertise to carry it out. Only Ben could do that and he needed a free hand if he was to succeed.

"Ben," Don B said. "Ben, do it right, is all I ask."

"Sí, *papa*."

"And if somebody's a threat, don't hesitate, Ben. You hear me?"

How could he explain to the old man the role Mary Lee played in the marriage? How could he explain how close the two women were? Nothing in Don B's long life prepared him to believe that two women could be as close as two men. Now that B. J. was pregnant, his father felt, she had reached her ultimate destiny in life, topped only by the delivery of a healthy boy. That she continued to have all the same interests she had before—the same loyalties and priorities—was something no man of Don B's years could understand.

If something happened to Mary Lee it would have a profound effect on B. J. She was not some ignorant peasant woman. She knew how to get to the bottom of a thing and she wouldn't rest until she found the explanation for what had happened.

In that sense, Mary Lee now led a charmed life. As long as Ben wanted a son, as long as his father prayed every day for the same thing, as long as Ben hoped to keep the tenor of his family life intact, for that long would Mary Lee live. How could his father understand such a thing?

"You can't let anything stand in the way," his father said.

"Right."

"Maybe a man feels his own problems come first," Don B

went on. "His own wife. His own life. Even his own son." He
spoke with such fervor that he was suddenly choked, as if
with emotion. "But I tell you, all this is second. You hear?
Second."

"Right."

"First comes first. You hear?"

"Right."

"And after first, comes everything else in the whole world."

18

The shopping center at Newport Beach spread out, baking in
hot California sunshine, reeking of gasoline and melting
asphalt. Mary Lee Hunter parked B. J.'s little orange Renault
5 at the far end of a row of what seemed like all the
automobiles in the world. She got out and surveyed the
one-story buildings spread as far as the eye could see: supermarket, hardware store, nursery-garden shop, do-it-yourself
center, auto accessories and repairs, four film theaters in one
and a hi-fi center.

The supermarket, she decided, would have the most telephones. She hoped they'd be inside, out of the hot sun and
soothed by interior air conditioning. It was now three p.m.
London would be waiting. She saw a row of a dozen booths,
all filled and several people waiting.

Loudspeakers bathed the immense hall in seamless music
which, devoid of the words once written to these songs,
stirred no memories in Mary Lee. They were, like the vinyl
tiles underfoot, wall-to-wall background.

Standing there, Mary Lee reviewed her recent activities
and found them far too hectic. Since her return from Paris
late Sunday night she'd had time to get to her office in
Westwood once, and corporate headquarters in Redlands
once. The first meeting had been the west coast representa-
tives of the Eastern brokerages handling the new zero percent bond issue. The bastards were holding out for an upfront
discount of 30 percent, but this was merely their opening
offer in the bargaining.

When she'd told her boss, Lederer, that she hoped to

whittle the brokerages down to 15, he got red in the face and began making vulgar noises of disbelief. "No way," he spluttered. "They can't back down that far. You never should have let them come in with an opening that rotten. Now they're stuck with it and so are we."

"I will get them back, fear not."

"Back to 15? Forget it." He had stared long and hard at her. "Where the hell did they ever learn to sell us that cheap? Christ!"

"It's only an opening offer," she insisted. "Trust me."

His stare turned as impersonal as an express train that rushes through a waystation without pausing. "Trust you," he echoed, deadpan.

Recalling that conversation and his look, Mary Lee realized that she had some miracle-working to do in New York and Boston next week. There were a lot of things she had to do before then, material she had to get together, letters she had to dictate, a mass of special pleading that mustn't look like special pleading, all designed to raise the brokerages' expectations of a quick, easy sale.

At the same time, she had to set in motion—and this was best done by phone, without committing anything to paper— rumors that the issue would be *so* simple and profitable to sell that she might turn to a different broker to handle it, not needing the awesome clout of the two with whom she was dickering and who were giving her a mildly hard time on discounts.

It was a process Mary Lee knew inside out, a combination of carrot and stick that had to appeal to the innate greed and laziness of the brokerages. Their idea of hard work would be to insert a few big tombstone advertisements in the *New York Times* and the *Wall Street Journal*, sit back and let customers come pounding in, cash in hand. Anything more onerous than that they refused to do.

Waiting now for a telephone booth to open up, Mary Lee wondered if she might simply lay off the whole issue on Ben's brokerage. It wasn't one of the biggest, but it did have unusual clout. And from Ben she had a far better chance of bringing in the job at 15 percent discount. That look on Lederer's face . . . that you-win-or-you're-finished look that promised her disaster without spelling it out.

She would be spending the rest of the afternoon now with B. J. in Newport Beach, after much agonized begging. "You have to," B. J. assured her. "Ben as much as *ordered* me to have you here tonight."

"Ben order? He's such a pussycat."

"Can you tell me why that word is a synonym for pushover?" B. J. had demanded over the phone. "No pussycat I know ever got anything but its own way. Please, Mary Lee. Be here."

The man in the nearest booth got up and left. Mary Lee sat down and dialed the operator. Her coin returned at once and she placed the collect call. She found herself hoping Curtiss would answer. She'd heard of Palmer and was a little in awe of him. He still had quite a reputation when Mary Lee had first joined the Federal Reserve. The gossip about Palmer was that the American banking industry had breathed a sigh of relief when he exiled himself to Europe. Mavericks worried Mary Lee. Of course, Curtiss had been described that way. Still . . .

"Yes," she heard Curtiss say, "we accept the call. Hello?"

"Curtiss, are you all right?"

"Yes." He sounded funny to her. "You?"

"Fine. Spent the night with B. J."

"You what?" An awkward pause. "And her husband?"

"No, he wasn't there. We expect him tonight. Why?"

"Don't see Bennett Brown. Don't sit around waiting for him. Get somewhere he can't find you. And don't tell B. J. where you are."

"I'm due in Washington tomorrow to make a presentation, but he knows that."

A longer pause at the London end. "If you go to Washington tonight, where would you stay?"

"Usually at that big place in L'Enfant Plaza. Or the Watergate."

Another pause. "Palmer says to go somewhere you wouldn't normally stay. He suggests the Hay-Adams."

"And then what?" she asked.

"Then I know where to get you."

"But B. J. expects me back. She'd never understand my running off when I've agreed to stay over."

"Drive to the L.A. airport and book the next flight to New York. Take the copter to LaGuardia and shuttle to Washington. Don't fly direct. The Hay-Adams, remember."

"Curtiss, do you know what I have on? A bikini and a beach robe."

"Seethrough?"

"Not quite."

He was chuckling at the other end. She thought she heard him ask someone to leave him alone in the room. After a pause he came on the line again. "I miss you."

"I miss you too." She sat back in the phone booth and tried to relax. "I don't understand about B. J. and Bennett."

"It's only a hunch. Did you tell them what happened in Paris?"

"No. I wanted to save it till I saw Bennett. He's very bright about these things. I think he could give me an answer."

"Your instinct is on the button."

"Meaning?"

Curtiss was silent a moment. "Meaning Bennett Brown could explain the whole thing to you, Mary Lee. Palmer and I have been trying to figure it out since the shit hit the fan here. We don't know where he fits into the picture, but it isn't down near the bottom."

"Do you really miss me?"

"A lot." He paused a moment. "That's quite a first impression you make."

"Knocked you for a loop, huh?"

Despite the fact that she could close the door of the booth, the bath of music seemed to engulf her in lush strings and ticky-tocky percussion noises. She felt as if all the loudspeakers were beamed at her alone and the phone booth was filling up with anonymous song that would soon be over her head. She gave a broad fake smile through the glass to two women looking daggers at her as they waited for the phone. His voice and his words had given her a warm feeling in the pit of her stomach as if he were the first man ever to have said them. He wasn't, but the feeling was. She was drowning in it.

"Curtiss," she said softly, "I am in love with you. But I guess you knew that."

"How the hell would I know that?" he demanded.

"Don't get upset. I love you. It's not the end of the world."

"You don't know me, Mary Lee."

"I expect the more I know you the more horrible you will become. But that cuts two ways. I'm not all that great. You just brought out the best parts of me."

"That works both ways, too." He was silent. Then: "I have a lousy history with women. Two divorces."

"Mine with men is pretty suspicious. No marriages. Having too much fun." She sat up straight. "Hey, Curtiss. This is not a proposal. I am not interested in marriage."

"Just fooling around."

"*Serious* fooling around."

"That's the best offer I've had in years. What?" Someone was telling him something. "What about some privacy?" he snapped back. "I am talking to the woman I love."

"Did you tell that man the truth about me?" she asked.

"Would I lie to Woods Palmer, Jr.? Especially about love? Listen, how urgent is this Washington meeting? Because Palmer has booked me into a suite here with a bed bigger than a Queen. Bigger than a King. Four people could lie in it and never find each other."

"Some orgy. I do have to be at the Washington thing. Maybe..."

She glanced at her watch and punched a button for the date. "Let me see what I can cook up with the front office. Then I have to tell B. J. what I'm doing, drive her car back, get a cab, pick up some clothes, get to the airp—"

"No. No word to B. J. And don't go home. I meant what I said, Mary Lee. Direct to the airport and onto a plane. Call B. J. from Washington. Not before. It's really important."

"It must be. You raised your voice."

He sighed. "I'm kind of tense. Since you left it hasn't been all that marvelous."

"Oh, Curtiss, I do love you."

"Well. It helps to know that. I hope it helps you to know I'm crazy about you. Not that it does much over a long-distance phone."

The women outside the phone booth were discussing her in unflattering terms. She couldn't lip read, but she didn't really need to. Or maybe, she thought, they are singing the forgotten words to all these forgotten Muzak songs.

"It helps me to have you," she told Curtiss. "We are both loners. I think that's really at the bottom of what's between us. Loners are hard to please. It's a matter of not trusting most other people. And then, when you find someone you trust, it releases something inside you. It changes you. You're another person because you've finally found someone you can rely upon utterly, their judgment, their sexiness, their bravery, their small talk, their style, everything about them including the toothpaste they use. Curtiss, I *approve* of you."

She swung open the telephone booth door. Music flooded in.

"Will you two fuck off? Go spoil someone else's phone call."
She slammed the door shut.

"What?" Curtiss demanded.

"Nothing. We were discussing love." She felt the two
women's concerted glare focused on the back of her head. "I
guess it's like the song, Curtiss. I found you just in time. I
mean, I don't *have* any one else. I have B. J. and she's got
me. I have three overpowering older brothers back home in
Maryland, but I'll be damned if I'd ever let them know I
need love and affection and advice and intimacy. You don't
open yourself up to a brother, not the kind whose idea of
humor is secretly to loosen your girth cinch so the saddle
slides off the horse in mid-stride. All three of them are still
waiting to see me fall flat on my ass as a financial officer."

She could hear him laughing. The sound came from far
away, six or seven thousand miles. It was clear but it had no
body to it, as if produced by microprocessor synthesis designed to override ambient noise levels of wall-to-wall Mantovani
strings. Then: "It sounds to me as if you know Bennett Brown
rather well."

"Very." She wondered how he'd take the next. "The first
time B. J. turned him down, he proposed to me. Next best."

"You make him sound sort of pitiful."

She snorted. "Bennett Brown is the most resourceful,
brilliant, motivated person I have ever met. I think that's
why I turned him down. I like a guy..." She paused. "I like
a guy with some loose space in him. Room to pause and turn
around. Room to loaf and do nothing. Ben is a driven man."

"Know his family background?"

"Just a nice Jewish boy from a poor family. Never met any
of them."

After a long pause, Curtiss cleared his throat. "If you think
of anything else, just place another collect call. Otherwise,
I'll hear from you after five your time tomorrow. I love you,
Miss Hunter. Take goddamned good care of yourself. I wish I
could be there to help."

"I wish so, too."

19

Bennett Brown, at thirty-five, had carefully avoided the intense publicity that attends youthful success in the United States. There were no published interviews, even in magazines devoted to business, nor had his unorthodox lifestyle become the subject of photographic essays in gossip magazines. While it is expensive for young business leaders to buy such publicity, it costs even more for them to avoid it.

In truth his story would not have fitted conveniently into the general pattern of the American dream. An intelligent editor, faced with the facts, might well have decided not to publish. This, of course, is a fantasy guess: no one ever had the facts about Bennett Brown.

The two most noticeable things about him, which he had managed to hide even from B. J. until some time after their marriage, was that he was perfectly capable of working a twenty-hour day for weeks at a time. He thrived on it. The second, perhaps even more socially unacceptable, part of his personality was that he still believed there were patterns to human existence.

This essentially nineteenth-century belief, given substance and resonance by such nineteenth-century thinkers as Darwin and Marx, imbued everything Bennett thought and planned. He was a seeker after patterns. When he found one which rang true to him he effectively grouped all his forces around it, squandering immense energies on realizing what power or profit there might be in such a discovery.

He was not blind to the randomness of life. Far from it: he believed there was a pattern to the randomness. Moreover, he believed there was a pattern even to those freak occurrences we call luck. Murphy's law—the cynical observation that if something can go wrong, it will—was not unknown to him, nor did he denigrate it. As a result, between his seeking of patterns and his awareness that they could be shattered in an instant by dumb bad luck, Bennett Brown for all his relaxed exterior movements was a very tense young man.

The twenty-hour day, if nothing else, seemed to bear this out. At the moment, about three p.m. in Los Angeles, atop one of the high-rise buildings in the Century City complex off Wilshire Boulevard, the west coast offices of Brown, Brown, Finch, Pierce and Cohen were closed. The markets in New York had closed three hours before. Still, many California brokerages remained open, those who classified themselves as consumer shops.

Brown's brokerage paid hasty lip service to small investors, but it was pre-eminently an institutional shop. Its business was devoted almost completely to the buying and selling requirements of large funds, trust departments of banks, insurance companies, large corporations and a few private individuals whose volume was as large as an institution's could be.

Retired gents who liked to sit around watching the tape and gently readjusting their modest portfolios as a way of passing each day, these off-the-street customers were not made extravagantly welcome at Brown, Brown, Finch, Pierce and Cohen. It was the big customers Bennett Brown wanted. He readily reduced fees in order to get high volume. He had his reasons.

Handling bits and pieces for a small-time plunger tells a broker nothing. Handling the fat put-and-take of a major corporation or bank tells him a lot. And when he handles a lot of the major institutions across the country, he gets an instant reading of the turns, shifts, leaps and drops of the market.

It isn't so much that major gamblers know more than minor ones, although they do. It isn't even important that the "little guy" is always wrong. The reason he's wrong is the important thing. It lies in the overwhelming weight of a market surge based on big, institutional movements.

Bennett Brown had made this the topic of his master's thesis at Harvard's School of Business Administration. He reasoned that market movements had long ago severed their connection with anything concrete in the business world. Yes, a major bankruptcy in, say, steel, would depress other steel stocks. But the daily guesses of the newspaper reporters as to why the market had gone up or down (often attributing it to something as arcane as a recent political poll or the discovery of oil in a new place) were not to be believed. They were merely the hurried attempts of journalists to fill a daily allotment of space with something that, at first glance, wouldn't sound too wildly hallucinatory.

Bennett put forward the conviction—this was in the mid 1960s when some of his classmates were marching in the south and others were burning draft cards—that the New York and American stock exchanges hadn't followed any logical link to the business world since, perhaps, they'd resumed normal activity after World War II.

It was at Harvard that he had come under the influence of the controversial Kondratiev theory of economic cycles. Nikolai Kondratiev, early on, had run afoul of Stalin in 1930 and paid for it by being sent to hard labor in Siberia. His crime, committed after decades of studying commercial data back to the eighteenth-century, was a new theory that booms and busts cycled in long waves. Patterns of sixty years were not uncommon.

Among the few western economists to see anything in the long-wave idea was Dewey of Harvard, who had no more attentive pupil in the 1960s than Bennett Brown. But the youngster's ideas had jumped well ahead of Kondratiev. A wave that long (Dewey had found a fifty-four-year cycle in British wheat prices that went back seven centuries without a variation), reasoned Bennett Brown, pretty much negated anything of merely passing business interest like strikes, bankruptcies, tight money, new industries, bad weather and the like.

He, and others, soon developed a psychological pattern for investing in the market. People bought, so the thesis seemed to prove, when they felt up and sold when they were depressed. The terms Bull and Bear were elevated to a pedestal of folk wisdom, after common practice had already decreed that the ebullient, optimistic bull always bought, while the soreheaded, sour-faced bear looked to profit on downtrends and other disasters.

Acting on his observation that market action was illogical and unknowable—after all, what one mortal could plumb the collective psyche of the investment public each hour of every day?—Bennett Brown decided that *his* brokerage firm would tap into the hopes and fears of the biggest bettors, the institutions. If the majority of them turned tail and panicked, Brown, Brown, Finch, Pierce and Cohen usually had an hour lead time before everyone else panicked. With that kind of advance notice, they made the buys and sells for their own accounts which would take maximum advantage of prior knowledge.

The technique, hardly an invention of Bennett Brown alone, was already in use among some of the more successful brokerages. But Bennett used real time computer probes every ten seconds of the day. They could instantly spot a trend and order appropriate action in less than another second. This was what made his brokerage vastly more profitable than most.

The moment his system flashed a buy or sell alert, a second program converted the alert into a series of orders flashed to a floor dealer. It had also been Bennett's idea to add an on-line voice simulator to the system so that the floor man received his orders in a human voice, with automatic repetition capability.

Somewhere in the brokerage offices now a telephone rang. Bennett Brown located it at the switchboard and sat down in the operator's chair. He flipped on two switches and settled the headset over his ears.

"Brown, Brown, Finch, Pierce and Cohen," he said.

There was a momentary pause at the other end of the call. "Uh . . . this is . . . uh, wait a second. Ben?"

"Yeah, Freddie. What's up?"

Alfred J. Marston laughed. "You're alone, I gather. Everybody's gone for the day. I just wanted to schmooz a second. You heard that UBCO took the bait on CIT, right?"

"I heard."

"Hertz may be even easier. There's a group in the top echelon of management might like to buy it back from RCA."

Bennett Brown's dark face lit up slightly. "Great. Encourage it."

"The new board meets next week. It's on the agenda to spin off both companies. I don't worry about the UBCO acquisition of CIT, unless we get flak from the Justice Department. But where is the money for these Hertz clowns to buy up the company?"

The dark-eyed young man sat in silence, thinking. "That might be a situation for the Lucchese group. I understand they're looking around for a big fat tax loss."

"Should I talk to them direct?"

"Through Sal Maggoranza, their comptroller. Mention my name."

"You're a fount of information, Ben."

As he hung up, Bennett Brown allowed himself a small smile. Doing Pino Lucchese's family a favor was never a waste of time. He glanced around the sleekly appointed office with a certain feeling of satisfaction.

The author of all this, having waited until the Century City office was closed, now patched in a conference call to London and Basel and waited for each line to clear. When he had both respondents on scrambler he flicked on a tape drive and began recording.

"Urs," he began, "any unusual market action? Do you get the feeling our mitt was tipped?"

"Nothing," the Swiss banker replied. "The target stuff is still being traded at normal levels and prices. Even a few down ticks. Nothing significant."

"Good. Where do we stand in London?"

Julian Sykes-Maulby cleared his throat. "All quiet on the Western Front, Ben."

"Then why is Curtiss in London, huddling with Palmer?"

"No idea. Is it important?"

"Only if you leaked something to Palmer I don't know about?"

"Mum as the grave. Purely social encounter."

"Funny coincidence. You bump into your old buddy and the next thing Curtiss is in London."

"It's just that, a coincidence." The Englishman seemed bored with the conversation already.

"I hope so," Bennett Brown said. "For all our sakes. And particularly for yours, Julian."

"Actually," he snapped, "I ought to be the injured party. You had some sort of bloodhound on us in Green Park, I take it?"

"More or less."

"I'm afraid I resent that a bit, old man. However," Julian went on in a lighter tone, "one can't be too careful, can one?"

"Right."

"I say, Urs," Julian went on, "as long as we're chatting on Ben's money, did you make that offer to the electronics firm?"

"Yes," the Swiss responded. "They took it. Had no choice, the way you scuttled them with the Kreditanstalt."

"Okay," Ben cut in. "I have your word, Urs, that the markets show nothing unusual in the target areas. And there's nothing showing here on any of the markets. So we can assume we're still for the moment in the clear."

"I think you can assume a hell of a lot more than that," the Englishman put in. "Not that it can't happen by a fluke, but I see no normal way Palmer or Curtiss can ever make the connection we don't want them to make."

"I agree," Urs said.

"You two never heard of Murphy's Law, did you?" Bennett Brown asked in a somber voice. Without waiting for an answer he snapped a fast "good night" and broke off the conference call.

Then he sat back in his terminal room high above Los Angeles and thought. He played back both men's conversations from the tape. Then he replayed Julian's responses. There was nothing to put one's finger on. The man had made all the right responses.

Then why, Bennett asked himself, do I feel the Brit is giving me a tale?

PART THREE

•

Council of War

20

"If you don't need me any more," Curtiss said, "I'm supposed to be in Rome, heading off a scam by the Minister of Finance."

Palmer eyed him coldly for a moment, as if, not having heard him when he spoke, he was recreating the voice out of a memory cassette. Then his face softened. He almost smiled.

"What can you do to protect UBCO from a government scam?" he teased. "The Italians have been blackmailing everybody blind since the end of the war. That whole business of having a legal Communist Party. It's no more communist than I am. Even its own members are tired of it. But it forces Uncle Sam to keep Italy in pocket money." A yawn overtook him. He stretched and leaned back in an upholstered chaise-longue to stare out of the picture window at Cadogan Place. "How about some tennis?"

"I don't have shoes or clothes or a racket," Curtiss said. "And it happens to be raining at the moment. Otherwise, sure."

"Never mind rain. To play tennis in London you have to learn how to play on wet courts. It's chiefly a matter of having non-skid soles. The sneakers yachtsmen use are probably best."

"Then, if I don't go to Rome," Curtiss went on in what was not really a *non sequitur,* "I think I'll go to Washington."

Rain drummed on the glass panes, a steady, soft noise. Outside, car tires whooshed through puddles.

"And rendezvous with the estimable Miss Hunter."

"Something like that."

"Probably the best idea," Palmer mused. "I don't believe she's in danger, but we have no way of seeing into the heart of Bennett Brown."

"Don't we?" Curtiss countered. "We know he's taken years to put this together. We know he knows I'm onto it. We have to figure he knows she's onto it. Only the fact that we haven't done anything with our information has kept him from including her in the general butchery."

"I'm not sure he's that much in control of the, um, enforcement." Palmer got up and stared out at the rain. "I have the feeling he's not supposed to touch any of the dirty parts of the machine. He's supposed to have deniability, in case somebody goofs, like those morons who tried to blast you out of your apartment."

"Those were imports from Sicily, I think." Curtiss joined him at the window. "But we can't count on getting dumdums all the time. They will ultimately send somebody who knows his job better than we do."

"Maybe . . ." Palmer paused. "What if we do nothing for the next week? I don't mean nothing. I am personally going to develop as much material on Brown as I can. But nothing overt. Whoever is monitoring share prices will see nothing attributable to our interference. They may calm down and say: 'Okay, we scared the shit out of them, they're neutralized.' Which is the way they work anyway, Curtiss. They only kill *in extremis*. If they can get the same effect with a threat, they prefer it."

"That is most reassuring," Curtiss said, deadpan. "Especially when you've been *in extremis* with them."

"Remember, the lad who wanted to grenade you was taken out by his own buddy."

"Louch tells me the guy was connected in Calabria. Son of some local *pezzo novanto*." He watched four tall red buses follow each other through the rain along Sloane Street. Tiny cars, taillights winking red, wove in and out among the buses like bees around flowers. "His takeout may start trouble in the mother country."

"Meanwhile," Palmer concluded. "Maybe they think they have us in fear and trembling."

"Maybe they have," Curtiss suggested. "Maybe I ought to get Mary Lee Hunter to a safe place."

"How could you get her out of the U.S. without them knowing?"

"Only if I hand-steered her."

Palmer grinned. "What sort of excuse can you give Bill Elston?"

"That," Curtiss retorted, "gives me an idea. She phones Elston and demands protection?"

"He politely refers her to the local cops."

"Um." Curtiss stopped and stared out at the rain. "It'll just have to be unofficial. I'll pop over there and—"

Palmer laid a hand on his arm. "They want you more than they want her."

Curtiss made a face. He said nothing for a long moment. Outside the rain hammered down on car roofs and umbrellas moving erratically across streets. Then: "What about this good buddy of yours, the errant knight, Julian? Does he have any clout with the coppers here?"

Palmer glanced sideways at him. "What do you know about him?"

"Feeds on wounded businesses. Helps wound 'em a bit, then gobbles 'em up. Finger in everything profitable which, for the UK, means he does most of his business elsewhere. The thing I don't know much about is your connection with him."

Palmer nodded politely. "We met in Sicily in 1943. You'll recall the American troops had an easy time of it. While the Canadians and Brits took heavy losses."

"We had some sort of deal with the Mafia, wasn't that it?"

"With Lucky Luciano, set up by Meyer Lansky. But our allies had no such protection. Julian had been detailed to try to get a bit of our Mafia umbrella over his people."

"And did he?"

"By the time we set it up, Sicily was finished. The Germans had been swept out via Messina. I told you the suggestion Julian made the other day?"

"About heading UBCO again? But did he suggest how you could go about it?"

"I didn't let him. I'm quite happy as I am."

"Ha." Curtiss left the window and limped over to the couch. One of the various falls he had taken the other night had left him with a bad knee. The pain was not intense. He would be over it in a day. But perhaps the damp weather was prolonging it. He sat there, nursing his knee in silence for a while. It wasn't his role to give Palmer advice, or make pointed observations. But the way the older man had slid into the present problem, up to his neck, indicated how much he wanted to get back in the swim.

"You know," Palmer said then, "if we could phone her on a secure line, we could tell her how to make a noiseless exit from the States."

Curtiss kept his face impassive. The old intriguer was at it again. "Secure on both ends? Not easy. Look, she's calling me tonight, some time after ten p.m. our time. From a phone booth."

"Here?" Palmer turned sharply towards him. He was silhouetted against the rain-swept window so that Curtiss couldn't see his face. "What can we do between now and then to secure this end?"

"Damned little."

Palmer didn't take kindly to this. "Let's try; I'm a good customer here. A word with the hotel security people ought to do it."

Curtiss shook his head from side to side. "Not good enough. A hotel like the Carlton gets a lot of VIPs, politicos, business types. There must be a dozen in-place taps on trunk lines."

"Then we'll demand they sweep the lines clear."

Curtiss's glance moved around the room, pausing at cornices, picture moldings, doorways. This was a fairly modern hotel, no ornate plaster rosettes, shells, acanthus-leaf friezes or other likely spots in which to spike a listening device.

"There are also in-place bugs in the big suites," Curtiss said. "They're left over from previous surveillance. Some have run-down batteries. But even if we sweep this suite from top to bottom, can we be sure?"

Palmer nodded decisively. "We'll do both things. That gives us a hell of a more secure position."

"What about remote eavesdropping? Parabolic reflector mikes? Those laser beams that 'read' the vibrations on your window pane?"

Palmer grinned broadly. "That's why we'll keep the TV turned on loud."

"The cheapest tap of all is bribing the switchboard girl to patch you into the call. You lurk in a phone booth and eavesdrop every word."

Palmer had opened a closet door and was pulling a dark blue, double-breasted, gold-buttoned blazer from a hanger. It was almost a duplicate of the one Julian wore. "My, my," he said then, "it does pay to have a misspent youth. What other tricks can you think of?"

"Whatever I know, I learned working for Mother UBCO."

"Fair enough." Palmer shrugged into the blazer and buttoned it. "I'm going to have a word with the security people downstairs. Eleanora and I will cover that end between us. All you have to do is figure out a foolproof scheme by which

Miss Hunter can get herself out of the States without any of Bennett Brown's associates knowing it."

"I figured that'd be my end of it."

"It's the easy part," Palmer assured him as he left the suite. Rain hammered against the picture windows. Curtiss sat nursing his knee and thinking.

The opposition's moves so far, he told himself, had been crude. Not that crudeness didn't work. Far from it. In Curtiss's experience it nearly always did. But it also alerted both the police and the intended victims. Now, with Mary Lee coming here from the States, she would be the focus of a different kind of opposition, the smoother kind that relied on remote control and layers of insulation.

This was the kind of opposition he and Palmer had been talking about foiling. It was the opposition they could count on facing from here in. Because it bore a "Made in U.S.A." stamp on it didn't necessarily mean it would be more successful than the Mediterranean kind. It only meant a higher level of concern and awareness.

Curtiss tried to ease his muscles into an appearance of relaxation. He stretched out his legs and leaned back in the upholstered sofa, emptied his lungs of air, took in a slow, steady draft of fresh air and tried to clear his mind of the residual fears and angers there.

I'm in love, he told himself. Think positive. I'm in love again. She's in love. And she's lovely. And we go well together and we know it and we're smart enough to know how rare that is.

He tried the lung-emptying routine again. But nothing worked.

21

B. J. answered on the third ring. "Mary Lee!" she responded. "Where the hell are you?"

"I just called to tell you where I left your car," Mary Lee began in a hurried tone. "I don't have a second, B. J. I'm—"

"Bennett is *so* pissed off at me. My God, what a fight."

"Because I ran out on you?"

"You'd think he owned both of us," B. J. responded angrily. "I gave him a large piece of my mind and when I could see he was itching to punch me out, I retreated to my bedroom and locked the door. Standard operating procedure."

"Ben would never strike you."

"No?"

"Not while you're pregnant," Mary Lee added. This brought on an attack of nervous giggles from both of them. Then: "B. J., the car's in the L.A. Airport long-term parking. I left the keys in an envelope with your name on it. The United Airlines info desk has it. Ask for Betty Sue Ann."

"You're making up names again. Betty Sue Ann what?"

"Betty Sue Ann Tronchowsky from Detroit."

B. J. whooped loudly. "Where are you anyway?"

"Don't tell Ben."

"No, that won't do. First you're dying to talk to him. Then he's dying to talk to you. Then you don't want to talk to him. Now he isn't talking to me. You will agree it looks fishy."

"It's worse than fishy," Mary Lee admitted. "I promise to tell you what I know some day. Not now."

"But what can I tell Ben?"

"Say nothing. I didn't phone you."

"You don't understand, baby. He's got a stolen-car report out to the cops and a missing persons as well. If I don't call him off, you'll end up in jail. Jet-Tech International Femme Exec Overnight Guest in Drunk Tank."

"That won't happen."

"Mingling with Prostitutes and Junkies, Financial Tycoon Spends Educational Night," B. J. went on, spinning out imaginary headlines.

Mary Lee failed to respond for a moment. "Say I called and told you where the car was. Say I'll call back around dinnertime tonight and talk to him. *If* he calls off the cops."

"And will you call back?"

"Swear to God."

B. J. was about to persist when she heard one of the outer doors open and shut. "Mary Lee! I think he just came in. Hold on. Ben?"

"What?" he asked.

"Guess who's on the ph—" B. J. stopped, realizing the line was dead. "It was Mary Lee. The car's in the—"

"Never mind." He strode past her into the dimly lit terminal room, threw some switches and, in a moment, B. J.

heard her own voice shriek: "Mary Lee! Where the hell are you?"

B. J. moved into the kitchen, found some ice cubes and made herself a cabernet-on-the-rocks. She stood there sipping it while the sound of her voice and Mary Lee's filled the house. Bastard was bugging her now? Had she said anything on the phone? Just your usual dumb, husband-supportive wifely phrases, fighting his battles for him, or trying to. Son of a bitch.

Ben came into the kitchen. "Sorry about bugging the phone," he began. "I had to." He took the wine from her and finished it off in one gulp. "Why is she being so cagey? Won't even say where she's calling from."

"Cagey? She isn't the one secretly recording my conversations."

"I said I was sorry." He turned and left the room. After a moment she could hear him talking on a telephone in the terminal room. "... United Air Lines yesterday afternoon," he was telling somebody.

B. J. moved closer to the door of the terminal room. "It has to be a flight East," he was saying. "She was due in Washington today for meetings. Try that first. Get me a flight number. I can take it from there."

His voice had sunk to a lower level, but she could still hear him. "*Porca miseria!*" he exploded. You have a nerve, Enzo. *Senta, telefonarmi subito!*" He slammed down the phone.

B. J. wandered back into the kitchen to refresh the drink she had hardly sipped. A business major from Wharton with an MBA from Stanford had had little time for languages. But surely what Ben was talking couldn't have been Yiddish?

22

Deeply ensconced between the thighs of a small, pert auburn-haired young woman, Julian almost didn't hear the discreet ping of his telephone. He muttered something indistinct and groped for the ringing noise.

"Jolly," Miranda Smith's voice began at once, "all clear?"

Sykes-Maulby delicately extricated himself from the peach-colored thighs and shifted to a sitting position at the edge of the bed. "Slight complication here."

"Not to worry, Jol. I'll take ten minutes. Tell the lucky lady to enjoy a nap. Knowing you, she requires one desperately."

"Most kind."

When he had hung up Julian turned to his companion. "Could you profit by a brief kip?"

"Could I?" the redheaded young woman asked rhetorically. "Lights out, tiger."

In Julian's drawing room a few books, mostly paperbacks on financial matters, graced half-empty shelves alongside tiny *objets d'art* he had picked up in his travels. Sykes-Maulby's collecting instinct resembled a pickpocket's since it was restricted to items small enough to fit inside a jacket without leaving a bulge. The usual Nabatean tear vase sat beside a lone Greek obol mounted on a wire tripod. In a small glass frame was displayed a 1923 24-cent U.S. airmail stamp in which the blue Curtiss Jenny biplane flew upside down in the dark rose border.

Julian had picked it up for three thousand pounds some years ago. Since it was currently worth seventy thousand, he was considering retiring it to his vault except that he loved to look at what was, for him, one of his prettier investment successes.

Gazing at himself in a long, rosewood framed pier glass, he adjusted the hang of his dressing gown. He refluffed his ascot. The front door opened softly to Miranda's key.

She looked, as always, fresh picked, quite dewy at ten p.m. for a mother of two adolescents. She and Julian kissed. "Jolly, you simply must let me re-do this, this lair. It's too . . . too . . ."

"Ballsy." Julian poured them each a tulip glass of champagne. They touched glasses. "Studsy," Miranda corrected him. She opened her bag. From it she removed twenty bags of fifty-pound notes with the imprimatur of National Westminster Bank stuck on the plastic film.

Sykes-Maulby's head did the computation only a shade less swiftly than one of Bennett Brown's computers. With fifty fifties in each bag some fifty thousand pounds lay before him. He deposited the cash in a wall Chubb behind the fridge. "Tell him it couldn't be timelier," he said on his return to the parlor. "I'm onto something marvelous. A license to steal."

"Jolly, you do skate close to the wind."

He eyed her petite face, framed in dark ringlets, that classic British beauty that combines high coloring in fair skin, as if the artist had a set of colors fresh from the factory. Julian tested the resonances in her statement, trying to decide if this were her own idea or she was relaying doubts from a higher quarter.

"Not at all," he countered easily. "It's the ultimate nick, sweet girl. I advise a major plunger what Euro-shares to buy in bulk. But first I buy them on my own. Then I sell them at higher prices. Safe as houses." He smiled, he hoped, infectiously.

"And when he twigs?" Miranda asked.

"I rarely make more than a 10 percent profit. Hardly of note if one considers it a commission."

Miranda frowned. "You do appreciate, Jolly, that a 10 percent profit on an investment held a month or less is equivalent to an annual profit of over 100 percent?"

There was an uncomfortable silence. "Dear me," Julian said at last. "You do have a quick mind, Miranda." He paused again. "No news on the appointments list? No hint the world may soon call me Sir?"

She shook her head. "He can hardly wish you such publicity, Jolly. You'd be infinitely less useful to him as a knight."

"Too true, more's the pity. But, perhaps, some day . . . ?"

She threw her hands daintily to each side, as if releasing a small bird. "In any event, I'm overjoyed to hear of your financial successes. I only warn you as a dear friend that you're liable to get caught."

"I appreciate your concern. More champers?"

She shook her head. "I'll have another shipment of cash next week," she said, finishing her drink and getting to her feet. "It may be a bit more. I never know."

She stood, abruptly ill at ease. Sykes-Maulby got up. "My dear girl, is everything all right?"

"Quite." She was swaying very slightly.

"You looked unsteady. *Figure-toi*, the suavely desirable Miranda off her feed. One's mind reels." He put his arm around her shoulder. He could feel her body off balance.

She shook her head and took in a steadying breath. "Just a touch of feminine *mal de coeur*. I m-mean, it's so bloody hard for us to meet at all and when we do all the poor sod has time for is to slip me the lolly. It's . . ." She broke down, spilling tears on his dressing gown.

"There, there." As he always did in the face of a woman's

tears, Julian felt that he alone was the cause of them. Being British, he knew, she would pull herself together in time. Meanwhile, inanities were in order. "There, there," he repeated.

"I do love him, Jol." She pulled back and patted her eyes with his breast pocket handkerchief. "And I'm turning instead into a bloody bonded Wells Fargo."

Julian surveyed her face, looking for signs of serious trouble. "As long as it doesn't lead either of you," he said in his least severe tones, "into accidental indiscretion."

"Dear God, no," she said in irony. "That's it, Jolly. End of outburst. Mandy's herself again. Good old reliable Mandy."

"How is Giles these days?" he asked, more to distract her from further self-directed shafts.

"Complaisant. Oh, such a model husband."

"Do you mean to tell me he knows?"

"Do you mean to tell me he doesn't?" she responded tartly.

"But . . ." Julian thought back over Giles Smith's private life. Did he have one? To hide, that is, and thus offer a trade-off for Miranda's private life. Or was it simply that her extracurricular activities could not possibly hurt a Foreign Office johnnie's chances?

"You haven't," he asked in sudden dread, "*talked* to him?"

"Certainly not." She gathered up gloves and her bag. "Birds in their nests agree," she said with false sweetness. "What is it the Americans pine for? One big happy family."

The redhead was still asleep when Julian slipped into bed beside her. The unsettling encounter with Miranda made him keep to himself rather than restage a triumphant reentry. Poor Miranda's nerves, he thought, are stretching thin. Himself possibly as desperate as she. Nothing a few good fucks wouldn't put right for them both. Still . . . Julian did relish serving his country in such a fascinating manner. The venerable ambience harked back to earlier centuries. He particularly enjoyed the gentlemanliness of it. Miranda passed him sums but required no receipt. In all truth Himself probably didn't keep track. Beneath him. But Miranda would.

Yes. His eyes narrowed as he stared at the ceiling. Careless of him to mention the joke he was playing on Bennett Brown. It could never get back to Ben, but it showed Sykes-Maulby that he had to put a tighter rein on himself. Miranda was amazingly lovely and generated phenomenal confidence. But at the same time she was beginning to show sharp signs of an intelligence and a vulnerability that could become dangerous.

In this business there was virtually no margin for error.

23

"I don't have to trust him," Palmer was telling Eleanora. "I'm not in bed with Julian."

She had propped herself up on two pillows and was lying naked in bed leafing quickly through one of those anonymous, useless magazines to be found in hotel suites all over the world, unreliable as tourism or shopping guides since they were only vehicles for advertising.

She had brought with her a tiny cassette player which lay between their pillows, its miniature headphones lisping faint music, far away, as if played by a toy band, only a sketch of what Mahler had in mind when he composed these shimmering chords and arpeggios.

Palmer had been half asleep, curled away from Eleanora like a large shrimp, the sheet up over his face to keep the light out. Now he turned on his back and gazed at her. "Remarkable breasts."

"Has he?" She pretended to be interested only in the magazine.

"Julian's? No, yours. Full, firm, no droop, hot pink areolas and nipples a man can really enjoy. Which are sitting up now like tiny penises." He reached across and squeezed each in turn.

Eleanora put away the magazine. "Isn't it amazing," she said, "how words still have the power to excite."

"The nipples and the penis are both what are known as erectile tissue."

"How romantic." She gave him a long sideways look. "You really come to life in big cities." She slid her hand along his arms. "This city tension. You tell me how much you hate it. But it fascinates you."

"Not in the least."

"And Julian Sykes-Maulby, surely one of the world's least reliable men, has only to mention this—what would you call it?—comeback scheme, and you're tormenting yourself over

him. Is he reliable? Trustworthy? I, who have met him twice
in my life, tell you he is neither."

"He needn't be. I'm not relying on him for a thing. Just
information. And what he tells me is very worrying."

The music seeping through the headphones of the cassette
player now sounded louder, more tempestuous, if sounds so
tiny could be thought of as being stormy.

She let the magazine slide off the bed. Palmer was lying on
his stomach, more or less. She half rolled on top of him so
that her breasts pinioned him to the bed. "Can you breathe?"

"Who needs to breathe?"

"Is it dark enough for you down there?"

"The cave of the sibyl."

"Soft cave," she said, rubbing back and forth. The short-cut
hair of his neck tickled her breasts. She felt the bed shift as
he turned over. One of her nipples was in his mouth. "Now
you see what it's all about," she murmured softly.

His hands began to stroke down the sides of her rib cage.
She shifted on top of him and reached for the headphones.
She clamped them on his head. "There is nothing like a hotel
bed," she said, more to herself than out loud.

She pulled her knees up so that she was riding him like a
jockey. She could feel him stiffen beneath her back and forth
movement. Pausing, she fitted him into her and began to
rock up and back, digging her heels into his thighs. He began
to move strongly beneath her to a different tempo, perhaps
Mahler, heard in private. She was laughing suddenly, almost
uncontrollably. He had pulled his knees up to lock her in
place. His fingers pinioned her shoulders to press down on
her as his pelvis thrust up.

There was indeed nothing like a hotel bed. Their own in
Morcote was softer and the ambience more seductive, all the
room lights being on a dimmer. But the idea of fornicating
among absolute strangers who heard or guessed, who came
and went, who changed the sheets, who passed one in the
hall. Glances. Thoughts. Prolonged aphrodisia. Constant state
of arousal. The way they had been when they'd first met.
That night in the hotel in Compiègne. Bell-tower. Heavy with
wine and good food. Strange sheets.

Beneath her his face had knotted, resisting his own orgasm. As it always did, the sight of him in this state triggered
her own climax. She forced the rhythm to slow. It was
excruciating as it inched closer to orgasm, closer. She watched

him come beneath her, a hard, twisting spasm and a cry of pure agony. Then she heard no more. Her own passion climaxed like a ring of fire engulfing her. He lay there, eyes closed, alone with Mahler.

Later, rolling off to rest beside him, she thought about their strange life together. They were a married pair if ever there was one, without the dubious benefit of a wedding ceremony. Their affair had now lasted even longer than her marriage to Dieter. He had died on the E-4 from Fribourg when Tanya was only five. They'd called it an accident.

She withdrew slowly from Palmer, her limbs suddenly cold. Bits of their early life together returned to her now without her asking, or wanting. An aura of violence had always surrounded him. The death of Dieter, who looked like him and had been killed for that resemblance. Others.

It wasn't something Palmer did. It wasn't his nature to attract violence. She knew about that hot vein of violence in Americans, but Palmer had never been that kind, loud, lawless, swaggering. With her beside him he had peacefully enjoyed the almost rural life they had on their mountain peak overlooking the Lake of Lugano. Was there some fatal synergy between them? Perhaps together they were a lightning rod that could attract strokes of senseless violence. Was it for this that Palmer avoided the heightened life of the cities? Because he wanted to reduce almost to zero the chance of lightning striking?

But here they were, after only a few days in London, surrounded by filmy plots of disaster and strange henchmen like Julian who inspired an almost physical distrust in her.

He stirred, stretched, took off the headphones. "Lovely," he murmured. "If I ever forgot what was important in life, you'd quickly remind me."

"Do I have that power?"

He nodded and stroked her flank. "You're cold." He pulled the sheet over both of them. "This kind of encounter is supposed to warm one up."

"At first."

He turned to look at her. "What's wrong?" The music lisped quietly, the headphones lying between them.

"Let's go back to Morcote. Now."

"Now?"

"Tomorrow."

"But I . . ." He paused. "I can't leave Curtiss to handle this one on his own."

"He's a resourceful young man," Eleanora told him. "And he's being paid by UBCO to do exactly what he's doing."

"Meaning I'm not."

"Meaning the affair is in capable hands. We can leave."

He gave up staring at her and regarded the ceiling over-head for a long time. Then, reluctantly: "You're afraid of the way it used to be with me. People being killed. I assure you—"

"One man is already dead in Paris. We don't mourn for him," she said, "but there he is. Death Number One."

"With any luck, we—"

"I don't want to leave it to luck, Woods," she said, sudden-ly hugging him to her. "I want to get out of London first thing tomorrow."

"We could be back in Morcote by lunch time."

"My most devout wish."

He rolled on his side so that he could embrace her. "All right," he promised. "There's a Swissair flight around nine a.m. If it means that much to you . . ."

They kissed.

24

The climb up the Alley of the Ten Thousand Virgins had winded Urs Rup. He puffed freely for a moment at the door of Margit's apartment before feeling in his pocket for the keys.

In the distance he could hear some young people shouting, then singing. A couple mounted the steps of the Alley and paused at the shop window beneath Margit's flat. They examined the old engravings in their ornate, gilded frames, and resumed their climb, in no way breathless.

Still breathing heavily, Urs sorted the keys on their ring: key to his office safe, to the safe in his house in the Gellertstrasse section of Basel, keys to the house and office doors, spare key to his wife's car in the likely event she lost hers, and the key that opened this door as well. He was beginning to walk around town like some janitor, tilting sideways with his ever-present bunch of keys.

He pulled down the points of his white velvet waistcoat and buttoned across it his faintly pink, faintly beige new silk jacket. His open shirt was also of silk, in broad stripes of magenta, cerise and Nile green. He mopped his face dry before opening the door. Margit had mentioned, only the other day, that of all the people she knew, Julian never seemed to perspire. That was all she had said but it somehow reverberated in Urs's mind.

He opened the door and walked slowly up the steep flight of stairs that twisted in a vague, undisciplined spiral as it mounted to Margit's flat. Winded, sweaty, he thought. But I'm slim.

His wife, also called Margit, also never seemed to perspire. Not even in the heat of summer after a romping set of tennis or a night of discoing. In his recently inspired sense of sudatory inferiority, he wondered if not sweating were a sign of higher birth, that aristocrats went into the world dry and faintly powdery to the touch while peasants dripped and sweltered like beasts of the field.

If so, his own ancestry was seriously in question. Taught that he was descended from hunters in the Alpine heights, part of Switzerland's natural aristocracy, Urs had never before been made to feel that he might in fact be nothing more than the offspring of gross, sweaty peasants, grubbing for their livelihood in the lowlands while the graceful Alpine marksmen, cool and dry ...

Margit (his mistress, not his wife) opened the door suddenly. "Are you planning to stand out there all night?" she asked. "I was beginning to think you were a burglar."

Inside, nestled comfortably on her long, batik-clad sofa, Urs rolled a joint of new leaf brought in this week by a client, a rock singer who had recently worked in Hawaii.

Urs inhaled deeply and held the smoke in. When he finally relinquished it, he sighed ecstatically. "Boss weed," he told Margit in English. "They call it Maui Wowie."

She laughed and switched into the Basler dialect of Schweitzerdeutsch, a clattering tongue with a choppy singsong to it. "Urs, you work so hard at it."

"At what?" He took six short, sharp inhales, stacking up the smoke in his lungs.

"At being the bad boy," she teased him. "At being the unruly son, the unorthodox banker, the scandalous husband."

A group of young people were climbing the steps of the

Alley of the Ten Thousand Virgins outside, screaming with laughter and quarrelling pleasantly about how many stairs they had mounted.

Urs let the smoke out stingily, unwilling to let it escape. It had a thick, clotted smell, like burning carrots. He could feel himself relaxing. He sighed out the last of it, his breath trembling with the effort. Again he proffered the joint to Margit.

"I'm fine," she refused. "What brings you here so late? It's almost time for you to go home."

Urs felt drops of perspiration spring up on his forehead. His armpits were damp. He inhaled more smoke, trying to feel tension being allayed. "I'm not going home tonight," he said after a while. "She thinks I'm in Lucerne for a conference at the Wilder Mann."

Margit hooted joyously. "Why did you pick that hotel? It's a notorious romantic rendezvous."

Urs nodded slowly. "I have my reasons." He knew all his actions, and his words, were slowing down. He welcomed this after a day of hideous tensions. "I happen to know she herself had an assignation there once."

"Recently?"

He was shocked. "Before our marriage, of course."

Margit nodded with false meekness. "Of course. And if she calls you there?"

"She won't." He sat back. The joint was down to a roach the length of his thumb nail. He picked up a bobby-pin Margit kept in the ashtray, used it as a tweezer to hold the roach and puffed on.

"But what kept you from me so long?" Margit persisted. "You left the office at three. Did you pull off a matinée with that art student?"

He sighed out smoke and reluctantly let the roach die in the ashtray. "It's no good cheating anymore," he complained. "Who told you about the art student?"

"That's not important." She took his hand, turned it over and kissed the palm. "I'm worried about you. Already you delegate too much of your job. And, Urs, you don't know how to delegate."

He made a face. He could feel his skin move chunkily, as if segmented under the skin. This Hawaiian herb was fantastic. Already the tingling in his skin seemed to be disjointing him. Pieces dangled free, a leg here, an arm there.

"Your father could never delegate, either. The only reason you're running the bank for him is that he finally had to slow down."

He sighed deeply, drawing from some pool of self-pity he had summoned forth. "What a thing it is to be married to two Margits. One at home is bad enough. But when my mistress begins talking like my father and mother and wife combined together with three heads on one body, red-faced, they are shouting at each other and crying real tears down their cheeks of red and orange and green like my shirt, stripes, blotched..."

He finally ran down, well aware that he was rambling incoherently. He sighed again and began rolling a second joint. A drop of sweat ran down his nose and dropped in the center of the small heap of marijuana cupped in a roll of paper. The spot spread out quickly.

"Damn."

Margit took it from him and finished rolling. "Is it too hot in here for you?" she asked, apparently without hidden meaning.

"Because I sweat like a horse? Did Julian find it too hot in here?"

"He? Icewater in the veins." She licked the joint closed and poked it into Urs's mouth.

"Did he?" he demanded.

"He's never been here, Urs." She struck a match. "Nobody has ever been inside this flat but you." She held the flame to the rolled cigarette and watched him puff smoke. "And my mother, of course."

"Is she doing well?" he asked politely.

"Yes. The hip is entirely healed." She sat back and watched him pack smoke into his lungs with short, efficient whiffs. "Speaking of Julian, he called you while you were servicing the art student."

"What did he want?"

"To bury his face between my thighs." She produced a sweet smile. "And if that wasn't possible by telephone, to talk to you."

"About what?"

"Urs, I can manage most of your daily routine without you. But you have never explained what you and Bennett Brown and Julian are doing."

He could see her suddenly enlarge, as if she were an

inflatable rubber doll, one of those sexshop specialties with a
vinyl vagina and dacron dugs. She grew huge. Her slim frame
swelled. Her breasts became gigantic melons. Her thighs
bloated. Her mouth was moving.

". . . and ended with an invitation for me to visit him in
London."

He closed his eyes. He was on the high seas, the ship
listing and falling with majestic slowness. He opened his
eyes. She had shrunk. Her nails were like talons. Her eyes
glittered.

"I don't trust—" He felt the rest of it stop in his throat
with a click.

"Don't trust Julian?" Margit finished for him. She watched
his eyes roll up in his head again. "That's not as crazy as you
think," she went on almost chattily. "I have always felt that
about the English."

"English what?"

"That they are out for themselves first. And there is no
second," she said. "Urs, are you listening?"

"Yes. You just accused the British of being very Swiss." He
giggled.

"I thought you'd dozed off."

"I hear all." He put down his joint and let it smolder
unused. "You don't trust Julian because of what? Something
he said?"

"Just a feeling."

"I have come to—" He stopped abruptly. He seemed to
have rolled off the batik sofa onto the floor. His face was
pressed against Margit's black patent leather pumps. When
he spoke, his voice was distorted because his lips were
twisted by the pressure of her shoes.

"—value your judgments," he went on casually.

"Urs, will you get up? I've never seen you like this."

"Undignified," the banker agreed in his most leisurely
tones, each syllable coming out slowly as a single word. "Sexy
shoes. Legs."

She planted one high heel on his chest and gave him a
quick shove. He fell back on the tan carpet and was snoring
in a moment. "Maui Wowie," she said aloud.

Margit, while not a big woman, had some experience of
handling her lover in similar situations. She got him by his
damp armpits and dragged him across the carpet into her
bedroom. There she stripped off his pinkish suit, white velvet

waistcoat, striped shirt, gold neck chains, cache-sex briefs, cobra boots and silk socks. Bracing herself, she first got his shoulders and head on the edge of the bed. Then, using his legs as levers, she finally worked him up onto the bed, where he lay in naked bliss.

As if there had been an audience watching this skilled performance, a group of revelers outside on the Alley burst into raucous cheers. Margit went to the window. Half a dozen students were crawling up the steps. Margit turned back to look at the prone body in her bed.

"Ah, Urs." She covered him with a sheet. "You really need a keeper, not a mistress," she told the inert form.

"I don't trust him either," a disembodied voice from the bed assured her.

25

Normally such a meeting would have taken place in one of three restaurants in the New York City area. Alfred J. Marston had eaten in all of them: the Lair near the New Jersey end of the George Washington Bridge, Mamma Serafina's in the Greenwich Village section of lower Manhattan, or Stella Amore on Lefferts Boulevard in the borough of Queens. In all three eating places, considered safe from eavesdropping or other surveillance techniques, syndicate matters could be discussed freely. If, by freely, one meant that it was all right for waiters and customers in nearby booths and tables to hear portions of the conversation. Marston considered this unacceptable since what he was discussing today with Sal Maggoranza was the feasibility of stripping a publicly held corporation.

He scheduled the sitdown, accordingly, for a noisy Irish pub and restaurant in Radio City called Charley O's, where it was almost impossible to hear what was being directly said to one, much less eavesdrop. Sal Maggoranza arrived on the dot at one p.m. and they silently toasted each other in Perrier with a wedge of lime.

"I looked over the prospectus," Sal said without preamble. Perhaps at Princeton, where he majored in economics, he had developed a case of Ivy League lockjaw that made his words come out in a strangled honk which contrasted appealingly with his curly black hair and ripe-olive eyes.

"You like?" Marston responded. "You see possibilities?"

"Not in the prospectus. What do I know about car renting?"

"It's so simple it hurts," Marston promised him. A waiter, lurking nearby, moved forward to take two orders of corned beef and cabbage, then retreated into the general din.

"At a car rental place you can get a Mini for say twenty bucks a day. Or a Caddy for say fifty. That makes sense to you, right? The big car should cost more?"

Maggoranza shrugged. "So?"

"It's a scam, Sally. The Mini costs Hertz say four thousand to buy new. They sell it used for say three thousand. It cost them say a thousand for the year they owned it. The Caddy cost them say ten grand new and they sell it used for say nine. It cost them the same for a year as the Mini. Dig?"

The financial manager of the Lucchese family looked unimpressed. "This is supposed to make me come in my jeans?"

"It's supposed to introduce you to the fact that the profit in car rental is made off selling used cars. Not renting them."

Sal Maggoranza was silent for a moment. "I'm waiting."

"Okay," Marston continued quickly. "Here's what a smart operator can do once RCA spins Hertz off. He can start by selling off the fleet for cash."

"So far, so good."

"Then he can close down everything but the profitable locations at airports. Where they're big enough, physically, he can convert locations to renting and leasing equipment. Heavy stuff, mostly for the construction business."

The Princeton man sat forward in his chair. "Now my ears are flapping."

"I thought they might, considering what a commitment your family has in construction."

"But, Freddie," Maggoranza warned him, "you look at any big construction site in the tri-state area, you're looking at stolen dozers, backhoes, mixers and trucks. It's a fucking jungle out there. These bullvans I got working for me, they think nothing of rolling up a truck and loading a dozer onto it. They got fake papers calling for an overhaul or minor repairs. And off goes the dozer, a hundred thousand bucks worth of iron, to some lot out on Long Island where I have to ransom the mother back again. I have to buy back my own dozer for twenty grand. You ever hear of such nerve?"

Marston concealed a smile, knowing that, while one of the other families controlled the stolen-equipment business, it could never get away with such a racket without the complicity of the Lucchese construction firms, who simply passed along the cost, known as "stealage," to the client whose misfortune it was to have hired them to build something.

"Those bastards are rough," he sympathized. "What do you think they take home in a year. A few million?"

The financial manager shook his head. "It's a half-a-billion-a-year business, Freddie," he said in awed tones.

"And Hertz is your passport into it," Marston pounced.

The waiter delivered two steaming plates of corned beef, cabbage and boiled potatoes. He was about to linger long enough to ask whether they wanted hot or regular mustard, but thought better of it and disappeared back into the noise.

"You heard me, Sally," Marston went on in an authoritative voice. "The network of Hertz locations gives you on-the-street availability. The thieves don't have to truck the stuff way out to Long Island. You just add it to inventory and put it up for lease. That way, look." He held up the fingers of one hand and ticked off his propositions. "First you add maintenance and depreciation of your own equipment to the customer's bill. Second, self-insure and add premium costs against stealage to your customer's tab. Third you add the rate Hertz charges you to rent or lease replacement equipment—your *own* stuff!!—back to you. Fourth you make a profit doing business as Hertz. Sal, I'm running out of fingers."

A faint smile turned up the outer corners of Sal Maggoranza's lips. "But, Freddie, what will it take to buy out the Hertz people RCA is selling the company to?"

"Buy out?" Marston echoed. "Not too much, once they start having all those gasoline fires."

26

It is not easy, Curtiss had told Mary Lee Hunter, to get out of the U.S. without organized crime knowing about it. This rather daunting idea stayed with her for the rest of the time she went through the motions of following Curtiss's advice.

It was more than daunting, she reminded herself now as she sat in an aisle seat aboard a 747, it was depressing in the extreme. Silently, unable to sleep and uninterested in the movie being shown, Mary Lee went back over both her instructions and her own performance of them.

It is not easy, Curtiss had said, because the mob controls most major airports as to freight—through its Teamster minions—and has a good idea of the passenger situation through informers, baggage handlers, suborned employees in the computer relay offices and a vast number of travel agencies used for steering vacationers to syndicate-owned resort hotels and gambling casinos.

"Anything in writing gets back to them quickly," he had explained. "They also have eyes and ears inside the big credit card companies. So charged items are something they can check on, too."

The evening before, Mary Lee had had a long conversation at the travel desk in the lobby of the Hay-Adams about planes back to Los Angeles. She had finally bought a nonstop leaving Dulles the next morning and had paid for it with her Diners card.

At the hotel cashier's she had got a cash advance on her American Express card. Carrying her large handbag—which had been her only luggage from the Coast, anyway—she had left the hotel around six p.m., walked half a dozen blocks, bought a dress and waited for a public bus that would take her to Washington National Airport.

"No cabs," Curtiss had warned her. "Cabbies remember faces, especially if the person asking them is also pressing a gun muzzle to their ear."

At the airport, she had avoided the Eastern shuttle to New

York and taken a regular airline flight, paying cash and giving her mother's maiden name. At LaGuardia Airport she had boarded a public bus to JFK International Airport.

"Don't go to British Airways or Pan Am or TWA," Curtiss had explained. "Everybody going to London will be there. Go instead to the International Departures building and shop around for a last-minute walk-on ticket on one of the airlines people don't think about when they go to London. Try Air India or El Al or PIA. If none of them pan out, you still have time to get back to one of the Big Three for their last flight."

As it turned out, El Al had one seat left to London. Mary Lee paid cash, then walked head-on into the most stringent security check she'd ever known. A young woman her own age, not in uniform, took Mary Lee aside. She eyed the big handbag. "That's *it?*" she asked.

"It's all I need."

"For a transatlantic flight?"

"My clothes are in London."

Eyeball to eyeball confrontation. Then: "Has this bag been out of your possession in the last forty-eight hours?"

"No."

"Have you checked it anywhere?"

"No."

"No lockers?"

"No."

"Has anyone you've been with recently asked you to take something to London for them?"

"No."

"Given you a gift?"

"No."

"An envelope?"

"No."

"A souvenir? Perfume? Scarf? Lipstick?"

"No."

"This might have been a friend?"

"No."

"Member of your family?"

"No." Mary Lee could feel her cheeks growing red. She shoved the bag at the security woman. It contained the new dress and her makeup. "Open it up. Take a look."

Her face stern, the woman locked glances with Mary Lee. Though her glance didn't waver, she seemed also to sense and evaluate the fact that Mary Lee was back in her standby costume: bikini and beach robe. After a long moment the Israeli scribbled something on the boarding pass. "That won't be necessary."

Passing through normal JFK security, Mary Lee ran into a second interrogation at the El Al gate. "Why did you book a flight this late?" a man asked her.

"It was the only stand-by seat left."

"But why El Al? There are plenty of seats at Pan Am or one of the others?"

"They're not in the International building."

Again that grave, eye-to-eye gaze. He turned her boarding pass over and scrawled something next to the other scribble. "Okay," he said eyeing her beach robe with the faint suspicion of a smile, "have a good flight."

If, after such treatment, she had expected something special about the flight, Mary Lee would have been disappointed. True, an almost unidentifiable liquid labeled "citrus" was indiscriminately served. And when she ordered a meal she got neither butter nor cream for her coffee. Otherwise El Al's crossing was like all others.

Unable to fall asleep, Mary Lee tracked back over her trail, wondering if she'd been followed. The false Los Angeles trail would probably remain credible at least till departure time at Dulles, by which time they could no longer backtrack and pick up her real trail. Or so Curtiss hoped.

But how was it possible for them to casually reach into the private heart of a free country and pull out confidential information at will? Curtiss had been rather matter-of-fact about it.

"Any computerized information is available to anybody," he had told her over the phone. "That's the state of the art in these United States. Either you buy yourself a terminal and tap in on the sly, or you buy yourself an authorized operator who sells you info on the sly."

"But, Curtiss," she had complained, "is this a free society? I'm horrified that I have to sneak around this way."

"There are much sneakier ways to do it," he had promised. "I'm laying out the easy, amateur way. It gives you, I would say, about a 95 percent chance of leaving without discovery. A pro who needed a foolproof exit, for whom only 100 percent security would do, would spend a lot more time and money and expertise on his departure."

"The idea of them sitting on this immense mound of stolen information . . . it's incredible."

"They don't keep track of everybody. Right now the name at the head of their list is yours. Next week it'll be someone else. On that basis, you see it's not really a very hard thing to do."

She closed her eyes aboard the 747 and tried in vain for sleep. Her gritty eyes followed some inane movie without listening to the sound track. Cars were chasing cars. She got up and went to the galley, feeling thirsty. Faced with cold "citrus" compound or warm water, she chose the water. Time passed. The sky outside was black. Then it was indigo. A hot pink-orange line appeared in the east.

At Terminal Three in Heathrow, she yawned uncontrollably. The walk seemed to go on forever, even with the help of motorized walkways. She was still yawning at passport control and customs. When she stumbled out into the public area where people were waiting for arriving friends, she spotted Curtiss at once. He shook his head, reminding her to get her own cab. Only when she was getting into it did he join her in the back seat.

"Carlton Tower Hotel."

He reached for her and they hugged, kissing slowly. She was half asleep already.

"Did you mention something," she asked, "about a king-sized bed?"

27

"What do you mean she can't be found?" Julian honked in a high voice. Bennett Brown's response over the telephone was so delayed he wondered if the connection had been broken.

"Vanished," came the somber reply at last. "A fake trail led back to California. That means she's in London."

"Want the eye kept peeled here, eh?"

"Yes."

"But, please. No cowboys and Indians here, eh? Nothing crude like the Cité Odiot. Scotland Yard is Scotland Yard and I have my own nose to keep clean." The line was dead. Brown had hung up.

The Englishman slammed down the phone and glared out

of the window of his office at the early morning sun on the close-cropped lawn and high trees of New Square in Lincoln's Inn Fields. He always found the sight of green restful to his soul and his soul was sorely troubled at the moment.

It was eight-fifteen a.m., much too early for anyone of Julian's class to be up and doing. He had lived abroad and picked up unseemly foreign ways, but no gentleman, and certainly no financier, appeared in any business office before ten. His only excuse was a breakfast appointment, and a tricky one.

Sighing, Sykes-Maulby tried to let the greensward soothe him with its restorative powers. The two immense locust trees near the fountain in the middle of New Square, stretching higher in the air than the buildings that surrounded them, gave an uplifted quality to this otherwise grim hour of the day.

Were the truth known, Julian kept the tiny office of his private investment trust in these dingy but prestigious surroundings among London's oldest law firms because of the soothing quality of the grass and trees. And the old-money ambience, of course. He had chosen a small suite on the top floor of Number 3, next to the law-book shop, because it gave him a diagonal, and thus more expansive, swath of green to contemplate.

The interior decor was Dickensian and the staff quite small, only his elderly secretary, Lavinia, tottering about on her five-inch heels, and an even more elderly accountant, Mr. Tooth, who had switched from bound ledger books and quill pens only in the last ten years, but now seemed quite at home with the simple computer terminals he used.

Most of the office was given over to a boardroom with a magnificent brass-bound rosewood table that seated twelve. It was for the benefit of his board, and the occasional new major investor who took a flier with the Trust, that Sykes-Maulby had chosen this excessively legal neighborhood, for much the same reason a quack might practise in Harley Street, respectability. Julian was no quack. He was, even this early in the morning, a shark.

Brusque, ill-mannered Bennett Brown, he found himself thinking. A genius with figures, a thorough cock-up as a human being. Still, Bennett Brown's family connections were fascinating if what one sought in life was cash flow.

Sykes-Maulby listened again to the phone conversation just

concluded, trying to find any note of the paranoia of yesterday's conference call with Urs listening in. Yesterday he'd been almost accused of treachery by young Mr. Brown. Almost accused of leaking something he shouldn't have to Palmer.

Which he had, and very deliberately, certain it couldn't get back to Brown. It was part of the Englishman's private plan that Palmer be indebted to him, whatever the cost to Brown's world-devouring schemes. He had, in fact, crassly betrayed Brown, but had done so in the full confidence of not being suspected.

That confidence had withered the moment Brown revealed he'd been under surveillance while talking to Palmer in Green Park. Thank God the watcher had no way of eavesdropping. That was one of the reasons Julian had picked a public park for the conversation. Not that open air talk was immune to bugging. Just that it would have taken Brown's henchman hours to procure and set up a system.

So, although he felt sure his treachery had gone unheard, Julian was shaken to learn he was so poorly trusted as to be shadowed around London. Or had the tail been on Palmer? Ah! Better.

He gazed benignly on the green grass and shrubs. Much better. You see? Even big problems become little ones after a bit of positive thinking amid Nature's greenery.

He pulled himself together. Because he was returning to Switzerland today, Palmer had asked him to breakfast at that ghastly hotel of his, where only foreigners stayed. It meant Bloody Marys with all sorts of peculiar things to eat: waffles or hominy grits. Hearing him get to his feet, Julian's secretary clattered around the corner of the rosewood-and-glass partition. "Ready to leave, are we?" she asked.

"Yes, Lavinia."

She brought him his hat and cane. "George has the Roller at the New Square gate."

Striding briskly forward in the summer sunshine, cane flashing, Sykes-Maulby watched his uniformed chauffeur open the door of the pewter-colored Rolls and usher him inside. This was one of the last, lean-flanked Phantom III Rollses made in 1938 before war production usurped everything. Its Mulliner coachwork had been polished to a discreet pewter gleam. Its tall radiator grille cleaved the air imperturbably. The heavy car sped silently west down the Strand, along the

Mall, through St. James's Park and entered Belgravia the
back way, across Pont Street and up Sloane Street.

As the Rolls waited at Harriet Street to turn right, a cab
trundled down Sloane Street and left-turned ahead of it,
bound for the same hotel. Julian saw a man and woman get
out of the cab.

Instinctively his glance followed the tall young woman who
carried an outsized handbag. What on earth *was* she wearing,
he wondered. Some sort of diaphanous pullover like a long
nightie? But translucent enough to show him that underneath, that lissome body was covered by only a bikini bottom.

His glance lifted to her face. He had seen that square chin
and small nose before. If behind those immense dark glasses
lurked china blue eyes, he believed he was watching a most
wanted apparition indeed.

The last time he had seen her pointed out, at a restaurant
in Beverly Hills, she had been wearing a brown suit over a
beige sweater and cream blouse, closed at the neck with a
large amber pin, a pretty picture of wrapped-up executive
female. This coryphée in gauze bore few resemblances.

But enough.

28

The guard around the perimeter of Don B's villa near Palermo
had been doubled. Gaetano Sgroi, his majordomo, had hired
six more local men, chosen and vouched for by the local
capo. The shape of the villa estate was roughly triangular. At
present a man patrolled each of the sides, relieved every
eight hours by a second man. That meant Don B's guards
could not sleep a normal night. But at this time he needed
them particularly alert. With the troubling of the guard, each
man would now be fresh eyed for his work.

"Gaetano," his employer said when he had inspected the
six new young men, "you will take the cook into town. She
must order double quantities of everything, and for a week at
a time. The fewer trips we make in and out of here, the
better."

"Sí, *padrone*." He paused, fidgeting. Then: "How do they

seem to you, these new ones? Don Calogero swears they are his finest, cousins and nephews all."

"But you don't agree?"

Sgroi wrung his hands together in misery. "I . . . you . . . Don Calogero is a man of great respect, *padrone*. What he says is clearly the truth."

It was not easy being majordomo for Don B, as Gaetano had often had cause to reflect. If he had been one of the Old Ones, steeped in the hierarchical darkness of the honored society, he would have known how to serve him more effectively. But Don B was an American.

Yes, of course he was one of the Old Ones, but from another land, where they had lost the sense of the slow wheeling of time, of nature's pauses and seasons, of the leisurely natural rhythms of the land and its people, of death and its helpers.

Don B demanded results and he wanted them quickly. He had no patience. And one could never counsel patience because he would have his head handed to him on a pizza pan. When Don B asked for an opinion, as now, he wanted it produced instantly, without reservations.

"But? But?"

"But to me they seem raw, untested," Gaetano finished quickly.

Don B said nothing. Gaetano Sgroi had been with him now for two years. He was of his native village in Calabria but had lived a long time among the Siciliani. He knew the ways in which they were different from Calabrese. If he were right, what a monstrous problem for Don B. Untested men can be trained. In time they become reliable. But the fact that Don Calogero had given him raw recruits was a symbol of something much more threatening.

Don B sent Gaetano on his way with the cook. He groaned softly as he sat back in the tall wicker armchair placed on his patio so that breezes could cool him. It was ominous: Don Calogero did not want truly valuable soldiers wasted in fighting a lost war. So he sent beginners.

Did it mean he felt Don Gino, seeking revenge, would be the victor? If so there was only one answer. The tall man who had rid the world of Gino's son Turi in Paris had jumped French bail and been smuggled by fishing boat from Marseilles to Genoa, where he was lying low. Don B picked up the patio telephone.

"Your health is good?" was his salutation.

"Yes."

"He who left us in Paris," Don B continued in a casual tone, "had a father."

"Had?"

"You take my meaning."

A pause. "Yes. But . . ."

Today the air was filled with buts. "If it is a matter of showing gratitude, my heart is full enough to the extent of a million lire."

"Could it be doubly full?" the tall man inquired.

A thing worth doing, Don B reminded himself, was worth doing right. "Agreed."

"Then it is as good as done."

"Within the next three days."

"Sooner."

Don B hung up the telephone with a satisfied half-smile, as if food he had eaten was digesting in pleasing calmness. Two million lire was cheap for the death of Don Gino *now*. And in his experience the tall man never failed. He had a talent for this kind of work.

In the distance, at the far end of the property, three black birds settled on the barbed wire. Don B frowned. By their grave, watchful demeanor they seemed to be ravens. Even at this distance he could see their sharply downturned beaks, like curved scissors. In the sunlight their black eyes glinted.

One of the housemaids approached. "*Padrone*, your visitor is here."

Don B moved with slow dignity to embrace the man coming out onto the patio. He was younger than Don B, in his late fifties perhaps, and dapper slim like a jockey. His iron grey hair was close cropped. Under a large, sharp nose, a hairline moustache bristled. When he spoke it was conventional textbook Italian with a strangely French intonation, uvular r's and pursed vowels.

"You never grow older, Don B," he said, patting the old man's shoulders as they embraced.

"While you, Achille, only grow younger."

The housemaid, in Gaetano's absence, brought out Campari, soda and ice cubes in a bucket. Don B busied himself with making drinks.

Achille Gamba held within the Unione Corse, the Corsican criminal organization, a position which resembled the post Don B had held before his retirement from America. Achille Gamba was the authority to whom any difference of opinion was brought. His personal probity made him the peacemaker of his warring families and allowed him to walk safely where others would have been killed. He supervised compromises no one liked but everyone obeyed.

This meeting with Don B was not business. Achille happened to be in Palermo to work out changes in the distribution system for Afghan, Iranian and Turkish Number 4 White injectible and morphine base.

There had for some time been a marshalling area for the fishing boats that carried such cargo west through the Mediterranean. Once they rounded the straits of Messina, they headed for one of the smaller Aeolian islands near Stromboli, where they off-loaded onto high-powered trawlers which took the stuff in to the Provençal coast of France or, via the Atlantic, to coastal ports in Brittany.

None of this had anything to do—anymore—with Don B. But Achille liked to talk to his elderly comrade. Both of them had a philosophical bent. Over the decades, Achille hadn't found too many like Don B, who could spin out an idea or two into a valuable afternoon of hypothetical discourse.

"I hear great things of your son Benedetto's work," the Corsican said, sipping his deep pink drink. "I am certain our own small contribution to the project will bring us substantial rewards."

"In time. It goes slowly because, as you know, old friend, to hasten it is to give our hand away."

"Exactly so." The Corsican held up the drink and peered through it, as if through a rose-colored monocle. He smiled softly. "Tell me, and only me, dear friend." He paused.

"Whatever you command, Achille."

"Tell me something I have been thinking about. We know what the end result of this project will be, no? That we harvest all the wealth of all the nations. That nothing moves without our word. That no profit is made without our tithe, no? That our banks finance our businesses and our deputies and senators and mayors and governors, our parliaments, our chiefs of police, our generals and admirals, all, all obey us."

By the time he finished this speech each man was grinning in his own cadaverous way with a kind of holy glee, lit from within by fires they refused to control. "You look very far into the future," Don B said then. "These things you will, of course, live to see and enjoy. I shall be long gone."

"But you will have left a living monument to your wisdom and devotion," the Corsican added. "None of this bothers me, old and honored friend. I am serene in my expectations because your son is the one man capable of carrying out the project."

The three ravens began to shuffle along the barbed wire, a grisly little shifting dance, as if the filament hurt their hard, curved talons. To the left they danced, then far to the right, silently, eyes bright.

There was an awkward little pause, which Don B finally took pains to bridge. "You speak of what does not bother you. Now tell me, my dear Achille, what does?"

"This is a more theoretical question, old friend. You and I read the newspapers, no? We keep up with the world. We know that some day soon, perhaps even as we speak, the big companies will falter. The big economies will shrink. We will have another of those depressions which sends its tentacles around the world and clutches at every heart, no?"

"So they say," Don B agreed.

Achille sat silently for a moment, as if choosing his words even more carefully than a man in his position normally did. "With respect, dear friend, what will it profit us to control a bankrupt world?"

Don B smiled broadly. He liked a good theoretical discussion, especially with a mind as quick as Achille's. "Do you imagine for a moment that Benedetto has not allowed for this contingency? The boy is already a genius, but his machines, his computers, would make even a blockhead like me a genius."

"You a blockhead?" Achille Gamba made a chuffing noise, as of a small locomotive successfully pushing a load of freight uphill. "You, the da Vinci of our hopes and dreams? It is easy to see where the genius son gets his brilliance, no? Tell me, and only me, how has he discounted this contingency?"

Don B raised a short, thin finger, gnarled with arthritis. "I well remember the day he told me of this. It was the same day he told me the woman of his choice had set a date for their marriage. Even then he had begun to put into effect with the funds at his disposal the beginnings of the project in which we all now participate. He said to me: 'Papa, the big bust is coming, the Kondratiev Wave has hit its beta peak. Any year now...disaster. So when you ask me, why do we buy this stock, but not the stock of another concern, the answer is, we only buy depression-proof paper. The other companies we will pick up cheaply after the crash.' This was the vision he had and it has so far proved prudent. But it is only half of his contingency plan. The other half is even more ingenious."

Achille Gamba chuckled with delight. He enjoyed sharing the inner workings of a real brain. "Marvelous, old friend, no? Because in his prudence he is also concealing our intentions. You follow? By buying this stock but not that, he confounds anyone who suspects our plans. He confuses our natural enemies, no? It is pure sleight-of-hand. Now tell me, and only me, what is his second move?"

Don B sipped greedily at his Campari-soda. Talking had made him thirsty. "Have you noticed the way in America our honored society operates its legitimate enterprises? If you were to investigate, let us say, how the manager of one of our supermarkets is ordered to do business?"

"In the normal way, no?" Gamba asked. "With the A list."

"Precisely. From the A list given him, he knows that he must buy only from certain wholesalers, certain suppliers, particular butchers, special frozen-food warehouses, use the facilities of only one cleaning and maintenance concern, one security firm for his night watchmen, one insurance company, a particular short list of truckers, only certain advertising agencies, one special bank..."

He gestured airily. "In America these A lists get quite long. They are made up, naturally, of companies we control. Even down to the employment agency that supplies him with workers and the union that organizes them." He smiled, listening to Gamba's guffaw of pure pleasure.

"Ah, America!" the Corsican sighed happily. "I begin to see your son's magnificent idea. When we own an Eastman Kodak, a Citroën, a Hoffman La Roche pharmaceutical company, we make them work together, favor each other. And—"

"And bring the depression to a quick conclusion!" Don B exclaimed with excitement. "Think of it, dear friend. Instead of the cutthroat competition of the open market, instead of what is called free enterprise, we have total control, quick recovery, a placid economy once more. In months, rather than decades, the Kondratiev Wave turns upward and life goes profitably forward ... under our control."

"Under our control," Achille echoed admiringly. His cheeks were flushed. The tips of his hairline moustache quivered with excitement. "I salute you, Don B!" he said, lifting his glass. "We are eternally in your debt."

"Ben's, not mine," Don B protested. "Such beauty of design. Of course it benefits us first. But also the man in the street. Him it keeps at work and content enough not to turn to the political left."

"The true essence of the system," the Corsican agreed. "Everyone must get a sniff of it, even to the bone one throws the starving dog."

Don B smiled. "Even more, my friend. By bringing back prosperity—on *our* terms—we make sure there are no starving dogs. Hungry, yes. Ambitious, perhaps. Starving, no." The smile widened to a grin. "And always ... greedy."

"Greed," Achille Gamba mused, almost to himself. "It is the universal cement. It binds the entire system together."

The older man's eyes twinkled. "And us at the top."

"You have taught young Benedetto well," the Corsican said then. "It is one thing to devise such a scheme and organize its working details. Opposition there will always be, from within as well as without our, ah, structure." He used the word with a certain elegance. "But in the finality of time, a scheme that creates too much opposition, too widely spread, especially among the common people, is a scheme doomed to failure. This Benedetto has so cleverly provided for. Amazing."

In the distance they could hear a car horn honking. Don B frowned. After a moment it stopped honking. Turning in his wicker chair, Don B could see the old, heavy Mercedes Gaetano Sgroi drove. It moved slowly into the compound and disappeared at last behind the villa where it would be unloaded into the kitchen.

Along the barbed wire the three ravens seemed to crane their short, glossy necks. Don B frowned again. He did not like the birds. Their lower tail feathers drooped like the black morning coat of an undertaker. He felt the skin across his shoulders prickle.

"Can you honor my humble villa by remaining for dinner?" Don B asked.

"Nothing would please me more, dear fr—"

The scream pierced the air like a broken shard of glass. It

hurtled through the lemon trees. It ricocheted off the walls with their high, cyclone fences. Don B rose in his chair, his face pale. Again the scream, a woman's, perhaps the house-maid who had brought their drinks.

Now the Corsican was standing up. They moved like dreamers, slowly with unwilling feet, in the direction of the screaming. Around the corner of the villa ran Gaetano, his eyes wide with fear, his open mouth distorted.

"Don B!" he shouted.

"*Silencio, cretino! Stai calma!*" His employer and the guest followed the majordomo as he retreated in the direction from which he had come, turning towards them, then away, in a perfect frenzy of fear and indecision.

"*No, signori,* I do not recommend you come any further," Gaetano babbled. "*O, dio mio, che disgrazia!*"

The three men were now in the rear of the villa by the kitchen doors. The Mercedes stood in the driveway, its trunk open. Two guards, carrying sawed-off 12-gauge shotguns, stared into the trunk. When they saw their employer ap-proach, they backed away with a curious air about them, half respect and half pity.

Don B looked into the trunk. Behind him he could hear Achille Gamba's slight intake of breath, not a gasp, but painfully audible nevertheless.

"Who is she?" he asked softly.

"My cook," Don B said, trying to keep his voice steady. "My cook of twenty-five years." Grimacing, he lifted her severed head from her body and gently patted down the ragged gray strands of hair. Slowly, he closed the staring eyes. He smoothed close the gaping mouth. When he had finished, the front of his suit dripped crimson.

"She told me to return here without her." Sgroi was babbling. "She wandered off somewhere. I had a *caffè* at the bar. How could I know they would—?"

Along the far wall, where barbed wire topped a tall stretch of cyclone fencing as an impregnable barrier against the outside world, the three black birds rose suddenly into the air, cawing loudly.

Their harsh cries hurt the ears, insistent, hostile, as if trumpeting news to the world. Holding the gory head to his breast, Don B looked up and watched them circling, diving, shrieking.

Achille Gamba glanced from his host to the birds and then

back to Don B's face and finally to the gruesome burden in
his bloody hands, took a deep breath and crossed himself.

29

At eight forty a.m., his first cup of coffee only half finished,
Woods Palmer, Jr., glanced coldly across the breakfast table at
Julian Sykes-Maulby. There was always something in reserve,
something hidden about Palmer. People who liked him said
that he hid a remarkable intelligence behind a rather cold
exterior so as not to intimidate others. People who didn't like
him wrote him off as a typically arrogant, unsympathetic
banker. People who knew him very well, people like Curtiss
or Eleanora, knew both faces were true.

"You treacherous Limey bastard," he told Julian in a cool
undertone that barely carried past his lips. The coffee aroma
was strong.

"I say!"

"You Brits can't be trusted any further than a pit viper."

"I say, Woods! Undeserved! Did you not hear what I said?"

"I heard, all right. Double agent. Playing both sides against
each other. Soldier of financial fortune. Julian, you stink."

The Englishman put down the fork with which he had been
fitfully trying to make a frozen pat of butter melt on a
lukewarm waffle. He put the fork down with such a sharp
click that others in the hotel's breakfast room turned to look.
Then he took a sip of coffee.

"Silly twit," he said, smiling deceptively for the benefit of
those tuning in late, "you're firing on your own troops. You
don't deserve my help."

Palmer sat back, well aware that what they had been saying
could not be heard but that there was no disguising the
tension between them. He tried to relax. Almost without
looking at his plate, he pushed around some hash brown
potatoes until they overran the liquid yolk of his eggs.

"Julian, this is Palmer you're talking to. I have had your
number for thirty-five years. You have as good as told me,
haven't you, that there exists a three-way conspiracy between
you, the Bank Rup and what we call for lack of a better word

the Mafia? That they provide the cash flow, you provide the impeccable financial front and Bank Rup launders the cash? What more d—?"

"In no way is it a tripartite conspiracy," Sykes-Maulby interjected. "There is an employer and there are two employees, Young Mr. Brown has sharp hooks in my hide. I don't use the word blackmail lightly, but that's precisely why I do his bidding. As for Urs Rup, as you know, he'd work for Beelzebub as long as he was guaranteed a 1½ percent handling charge."

"I don't believe any of it," Palmer responded in a quiet, deadly tone. "What could anyone have on you any more damaging than what's already common knowledge?"

Julian's laugh attracted attention again and this time Palmer had the sense to smile, as if a joke had passed between them.

"As for Urs," Palmer continued coldly, "no Swiss banker puts all his eggs in one basket, even one as grandiose as Brown is offering. You yourself told me they're college mates. So delve deeper in that devious brain, Julian. Give me some better excuses."

He glanced at his watch. "On second thoughts, to hell with you." The cooling coffee had taken on a dead, inanimate smell. He got to his feet. "I've got a plane to catch."

Julian arose with him. The two men stalked through the lobby and into a waiting lift, got out on the fifth floor and walked without speaking to the door of Palmer's suite. "Goodbye, Julian," Palmer said in a firm voice. "You'll excuse me if I don't shake hands."

"You fucking sod," he exclaimed. "Open this door at once."

"I don't want you upsetting Eleanora."

"I didn't meet you at this ungodly hour to be insulted, you brainless ninny. If I'm to be insulted, you're going to listen to reason."

Palmer knocked on the door, Eleanora opened it. "Argue inside," she said.

They entered. Packed suitcases stood about, waiting for the porter. Eleanora surveyed both of them. "Were you yelling like that downstairs?" she wanted to know.

Palmer waved her off. "This snake," he said, "is in league with Brown. They're both behind that nasty business in Paris against Curtiss."

"He told you this?" Eleanora asked.

"Yes," said Julian. "We criminals always confess in advance."

"I don't suppose either of you ate anything?" She went to the phone and called Room Service. Then she dialed Curtiss's suite.

After a long wait she said: "I'm sorry, Curtiss. This is a horrible moment to interrupt you, but you have to come up here. I think you'd better bring your friend."

By nine-thirty, staying alive mostly on black coffee, the five of them sat in morose silence, churning over the news Sykes-Maulby had given them. A fresh coffee smell filled the large, sunlit room, a smell mingled with the faintly smoked odor of saddle-leather luggage. Mary Lee Hunter looked, if anything, fresher than the rest but, as Eleanora told herself in private, the American woman was the youngest person in the room.

Eleanora herself had the advantage of being perfectly turned out in a khaki traveling dress and elegant sandals while Mary Lee, perhaps five years her junior, had hastily pulled on a wrinkled dress that had been bought in Washington. A day in the bottom of her bag had done it no good at all. She smelled of soap and sex, in that order.

"We have to think of this," Julian said in a tired voice, "as a council of war. I do loathe clichés, but we must indeed bury the hatchet and come up with something useful in the way of defense."

"Stop forging Anglo-American alliances," Palmer muttered. "We've missed our flight. There isn't another till after lunch. I want to thank you for starting my day off so brilliantly, Julian."

"English-Speaking Union. Why do you Yanks resist it so? When you let the silly Persians take all those hostages of yours, who hid four and smuggled them out? The Canadians. There isn't any former colony of Great Britain that wouldn't have done the same, old man. You are all us. We are all you. I mean, damn it, can you really trust a France? An Italy?"

"Curtiss," Palmer begged, "tell him to shut up?"

"But with an Australia or a Canada behind you, what cannot be accomplished? The world can be moved. The—"

"Julian," Curtiss cut in, "he asked me to ask you to shut up." He rubbed the day-old beard on his cheeks. "I could listen to you forever. You know that. But older people have a lower tolerance." Sykes-Maulby frowned at him. American humor again? He addressed himself to Mary Lee. "Now that you're fully in the picture, Miss Hunter, there is something more you should know."

"I'm not sure I need any more reality."

He smiled charmingly. His nostrils flared, as if inhaling a potent perfume, and he instantly caught the aroma of the sex act, that unmistakable combination of male and female odors. Given a bit of makeup, he thought, and a change of clothes, she'd be downright *ravissante*. Who was rogering her? Curtiss? "I'm not familiar with the various data processing and retrieval systems in use at Jet-Tech," he said smoothly. "But I do know that a day or two after Curtiss's original report reached your desk, Bennett Brown knew its entire contents."

"What?"

"Not verbatim, but in a rather concise summary."

"No such summary exists," she told him. "And I definitely did not code any of Curtiss's report into my Gameplan projections. I had no place for it in the program. I simply filed it."

"In one of those sliding-drawer things?" he asked.

"Right. This was over a year ago. It didn't reach Bennett by an illegal tap on our electronic systems. It got to him the plain old-fashioned way. Somebody swiped it, made notes and put it back."

Palmer took in a slow, exasperated breath of air. "That's Mafia m.o.," he said in a fed-up tone. "The old-fashioned scams are still the best. They have in their pocket one or more of your office staff. The same way they pocket a businessman or bank manager. They find someone who likes drugs or money or women. Or doesn't want his wife and children firebombed. In other words, they find an average person and apply the screws until, whatever they want, he does."

Nobody spoke. Eleanora got up and moved among them, filling coffee cups from a large silver pot. Steamy aroma filled the room. She sent a plate of croissants around, with no takers.

Palmer turned to Julian. "What I don't understand is why UBCO is so key to their operation?"

The Englishman shrugged. "It's the biggest commercial bank in the world. And what they're doing is the biggest piece of commerce in history. It's *big*, old man. Naturally, only a big bank will do."

"Is that another of your snide cracks?"

Sykes-Maulby closed his eyes and sat back in an upholstered

armchair. Behind him, the summer day glared white, silhouetting his long, aquiline nose and powerful chin. He was watching Mary Lee's nipples pressing through the thin stuff of her dress, but no one could see this because of the blinding sunlight. "I suppose so, yes. You Americans have this passion for bigness. Why can't the American families of organized crime be satisfied with owning a few companies, a few brokerages, a few banks, their share or even a bit more of the goodies? We'd certainly let 'em, we fellow scoundrels and pirates. Why not? But must they go for the whole thing?"

When no one responded, Curtiss cleared his throat. "Because winning means winning everything."

Palmer tapped the Englishman's knee. "I apologize for all the insults. I'm on edge. Big cities do that to me. It's why we're clearing out for Switzerland. I realize you're playing a dangerous game and I appreciate your being frank with us. The only thing I don't see yet is what we can do about it."

"To begin wi—"

"And don't tell me I'm supposed to go back to Manhattan and wrest control from the weaklings now running UBCO. Because that's out."

The Englishman spread out his long hands to either side, palms up. "Then forget it, old man, and hotfoot it back to Morcote."

Another morose silence engulfed them. Outside the window they could hear the growl of a tour bus engine and the squeal of taxi brakes. Curtiss got to his feet and glanced outside. He stayed there, letting the sun warm his face through the plate glass. Behind him Mary Lee watched him without any pretense and Eleanora watched her watch him. Then her glance shifted to Palmer. She wondered if he felt attracted to the younger woman, exuding the odor of sex.

"My job for Bennett Brown," Julian said then, "is to keep him advised on British and European companies. Which look depression-proof, which can't survive a crash. Which has ownership spread so widely that one could control it by a relatively small holding of stock. Which is so family owned as to be impervious to a takeover. Or in which the family has fallen out, making the firm ripe for plucking. He feeds this into his machines and tells his electrons to chase things around till they come up with answers. Then he issues a buy order and Urs Rup executes it. You see how chains of command are made to disappear? Urs buys in the names of a

numbered account, of course. So, let us say that at Bank Rup,
Account Tango-447 then buys a carefully calibrated percentage of St. Gobain glassworks in France. Or some of Brown-
Boveri in Switzerland? Mercedes-Benz or the inheritor companies to Krupp? Bennett Brown has a weakness for
manufacturers, not service companies. He feels people will
need *things*, even at the depth of a world depression. In any
event, first Tango-447 buys, then Bravo-119 buys. Then
another numbered account and another. And only Urs knows
they are all Bennett Brown. Urs and now us."

"And now us," Palmer echoed. "And Bennett Brown knows
we know." He turned to Mary Lee. "Did you talk to him in
the States?"

She shook her head. "He wanted to see me, I suppose to
learn what I was planning to do with what I knew."

"Such as?" Curtiss asked, turning away from the window to
face them. "What has he done that's illegal? If we blew the
whistle, what possible penalty would he face?"

"Once found out," she suggested, "he has to abort the
whole project."

"Why?" Curtiss persisted. "I know the worst sin is being
caught, but how does it hamper him? Our society lives with
the knowledge of far more shameful secrets than this one. We
open our newspapers each morning and it's back to Zola
again. To start the day, we have to swallow a toad. Because for
the rest of the day we're asked to swallow much worse."

Palmer glanced strangely at his protégé. "What turned *you*
on?"

"Just a dose of reality," the younger man told him. "We're
living some sort of dream existence here. Suppose Bennett
Brown and his family and every goddamned one of their
associate families ended up owning everything from U.S.
Steel to Coca-Cola. What would that mean to the guy in the
street? Zilch!"

"Oh, come now," Palmer began, "you d—"

"He's right," Julian interrupted. "What could they do that
would hurt the man in the street more than he's already
hurting? It's *we* who don't want them to take over. Nobody
else really gives a damn, I think. But *we* do."

"Cynical nonsense," Palmer burst out.

Eleanora got up and moved behind his chair. Her hands
fell gently on his shoulders, as if by accident. He glanced up
at her almost with irritation. The hollows under his cheek-

bones were like caverns in the harsh sunlight from the window.

"I expect it of you, Julian," he went on, "because as you so rightly put it before, scoundrels will always make a place at the table. Plenty of prey for all. But I don't expect it of you, Curtiss."

"I asked what such a takeover would mean to the average person. And the answer is still the same."

The two men watched each other, Palmer with growing anger, Curtiss with doggedness. "If the public agree with you," the older man said, "then the public is a great fool." He took an unsteady breath. "If there is no real difference between us and them, then we are all fooling ourselves. But I happen to believe there is a difference."

"Then why have you opted out of it?" Curtiss asked.

The large room with its picture windows, the five people in their sofas and chairs, locked luggage scattered here and there, Curtiss standing, Palmer glaring into the sunlight, smells of coffee and leather, of men and women, all seemed to focus down now to one painful spot of light in which the faces of the two men intruded harshly like badly designed clowns, the makeup for tragedy, not laughs. The Englishman's eyes were hooded, watchful. But he said nothing. He had already declared himself.

"I opted out," Palmer said slowly, "because of the fatal inflationary drift into debt. The banks were greedy enough to give the public what it wanted, unlimited credit, and extended the same poisoned gift to industry and government. We're living with the results right now. Terminal credit glut. That's the cross I bear. But there's no connection between that and what we're considering here."

"I don't agree." Curtiss gestured unhappily. "You act as if a bank is something unique, staffed by creatures from another race. It's only a business whose business *is* business. If you look at the board of UBCO, or any bank, you find it full of directors who represent other businesses. You can't separate a bank from its debtors. They are one and the same."

Palmer buried his face in his hands. Eleanora's fingers began soothing him at the back of his neck where it met his shoulders. She pressed and stroked, pressed and stroked. Finally he looked up at Curtiss, not directly but to one side, almost shyly.

"Let's talk about this some other time," he said in a conciliatory voice. "Right now, we've got a separate problem."

"I don't think so," Curtiss said almost apologetically. "I think what we had was Brown panicking. That turned on the Paris attack. But he's had the chance to see that he's safe as hell. So I think he's stopped panicking. You talked to him this morning?" he asked, turning to Sykes-Maulby.

"He was his usual truculent self. But calmer, definitely." Julian hesitated. Then: "If I may say so, and for what it's worth, I did suggest he ease off the dramatics."

"Maybe he took the advice." Curtiss turned back to Palmer. "We can't be sure for a while. Meantime, we can at least send out some sort of alert to the SEC, can't we?"

Palmer shook his head. "To do what? And half of what he's buying isn't under SEC anyway. It's European. No, we get to him through Rup."

Abruptly, Eleanora stopped the massage. Palmer glanced up at her. "He's the weak link. The technical ability to do all this resides with his bank. It would take Brown quite a while to find another Swiss bank as responsive to his special needs."

"Woods," she said. Then stopped.

Watching her, his face changed. "I'm doing it again, right?" He looked faintly sheepish. "Weaving webs. Life among the scorpions." He stood up. The room was utterly silent. Not even traffic could be heard through the window panes. "We're going back to our mountain retreat. Big cities get my blood riled up. I even start quarreling with Curtiss. Gentlemen, as Goldwyn once put it, include me out."

"Not so fast," Julian snapped. "If Rup is the weak point, you are the one to snap it. You're going back to Switzerland? Go to Basel first. I won't take long. I promise you Urs is as vulnerable as a newborn lamb."

Palmer glanced at Eleanora again. "What do you think?"

"Does it matter?" Her accent, always very faint, had become the tiniest bit stronger, "metta" for "matter." Her face was impassive. Only a sharp horizontal slash of red across each cheekbone indicated that anything was wrong.

"Yes it matters. If you say no, it's no."

"Dear Got," she exclaimed, "I am not your muttah, Woods. Nor am I your keepah." She stopped and put her hand over her mouth, hearing the deterioration in her pronunciation. Then, in a quite different tone without any accent, she added: "Do as you wish. Do as you feel you must."

"Is that a yes or a no?"

She laughed unhappily. "I suppose the least I can do is stand by in case you—" She turned to Curtiss. "What's the phrase?"

"In case he goofs up."

"Right." She turned back to Palmer and kissed him once, slowly, on the mouth. "In case you goof up."

The Englishman listened intently. American slang, like American humor, almost always eluded him. But the end result was that Palmer would try to take Rup out of the picture. And that, Julian promised himself with secret glee, is absolutely perfect.

Bennett Brown might be a genius at manipulating computers, but Julian Sykes-Maulby happened to be a genius at manipulating people.

PART FOUR

•

Countermeasures

30

Today the copter pad and STOL-strip at La Costa were unusually busy. The resort, built with Teamster Pension Fund and other mob money, is the last word in what was once considered a *de luxe* resort. On its extensive grounds near San Diego it has championship golf courses for the old-timers, fast-surface tennis courts for younger folk, private cottages for those who shun attention and the usual complex of suites and public rooms for those who want to be seen.

To most of the men arriving by private copter and plane today, it was a matter of indifference whether they were recognized or not. La Costa was no longer to their taste, most of them. It was clearly to their fathers' taste, but this next generation, bearing MBAs from various prestigious universities and corporate credentials of impeccable provenance, were too keyed up to enjoy anything more strenuous at play than a sun bathe at the pool with dollar-a-point backgammon as a non-destructive time-passer. A little herb, a little snow, a few recognizable young TV actresses for the orgies and they were content.

Among these, his peers, Bennett Brown was considered an ascetic. He didn't drink or smoke—anything—and he was a total bust at an orgy, sitting there with an abstracted, faraway look on his face while getting blown. "Benny," one of his peers had yelled at him during such a session, "if we program her mouth in COBAL or FORTRAN, you can get a print readout . . . and come."

Today, however, no orgies were planned. It was a Friday meeting with a one-item agenda. What anyone did afterwards was up to him. Some might hang on and party for the weekend. Some, like Ben, would go home. But all of them, before sundown, would have telephoned their reports, suitably scrambled, back to the organizations of which their fathers or uncles were the titular heads.

Bennett Brown arrived alone, piloting his Vertol helicopter from his seaside compound near Newport Beach. He felt no uneasiness arriving last even though the meeting couldn't start without him.

Left to his own devices, he rarely called meetings, distrusting them as sources of rumor and gossip and the silly decision-making typical of any collective form. Still, this group of young executives, while in no way as powerful as the *Consiglio d'Amministrazione*, carried tremendous weight in the legal sector of the families' operations. So, when a meeting was called, Bennett Brown showed up.

"Took your sweet time, huh, Benny?" the chairman asked as Brown arrived in the cottage near the 16th hole of the championship golf course.

No one stayed in this luxury cottage overnight when they visited La Costa, not even the President of the United States and his wife. This was a special safe house swept daily for listening devices and shielded by tall evergreens from remote surveillance. A small squad of security men made sure no golfers, hacking out of the rough, came close.

It was here that total-security meetings were held. In the history of La Costa there had been many of these, melding business and political leaders with go-betweens like Jimmy Hoffa or his wife, moneymen, gangsters and those who no longer answered to that description, primarily alumni of the old Mayhill Road mob in Cleveland, now helping manage La Costa.

Bennett Brown gave the chairman a withering look. "Alfie, if I tell you I ran into clear-air turbulence over Orange County Airport would you know what the hell I was talking about?"

Alfie frowned. "Get your notes. We want a brief, I said a brief, report. And then stand by for questions, baby, because you are gonna get 'em."

Unzipping his aluminum-colored nylon anorak, Bennett chucked it underhand across the room where it landed on a sofa easily ten feet long and upholstered in crinkly tan glove leather. He stood for a moment in jeans and a tee-shirt lettered: IF YOU DON'T SEE WHAT YOU WANT, FUCK OFF. Then he pulled a folded wad of computer printout paper from his rear pocket and sat across the wide circular table from Alfie. He nodded to the rest of the men—six in all—and got down to business.

"Alfie says brief," he began. "Since my last oral report a month ago, we have been maximizing increment at a rate of 1.21 every 30 days or 14.5 percent per annum. We took on the following buys: another 4.9 of General Health, that's 14.7 to date; in two takes we bought 9.8 per cent of Aramco, that shook 'em up a bit so we'll lie low for now; Squibb another 4.9; the Glaxo pharmaceutical people in England, half a take, leaving us with seven and a third total; UBCO common we now hold 14.7, up one take from last month; we're starting this month to buy into ICI, that's a Limey conglomerate, and Sandoz, a Swiss drug firm, 4.9 each."

He stopped. In the silence he looked around at his fellow Young Turks. Although a few of them wore golfing slacks and sweaters, the majority had come in three-piece business suits, white shirts and dark ties. Young-old, Bennett Brown thought. Their fathers' mentality grafted onto a graduate degree from an OK college. Not many original thoughts would get born here.

"*Allora*," he said, smiling in a less than friendly manner, "*mi dica*."

Alfie produced another of his self-conscious frowns. "There isn't anything in the report you didn't give us by fax at the start of the week."

Brown's smile broadened to a you-really-are-hopeless grin. "Nothing's happened since Monday."

Sal Maggoranza, in a J. Press suit that somehow converted his chunky body into Ivy League Lean, sat forward. "What is this General Health stuff we control?"

"Outfit somewhere in the midwest. They own sixty major private hospitals in the States and about a dozen in Europe. About eighty nursing homes. Street clinics, methadone mostly. Abortion centers. They're also getting into fat farms, tennis camps, the whole range of health-related services."

Maggoranza nodded. "You planning some kind of crisscross with our pharmaceutical holdings?"

Ben shook his head negatively. "No point to it."

"That's good." The financial advisor for the Lucchese family made a sour face. "Reports from Europe say that whole Volvo-Shell deal is coming up lousy."

"What reports?"

"It never did make any sense to me, Benny," Sal went on as if he hadn't heard. "You have a fetish for vertical organization. On paper it all looks neat. But in real life it pisses a lot of people off, let me tell you."

Ben tried to control his anger. "What makes you an authority on organization?"

A chubby young man in black Porsche aviator spectacles cut in almost apologetically, as if unworthy to mediate such a clash of titans. "Ben," he began, "while we are discussing technical matters." He paused, sure of having everyone's attention. "I did a study on that European portfolio of ours. Maybe you noticed. As soon as we buy a stock, there's a sharp upcurve in price and then a massive unload. It may take a few weeks, but when it's all over, the damned stock bottoms out below what we paid for it."

"You have to expect that, Bobby," Brown told him. "It happens any time there's a fat buy. If you had inside info on the action of some other stock the way you know ours, you'd see it happens to all kinds of shares, not just the ones we pick. It's the little guys chasing after us."

"Ben," a delegate in charcoal gray spoke up. "I'm behind you all the way. You know that. I was one of the first to recommend we get behind your idea. But now that we're committed, my people get ootchy. They're looking at maybe a billion of their own cash they don't have control of."

He stopped, shot his cuff and glanced at the octagonal face of an immense electronic watch strapped to his wrist. He took a gold mechanical pencil from his breast pocket and touched tiny buttons on the watch.

The meeting room was filled with a melodious mechanical bleeping. Then the man in charcoal gray looked up from his wrist. "If all we did was put that nestegg in money funds, Ben, we'd have cleared 140 million the first year."

"Charlie, that thing on your wrist didn't tell you that. It won't hold that many zeroes." Ben gave him a jeering grin. "You worked the damned thing out at a desk computer back home because your old man told you to."

"So?"

"Second, what kind of tax would you be liable to on money market profit?"

"Never mind. With this project of yours there's no profit at all."

"You know the projection. Not for five years."

"I don't think my people will hang cool that long, Ben." He covered over the little marvel strapped to his wrist and tried to look magnanimous. "I'm your Number One booster, baby. Do I have to tell you that? I buy your whole schtick, even the K-wave analysis. But I'm not running my bunch. Other people are who wouldn't know a K-wave from a plate of scungilli."

"So therefore?" Brown demanded.

"Therefore I'm catching flak."

"Can you keep things steady till the end of the year?"

"Why?" the chairman cut in. "What's happening then?"

"I'm starting to put together a report, in lay language, something even Uncle Luigi can understand, lots of graphics."

Charlie brushed something invisible off his charcoal gray lapel. "This report better be good."

"It'll be a video cassette," Brown promised. "Better than a home porno flick."

The murmurs around the table seemed to Bennett Brown to indicate that he had effectively stalled matters till the end of the year. None of the others had much more to say, but it was obvious Alfie, as chairman, had something on his mind.

"Speaking of catching flak."

He said nothing more for a long moment, wanting to make sure everyone had directed his attention to the chair. "We have picked up serious flak out of Paris."

He wasn't looking at Brown. He was looking almost anywhere else but. "One casualty, two bail jumps, cops nosing around."

Bennett Brown eased back in the heavy captain's chair and laid one arm casually over the curved back of it. He hadn't expected this to cross the Atlantic so fast, nor had he foreseen it would be brought up in the financial meeting. The young men seated around the table, like he himself, kept hands off field operations, always had. There wasn't a police record in the crowd, unless you counted a speeding violation or two. These were the Mister Cleans of the organization. They touched nothing so that nothing could touch them. But here was Alfie, bringing up something the rest wanted deniability on.

"I wouldn't bring it up," Alfie went on, as if mind-reading, "but there is a terrific rhubarb Back Home. The casualty was a man's son. A man of great respect."

An uneasy silence settled over them. None of these economists, math geniuses, management stars or marketing spe-

cialists could be comfortable with what Alfie had deliberately
thrown down on the table, Bennett knew.

"What's the point of this?" he demanded of the chairman.

"Maybe you can tell us."

"No," Bennett Brown disagreed, "this is your party. You
tell us."

"It's a delicate question."

"It sure as hell is, Alfie," a beefy, fullback type in a dark blue
pinstripe grunted. He had recently undergone hair trans-
plants across the top of his forehead, but had not yet learned
to comb them so that they lost their clumped look. "You gotta
nerve asking us to consider something like this." He brushed
nervously at the delicate wisps of hair.

"Nobody has to consider it but Benny the Brain here,"
Alfie countered. "Our information connects it back in his
direction."

"You fathead." Bennett Brown was on his feet. "You've got
the tact of an elephant in heat."

He moved across the room to the anorak he'd thrown onto
the sofa. "Did you ever hear of chain of command, birdbrain?
Or of the compartments we're split up into? Or the reason
we're compartmentalized?" He began pulling on the jacket.

"All well and good," Alfie persisted doggedly. "But the one
thing we were promised on this project was that it would be
absolutely clean, start to finish. Nothing in it for a cop to bat
an eye over. All of a sudden, not some punk button man but
the son of a *pezzo novanto* in the old country dies and some
paisano won't rest now till he tastes blood." He was gesturing
pleadingly, hands turned palms up, cupped as if to receive
charity. "Benny, it's not right."

Brown sat back down in his chair. "Okay, Alfie. I had
nothing to do with it, but I'll be the first to admit it was
wrong. Now what?"

"Can we get some kind of assurance it won't happen
again?" Alfie almost begged.

Bennett Brown raised his right hand. "I give you my
word."

The fullback in pinstripes growled approvingly. "And let's
not hear any more about it, Alfie," he added. "My people are
jumpy enough without some vendetta to worry about."

Not meaning to, the beefy man said a word that stopped
any more from being uttered. He looked around him, as if for

support, and saw that everyone was busy pretending he hadn't heard the word.

Hoping to change the subject, for the benefit of everyone's morale, he turned back to Ben. "Listen, baby," he began chaffingly, "since when do you drop plums like that Hertz scam only in the Lucchese pocket? My people could use a gift like that, too. You got anything else up your sleeve you can spread around?"

Sal Maggoranza made a rude noise between pressed lips. "You want in on the Hertz deal?" he asked challengingly.

The beefy man smiled grimly. "You got something to offer besides scraps?"

"I got," Maggoranza asserted. "You want, talk to me after the sitdown. That goes for anybody else wants a little Hertz laid off on him."

The beefy man turned back to Bennett Brown. "Any other dividends coming down from this operation?"

"More all the time," Ben promised. "We're matching up pieces of RCA that manufacture electronic stuff with parts of Jet-Tech that use it in their space equipment."

The chairman emitted a noise somewhere between a chuckle and a snort. "Christ, Benny, I hope to shit you guys know what you're doing."

The aluminum anorak was supposed to trap a person's body heat inside. Despite its light weight, it kept a man warm. Nevertheless, Bennett Brown shivered.

He looked for an open window or an airconditioning vent to close. The room was almost hermetically sealed. Outside the California sun poured down on golfers in the distance, on carefully clipped greens and long, sweeping fairways. One tree nearby, a cedar, stood like a sentinel. On the lowest branch where needles had begun to fall from one bald spot, a black bird with glossy feathers and the hammerclaw tail of a mortician in full dress, cocked his head. He seemed to be looking back through the window at Bennett Brown.

Harshly, he let out a raucous caw and flew away.

31

"Yes, Freddie," Bennett Brown said into the scrambler telephone. "I understand. It wasn't easy for Aldo's people to lose her, but they did."

"Hey," Alfred J. Marston countered, "they're only human. Besides the London guys are certain to pick up her trail."

Ben shook his head, wearily and in suppressed anger. "They're even stupider than Aldo's bunch. We're working with real low-end material these days." He paused and tried to get a more commanding note in his voice. "Now, here's a chance to get something right, Freddie. Take the shit out of your ears and listen close. Countermeasures. We now have to take countermeasures. Got it?"

"On who? The girl?"

"The girl, this guy Curtiss and throw in Palmer as well."

"What degree?"

"No rough stuff. I want the stuff pouring in by remote control. Pull in the IRS contacts. Get on the horn to the CIA buddies. And whatever we need on Curtiss is right there in the UBCO files. Get it. The name of the game is harassment."

"All that clout?" Marston asked. "Just on three nobodies?"

Ben shook his head in total desperation. Why did he have the feeling more and more these days that nobody understood the issues but him? That nobody appreciated how close they were either to disaster or victory?

"Do it, Freddie," he almost whispered. "Just shut up and do it."

The plan of the 39th floor of the UBCO Building, which occupied an entire block front along Fifth Avenue, was fairly open. Light from the all-glass wall on the avenue flooded most of the floor, where thirty large, attractive desks sat in rows with a lot of space between them. Here a variety of men and women worked in what they believed was relative privacy, even though their desks had no walls around them.

The overseeing officer for each of their sections—there

were three—sat in a proper office at the far end of the room away from the avenue.

It was in one of these strategically designed offices that Bill Elston sat. The desks outside which belonged to his department, Internal Security, were few indeed, only four. His department, in fact, was quite small in the UBCO hierarchy since he commanded in the field less than a dozen people like Curtiss to handle various areas of the U.S. and the world.

Yet, in the nature of things, banking being as security-conscious as it is, Internal Security had as much power within the UBCO organization as, perhaps, the KGB did in Russia. Not that it was feared, nor used as an instrument of repression, but perhaps because it maintained dossiers on every employee of the bank, folders of information that went far beyond that submitted to Personnel by people seeking employment. And, unlike the Personnel files, these were secret.

The dossiers were magnetically encoded on floppy disks which had the latest state-of-the-art security safeguards protecting their storage, retrieval and use in a computer. On this particular morning, Mrs. Mulvey, who worked at the second desk from the Fifth Avenue window wall, walked into Elston's office while he was on the telephone. She indicated the safes that held the dossiers and Elston nodded silently. As she turned away he could smell her perfume, a musky odor he associated with thighs.

Mrs. Mulvey first switched on the small office computer terminal that stood in one corner of the office. She tapped its keyboard a moment, putting the name of an UBCO employee into the computer with a command. The computer responded with the employee's personal UBCO number. This Mrs. Mulvey copied down and took across the room to a bank of safes along the other wall.

She knelt beside the second safe on the left. Its heavy steel door had no dial over the latch handle, only a small black plastic rectangle with ten buttons, bearing the numbers from 0 through 9. Mrs. Mulvey punched in the personal number she had got from the computer. The door clicked and she was able to swing it open.

Hundreds of floppy disks in paper envelopes were stacked inside. She found the one she wanted, removed it and locked the door. Back at the computer she punched in an access code, a kind of second electronic key, before she slid the disk into its slot. Otherwise it would have been wiped magnetically clean against unauthorized use.

Now Mrs. Mulvey tapped some new commands into the keyboard. Silently and unseen, a pickup reached to the proper place on the disk and began reading off information encoded there. On the video screen a dossier began to print. A lot of information had been programmed into a dozen lines by using abbreviations. Mrs. Mulvey switched on the printer which reproduced the same lines on a roll of paper. She returned the floppy disk to its safe, tore off the paper and brought it to Bill Elston's desk.

"Too early to tell," he was saying into the phone. "These things take months to sort out. The new government could go under before then. Or another strong man could appear." He paused, listening. "Yes, I can certainly do that in the interim. Okay. Call any time." He hung up and glanced at Mrs. Mulvey.

"Signature," she said, putting the piece of print-out paper before him. This, too, was part of the security routine. Without Elston's signature, no secret dossier could leave this room, even for use at a desk outside.

Elston took up his pen and paused, reading the top line of the dossier. "Curtiss?" he asked then. "Who wants to know about Curtiss?"

Mrs. Mulvey made an I'm-trying-to-remember face, eyes swiveled toward the ceiling. "It's, uh, from Operations."

"Who in Operations?" he persisted.

"Wait a second." She left the room and he could see her return to her desk, a short woman in her middle years who had kept her figure and dressed quite stylishly. Elston watched the backs of her legs as she bent over her desk. Then she came back, holding a light green interoffice memo slip. She put it down beside the dossier. "Harry Kummel," she said.

Elston sat back. He held one of the pieces of paper in each hand. His glance swiveled back and forth between them. The green memo slip simply requested the file on Curtiss, nothing more. It bothered Elston. He didn't like people asking for a file on one of his own people. "Kummel doesn't have clearance for this," Elston said at last.

Mrs. Mulvey stood there, saying nothing. She had done her dark hair differently today, Elston noticed. Her new perfume was distracting. He put down the slips of paper and dialed Kummel's private number, which he alone answered. He was surprised when his secretary replied instead.

"I'm sorry, Mr. Elston, but he's out the rest of the week."

"Do you know why he asked for the Curtiss dossier?"

"I beg your pardon?"

"You typed—" Elston paused. "I think you typed a request dated yesterday for a confidential dossier. Was it for Mr. Kummel?"

"I don't recall typing it, sir."

Elston paused. The typeface in which the request had been done was one of the normal IBM faces used by UBCO. Elston happened to know it was in use only on electronic machines, the latest kind that could be driven directly by magnetic tape or a computer. Not the old-fashioned kind Kummel might have sat down and used on his own.

"You haven't had any requests about a Curtiss?"

"Not through me, Mr. Elston."

"And your name?"

"Peggy Fluck."

Elston's mouth opened, closed. There was a long pause. Then the girl asked: "You're *not* going to ask me to spell it, are you?"

Laughing, Elston closed off the conversation and hung up. The memo had a regular signature on it of Harry Kummel (E. Henry Kummel, vice-president) and below this was the code "EHK/pf." Someone with the initials P.F. had typed the request.

Which she said she hadn't. Elston let out a long sigh. "Leave this with me, Mrs. Mulvey," he said.

She nodded, turned and left his office. He sniffed the air like a hound. He saw that she was wearing heels higher than usual. It crossed his mind that she had generally upgraded her appearance quite a bit in the last few weeks. Making a note to check into her marital status, he put his mind to the problem of who was asking, in this devious and unauthorized manner, for Curtiss's dossier.

Someone was trying to pull a fast one, either Kummel or his secretary. Or . . . Mrs. Mulvey. And Curtiss was the target.

Moves like this simply didn't happen at UBCO. Routines simply weren't bypassed. It was most unusual. Like Mrs. Mulvey's new, sexier look, unusual things worried Bill Elston.

At two in the afternoon, Mary Lee had awakened, ravenous for food. She and Curtiss wandered out into Knightsbridge in the general direction of Harrods. Turning up off Brompton Road, they found a wine bar called the Loose Box with an entrance on Cheval Place.

The basement room was still crowded, but a sort of booth for two quickly opened up. They had pâté, Greek salad and a glass of Beaujolais. At three-thirty they left the Loose Box for Harrods, which Mary Lee had never seen before. Much later, in the clock department on the ground floor, Mary Lee discovered the time to be five p.m.

"Have to call home," she said in a panicky voice. "My cleaning lady— I didn't leave money. What time—?"

Curtiss counted back on his fingers. "It's nine a.m. in California."

Back in the hotel, Mary Lee waited for the connection to go through. "Velma!" she shrieked. "It's me!" She paused. "Just wanted to tell you I'd be gone till the end of the week, so—" She waited. "Yes. Yes. Okay. Who? No, forget it. Just junk mail. What? Bureau of Internal Revenue?" Her glance raked sideways at Curtiss, who was lying half asleep beside her.

"Better open it, Velma. Yes. Sure, if you don't mind." She paused. "Yes. I see. What kind? Field audit? Let me get this. I'm supposed to call a Mrs. Zurke? To set up a date for a field audit?"

Curtiss rolled over on his side, eyes open, and watched her.

"Okay. Internal Revenue can always wait." She laughed. "That's sweet of you, Velma. I appreciate it. But I just wanted you to know why I wasn't there to pay you. You understand? That's *so* sweet. Yes. Yes. Yes. Bye!" She lay back on the bed and smiled at him. "What's the matter?"

He smoothed her bare arm. "Do you do any self-employed work?"

"No."

"So all year long Jet-Tech forwards your IRS withholding? You're never in arrears."

"Never. Curtiss, will you stop scaring me to death?"

"I'm just wondering why you qualify for the extreme punishment of a field audit."

"I don't know. They spot-check, I guess."

"That's for office audits, where you visit them. A field audit is where they descend on your own office or home. It's brutal."

"Now you *are* scaring me."

He eyed her sideways. "I'm not. But you never know. Maybe somebody else is trying to."

Station Basel is located not far from the very modern State Theatre, in a section off the Barfusserplatz where many of the cinemas are found. It is situated in a very old building scarcely twenty feet wide but four floors high, dating back to the late sixteenth-century.

Station Head is a polyglot bachelor of middle years who majored in languages at Brown. His assistant, who only speaks German in addition to his native English, is a much younger man, Herbert Muckerman, one of the newer breed, married with three children enrolled in the American School.

On this particular morning, because he had a great deal of paperwork to clear up, Muckerman made the earliest appointment possible with his opposite number in the Bureau des Étrangers. As he walked, his rimless glasses glittered in the sunlight. Perhaps "opposite number" was pushing the comparison too hard. The Bureau was not, after all, the CIA. Whereas Muckerman was.

"Good morning, Herb," Herr Sefli said, extending his hand.

Muckerman sat down across from Sefli's plain oak desk. "Coffee?" the Swiss asked. He, too, wore rimless spectacles. Strangely, as if summoned up by the words, the aroma of coffee grew stronger.

"I'm caffeined up to the eyeballs, Hansl."

Sefli nodded. "I have the, er, file folder of which you spoke yesterday," he went on in a suddenly much lower voice. He opened a desk drawer and removed a plain manilla folder on which Muckerman, who could read most print upside-down, could only see the initials "USA."

"Hansl, you understand this is basically routine."

"*Natürlich*. All investigations are routine," Sefli said in a kidding tone.

"No, seriously. This man isn't suspected of anything, basically. Is that clear?"

The Swiss's eyeglass lens twinkled coldly as he nodded. "Don't work at it so hard, Herb, dear fellow. We professionals understand each other."

Muckerman sat back, not at all reassured. Then: "Basically this has to do with that enclave of his in Morcote. House, guest house, tennis courts, pool. It's about ten acres, heavily fenced in."

Sefli shook his head minutely. "Our office in Lugano will have more material. If it was real estate about which you had questions . . ." He shrugged.

"Basically, I simply want to initiate an investigation," the American assured him. "Our information is that at the time he bought the property, under your laws he couldn't take direct title. He had to work through a Swiss nominee."

As Sefli bent down his rimless glasses glittered again. He opened the folder and paged through it for a moment, shielding it from the American's sight. The smell of coffee was everywhere. Obviously it was being made fresh in another office nearby. "Yes," Sefli agreed at last. "There was a nominee. But, as you know, the laws have been relaxed. He now owns the property directly."

Muckerman moistened his lips. "Our information is basically in opposition to that, I'm afraid. Our information is that he himself is nominee for another, a hidden owner."

"You are accusing him of fraud?"

This time it was Muckerman's lenses that flashed as he shook his head vigorously from side to side. "I didn't *say* that, Hansl. I merely said—"

"I heard. You are suggesting we open up the books and get the name of this hidden owner?"

"Basically, yes."

"Which you need for some project of your own?"

"Yes."

"But lack the capability to determine for yourself."

The American's eyes widened in anger, but he held himself under control.

The main idea here was to stir up the Bureau and have them, in turn, stir up some dirt down in Morcote. Even if there were no dirt, they would produce a cloud of suspicion and inconvenience. It would disturb and alarm neighbors, shopkeepers, local laborers and the like.

"Yes," Muckerman admitted in a choked voice. "Basically we need your help."

"Very well." Sefli snapped the dossier shut with a sharp noise. "But there has to be a *quid pro quo*." The Swiss pulled an orange folder towards him. "Your people in Basel have collected thirty-seven parking summonses in the last two months. You do not have diplomatic immunity, you know. I expect appearances in court and I expect payment of fines. Is that clear?"

Muckerman frowned in disbelief. "That's the *quid*?"

"It may seem piffling to you, who have great projects coming out of your ears, but we Swiss are mainly interested in keeping our streets in order. You pay the fines. We do your dirty work in Morcote."

Muckerman, grinning, stuck out his hand, which Sefli shook.

"I don't suppose," the Swiss said in a dreamy tone, "we'll ever know what this poor fellow Palmer did to irritate you."

32

The international airport at Lamezia, in Calabria, is very special. For one thing, in a land that is mostly shoreline and mountains, it represents one of the few flat places big enough for a jumbo jet to land. For another, Lamezia took a decade to build because the Mafia bought up the rich alluvial plain and sold it to the government at the price of gold nuggets. For a third, the planners in Rome had placed the field so it was bisected by high tension power lines which took another five years to reroute safely.

And, for a fourth and last, Lamezia International Airport's most modern, advanced, high-tech hangars and terminal buildings in the world remain largely empty and unused. Nobody knows the reason, except that very few flights ever actually *use* Lamezia. Travelers still prefer to land down the coast at the toe of the Italian boot in Reggio Calabria, even though it is too small for jumbos.

To this costly boondoggle of Lamezia Airport, however, a few flights come daily from Rome and Milan, small DC-9s that have no use for its vast runways. The tall man got off the afternoon flight, which arrived three hours late and was, consequently, the evening flight.

He used a credit card and driver's license in the name of Ugo Pastore to rent a car from the bored airport clerk, got in and drove the few miles to the *superstrada* that cuts across the instep of the boot from the Tyrhennian Sea to the capital city of Catanzaro, on the hills above the Ionic Coast.

As he drove, the tall man hummed softly, a little song his mother had sung. It put him in the mood for Calabria since it was in the local dialect. His mother, and no one else since, except Don B, had called him Tonino. Since he had no father, he had taken his mother's name, and, at an early age, exchanged it for a variety of aliases.

At twelve he was already wanted in Messina, under the name of Antonio Tedesca, for grand larceny, auto. At fifteen, under the name of Tony Maschetto, the Rome police wanted him for assault and battery.

His last names tended to be nondescript, but his first names were often a variation of one theme: Nino, Tino, Tonio and the like. Once he had made a reputation for himself and was firmly connected, there were no more wanted bulletins. Most veteran police or *carabinieri*, seeing a body killed in a certain way, made a mental note that it was the tall man's handiwork and then forgot about it.

To be protected, in Italy, is to be protected for life.

He had rented a car as nondescript as his current name, Pastore. The little gray 127 had pep and handled well as he sent it along the *superstrada* at 130 kilometers an hour. The easy part of the journey he wanted to get through quickly. He would need more time for the harder part.

This came after a while when he turned off the good road and started up over the Zomaro range of mountains to the Ionic coast on the far side. Few people made the trip this way. They took the good road to Catanzaro and the sea, then doubled back on the coast road, SS 106, to whichever town they wanted. Tonino, the tall man, would not make the journey as the others did.

Instead he shifted into third and second to force the little 127 up steep, narrow mountain roads, zigzags and switch-backs across an almost sheer face of rock, climbing always until the unprotected drop was thousands of feet. The air was cool. A brisk wind sprang up to make the light car even harder to keep on the road.

After almost an hour, during which the road gave out several times and only a sandy track proclaimed its direction, the 127 reached the highest peak. Tonino stopped and lifted the bonnet to let the engine cool. He surveyed the wild landscape and the Ionic coast below.

These were folded mountains of chalk, clay and aggregate that had been pushed up from the bottom of the sea by one of the great volcanic catastrophes of antiquity. Even now this was a *zona sismica* where quakes were common and most buildings, no matter how reinforced, bore great cracks.

The cool wind sighed through pines and eucalyptus, rustling the yellow acacia flowers, stirring the brilliant branches of broom and the tiny violet flowers of wild oregano. Tonino took a deep breath and almost tasted the mingled odors. Under the few ancient spreading oaks little grew except spiky purple heather. Tonino walked a few yards into the brush, stooped and picked a wild artichoke no bigger than his broad thumbnail. He munched it slowly.

The town of Sabbia D'Oro was an ancient one. The Greeks had used it as a place to water and provision their biremes on the long trip from Athens to Syracuse, in Sicily. It could not be seen from this height, Tonino knew, not the original Sabbia D'Oro on the coast. But in the fifth century and after, when the Saracens had plundered this coast, the townspeople had fled into the hills and built a fortified Sabbia D'Oro. This was Tonino's destination.

It lay only a few miles below him now. History had reversed its destiny yet again. Once a seat of power, its prosperity had continued well into the nineteenth century, while its namesake on the coast had been racked by malaria. Then, in the twentieth century, with the use of DDT, the mosquitoes disappeared and the coastal town had come back into its own with hotels, lidos, restaurants and shops. Sabbia D'Oro Superiore, as the old mountain town was known, had begun to lose population right after World War II. It was now, if not a ghost town, then certainly one of many empty houses and old people. The young ones had long ago left.

One who had not was Don Gino Scarapace, nor had his counselors and the other elders of his family. This mountain fastness where every crooked, narrow street was known, every window a familiar friend, provided him with a feeling of security the modern town on the shore below did not.

And it was quite possible, with the telephone and the automobile, for Don Gino to control the same territory his uncle had once controlled by mule and on foot. Nothing much changes in the daily business of organized crime. The goal is power. The methods rarely alter from one decade to the next, even from one century to the next. The raw material of power is people. The motives that move them change almost not at all.

Tonino, the tall man, quickly stripped off his city trousers and pulled on an old, baggy pair of work trousers. He removed his elegant alligator shoes with their pointed tips and pulled on a pair of green rubber mud boots. Over his plaid shirt he slipped a hunting waistcoat with loops for 12-gauge shotgun shells. He opened a box of a particular cartridge used by deer hunters. Here in Calabria the largest game would be the occasional fox or rabbit. One of these deer shells would blow a small animal apart, for it carried a fat explosive slug designed to stop a large buck. He loaded two of these into the double-barreled deer gun and stuffed four more in his pockets, then poked a few ordinary shotgun shells into the loops of his waistcoat as camouflage.

He got back in the 127. The sky in the west was still bright. The sun had not yet dropped over the sharp ridges of the Aspromonte range. Driving more slowly, Tonino arrived at the outskirts of Sabbia D'Oro. The town clung to the rocky massif like a collection of squared-off barnacles. He parked the 127 well off the road at the top end of town before the first farmhouse, shouldered his gun, locked the car and started off on foot in the growing twilight.

Tonino, the tall man, had the natural sixth sense of a hunter and a good knowledge of the town itself. He had been there before, as a boy of seventeen, on the run and grateful to find shelter among people who had no use for the police. It was twenty years later, but he could scarcely have forgotten Sabbia D'Oro although he had worked in many grander and more colorful places, even America, in towns like New Orleans and Dallas.

Cradling the gun across his left arm, the breech broken open, the tall man moved confidently along the road towards the main piazza across from the church, where the elders gathered at sunset to talk and sip an *amaro* and smoke cigarettes or stubby cigars.

Just before the piazza, he cut to the left and took a narrow street that seemed to go off on a tangent. It passed a row of hovels, slowly disintegrating into rubble, and started a sharper descent to the lower town. Just there an even more narrow *vico* led to the right, upwards to the piazza. It was a lane no one took, evil-smelling and too uneven to keep one's balance. It brought Tonino, the tall man, to the rear of the bar on the piazza without anyone seeing him in the growing darkness. He stood motionless for a long moment. Then he closed the breech of the gun with such control that its click was almost silenced. He cocked it in the same controlled manner, muffling the sound.

Now he stepped into the rear of the bar, a sort of storeroom where cartons lay open and closed, empty or filled with wine or cigarettes. There was no crime in Sabbia D'Oro. He could hear the careful mutter of voices beyond the main part of the bar and in the piazza before it. Someone was speaking. He moved easily through the hanging strips of plastic over the connecting door. No one had yet seen him.

Around two tables sat seven old men, their glances on the television screen hung over the bar. The nightly *telegiornale* news program had begun. Slowly, the tall man's glance moved from one to the next. Don Gino was the only man not watching the program. He was instead working his lighter to ignite his cigarette, caught in a lengthy amber holder.

The lighter sparked. Tonino, the tall man, holding the deer gun at his hip, leveled it at Don Gino's heart.

At three yards he could not miss.

33

At the corner of Cheyne Walk and Cheyne Row, in that part of London's Chelsea that leads south across the river over the pretty, old-fashioned Albert Bridge, stands a pub called the King's Head and Eight Bells. It has a reputation for good, if English, food. Curtiss and Mary Lee had no way of knowing this as they walked in. They were looking only for a place to sit down.

Having settled into the front room of the King's Head and finished off pints of lager and glutinous cottage pies, they had reached the point where they had either to talk or to sleep. "Dessert?" Curtiss asked out of protocol.

She shook her head. "Unless they serve Spotted Dick."

He peered at the chalked menu. "Nope. Not even Boiled Baby." He sighed and leaned back in weariness. "Talk to me."

"The thing that's bothering me," Mary Lee went on then,

"is why you didn't want me talking to Ben. Or even telling
B. J. what I'd done until it was too late. The echoes of that
are beginning to deafen me."

Before she'd left London, Eleanora had insisted on giving
Mary Lee a pair of her own jeans and some summer tops.
"You don't want to buy anything in London," she'd told the
Executive Vice-President, Financial, of one of America's larg-
est corporations. "Everything is so horribly expensive here."

"But you'll need these, won't you?"

Eleanora had prevailed. "So European," Mary Lee told
Curtiss in private. But having seen the prices in the windows
along King's Road, she felt pleased to be wearing Eleanor's
sun-bleached Levi's, although they didn't come down far
enough, and a rather smashing horizontal-striped cobalt-and-
rose rugby tee-shirt that emphasized her breasts.

"You told me you used to date Bennett Brown?"

She slid her arm around his waist. "I used to date Ben. A
few disco scenes. He knew all the moves, but Ben is a very
proper young man, except for the way he dresses. But he is
not very laid-back-California, if you know what I mean."

"The chemistry wasn't there between you?"

She squeezed his waist again. "The thing that put me off
Ben was that he never bothered to conceal what he wanted
from me."

"Ah-ha."

"A child." Mary Lee made a no-that's-not-it face. "I don't
mean he was that crass about it. Ben is not all that sexual a
person. He lives inside his head. I mean, if you . . ." She
stopped, remembering her conversation in front of the mirror
with B. J. "Never mind. What I'm trying to say about Ben is
that he was even then an empire-builder. A dynast. He had a
very short list of what he wanted out of life: great power,
great wealth and a great son to leave it to."

"In that order?"

"The other way around. It kind of gave me the creeps. He
already had money. His brokerage was doing very well. As for
power, well, you and I are the same about that, aren't we,
Curtiss? Neither one of us needs it for its own sake?"

She stared into his eyes, as if daring him to evade the
question or try to lie about it. "Nobody ever asked me that
before," Curtiss replied. "In my career I've never been close
to getting power. It hasn't been a possibility."

"But you've worked with powerful people. Palmer?"

"Head of the biggest bank in the world? Palmer controlled more money than anybody on earth except the President of the United States and the Premier of the Soviet Union. That's power."

"And?"

Curtiss shrugged. "He gave it all up. For peace and quiet. Or out of guilt." He glanced away from her for a second. "I think it was for love."

"Curtiss! He's a romantic? He sure didn't come on that way."

"I guess guilt was the biggest factor," Curtiss said. "Palmer really deep down feels that he and the other bankers have led the world to the brink of chaos and death."

"My God!"

"You ought to hear him some time, going on about the systematic starvation of the Third World. How us fat cats get fatter by choking poor nations to death. Oh, he can really spoil your appetite for cottage pie and a pint of beer."

"I had no idea he was such an idealist."

"Eleanora brings that out in him." Crutiss was silent for a while. Then: "About Ben. Did he seriously claim to be Jewish?"

"Said the family name had been Bronstein."

"You ever meet any of the Bronsteins? Has B. J.?" He picked up his beer.

"His mother's dead and his dad lives abroad."

Curtiss, who had been sipping his beer, suddenly spluttered foam on the table. "Lives abroad!" he hooted. Then, more sedately, "Mary Lee, you and B. J. have only his word that he's Jewish."

Would somebody want to pretend such a thing?"

"Yes." He thought for a moment. "After both of you turned him down, how come B. J. married him?"

"This is the part of it neither of us understands," she said. "To this day, B. J. can only remember a Las Vegas weekend that ended up in marriage. That kind of thing is always lurking around the corner for any West Coast girl who doesn't watch her step. But the part she can't understand, and neither can I, is that she got married again in a religious ceremony. And stayed married."

"The chemistry had changed," Curtiss suggested.

"No, more mysterious. The *state* of being married changed the chemistry. I can't explain it any better. *Being* married, especially now that she was past thirty, seemed to do something to B. J."

"Like what?"

"Am I married?" Mary Lee countered.

"I was, twice." He stared into his beer. "Even if you do it on a Vegas weekend, stoned, *being* married kind of grabs you by the throat. Like Christmas."

"Like what?"

He gestured vaguely. "You know that peace on earth feeling? Even though you know people are dying of starvation and torture as often on December 25th as any other time? Cultural brain washing, dozens of childhood Christmases. My second wife is Danish. They do a very sweet, innocent, childish ceremony when you get married in Denmark. It's . . . it stirs up great gobs of goo from deep down inside."

She nodded slowly. "Great gobs of goo. That's what B. J. was suffering from, all right. And then he pounced."

"Yeah."

"B. J. and I grew up together. Went to the same grammar and high school. Dated the same boys. I mean, we both had our first periods a week apart. My mother is her godmother."

He pursed his lips, then produced something like a smile. "Were they at the wedding, your folks?"

"B. J. and Ben got married the second time at my parents' home."

"What did they think of the groom?"

But she hadn't heard the question. "It was a pretty wedding. My folks have this rambling place not far from the river. There's a kind of pergola down by the water's edge. We had the choir and the minister down there and picnic tables for the reception and a strolling band. Dancing. With the house and the trees in the back and the river with little sailboats along it. Such a lovely day. Clear blue sky. And my brothers had done all the things one does. I mean, a stag party the night before and Ben falling down drunk. He doesn't have much of a head for liquor and they . . . well, let's say my brothers are the drinkingest bankers in the whole United States."

"What did they think of the groom?"

She still hadn't heard. "At the end my oldest brother—he's about forty now—he has this 60-foot cruiser, sleeps six, plus two crew. He had it tied up at the dock by the boathouse and he had the band pipe B. J. and Ben aboard. And off they sailed! God, it was romantic. Talk about a honeymoon!"

He watched her face. "Kind of what you had in mind for your own wedding?"

"Me?" She frowned. Then, out of nowhere: "What did they think of the groom? Everybody loved him. They said, if they hadn't known they would never've guessed he was a Jew. Believe me, I did some deep cringes over that. But you have to understand this tidewater bunch. The Marylanders and Virginians consider themselves something special. They actually felt they were paying him a sincere compliment."

"Was that their only reaction?"

"Just a bit curious about there not being any of Ben's family on hand."

"They might've been *too* Jewish."

"Stop it. You don't hold me responsible for that pack I ran away from. I'm my own girl, Curtiss, not theirs."

"How about mine?"

"Your girl?" Her face grew serious. "Yes, I am your girl. Are you my fella?"

"Yes. You can see I don't learn much in life. I should know by now that women and me are incompatible. Not at the start. Later."

"How much later?"

"I'm hoping never."

"I'm hoping so, too." She hugged him tightly for a moment. "Okay. Tell me. What's the story with Ben?"

"You really like him?"

"He's good to B. J. If she's unhappy now, it's no more Ben's fault than hers. For a genius, he's kind of sweet. I like him and I trust him. So does B. J."

"You trust me?"

"I love you. That *means* I trust you."

"I trust you," he said. "With me, that's true love." He sighed unhappily. "What's going to become of us, Mary Lee?"

They stared at each other for a moment. Then his glance swept around the room, checking faces. When he spoke again, his voice had lowered almost to a whisper, delivered directly into her ear. "Benedetto Brown, son of Bruno Benedetto, known as Don B, retired *capo* of a major family of organized crime. Through the old man's clout, Ben has organized a huge investment consortium using funds from all twelve major crime families in the States. Using Swiss bank secrecy, the consortium is buying up every depression-proof company in Western Europe and the U.S. The moment he learned you were coming to see me in Paris, he panicked, or perhaps his father did. The result was that business at the Cité Odiot. One of his consultants is Julian Sykes-Maulby, who is selling him out for his own purposes. How successful Ben will be depends more on such associates and on his father's influence than it does on his own plans, which are probably impeccable. Human error will do him in, perhaps other people's error, since he never makes mistakes. Or he'll win. Big. And if you're alive, you'll count yourself lucky to know him."

In the other room of the pub someone let a tray of dirty glasses drop to the floor. Mary Lee blinked, but her eyes never left Curtiss's face. After a long moment she tried to say something, but her dry lips moved soundlessly instead.

After much longer, she managed to clear her throat. "Let's get back to the hotel," she murmured in a low voice.

Asleep, Curtiss seemed to grow younger, she noticed. His face regressed to an earlier, perhaps happier time. The faint shadows under his eyes disappeared. Closed, his eyes lost that hungry look of theirs, a kind of lust for facts, details, ideas, places, things. Talking to him with those eyes on you was as daunting as talking to Bennett Brown. Aside from the obvious analogues of age and intelligence, and the fact that they had each attracted one of the inseparable B. J.—Mary Lee axis, there were other, hidden similarities.

The cool young man, Mary Lee thought, watching him in sleep. She had fished her appointment book out of the rat's nest of her large handbag and was paging slowly through the past few days and the next week, trying to decide where and how to re-enter her normal life.

She picked up the telephone and moved it on its long cord to the far corner of the room, hoping her voice would not awaken him. It was nearly five o'clock at Jet-Tech's executive offices in the huge industrial park near Redlands, California. The swing shift that worked on rocket guidance systems would be arriving now, parking in the gargantuan lot that could hold ten thousand automobiles, if need be.

The office and technical staff would be closing desks for the day. In the research building the lights would remain burning until quite late where the team working on supercooled magnets would be playing their games against Mother Nature, games that included such costly fantasies as anti-grav boosters and proton-beam communicators. She dialed out.

The telephone rang seven times. Mary Lee was on the verge of hanging up when a man's voice asked. "Yes, what is it?"

"Dave? It's Mary Lee Hunter."

"I was all the way down the hall at the elevators." He cleared his throat. "You in the States?"

She listened to the wary edge to Dave Grissom's words. He was the comptroller and, as far as long-range planning went, subject to her directives. But in day-to-day tactics he had the practical power of being Mage of Numbers.

"Not till tomorrow, Dave. I'm just checking on the Friday meetings in New York and Boston and thinking I might fly directly there instead of trying to get back to Redlands first. What's the New York situation?"

"Breakfast meeting downtown with Merrill Lynch, one of those skyscraper dining clubs the Wall Street boys love." He riffled some pages. "Then we air shuttle to Boston for a lunch meeting with the bandits at Doheny Brooks."

This man, Mary Lee told herself, who was supposed to have been pumped up into the job that instead went to me, an outsider, is too smart to ask where I am. He's too smart to want to give away any anxiety he might have.

If Dave wasn't Ben's man at Jet-Tech, feeding him inside information almost the moment Mary Lee got it, then it was someone a peg or two down the line. But in the absence of an exact ID, Dave would be Number One traitor.

Imagine it, the consummate nerve of Bennett Brown, that whole fake façade of being Jewish to avoid any connection with an Italian background. With organized crime moving ever more boldly to fill its sector of the business establishment, having an Italian name could be a liability. Despite the existence of millions of honest Italians in the country and thousands in the financial field, when a whiff of mob intervention was suspected the finger always pointed to the nearest Italian name, innocent or not.

"We've had an IRS audit team here," he said with sudden ill humor. "Trying to audit your 1980 return. As if you'd been working for us then."

"Why come to the office?"

"Gestapo tactics," Dave Grissom said. "Strike the fear of God in all you sinners. I sent the bastards packing."

"Good for you, Dave." She felt a strange crushing sensation in her throat. She didn't ask for or need favors from Dave Grissom. What was happening back home? Had the IRS gone mad? Didn't they have anything better to do than harass a taxpayer whose entire income was on withholding? Her money reached Uncle Sam, monthly, even before she got her share.

"I hope you told them that for calendar 1980 I was still working for the Federal Reserve."

"It made no impression. IRS has stopped using accountants as agents. These goons could hardly read or write."

She was silent for a long while, trying to analyze the echoes of all this. Dave Grissom doing favors for her, acting upset that the IRS was harassing her? Bennett Brown's spy, being kind? Perhaps he wasn't the traitor inside. Still, he lusted for her job. Tread carefully here.

"Well, Dave," she picked up then, "I can't say you've made my day. But it's nice to hear a friendly voice. I'll try to check into New York Thursday afternoon."

"Terrific." He said it as he always did, "trific," an imitation of the way Paul Newman had been saying it in one movie after another, as if it were a synonym for "rotten."

There was an awkward pause. Mary Lee wanted to know if either of the brokerage houses had indicated a loosening up in their demands for a high discount on the new zero percent bond issue. But she didn't want Grissom to feel he was doing her a favor by filling her in. In the male game they all played, "beholden" was a nasty word.

"I'm going to try out my early morning curve on the Merrill Lynch people," she said then. "You warm up in the bullpen for the Boston game."

He laughed sourly. "Those thieves had the supreme nerve to call yesterday and ask why they hadn't heard from you."

"As if I had anything to say except '15 percent.'"

"I think," Grissom said, "it kind of shook 'em up that nobody at our end was begging. There's nothing like a long silence to unsettle the stomach."

"Don't kid yourself, Dave. A broker has the stomach of a goat." She was silent a while, digesting the news that the New York firm was getting uneasy. Good enough. "Keep the faith," she said, getting ready to hang up.

"Oh, I was on the pipe to UBCO yesterday," Grissom reported.

"About what?"

"Nothing big. Kummel was giving me a sales pitch for a different brokerage, in case we strike out with the two we have."

Something hard and cold seemed to touch Mary Lee below her left breast. She winced and rubbed herself there. "What was the suggestion?"

"Brown, Brown."

She nodded slowly, still massaging the area over her heart. "Let's try to score with the two we have," she managed to say. "If we fail..." She let the thought finish itself.

"Trific," he said in that same disgusted tone.

She hung up and stared at the open pages of her spiral-bound appointment book. Today was Wednesday. She had to fly out tomorrow, leaving Curtiss in the middle of things.

She turned to watch the sleeping Curtiss. One arm was flung up across the bed onto her pillow. The other had come to rest over his penis, as if protecting it. The sheet had worked its way down until it barely covered his calves and knees. She got up and cautiously raised the sheet to cover him. He muttered something. She stood there for a long time.

He was being peculiarly *fair* to Ben. "You've got to bear in mind," he had told her after unveiling the new, true Ben, "nothing he's doing is illegal."

"Sicking gunmen on us in Paris is legal?"

"We don't know whether he ordered that or his father did." Curtiss had been maddeningly evenhanded about the whole thing, as if Ben were some kind of protected species. "His father is of the old school. He believes only the dead make suitable business partners."

And he'd been even more infuriatingly fair about a hard-bitten pirate like Julian. "No, you have to put him in perspective," Curtiss had urged her. "He's in the great illegal, immoral tradition of empire. Britain no longer has imperialism. Anything goes. No quarter asked, none given, and devil take the hindmost. The epitome of Tory chic."

"He'd adore that description."

"Yes, I forgot that part of him. Ego galore. Latter-day James Bond. Palmer says he's the foremost cocksman in the Common Market."

Gazing down at Curtiss asleep, Mary Lee felt an attack of giggles overtaking her. She moved away and stood at the window, watching night over Cadogan Place, the sky faintly pink with the up-from-under illumination of London streetlights.

Managing Jet-Tech's tangled finances out of the bind they were in was a task of such awesome responsibility that the company paid well for Mary Lee's expert guidance. Like a lot of space-age companies, Jet-Tech was too much dependent on government favor, too overstaffed with ex-Generals and other shady types who cooked up cost-plus-overrun plums for the taxpayers to subsidize.

Without Defense Department contracts, Jet-Tech would have gone bankrupt years ago. But, like Lockheed and Chrysler before it, government-guaranteed loans and renewed contracts bailed out Jet-Tech again and again. It was not what Mary Lee and B. J. had been taught to regard as free-enterprise capitalism. More like state-subsidized socialism, if the truth were known.

That was why this new zero percent issue was so important. Lederer and a few others on the board of Jet-Tech realized how important it was for the company to get free of its military contract habit. New money from civilian sources would help Jet-Tech kick the habit for good.

Viewed in that light, what Bennett Brown was planning had an almost legitimate reek of free enterprise. Paid killers to one side, he was breaking no laws, simply figure-skating around them. And one couldn't even say he was on thin ice. The idea of secretly buying control of a company was as old as history. But the idea of secretly buying all the leading, profitable companies was a new concept. And she had the immense bad luck to be the best friend of the wife of the warped genius who'd dreamed it up.

As she stared out at the night, Mary Lee's eyes narrowed slightly. It had abruptly occurred to her that, just as Urs Rup might be the weak link in the conspiracy itself, B. J. Brown was a Fifth Column agent inside it. Or to put it more practically, the baby inside B. J. was the real undercover mole.

34

In the summer the sun of Calabria dips below the surface of the Mediterranean by long past seven in the evening. But the sky in the west retains a kind of pearly opalescence for another hour. Slowly pink darkens to burnt orange and blue becomes indigo. Then, especially in the full of the moon, the orange disk begins to rise out of the opposite sea, crossed by pale striations of pewter. By nine or ten o'clock a bright silver-blond flare of light beams across the waves preceding the moon as it crosses the sky.

Standing on the patio of his villa, a darker shadow among the others cast by moonlight, Don B remembered those summers of his youth. If he had been a man under weaker self-control he would have sighed unhappily, openly pitying himself. Here in Palermo, on the northern shore of the island of Sicily, one never saw the moon cut its swath of light across the rippling sea. Instead it beamed down coldly, a serenely contemptuous spy, bland and most secret.

It had been three days since Don B had talked to the tall man in Genoa. Three days since he had given his orders and been promised fast results. The death of Don Gino was by now an accomplished fact, since the tall man never failed. But why had he not telephoned to put Don B's mind to rest?

Shaking his head slowly—the utmost he allowed himself in anxiety—Don B retreated inside the walls of his villa. He roamed on carpet-slippered feet, silently, from room to room and window to window. He knew the guards' routine to the minute and managed to be at the appropriate window when they changed position along the walled perimeter.

In the stillness of the night he listened to their small sounds, a cough, the scrape of shoe leather on cement, the faint woosh a cupped match makes being struck. He monitored these sounds as a doctor with a stethoscope listens to a patient in intensive care. Don B knew that if he remained alert in this manner he would be the first to know if something went wrong.

Thus, he was quite tense, so keyed to every sound that he might be a jungle animal except that animals, eventually, sleep. Even the most beleaguered find a lair where slumber is possible. For the lion, however, there are no such hiding places. This was Don B's third night of watching and listening. He could feel fatigue wearing him down, loading his eyelids with great weight.

Besides, it was by telephone that the news would come, was it not? He had only to retire to his bedroom and wait for the ring of the phone. And sleep until it came. It was nonsense to get himself worked up this way.

And yet. Don B had employed the tall man for many years now. Even when he was in the States, Don B had fulfilled several contracts through him. It was Don B and his European associates who had first placed the palm of their hand over the tall man, giving him the support that protected him from harassment by the police.

For this protection, Don B ranked among the most honored of the tall man's client/sponsors. He was thus entitled to fast, ruthless, accurate service. Above all, results instantly reported.

Perhaps the job had taken him longer than the tall man anticipated? Even an expert is entitled to miscalculate his ti—

Don B grunted angrily in the darkness. His brain was softening. An expert *never* miscalculates, especially as to timing. That was why one used an expert.

Then what? What quirk or unexpected twist of fate? Don B had deliberately, as is the custom, cut himself off from any knowledge of *how*. Knowing was dangerous. One could be made to tell how. Even so, Don B was beginning to regret not knowing. In his mind's eye he could have followed the tall man's path, estimated his chances, his timing, perhaps accurately enough to know when the call might be made and he could sleep soundly, knowing his enemy dead, the vendetta uprooted at its source, never to flower into more blossoms of blood.

As it was, and by his own doing, Don B was in the dark. A grim smile distorted his thin mouth as he sat in literal darkness, knowing nothing. Thus did so many powerful men sit out the nights of their lives. Presidents, premiers, dictators, chairmen, generals... sitting without light or knowledge while distant hirelings and followers ignorantly carried out orders.

He heard the guard on the west wall shift position nervously and try to settle down. The man released the bolt on his automatic, removed the magazine and clicked it back in several times. All this Don B listened to. He understood the man's nervousness. Indeed he did.

Finally, he made up his mind and went to his bedroom. He locked the door. The grating on the windows was fashioned of one-inch iron rod. Chicken wire had been welded to the outside surface so that if a grenade were to be thrown through the grille into the room it would instead drop to the earth outside. The blast would be shielded from him by the wall of the house. Much thinking had gone into security. Something on the order of an anti-tank rocket would be needed to penetrate the bedroom.

Don B removed his embroidered dressing gown and stepped out of his carpet slippers. He stood for a moment at the window grille and watched the moonlight in the garden outside. Only low-lying plants grew here. There were no hiding places within fifty meters of the house, no tree trunks, no ornamental walls or heavy ceramic pots. Like the nervous guard on the west wall, Don B released the magazine of the Browning .9 and clicked it in and out several times. Then he placed it under his double pillow.

Again he went to the window to inspect the moonlit night. Leaves fluttered faintly in a light breeze. The smell of lemons came to him, the odor of eucalyptus. On the branch of an oak at least fifty yards away something small and black sat, one of those birds that seemed to infest the villa grounds by day, swooping and circling, cawing loudly, broadcasting dark, occult warnings.

Don B watched the indistinct form of the black bird, asleep, claws clutching the branch, beady eyes closed. The moonlight even cast him a shadow. No. Another bird. No. Three birds.

Don B stepped back from the window. A chill seemed to shoot across his shoulders. Icy with dread, he crossed himself.

35

Dropping below supersonic speed, the British Airways Concorde flashed high over the Atlantic beaches of Ireland, descending rapidly as it crossed the Irish Sea into a normal flight pattern before it arrived at Heathrow three and a half hours after its New York departure.

Its beaklike cockpit dropped to a new altitude, as of a bird searching for worms. A dismally small handful of passengers filed out through customs. The tall, dark young man in the sun-bleached bluejeans, the tee-shirt lettered BE REASONABLE. DO IT MY WAY and the aluminum colored nylon anorak passed quickly out into the cab area where a high-sided pewter-colored Phantom III, the last made before the war, waited for him.

He tossed a thin briefcase on the back seat as he nodded to the uniformed chauffeur. It was doubtful whether Bennett Brown recognized the antique car's Mulliner coachwork, but the imperious way it towered over traffic, dominated only by doubledecker buses, made him understand what the Rolls name had once meant.

"Sir," the chauffeur remarked, "I'm directed to take you to the Kinnerton Street flat unless otherwise ordered."

"Fine. And Mr. Sykes-Maulby?"

"Awaits you there."

Bennett Brown settled back in the pale tan glove leather upholstery and admired the way the driver deftly wound through airport traffic and onto the motorway. The heavy car surged smoothly toward the center of London. Sources had picked up the fact that Miss Hunter had booked herself back to New York tomorrow, which was what had brought Ben here today. But there was another reason. With Ben there always was.

The car turned off Belgrave Square, led on into Motcomb Street and turned right into Kinnerton Street. It stopped at one of the lanes leading off to the left. But first the chauffeur got out to remove a steel post blocking the way. Then he drove the pewter-colored Rolls into the courtyard, replaced the post and ushered his passenger into the vestibule of the Sykes-Maulby town house.

"Ben, my boy." Julian met him at the door of his flat with freshly poured tulip glasses of champagne.

The two men sat down at opposite ends of a long couch. Bennett Brown set his glass, untouched, on the glass-and-walnut-and-brass cocktail table. "I appreciate being able to bunk here tonight, Julian," he began. "I'm only here the one night and there's no reason the whole world has to know."

"Rrright," Julian said, trying to imitate an American he'd once swindled in Houston. "Can I help you with any of your work?"

"Not really." Ben glanced around him. "Nice place. Handy."

Julian raised and lowered his considerable eyebrows several times. "And hardly more than a short walk from the Carlton Tower."

The younger man gave him a weighing look. "You think I'm here to collar Mary Lee Hunter." A statement, not a question. "But I'm really here to collar you, Julian."

"Collar away."

Ben said nothing for a moment. "You usually have it neatly typed up."

"Dear God." Julian touched his forehead with two fingers, indicating absence of memory. He got up from the couch and returned a moment later with a black plastic bound booklet. He spread it open on the table before Bennett Brown. "All there. With the usual optional target-of-opportunity tag at the end."

Ben paged slowly through the typed lists of securities, a page per company, with current prices of common and preferred, as well as the most recent bond issues and a brief curriculum vita of the business, the industry in which it operated and prospects for both in the coming crash.

The British, Dutch and Swiss securities came first, followed by some rather more dubious issues from other countries in Europe. "I'm not recommending anything German this time around, Ben," Sykes-Maulby explained. "The Deutschmark is going through a thin patch. Terrifying unemployment problems. The Jerries are so bloody conscientious since their Nazi days that they included all those Turk and Calabrian and Yugoslav *Gastarbeiters* in their social security and unemployment insurance coverage. Some of these guest workers have been there donkey's years. They're entitled and so are their cousins, whom they reckon by the dozens, and their mothers and their fathers and their aunts."

Ben glanced up at him, pretending not to recognize the Gilbert and Sullivan tag. He had found it better if he seemed not to understand the British humor or pronunciation. It put them off their game.

"You've got a similar welfare set-up here in the U.K.," he pointed out. "But I see a lot of British securities on your list."

"We've had our devaluation, in fact a host of 'em. The Jerries haven't yet."

Ben nodded. "Okay. Looks good. I don't think we'll do much with the bottom end of your list but we'll start reaching out Monday for the good stuff. That reminds me."

When he said nothing, Julian sipped his champagne with a let's-get-it-over-with air. "That reminds me," Ben repeated slowly. He was watching the Englishman's face rather closely. "I had a meeting with some of my consortium people last week. Lots of questions. Nothing I couldn't handle, but one thing got me to thinking."

"Yes, old man?" Sykes-Maulby sounded bored.

"One of the smarter guys, Bobby, normally on my side, told me he'd been tracking our buys over the past year or two and had found a pattern. He said after we bought there was a drop in price. In other words, it seemed to him we were buying at a premium which evaporated once we'd completed our buy."

With a rock-steady hand Julian was refilling his tulip glass. He let the bubbles subside for a moment. Then: "But surely, Ben, you told him that was the follower-leader effect. The little fellows tumbling in after us and getting trimmed when the insiders took their profit."

"That was what I told him, Julian."

The younger man transferred his glance from the Englishman's face to the bubbles in his own glass. "That was before I set up a search-and-compare program for our computer. I sent it back over a ten year period, which is longer than Bobby studied. Back to when I first started making buys in Europe. I was just testing the waters then, of course, and I didn't have the benefit of your advice, Julian."

Again an oppressive silence. Eyes fixed on the bubbles in his untouched tulip glass of champagne, Bennett Brown seemed hypnotized. He glanced up suddenly and his black eyes zeroed in on Sykes-Maulby like some military aiming device. "See, I've been relying on you for almost two years now."

"Just about," Julian agreed. "And no complaints."

"Right. But it's about two years ago that this phenomenon of Bobby's cropped up. Before that there was no run-up before our buy, nor a run-down after..."

The Englishman sipped his wine. "It may be because your purchases were modest before I joined the team, old man. Once you felt you could rely on my advice, your volume rose quickly and this follower-leader effect set in."

Ben was silent for an extremely long time. Finally he smiled softly. "Julian," he said, "when you Brits are good, you're real good."

Sykes-Maulby crossed his long legs with a pleased look. "I'm *say-o* glad to hear you say so, dear boy." He indicated the typed booklet. "Then you approve?"

"I thought I'd said that. We'll start buying on Monday."

Julian nodded. "What are your plans tonight, Ben? Theater? Dinner? I'm entirely at your disposal."

"Before I decide, I have to make a call."

"By all means." The Englishman indicated the telephone and got to his feet. "I'll leave you alone."

Ben waited until the older man would have reached another room. Then he dialed a number in Sicily. His father answered on the second ring.

"*Serafina c'è?*" Ben began, using a code question to learn if scrambling were necessary.

"Ben!" His father's voice rose to a yelp. "I was expecting..." He paused.

"Somebody more important, right?" Ben kidded him.

"*Sì.* No. You get me all mixed up, you dumb kid." He managed a laugh. "Somebody who shoulda called me two-three days ago and hasn't."

"Listen, I'm in London. In case you need me."

"Gimme a number."

"That's all right," Ben stalled him. "You know our gentleman here."

"Ah. *Sì.* But I'm okay, Ben. No problems."

"Just in case. A father," he added, still kidding him, "should always know the whereabouts of his son."

"That's what you t'ink," Don B said in a somber tone. "Still, I appreciate it. You're a good kid. *Ciao.*"

Ben hung up, his antennae still vibrating with the strange tone of his father's voice. It was expectation, yes. It was frustration, too. But there was another note in his voice and Ben could not put a name to it. He got out his wallet and found inside the scrap of paper on which he'd written the phone number of the Carlton Tower Hotel. He dialed it.

"Mr. Curtiss's room, please."

The voice that answered was also a man's, if anything even thicker with caution than that of Don B. "Miss Hunter, please," Ben asked, keeping his own voice very neutral.

"Can I tell her who's calling?"

"I'd rather surprise her. I'm a friend."

Silence. Then: "Do you mind?" Curtiss asked. "It isn't that she doesn't adore surprises. It's me. I don't adore them. I think they suck."

Ben found himself grinning. "I'm phoning all the way across the Atlantic to give her a little surprise and I'm catching flak already."

"God, it's one of those days," Curtiss sympathized.

"And you're just not going to put her on without knowing my name."

"What do you say?" Curtiss asked, obviously addressing someone else.

Mary Lee's voice, on the extension phone, sounded wary. "Hello, Ben. Surprise yourself."

"Bingo! God, it's good to hear your voice, Mary Lee."

"How's B. J.?"

"Just fine. Sends you her love."

Mary Lee was silent for a moment. "How'd you locate me?"

"It wasn't as hard as you think," Ben assured her. "There aren't too many hotels where Americans stay in London."

"Under my pen name of Curtiss?" she pounced.

"Why do I ever try to fool you, Mary Lee?" Ben asked contritely. "You are ten times smarter than I'll ever be."

"Careful, Ben. The shit's up over my ankles already."

"I have to talk to you, sweetheart."

"Isn't that what we're doing?"

"I mean face to face."

She was silent for a moment. "If you know my hotel, you probably know I'm booked back to the States tomorrow. I'll set something up when I get there."

"Well," he stalled, "you see how it is . . ."

"What he's saying," Curtiss cut in, "is that he's here in London, probably calling from the lobby downstairs."

"More or less," Ben agreed.

Now neither of them spoke. "Look," Ben went on pleasantly, "they do good steaks downstairs. Why don't we—"

"No, look," Curtiss interrupted again, "let's make it seven-thirty at Langan's Brasserie. It's on—"

"I know where. Seven-thirty on the—"

"See you, Ben," Mary Lee cut in. She hung up and Curtiss did an instant later.

Ben put away the phone and wandered through the flat without finding Julian. Although the place had been carefully described for him, even blueprinted, he had never actually stayed here before. He glanced out of the courtyard window and saw the chauffeur dusting the pewter flanks of the Phantom III with a kind of feathery thing. Bennett Brown craned his neck to try to see the flat below. It, too, had been described for him, including its three escape routes, by Enzo, Don B's man in London.

Remembering, thinking of his father, Bennett Brown suddenly put a name to that extra vibration in Don B's voice. It had been fear. The old man was scared.

36

Andreas Hutli is a symphony conductor, still in his thirties, one of those eternally circling planets that seems to conduct every leading orchestra at least once a year, issue best-selling recordings on three labels, stage television premières of new works, get married to film stars and endorse a particular brand of magnetic tape cassette, all without dropping a baton. That he is also Swiss, and therefore cautiously bourgeois underneath it all, is not widely known.

Certainly today, as he walked into Zum Goldenen Stern in Basel, the essential man was well camouflaged under a chiffon openwork shirt, trainman's red bandanna, fawn jodhpurs and smoke-colored jackboots. The only person in this rather staid restaurant who nearly outshone Andreas was his banker, Urs Rup, in a cambric blouse, massive gold chains and a paper-thin chamois jacket and jeans.

The sight was unusual at Zum Goldenen Stern, one of

Basel's better restaurants. It sits close to the river in a very
old part of town where paper-mills used to employ water
power produced by rivers flowing into the Rhine. It is a
favorite place for all-male lunches because the immense
portions provide good cooking with a patriotic Swiss theme.
Considering the tentative grip the Swiss have on a cuisine of
their own, the Stern ranks as a good try.

It was not food the two rather outlandishly dressed young
men wanted, at least at first, but a slightly chilled bottle of
dark rosé Dôle, which they began to drink as if terribly
thirsty. The musician wanted to get the banker's opinion of a
new testimonial contract that would have him advertising TV
sets all next year in return for a lump sum.

Urs Rup shook his head violently. "No lump sums, Andreas."
Quickly he sketched his idea of a low upfront payment and a
percentage override on appliance sales.

Hutli's head began to nod just as violently in agreement.
"Perfect thinking," he responded. "Look, Urs, my agent has
negotiated a higher royalty rate on the new albums. I want to
do something crazy with the extra money. Something wild
and risky and insanely profitable."

Looking sage, Urs Rup slowly rolled himself a thin joint
and lit up. He inhaled deeply and passed it to Andreas, who
glanced guiltily around him before taking a drag.

At that precise moment, as if waiting to catch him *in
flagrante delicto*, a tall, thin man in regulation bankers' attire
seemed to materialize at the younger men's table like an
avenging genie.

"Urs Rup," he intoned in a strangely penetrating voice. To
the musician it seemed as if every important Basler in the
restaurant had heard.

The young banker was on his feet. "Palmer, what a surprise,"
he said quickly.

"And here's another celebrity," Palmer said. This time
every eye in the room had to be on them, Andreas felt sure.
He could feel himself break out in a sweat as Urs made
perfunctory introductions.

American, Hutli thought feverishly. CIA? That disapprov-
ing look of his, as if he *knew* something. But, dear God, what
was there to know?

"It's good to see you in public so soon," Palmer said in an
insinuating tone. "I thought—" He stopped himself and

looked in embarrassment at Andreas Hutli. "But I'm sure you two have no secrets from each other."

Neither of the younger men spoke, nor daréd eye the other. The musician was sure now it was the marijuana cigarette. This was some kind of officer from some international drug control commission. As if fulfilling his wildest fears, Palmer picked up the joint from the ashtray and smiled at it. He put it down again. "Urs," he said, "I'm sorry. I had no idea."

"What are you talking about?" the younger banker demanded unhappily.

Palmer's head inclined infinitesimally in the direction of Hutli. "I've said too much as it is," Palmer responded in a flustered tone. "But the police didn't tell me not t—" He stopped again, mortified. "I do apologize," he said. Then, turning to the conductor. "I would never knowingly cause pain. Dear me."

He backed away from the table and seemed to disappear off the face of the earth, as if swallowed up. Urs, who had got to his feet, now stood there for a long moment, cursing the fact that he was blushing and Hutli could see the blush.

"What did he mean?" Andreas implored.

Urs sat down and sloshed Dôle in both their glasses. "I've no idea. Man's insane."

"Urs, please. You know how open I am to scandal. People like me live entirely in the public eye. Who is that man?"

"American banker." Urs seemed unwilling to talk. "Busybody."

"*Mein Gott*, something to do with Bank Rup?" Hutli sounded agonized.

"I told you, Andreas." Urs tried for a soothing tone. "I have no idea what he's up to. But as soon as we finish lunch I'm damned well going to find out."

"We have finished," the conductor said in a nervous tone. "I couldn't eat a bite."

37

"It's too dangerous," Curtiss told Mary Lee Hunter, "I'll meet him. You stay here in the hotel."

"We both go or not at all."

Curtiss grimaced. "We are talking about the man who may have put out a hit on me last week in Paris."

"Curtiss: both of us or neither of us. I am not about to lose you. If you're going down in a hail of bullets, I want the body beside you to be mine."

"Touching." He smiled at her as he turned back from the picture window. "There's no sense trying to guess what he's up to. But we'd better agree what we're up to. We're trying to defuse him, right? Calm him down?"

"But he's very bright," Mary Lee cautioned. "He knows we know. All we can try is to convince him that we won't do anything with our information."

"That shouldn't be too hard," Curtiss responded in a thoughtful tone. He glanced at his watch. "We're supposed to be there in fifteen minutes. The most dangerous error you can make in this business is letting the opposition know where you're going to be and when."

"Which error we've already committed."

He shook his head. "No, he has." He scribbled something on a piece of paper and handed it to her. "I'm pushing off. Give yourself till half past seven, then go downstairs and take a cab to the address on that paper. Don't take the first cab in line. Take the second or third. When you get to that place—it's a wine bar—go downstairs to the phone and call Bennett Brown at Langan's Brasserie. Got it?"

"And tell Ben what?"

"Tell him you changed the dining place. Give him the address of the wine bar. He'll arrive a few minutes later and I'll be a discreet distance behind him."

Her face had grown pale through this. "Curtiss, you don't really expect trouble?"

"None at all."

She frowned down at the piece of paper. "Is this a joke? L'Artiste Musclé? What kind of name is that?"

"It's a wine bar. Don't order the house red." He put out his hands and lifted her to her feet. "Remember, not the first cab in the rank."

"God, Curtiss."

"I don't remember saying it lately but I love you." They kissed for an instant. Then she put her arms around him and they kissed for a long time. "When we get out of this," he muttered, "we'd better think of something really marvelous to do with our lives."

He found his way out the hotel's rear delivery entrance to a private parking space that led into Harriet Street. Moving at a jog, he followed the alleyway out onto Lowndes Street, where he picked up a cap at the Lowndes Hotel. When the driver brought him to Stratton Street he leaned forward:

"Go past Langan's a few doors and pull over. Keep your meter running."

He glanced at his watch, then sat back in the cab to one end of the rear seat so that he could glance obliquely through the rear window to the entrance of the restaurant. He waited.

At seven twenty-nine a tall young man with dark hair and black eyes came down the street on foot wearing an aluminum-colored anorak. He stopped at the entrance, checked his watch and entered. Curtiss couldn't be sure of his identity, but he was positive of his nationality. With a tee-shirt reading I DON'T THINK A HELLUVA LOT OF YOU, EITHER he could only be American.

Curtiss peered through the evening light at Stratton Street, analyzing passers-by and loiterers alike and finding none of them very suspect. At seven thirty-five the dark man in the aluminum anorak came out onto the street with someone in a *maître d's* formal attire. They conferred for a moment, the restaurant man gesturing and pointing. The young man nodded and took off in the direction of Piccadilly.

"Sorry, driver. The ride's over." Curtiss pushed two one-pound notes at the cabby and followed the dark young man.

Along Piccadilly buses and cars were growling past at reduced speeds as the pre-theater crowd started to converge on the Shaftesbury Avenue district. Ahead of him, Bennett Brown passed the Green Park tube station and pushed on past Clarges and Half Moon Streets. He had stopped to speak

to no one and his walking pace had been fast enough to keep
Curtiss scrambling.

At White Horse Street he turned right into the curving
lane, barely wide enough for a car to traverse. At the far end
of it, Curtiss knew, lay L'Artiste Musclé, a French wine bar
with good food he remembered from his last visit to London.
He had no way of knowing if Mary Lee would be seated at an
outside table or not.

He watched Bennett Brown slow his pace and come to a
stop, surveying the corner establishment, starting to fill up
now with diners. At the precise spot where the windows
curved around the corner stood a table with three chairs. On
it were three glasses and an open bottle of wine. Mary Lee
Hunter, wearing Eleanora's Levi's, a pale mauve body-hugging
tee-shirt and high heeled sandals she had bought today, lifted
the bottle and poured her own glass full. She looked up, saw
Brown and filled a second glass. She refrained from looking
past or around him, Curtiss noted approvingly.

He stood in the doorway of an oriental restaurant and
watched them without being able to hear anything they said.
Both of them were slugging down wine at a rate unknown in
any European country. The dark young man was gesticulating
and Mary Lee was shaking her head. Then Brown sat back
and looked unhappy. Curtiss stepped out of the doorway and
approached.

"Sorry I'm late," he said, taking the third chair as Mary
Lee poured his glass full.

"Tailing me, huh?" Ben asked politely. "That was the
reason for changing the venue?"

"Right." Curtiss brought the glass to his lips and watched
Bennett Brown over the rim. Their glances met and Curtiss
noticed the bottomless quality of eyes whose irises were the
same color as the pupils. Otherwise, with his unruly hair of
uneven length and his small, careful mouth, he looked a lot
like a graduate student in a discipline like law or medicine.

"You expected me to bring along muscle?" Ben teased.

"I still do," Curtiss assured him with mock gravity. "Can
we get down to business or are you hungry?"

"My gut's out of whack with the time zone," Ben responded.
"Mary Lee?"

"Nothing yet. Ben, tell me how B. J. really is."

"I told you fine. She doesn't know I'm here, much less
seeing you."

Mary Lee nodded. "What else doesn't she know?"

The silence was short, but unhappy. "Hey, look," Ben began, holding both his hands up, palms out, in a traffic-cop gesture. "I don't mix family and business, Mary Lee. You know that. It gets me a little sick to my stomach even having to discuss all this with you. Because as far as I'm concerned, you're family."

She managed a gracious smile. "Family that's causing you a lot of trouble."

He glanced sideways at Curtiss. "It didn't have to be that way. This guy's ideas would have stayed inside his skull if you hadn't tapped him."

"As far as I'm concerned," Curtiss began, "that's where they stay. The only thing that's happened since I let Mary Lee in on them is grief." He kept his eyes focused on his still full glass of wine. "I think Mary Lee feels the same way, but she can speak for herself."

"We've talked about nothing else now for a week," Mary Lee picked up, "and we've reached the same conclusion. Forget it."

"Why?" Ben pounced.

"Why not?" Curtiss asked. He had laid one arm back behind the finial of his chairback and looked very much at ease, lolling in the evening here in Shepherd Market, watching couples pass by, following for a moment the rounds of prostitutes on their early-evening tour of duty.

"What difference," he went on after a moment, "does it make who runs what in our society? You tell me: would you run Jet-Tech any differently, once you bought control? What it comes down to is profit. To whom does the profit go? To your bunch or some other bunch? Who gives a rat's ass where it goes? We could stand on our heads, stick pins in the SEC and sing a chorus of the 'Star Spangled Banner' and in the end it wouldn't make a goddamned bit of difference to us or the rest of the world whether you won or lost. Face it, Brown, this is an ego trip for you. You're peeing your pants with anxiety. So it feels hot to you." He grinned. "It's just cold piss to the rest of us."

Mary Lee flashed him a look of gratitude so rapid that Curtiss was sure Bennett Brown hadn't seen it. "Curtiss is right, Ben. The vast majority of us have no stake in what you're doing, win or lose."

"No?" The dark eyes swiveled to her. "How'd you feel if I took over Jet-Tech and let you go?"

"And put Dave Grissom in my job?"

He blinked. Curtiss realized that Mary Lee still had the inner power to shake this cool customer. "Grissom is not my man," he said automatically. "I'm saying you've got a stake in protecting your own career, your own success. Him," he indicated Curtiss with a dip of his dark head, "he's a loner. But you play the organization game, Mary Lee. That's why you've gone as high as you have."

"What does that mean, Ben? You'd make sure I'd never work in any major corporation again?"

"Did I say that?" He sounded actually hurt. "Would I put a blacklist on you? You're part of my family, Mary Lee. What do I have to do to convince you of that?"

A waiter with two earrings in one ear and platinum hair approached their table. "Ready to eat?"

Curtiss shook his head. "Come back in a while."

All three were silent as the waiter retreated. Curtiss smiled dreamily. "Can I call you Ben?" he asked.

The dark young man shrugged.

"Ben," Curtiss pushed ahead, "you have to remember something neither of us fully appreciates. You and I, we're brainwashed into thinking that organized crime is a vast shadow in which monsters lurk, bloodsuckers on the body politic. But most people don't feel that way at all."

"How's that?"

"Most people take a very pragmatic view. They feel *all* bosses are bloodsuckers and when they themselves get to be a boss they'll suck harder than anybody."

Ben laughed. It seemed to escape from him, after which tight self-control clamped down again, masked by a very reasonable, even neutral tone of voice. "That's a pretty sour view of human nature."

"But if I'm right," Curtiss went on, "people couldn't care less who takes the profits, as long as they have theirs and the chance for more. In fact, that *is* success. To climb a bit higher, even if you step on somebody's head."

"That's not how Mary Lee became successful."

"No. She and your wife are the product of big corporation guilt. One day the boss looks around and says: 'the next bright broad who passes by, nail her.' The trick is being the next to pass by."

"And to be bright," Mary Lee added. "Gee, Curtiss, you really know how to flatter a broad."

"Come on, if you'd been born ten years earlier, you'd have

been unsuccessful in a business career, for the reverse of the same reason you're successful today."

"Precisely my point. Mary Lee has a stake in who runs things." Ben turned to her. "This guy is some kind of anarchist, baby. I don't put down anarchy. It has its uses. But you were born a capitalist. It's in your genes."

She nodded. "I know an older man like that. Banker's banker. Put in more time shoring up free enterprise than all of us together. And now he's had it. Sees no hope. Couldn't care less who's at the helm."

Bennett Brown made a lip noise, as of a baby refusing a nippled bottle. "Fucking Palmer, huh?" He turned back to Curtiss. "You're getting too old to let him keep jerking your string."

Curtiss responded with an easy movement of his arm, as if brushing away smoke. "I don't need to be Palmer to see that you're heading for a fall, Ben. They tell me you're into long waves and that whole Kondratiev bag. Of all people, you should know that about the time you've bought it all, it turns to dust in your hands. I, for one, couldn't care less if you're holding the bag or somebody else. You're welcome to the whole mess."

Bennett Brown sat back and stared at Curtiss. After a long moment he poured wine for himself and Mary Lee. Then he sat quietly, staring into the ruby depths of the wine. Curtiss, who did not seem to mind having his eyes stared into, began to miss the contact. He knew Brown was trying to figure out where Curtiss had heard about the Kondratiev connection. He might conclude that Sykes-Maulby had been blabbing which, indeed, he had.

Intent on Brown, Curtiss failed to notice that Mary Lee was watching him with an inner intensity, as if he had just given her the news that a loved one had died.

"Curtiss," she said at last, "if it's all going down the drain, what am I doing at Jet-Tech? What am I doing in business? What kind of success have I worked hard for if it just—what did you say—turns to dust in my hands."

"You'll have to ask Ben," he responded with some maliciousness. "He's the expert on success, not me."

Bennett Brown looked up with the air of someone who has weightier matters on his mind. "This is horseshit, Mary Lee. You wanted success. You slaved for it. You got it. The success is in the winning. It doesn't matter how long it lasts. There was a challenge and you sure as hell met it."

"Oh, no."

Her voice had gone up half an octave. "Don't sit there and tell me that," she said. "The two of you cool young men. Don't just sit there telling me I blew my youth on an illusion. Do you have any idea how *hard* it is to get this far this fast for a woman? How you have to be twice as bright and work twice as hard as a man? What it means in deferments? Fun deferred. Pleasure, relaxation deferred. The weekend I had with Curtiss in Paris, do you know it was the first in my whole miserable life? Ask B. J. sometime, Ben. For a woman to get this kind of success, she has to give up a hell of a lot more than a man. And there sit the two of you like a pair of bookends telling me it was all for *nothing*."

By this time people at other outdoor tables had turned to listen. One short, dark-haired woman at the end table started to applaud. Curtiss waved to her nonchalantly. Then, to Mary Lee: "You have painted the problem so perfectly I can't add a line." He reached across to pat her hand. "Universal economic depression affects everyone, regardless of sex. It's dull and it's boring and the only exciting thing is that we don't know when it'll happen."

"Or if," Ben put in.

Curtiss made an open-wide gesture of if-you-say-it-it-must-be-true. Then he put his hand back over Mary Lee's on the table. "I stand corrected. It's a question of when or if. Somehow I don't think that improves the odds."

She gave Ben a crooked smile. "Not if the boy genius here is manipulating all the major profit centers." She took Ben's hand and laid it on top of Curtiss's so that all three of them seemed to be making a pact. "Ben," she said in a firm voice, "bygones are bygones. We're friends again. Yes?"

"We never stopped being," he assured her in an equally firm voice. "I love you, baby, always will. And if this goon is your heart's desire, I love him, too."

Curtiss beckoned the waiter with the double earring. "We're ready to eat."

But Ben was getting to his feet. "Not me, kids. Gotta late date. Keep well. And, Mary Lee, get back home as soon as you can, okay?"

All three were standing now. Mary Lee kissed Ben, who then shook hands firmly and formally with Curtiss. He flashed them a grin as bright as his aluminum anorak and walked off quickly along White Horse Street in the direction of Piccadilly.

Mary Lee sat down and peered at the hand-scribbled menu. "They seem to have a lambstew, if that's what *ragoût d'agneau* means." She glanced up at him. "Sit down. I'm starving."

"Later." He took her hand and half-hauled her back on her feet. Putting some money down on the table, he led her off around the corner of the wine bar in the opposite direction to Ben's. As they left, the short dark-haired woman called: "Spot on, luv!"

Curtiss started running, dragging Mary Lee behind him. He dodged left around a greeting-card shop and ran west along Shepherd Market until they reached the far exit to Curzon Street. They turned right, still running. At the Mirabelle restaurant, a cab let out two men, animatedly conversing in an oddly accented French.

Curtiss jumped into the empty cab and pulled Mary Lee in with him. "Leicester Square," he told the driver. As they moved off, he stared back at one of the men who had been speaking French, a dapper gent with a hairline moustache. Then Curtiss turned back to Mary Lee. "Sorry."

"Obviously you don't believe Ben is our true friend."

He shook his head. "I don't even believe half of what *I* was saying. The problem is: how much did Ben believe?"

38

Achille Gamba, still conversing in rapid Corsican French with his London associate, Ettore Charmat, stood in the foyer of the Mirabelle restaurant and looked around him for familiar faces. The Mirabelle had a certain elegance that attracted a particular type of customer. Gamba, who knew most things criminal as well as he knew the multiplication tables—that is by rote—understood the special position of this terribly expensive place.

"*Figurez-vous*," he told Charmatt in a suddenly lowered voice. "The upward striving lower middle class of Britain, the grubby council and borough officials, the county sheriffs and bureau chiefs in charge of issuing permits for everything from building a coliseum to spitting on the pavement, these mangy curs whose chief resource is not their salaries but their ability to sell favors, whose wives possess faces like an open bag of burglar's tools. Tell me, Ettore, what is their highest aspiration?"

"*L'argent*."

"Money they crave, but their aspiration is to dine at the Mirabelle. *Vraiment*, this very place."

His companion began to scan the faces of those waiting to be seated. "I see a few colleagues tonight," he murmured.

"Yes, it is here they take their corrupt political friends. A wad of twenty-pound notes is all very well under the table. But the table, Ettore, must be here at the Mirabelle."

Both men chuckled softly as the headwaiter, recognizing them, beckoned. They moved with quiet dignity to their table, only their eyes flashing here and there around the plush-encased restaurant.

"And those three in the corner?" Charmat asked in a barely audible voice as he and Gamba sat down. "You saw?"

"Doctor Hakkuk is the tall one's name. The other two I have seen in Corsica within the last month."

Charmat gave him a wondering smile. "Your eyesight, Achille, only grows sharper with the years. And your memory."

"Dangerous men are worth remembering."

"Arabs?"

Gamba shrugged. "Possibly. Druses. Dervishes. Parsees. Within the vast stretches of Islam many minorities languish. Those two have been trying to pick up a connection for something quite insane they are planning here in London."

Pretending to read the menu, they instead inspected the three men at the corner table. "Terrorists of course," Charmat said. It was not a question.

"They are charged with financing terror," Gamba corrected him. "The operation they intend here will net millions. I told my people back home to give them a wide berth. It was too tricky. Too, ah, what shall I call it? Too devastating. One must draw the line somewhere."

"What sort of operation?"

The Corsican shrugged uneasily. "A ransom caper. I don't want to be more specif—" He stopped talking. A runty man with shoulders almost as broad as his height sat down with the three men in the corner.

"You saw?" Achille Gamba breathed softly.

"Enzo Tagliabue. Don B's man in London."

"For thirty years his man. Don B would surely not approve of the company he is keeping tonight."

"Then what is to be done?"

Gamba smiled thinly. What he liked about Charmat, as an associate, was his practical mind. Something was wrong? Fix it. "I shall speak to Enzo," Gamba promised.

"And then?"

Gamba shrugged. "If that is not enough, I shall speak to Don B."

39

In the old part of Basel, not far from the Alley of the Ten Thousand Virgins, is the city's newest hotel, Hotel Basel, designed to fit in with its often medieval background, low pleasant buildings surrounded by crooked cobbled streets which defy cars to traverse them. As a result, most traffic is pedestrian.

The two young women who left the three-story building across the street stopped for a moment, then headed on foot towards the Marktplatz. In the distance they might have seen the rich brown-red Rathaus, Basel's ancient town hall, recently renovated. Because they were busy chatting, it is doubtful that either of them actually studied the Rathaus as they rounded the corner toward the Post Office and headed for lunch at the Safranzunft, a restaurant in the antique headquarters of one of Basel's oldest guilds, that of the keymakers.

Eleanora hardly knew Basel, but her friend Elfi was a native. They had met some twenty years before as schoolgirls in Holland, their common bond the German language. Now Elfi ran her own translation bureau in Basel. Sitting in the Safranzunft's upper ground floor dining room, they barely examined the menu, choosing to share a double portion of fondue and a bottle of chilled Fendant white.

Eleanora, who was tall for a European woman, easily five feet five inches, and beautiful in a dark way, rather like a rose, smiled happily across the table at Elfi, who was petite, with pale blond hair and those hectic spots of natural color

across her cheekbones that many Swiss inherit from moun-
taineer ancestors.

"It must be a terrifying grind," she was telling Elfi. "Nobody asks for anything exciting to be translated, eh? Only the
dull stuff."

Elfi frowned and switched to English. "The noun is 'grind'?"
she asked. "As in the verb 'to grind'?"

"An idiom," Eleanora came back in German, "backformed
from the verb. Something dull and perhaps necessary. The
daily grind. Meaning the boring daily routine. Also a second
meaning; one who grinds away, as a student who is forever
studying. Grind."

Elfi nodded in appreciation. "Your English was always so
much more precise than mine. My French is perhaps a shade
better than yours. But now that you live in Italian Switzerland,
your Italian must be superb."

"*Meraviglioso*," Eleanora responded and both of them clapped
their hands over their mouths to stifle an attack of giggling.

"Do you really speak only Italian in the Ticino?"

"Not Woods and I. But in the shops. The workmen who
clear our land. It's a very precise Italian, easy to compre-
hend. But . . ." Eleanora stopped. "It's like the espresso coffee
they make in the Ticino. *Un po' noioso.*"

Elfi gave her a reproving look. "The girl has everything and
still she's a little bored. Poverina."

"Life is very even in tenor. Very calm. After a while,"
Eleanora confessed, "we get on each other's nerves and are
afraid to discuss it. So we visit Paris or Milan or New York.
He invariably finds something to dislike and again, I am
afraid to say that I quite enjoy big city life, at least for a few
months now and then. We are like Robinson Crusoe and his
Woman Friday. And Woods is, after all, to be sixty in a year
or two. So this is an irreversible situation."

Elfi listened to this with small intakes of air, tiny gasps of
sympathy that were partly vocalized into a series of "tschou"
sounds that doves make as the evening light grows dim.
"*Nai*," she said at last, "there I disagree. Nothing is irreversible. You remember Franzl?"

Eleanora rolled her eyes. "*Sehr schön.*"

"When was it he lived with me? 1979? Out of work. For all
of March, April and May he was impotent. Nothing I did
could bring him to life. He brought home pornographic
magazines. We went to the sex shows they have across the

river in Germany. I even got my cousin Magdalene to help. Imagine, the three of us in bed. A tragicomedy. Then, in June he finally got a job, in Zurich. He had a month before he was to start work. All of a sudden he ... I mean ..." she glanced around her. "It was like a flagpole, Elli. It was like a gatepost. So there is nothing irreversible."

Eleanora hid her laughter behind her napkin. Then: "Where is Franzl, now?"

Elfi gave a shrug as petite as she was. "We have lost touch. He used to visit me at weekends, or I him. But we have other interests now."

Eleanora sat silently for a long moment. Then the waitress brought the big metal fondue bowl with an alcohol burner flickering under it. The bits of bread and the long two-tined forks stood by until the cheese mixture was hot enough.

Eleanora sipped her wine. "You see what it is," she said then. "You have the translation bureau. You have five women with you. And you have all the hundreds of customers to be found in a town like Basel, with its international business connections. You have independence, Elfi. If you want to drop Franzl for someone else, you just do it. You're not tied to—" She stopped herself.

"Don't think my little business makes me rich." Elfi stared at the pale blue alcohol flame. "Most of my girls are simply bilingual typists. Only I and one other are really multilingual. The work never lets up, never."

"But if you wanted to take a trip for a week, you could."

"I do that quite often. My new friend works for Swissair and he gets the discount on air tickets."

"How marvelous," Eleanora enthused. She speared a bit of bread and dipped it deep into the molten cheese mixture. Then she brought it out and blew on it gently for a moment. "I'm sorry Woods isn't here for this. He adores fondue."

"Busy?"

"He's scaring a Swiss banker to death."

Elfi's hand went over her mouth. "Don't tell me. He can make a banker tremble?"

"Woods can make anyone tremble. He has a very intimidating manner when he wants. And he has some very incriminating information about this particular gentleman."

Elfi's eyes widened. "I had no idea he was so fierce, your man."

"Yes." Eleanora nodded, as if also saying yes to something

Elfi had left unsaid. "It is a very secure existence, Elfi, being under the protection of a man with money who, moreover, loves me as I love him. But I see your little bureau and the life you lead, and I say: she is as secure as I, and she owes it to no one but herself."

After a moment's pause, Elfi's friendly glance grew embarrassed, as if caught in some shameful sort of secret. "You and I," she said in a low tone, glancing around the restaurant, "we treasure our independence. It is not usually thus with women of our generation. The young girls, yes."

Eleanora's answering look was almost wary. "Nor our mothers'." She dipped another bit of bread into the liquefied cheese. "Perhaps we are the link between our mothers and any daughters we may have." She withdrew the coated bread and let it stand in the air, cooling.

"You don't sound convinced."

Eleanora's face went deadpan. "Independence is important. So is a good life with a man."

"And when the two clash?"

"When?" Eleanora demanded. "You must mean if."

40

From the Fifth Avenue window of UBCO headquarters in Manhattan one could crane one's neck to the right and catch a tantalizing glimpse of Central Park, further north at 59th Street.

The sliver of brilliant green, shimmering through the city's heat haze, teased Bill Elston as he stared at it. He would like to be out there now, heat and humidity notwithstanding. He would like to stand on that corner and watch the tourists climb aboard the horse-drawn carriages for a ride through the park. He would like to sample the marinated veal bits, speared and grilled by the cute young girl in the halter-top and short shorts who ran the pushcart. He would like to see New Yorkers sitting around the edge of the Pulitzer Fountain where Scott and Zelda once took an impromptu bath, the newcomers only going as far as taking off their shoes and stockings to cool pavement-baked feet in the running waters. He would like to be anywhere out there, anywhere but in here.

The secret life of any big corporation, especially a bank, is supposed to run blandly, a sort of steady, even flow of cream sauce that smooths down temporary peaks and fills in unwanted valleys. It is assumed that officers and employees themselves will see to this. It is not the function of a security chief like Elston to keep ladling cornstarch into the mixture.

In practice this leads, of course, to a lot of hyprocrisy and intrigue. Human beings are naturally up to no good, Elston told himself now, and it's unrealistic to expect that they'll all be little Goodie Two-Shoes. Oh, they'll *pretend* to be. Mrs. Mulvey was a case in point.

Veronica Mulvey, age forty-four, an UBCO employee for more than ten years, a widow for two, not unattractive in a big-breasted way, pushing forward like a pouter pigeon on small, skinny legs and high heels, had been thoroughly checked out by Bill Elston. It had taken him, or rather the detective agency he'd hired, a week. And now that he knew Veronica Mulvey and her associates inside out, Elston was angry and sick.

And mad as hell at himself.

He stood revealed in his own mind as a careless idiot. Mrs. Mulvey came out of it looking weak, unreliable and more than a bit nasty. According to the detective agency she'd begun seeing this man about eighteen months ago, which accounted for her general sprucing-up. The money for it came from the man, together with languorous cruises to the Caribbean and a few sizzling weekends in Las Vegas. This was not the classic con game in which the victim went so deeply into debt that she had to start filching bank funds. In this version her lover spent thousands on her and wanted nothing in return but her own luscious self.

Until last week, that is, when he suddenly wanted Curtiss's dossier. When Veronica Mulvey weakly remonstrated, he gave her the name of Harry Kummel as one which would "cover" should the occasion arise. It wouldn't, of course.

"But how can it?" Elston could picture the lover saying. "This thing is cut and dried. You only need Kummel if your boss catches wise and how could he?"

As for E. Henry Kummel, the detective agency had also amassed a secret dossier that disgusted Elston with his own carelessness. Imagine not knowing what one of UBCO's vice-presidents was all about. Kummel had been treasurer of a Brooklyn commercial bank UBCO had merged with some years back, a bank with close gangland ties and a portfolio of bad debts the mob had hung on it.

He had reams of material from the private agency. Some of it had been in their files, or the police's, for years. Possibly the FBI had a lot of it, too. Only Internal Security hadn't had it. Well, better late . . .

Puffing out his cheeks in a disgusted way, Bill Elston turned from the window and marched back through the immense bullpen area of desks to his own office at the far wall. He passed directly behind Veronica Mulvey, hard at work at her desk. She had no idea that in a few minutes she would be summoned to the office of Charley Oakburn, Executive Vice-President, Operations, together with Kummel, another officer named Hearst who seemed to be in this with Kummel, and Bill Elston, arms filled with several pounds of dossiers and agency reports.

In all his years Elston had never run across a case in which one of his own Internal Security people had been suborned to provide confidential material about another. What bothered him most was that he couldn't swear it had *not* happened before. Only that he had not caught it.

It had been a nasty surprise, both to find his own acumen so faulty, and to realize how vulnerable to cheap, fleshy subornation one of his employees could be. They had tampered with the soul of Veronica Mulvey like burglars learning the combination of a safe. Money she would have turned down. Love, no.

But as he gathered together all his material and went upstairs to speak privately with Charley Oakburn before the actual meeting, Bill Elston had no idea this was not the only nasty surprise waiting for him this morning.

The intercom on Charley Oakburn's desk buzzed twice. He picked up his phone. "No," he told his secretary. "Hold all calls." He glanced at his watch. "Till noon."

He hung up and turned back to face the two men sitting across his rather grand desk. Charley Oakburn was not, by any definition, a career banker. He had barely graduated Yale, but he had crewed a number of America's Cup races and as skipper had actually won a few. His personal fortune was not large, but so well placed for him by his father that he had found himself on the boards of nearly a dozen East Coast companies, men's and country clubs and amateur sports groups. His eleven lines in *Who's Who* were impressive, but expensive in terms of membership fees and the cost of maintaining the appearance that went with his position in life.

At about the time his eldest son entered Yale, the old management at UBCO had arranged an executive position for Charley. The old chairman of the board, Lane Burckhardt, had been quite a keen yachtsman. The job created for Charley was not onerous, hardly more than chief-of-protocol work, but it did carry a vice-president's office and salary. In those days UBCO had only a dozen or so vice-presidents. It had several hundred now so it had been natural to move Charley up a notch to the almost purely honorary title of Executive Vice-President, of which UBCO had only twenty. This had been done long before Burckhardt's era and just after Woods Palmer quit the bank.

Charley's tanned, handsome face radiated confidence and power as he smiled at the two men across from him, lower-level executives from CIT, the subsidiary of RCA that UBCO was about to buy. Or had already bought. Charley had no head for details unless they were directly related to yachting. All of his banking decisions were made for him by his executive assistant, Harry Kummel.

And Harry had said...? Charley Oakburn frowned in thought. Had UBCO bought CIT or not? He quickly replaced the smile on his face. "Lovely to work with you chaps," he told the two CIT men. "Consumer finance, all that. Lovely line of work these days, eh?"

The older of the two, a man named Hodge, produced a noise somewhere between a sniff and a snort of rage. "Not so you could notice," he told Charley Oakburn. "At the moment we're paying sixteen for cash and we don't dare charge our customers more than nineteen. In our business nineteen's a magic number. People think twice before taking out a loan if the interest gets as high as twenty."

That was what Harry Kummel had said, Charley remembered suddenly. Reassure them about the prime rate. Reassure them about the overnight rate. "You chaps needn't worry over that for one moment," he assured them now.

The two CIT men exchanged glances. "Rates are going down?" Hodge inquired. "It's news to me."

"Well, but, that is hardly your problem now," Charley Oakburn responded. "I mean, once you're part of the UBCO family, the published rates have no meaning for you."

Hodge produced a cynical grin. "That so?"

The desk intercom buzzed again. "Marie, I told you—" Charley's craggy good looks set in a petulant mold. "Oh, yes. But not now. Have him wait outside." He hung up. Tricky as it might be to slide his way through this meeting with the new CIT people, the meeting to follow would be far more difficult and with his own man, Bill Elston.

Another man in his position, put there by an Establishment network of old boys who liked his style at the tiller of an America's Cup defending yacht, would have in time developed delusions of grandeur. Not Charley. He never for a moment considered himself competent in any aspect of banking except to present what others had prepared for him. He was, if he said so himself, with his boyishly slim figure and ruggedly handsome face, a master presenter.

In his role as Mr. Façade, he was really only welcoming these new CIT chaps as a signal that they would get top support at UBCO. Nothing more was needed from him than welcoming handshakes and five minutes of supportive chit-chat. The meeting to follow, which Charley had deliberately tried to forget, would be traumatic.

"In any event," he told the CIT chaps, producing a smile wider than any they had seen before, "we do take the family thing very much to heart. When you're part of the UBCO family," he said, getting to his feet, "you're back home."

Not quite understanding, both men stood up. Handshakes were extended. Charley escorted them to the door and opened it for them. With quick, light, but firm, pats on the back he sped them on their way. Beyond them, standing at his secretary's desk, he could see Bill Elston slowly leafing through the fattest folder of papers Charley Oakburn had ever seen.

His heart sank as he gestured Elston into his office. As the Chief of Internal Security sat down, he plunked the folder on Oakburn's desk. "Charley," he began, "how long have we known each other? Ten years?"

Oakburn sat stiffly in his chair. "Yes. Why?"

"You came in right after Woods Palmer left," Elston continued. "And Harry Kummel came in after you did."

"What has Harry got to do with this, Bill?"

"Everything, I hope."

"What the hell is that supposed to mean?"

"Otherwise," Elston said in a slow voice, "I'm going to have to pin it on you, Charley. And that won't look good at all." He paged slowly through the thick folder and stopped at one entry, then moved on to another. Finally, he looked up. "Tell me," he said then in a voice of compassion, "was it just that you had no idea what was happening? Or were they purposely keeping you in the dark?"

Charley Oakburn's jaw tightened. "I don't know what the hell you're talking about, Bill. Would you care to start at the beginning?"

"I sure would," Elston admitted. "But what I've got is the tail end of it, the most recent example. For instance, I don't know how far back it goes. Back to when Kummel came aboard? Later? And I don't know who else is involved. That's partly because it runs right to the top." He frowned. "You."

Oakburn's voice was thin but steady. "I still don't know what the hell you're talking about. But I *am* getting a little hot under the collar."

Elston surveyed his superior officer and saw no signs of heat, just the usual unruffled male-model exterior. "This stuff," he said then, touching the fat folder with his knuckles, "proves that E. Henry Kummel is fronting for the mob, Charley. He's been clever and careful, but he made one mistake. He suborned one of my own people into supplying him with a dossier on another of my people. It was supposed to go by me in a cloud of routine dust. Maybe it has before. Maybe I've been a patsy on several occasions. But on this one I wised up fast and started digging." He rapped the folder again. "This collection of information is like the tip of an iceberg, Charley. An old salt like you knows how much must be hiding below the surface."

The two men were silent for a while. Then Charley Oakburn sighed. "Damn it, Bill, is that what you're going to confront Harry with today?"

"I'm confronting both of you with it, and one of my own people, Mrs. Mulvey. And maybe one or two others. But you're getting a preview of it, Charley, because whenever they need top clearance, there's your goddamned initials or signature. I want to think they played you for a chump. Stupidity we can live with. I don't want to think you've been sailing under false colors. That we can't hush up or white-wash. We can only cut it out like a goddamned cancer."

Something was ticking slowly at the corner of Oakburn's massive jaw, right below his left ear. Elston watched it for a moment and realized the man was tightening and relaxing his jaw muscle. The tempo of it grew faster and more erratic.

"I plainly don't like your tone of voice," Oakburn said then in a voice that was still thin but no longer steady.

"It isn't in me to stay polite, Charley. I'm as mad at myself as I am at you. I should have seen this thing years ago and acted then. Shit. Woods Palmer hired me when he had his own back to the wall, fending off one of these Mafia takeover attempts. They're patient. They can afford to wait. And this time they've won. I've let them win. To what extent you've been guilty is something we'll get to the bottom of in time."

There was a knock at the door behind Elston. He swung half way around. E. Henry Kummel entered, but without Mrs. Mulvey. He stood in the doorway, a pleasant, slightly plump baldheaded man in his early fifties whose half glasses, perched on his nose, gave him a family-doctor look. His small eyes were green, Elston noted with something of a shock, brilliant green-blue.

He looked from one man to the other. "Charley," he began in an easy, no-tension tone, "I'm going to be five minutes more. Will it keep till then?"

"Ask him," Oakburn snapped, indicating Elston with his thumb.

Kummel frowned, but politely. "Five minutes, Bill?"

Elston's face contorted into a half smile. "Five minutes, Harry."

Kummel's glance moved back to Oakburn, then to the folder on the table, then returned to Elston. "Three minutes tops." He grinned charmingly and left the room.

"You think he'll come back?" Elston asked of the air at large.

At a desk in an adjoining office, Kummel tapped a number into a telephone and waited. The doctorly look was gone. His eyes had narrowed to green pinpoints as he glared at the telephone. He waited impatiently.

"Mr. Maggoranza there?" he asked at length. He glanced at his watch. "It's only noon." He listened for a while to some explanation. "All right. Very important. Tell him to meet Mr. Kaye for a drink at six p.m. sharp. He'll know where." He paused. "No excuses. It's a matter of life and death."

He put down the phone and got to his feet. Then he took up a post by the thin door that separated this office from Charley Oakburn's. Through it, as he had before, he could hear Bill Elston's voice raised in a kind of controlled anger.

". . . bottom of it, Charley, if it's the last thing I do," he heard Elston exclaim.

Alone for the moment, E. Henry Kummel smiled slightly.

PART FIVE

•

The Siege of Kinnerton Street

41

The cab dropped Bennett Brown in Kinnerton Street. As he walked into the courtyard he thought he saw a man in a dark suit blend back into the shadows behind the pewter Phantom III. Without checking stride, Ben entered the building, using the keys Julian had given him, and went upstairs.

In the drawing room Sykes-Maulby sat leafing through a magazine. "Back so soon? Did you have a meal?"

Brown shook his head. He pulled off his anorak and chucked it across the room into an armchair. Then he sat on the same sofa as the Englishman. "Not hungry. Did you ever mention my name to your buddy Palmer?"

Julian slowly put down the magazine. His long face with its long nose looked utterly bored. "Never, I do assure you."

Ben said in a flat voice: "I have ways of knowing."

Julian drew himself up. He was dressed in a variation of his normal daytime attire, a smoking jacket rather than a blazer, a thin strip of Liberty silk paisley replacing the school tie. "My dear, Ben," he said in a disinterested tone, "If you've detected a leak it may well be at the Swiss end. It was not I."

When the younger man remained silent, Sykes-Maulby went on, as if nothing had been said: "You sound cross. Food will do you good. And a drop of champers." He got to his feet. In the small kitchen he made clinking sounds. "Pâté and biscuits all right?"

"I'm not hungry, Julian."

"To hell with that, old man. I am."

Ben went to the telephone and dialed a number. Someone answered in an American voice after half a dozen rings. "Yeah?"

"What'd they do?" Ben asked.

"Huh?"

"After I left them."

"How would I know?"

Holding the telephone, Ben's knuckles tightened. "Let me talk to Tagliabue."

"Not here."

"Asshole." Ben slammed down the phone. He paced to the window and saw that a second shadow stood next to the first. They were taking no precautions about being seen. Something about their general shape, tall and slim in well-cut suits, told Ben they weren't anybody his father's London man, Enzo, would have sent on a job. Where the hell was Enzo, anyway? And why hadn't he left someone responsible at the phone?

"*Mangia, ragazzo caro,*" Julian said setting a tray on the cocktail table. Two glasses, the usual bottle of Veuve Clicquot in its orangey Ponsardin label, various crackers and a wedge of light, grainy pâté stood waiting for Ben. He felt his throat close over sickeningly as he surveyed this.

He sank down on the sofa again, a sense of something heavy and dangerous hanging over him. Wherever he went in the world, his father's men were able to produce a shield around him, an invisible field of force that obeyed him as it would Don B. He was not used to having his phone calls treated cavalierly.

He was also not used to being watched by people he hadn't arranged for. He was not used to dealing with slippery Limeys. He was especially not used to letting freelance smartasses like Curtiss escape with ther skin intact. He knew far too much, even to the Kondratiev side of it. As soon as Ben could separate him from Mary Lee, Curtiss would have to go.

And yet, Ben thought as he watched the Englishman pour two tulip glasses of champagne, Curtiss had been right on the button. There *was* a risk, trying to take over during the downward plunge of the long wave. If only for that alone, Curtiss had to go. If his estimate of the risk ever got back to some of the smartass MBAs who represented the money side of their families in the Gameplan consortium, the whole thing could blow up in Ben's face. Not dust. More likely blood and brains. His own.

Without realizing what he was doing, he had taken a glass, raised it silently to Julian and downed half of it in one bubbling gulp. He coughed. "Reason I wondered about you and Palmer," he picked up suddenly, as if only a second or two had intervened since his last accusation, "is that I found

Palmer's man Curtiss to be super-knowledgeable about my business and yours. It struck me somebody had been talking."

"That could well be," Julian admitted. "But there is another s—" The telephone rang. "Excuse me." He got to his feet. "Dearest girl," he said in a joyous voice. "Oh, really?" He was staring up at the ceiling as he listened. "Wee complication, however." He laughed. "Not that, for once. Not to worry. Carry on, ducks." He hung up, went back to the sofa, sat down and spread a bit of pâté on a cracker.

"But there is another side to it," he began again. "The weak link has always been Urs. I have my vices, as we all know, but they do not render me *non compos mentis*. Urs, however . . ."

"Who was that just called?"

"A rather attractive young woman named Miranda."

Ben managed to keep his face blank. Thanks to Enzo Tagliabue, he knew all about Miranda and the man Sykes-Maulby called Himself. Enzo had checked this house often once Julian had been folded into the consortium as an adviser. There was very little about the comings and goings, including the three escape routes, that Enzo hadn't reported.

"Look, Julian," Bennett Brown said then, "if you're putting off a date because I'm here, let the good times roll."

Sykes-Maulby grinned broadly. "I may just," he said then. He glanced at his watch. Then he yawned. Finding the canapé he had made, he munched on it for a while. "I don't suppose . . . ?" He stopped. "I mean, I could find a friend for you, old boy. No." He shook his head. "'Benedict the married man,'" he quoted. "Quite right, too. Baby on the way, all that."

Ben left his drink unfinished and returned to the window. There was no one in the courtyard. It was obvious they had been bodyguards for Himself, sweeping the area to make sure it was clear before either Himself or his mistress made an appearance.

A tiny blue Mini rounded the corner from Kinnerton Street into the lane and pulled up to one side of Sykes-Maulby's ancient Rolls, looking rather like a newborn colt with its mother. The door opened and an attractive woman with dark ringlets got out. She brought keys out of her bag and disappeared from Ben's view, heading for the entrance to Julian's house.

"Anything stirring out there?" the Englishman asked, coming up behind Ben.

The younger man shook his head. He often found quite irritating the way Julian spoke, using words like "enna-thin." Should he hang around at the window, driving the man crazy with anxiety? Or was it too boring to rib the Limey about his sainted national hero. Probably Himself came in by the Lowndes Square route. Ben was too tired to find it amusing. He turned back into the room.

A man in a slim, well-cut dark suit was holding a Cobra .38 on Julian, the short barrel level at his stomach.

Slowly Sykes-Maulby's arms went up over his head. Ben stared at the man's face, dark and hard to see in the intimate lighting. He looked like a *paisano*, but there was something about the way he wore the English-cut suit that made Ben mistrust this identification. Mediterranean? That sharp nose. Those high horizontal cheekbones. That faintly bluish cast to the lips. Turkish?

"You, too," the man said, flicking the Cobra's muzzle sideways at Bennett Brown. "Hoist 'em."

Ben obeyed. The slang told him the man watched U.S. television. "You have to be crazy," Ben said then. "This place is swarming with cops."

"Swarming. Not with cops." The man shifted the revolver back to Julian's midriff. "You know better than to act up, my lord?" His smile revealed perfect large white teeth. "You know there's a man in the flat downstairs with a gun in the right ear of the Honorable Mrs. Smith. Either of you get smart, she dies."

"What do you want here?" Sykes-Maulby demanded. His face had gone quite pale, Ben noticed.

"We want the missing guest." Again the toothy smile. "And when he gets here, the party begins."

The Englishman turned on Bennett Brown. "Is this some of your doing?" His voice was shaking with anger. "Are these your associates?"

"Try not to be any more of an egregious asshole than you already are," Ben sighed unhappily. "Listen," he asked the man with the gun, "is this strictly a cash heist or what?"

"Or what," the man mimicked.

The Englishman's face lost every vestige of color. He groaned. "You're not one of these bloody fanatics?" he demanded of the man with the gun. "Because we can't have it, do you understand?"

Teeth flashed as the man chuckled. "You have it, my lord. Oh, yes." He gestured with the gun. "Lean forward against the wall, both of you."

He fanned them for guns, then stepped away. "Sit down. This may take a while."

The telephone rang. Calmly, the man went to the phone and picked it up. "Yes?" He frowned. "One moment, please." He muffled the phone by pressing its mouthpiece against his thigh. "For you, Mr. Brown."

Ben got to his feet. "Watch what you say," the man warned him. "Get rid of the call. You'll talk to him in the morning. Understand?"

"Perfectly." Brown took the phone. "Who is this?"

"*Benedetto, caro,*" his father burst out. The connection to Palermo crackled with noise. "I am sorry. All of this is my fault. Enzo has sold me out in London. And here I am surrounded. My guards have deserted me. The villa is empty. I don't think I can hold out mu—" The line went dead.

"Hello? Hello?"

The man with the gun grabbed back the phone. He listened for a moment, then hung up. "What happened?"

Ben shrugged, trying for that look of bored disinterest he had often noticed Julian relying on in an emergency. "No idea."

The man hung up the phone. Then, as an afterthought, he yanked the cord out of the wall. "Okay, that's that. Back on the sofa, Benedetto," he added in a mocking tone.

42

Near Palermo, the night sky over Don B's villa was filled with small, moonlit clouds wandering across an intense indigo vastness like sheep. The elderly man, small as a jockey, huddled inside his own bedroom suite, listening to the night.

The perimeter of the enclave was unguarded, the villa deserted of help. The decapitation of his cook had ensured that. Now, without a telephone, his isolation was complete. He could taste it. If the tall man were to call him to announce the death of Don Gino, he would be unable to.

The bedroom suite had been designed as the castle keep of the place, impregnable if necessary. It included his bedroom, a separate sitting room and bath, even a larder of canned and dried food. Tough window screen kept out such possible weapons as smoke or tear-gas grenades. The walls were eighteen inches thick, of poured concrete whose core was one-inch-thick iron rod, that most impregnable of building materials the Italians call *cemento armato*, armed cement, ready to resist anything from a quake to an anti-tank missile.

Its flat top, as broad as a tennis court, offered no cover. The one escape hatch on the roof could be opened only from inside. Otherwise, the suite was as unbreachable as human ingenuity could make it. It was not an artifact of peace. The spirit of war infused its every corner and curve.

And war had been declared. The open announcement had been Rosanna's severed head. But the more serious declaration had been silent: the failure of the tall man to report success. As always in life, Don B realized as he sat there in darkness, silence speaks loudest. The taste of his defeat was like brass in his mouth.

He glanced at his watch. At eleven he planned to turn on the *telegiornale* program. If a man of respect such as Don Gino had died, surely the television would carry such news and, with it, deliverance.

Meanwhile, he brooded over the treachery of Enzo in London. For thirty of his forty-five years Enzo had served Don B in London, no matter where Don B might be, in America, in Calabria or, as now, in Sicily. For thirty years he has been trustworthy and honorable. Overnight, he had deserted his responsibilities. Don B had only learned of this through the Corsican, Achille Gamba, who had telephoned earlier this evening from London.

Gamba had first spoken to Enzo to warn him that a terrorist group had been splashing money around Corsica and Nice seeking to buy information. They were to be shunned.

No one in organized crime is against terrorism, *per se*, since it helps disestablish a city or nation and leave it even more at the mercy of its underworld. By shattering the normal shield of the law an act of terror shows the average citizen that he has been abandoned by the very people to whom he pays heavy taxes for protection.

But there is a contradiction at the heart of all this which Gamba and Don B understood quite well. Within any status quo, the mob finds its niche, pays its bribes, arranges its conduits of information and settles in to do business. To disrupt that status by an act of terror means that doing business becomes chancy. Police are shifted. Well-corrupted officers slip away to other jobs, leaving a fresh bunch hungry for bribes. Suborned politicos fall, while their successors flounder about, not knowing which bagman is which. The strategist of organized crime knows that his business relationships with terror groups give him the most trouble and present the greatest risk.

Achille Gamba had learned that this particular group planned nothing less than holding for ransom one of the highest-ranking men in Britain. The crime would have had too destabilizing an effect on England. It would bring forth all the disadvantages of chaos and none of the benefits.

Enzo had agreed to watch himself with such political savages on the loose. But to Gamba a worrisome note of insincerity pinged like a warning in the background. So he had promptly put the matter to Don B by telephone. Only Don B understood what Enzo had to sell: that the apartment of the English milord who worked with Ben was the very place used for illicit assignations with a married inamorata.

This was immediately confirmed when Don B called Enzo and was unable to get anyone to put the man on the telephone line. It was unheard of, a hireling of Don B, his own cousin as a matter of fact, showing so little respect. Showing, in fact, disrespect. A capital offense.

Since Ben stood at that moment in the heart of the matter, Don B instantly called to warn him. Then the phone had been cut.

Don B shook his head slowly, his only outward expression of being upset or angry. As a matter of fact he was neither. He was resigned. In his dry mouth, his own death had the flavor of a bullet, the greasy taste of lead and the dangerous tang of brass. He had lived a good life, measured by what counted. They would come for him tonight or tomorrow and he would stand proud. But perhaps, before then, would come news that Don Gino was dead.

Kneeling by his bed, Don B folded his hands and began to pray.

43

The tableau had remained the same for nearly fifteen minutes. The dark, sharp-faced terrorist in the well-cut suit sat upright in a straight chair near the window. From time to time he craned his neck to look down into the courtyard. But most of the time his glance shifted from one end of the sofa to the other, where Bennett Brown and Sykes-Maulby sat, talking sporadically, falling silent, sipping champagne and listening, as the terrorist was, for the sounds of new activity outside.

"This couldn't have happened," Ben remarked, "at a worse time."

Julian's sharp, hard laugh was more of a bark. "Do you have any idea for whom they're waiting?"

Ben thought for a moment. "I even know who sold them the floor plans and the alarm system wiring chart."

"What?" Sykes-Maulby sounded shocked. "One of yours?"

"Whatever they paid him he's got no time to spend it. He's a dead man."

They brooded in silence for a while. The Englishman looked up. "What did you mean it couldn't have happened at a worse time?"

"That phone call was my father. He's pinned down in Palermo. I'm pinned down here. These bastards have made it possible for somebody to kill my father without me being able to lift a finger."

"Is that what angers you?" Julian sneered. "It doesn't bother you to think of them holding my man for ransom?"

"Those will be the big headlines," Ben agreed almost amiably. "My God, could anybody think of a bigger story? But you know Italians, Julian. The polar ice cap could melt. Mars could be on a collision course. But my father's well-being would come first."

"Senti, ragazzo," Sykes-Maulby murmured in an undertone. Then, continuing in Italian: "Before my man arrives, we can still overpower this shit and you can be on your way to Palermo."

The unaccustomed quiet of the words made the terrorist look up from the Cobra .38 he cradled in both hands. "Be careful," he warned. "You don't know what languages I speak."

"*Sí, dottore,*" Ben called to him. "Can I take a leak?"

A sneering smile showed most of the man's bright teeth. "In the bathroom? You think I'm stupid? Use the kitchen sink."

Ben got to his feet. "It's too high."

"Then piss in your pants."

Brown walked slowly into the kitchen. The terrorist followed until he was standing in the doorway, able to watch both men by shifting his eyes through an arc of ninety degrees.

"Snap it up," he ordered, dimly sensing his problem.

The Englishman was on his feet now. "Next?" he asked, approaching the man with the gun.

Suddenly aware, the man shouted: "Stop right there!"

Behind him Ben moved back to him on cross-country sneakers. The man whirled. "Hold it! No more walking!"

He was less than a yard from each of his captives, but the angle was fatally against him. He hadn't had time to see Julian pick up the heavy champagne bottle being held behind his right leg. Ben had.

He took a step towards the man. "I'm finished. Let me out."

The man's bright eyes in their muddy whites seemed to grow wider. "You think I'm stupid?" he demanded.

"As long as you have that .38, fella, I think you're Einstein." Ben smiled engagingly. Then, out of nowhere, he suddenly doubled over in a fit of coughing. The man with the gun stared wild-eyed at him for only a second. It took less time than that for Julian's up-from-under swoop. Holding the Veuve Clicquot by the neck, he swung in an arc that ended when the reinforced bottom smashed into the man's chin.

Both Sykes-Maulby and Bennett Brown heard the sharp click of bone. Ben swiveled sideways and wrapped his hands over the gun to prevent it from falling. The Englishman caught the dark man under the arms and let him settle slowly in the doorway. Then he brought the champagne bottle down hard on the area where his neck ran up past his ear to his temple.

He stepped over him and joined Ben in the kitchen. "We

don't have long. Himself gets here any second. There's a
fire-escape ladder down the wall from the kitchen window."

"They'd pick me off."

"No. I'm going down the front stairs. They won't notice
you."

"They'll chop you down."

Julian frowned and pulled at his lower lip. "I don't think
they want a lot of noise now."

The frown deepened. "Too right," he growled, "We'll both
take the escape ladder. I'll go first and get into the flat below."
He took the Cobra from Ben. "You keep on going. There's a
pub down Kinnerton Street. Report the whole thing to 999,
then buzz off on your family business."

"What do you expect to pull, even if you do get into the flat
without them seeing you?"

"My problem, old man. Let's go."

44

The Rabbit Castle, to give it its English translation, managed
to combine Swiss cleanliness and lowdown seediness in one
crowded restaurant not far from the Hotel Basel. It was its
nearness also to his mistress's apartment on the Alley of Ten
Thousand Virgins that made Urs Rup choose it as a place
where he and Palmer could talk with some degree of privacy.

Nobody who was anybody ate at the Rabbit Castle except
noisy students and those few elderly indigents that even a
neat Swiss society somehow cannot manage to make disappear. The atmosphere steamed with perspiration and cooking
smells as Palmer pushed his way to the far end of a long
table. He ordered a Feldschlosschen light beer and sat back,
letting noisy waves of laughter, argument and table-thumping
wash over him.

On the whole, he felt he had Urs Rup where he wanted
him: scared and panicky. The opening gun had been to
surround him with an odor of criminality. That he happened
to have been lunching with an extremely nervous and very
well-known client was a bonus. Palmer's subsequent interview with Urs had been more specific: connections with

organized crime, unauthorized personal speculations in foreign securities, drug use, *und so weiter.*

There is very little behavior officially forbidden to a Swiss bank. But there are many things a banker cannot be seen to do. Urs was guilty of most of them. It only remained to play a toccata of guilt on the keyboard of his soul.

Palmer grinned at the figure of speech. Eleanora would like that one. When he got back to her tonight, he'd have to remember it. She needed cheering up. Knowing how much she hated big cities, even Swiss ones, he knew she was anxious to return to their mountain solitude in Morcote. Of course, she would never say so right out. But Palmer knew she was aching to get back.

At that moment, Margit, Urs Rup's mistress, entered the Rabbit Castle and stood in the doorway. She had met Palmer once before but couldn't be expected to know him by sight.

Palmer examined her at his leisure. She was a well-fleshed woman without being fat. The way she'd dressed for a visit to this student hangout told Palmer her arrival was not accidental. The extremely tight bodyshirt and even tighter white jeans gave her almost the look of a very expensive *bratwurst,* one that promised to be delicious to eat. Obviously Urs had asked her to join them, probably as a witness.

Palmer beckoned. She sat across the table from him, examined his stein of beer and took a long drink from it. Palmer enjoyed masterful people setting their own stage for themselves. He'd done it often enough and appreciated a good performance.

"*Zweimal,*" he shouted to a passing waitress. Her raddled face swiveled towards him, nodded, moved on.

"A pleasant variation from having to look at Urs," Palmer began. "Will he be late?"

"Very."

Palmer frowned. "He's not coming?"

"You're very perceptive, Herr Palmer." She finished off the rest of his beer just as the waitress brought two more. Margit handed her a ten-franc note, then pushed Palmer's beer across to him.

"He sent you to buy beer," Palmer remarked in a dry tone. "Where the hell is he? Flown the coop?"

"*Ganz* perceptive," Margit agreed.

"The crafty little bastard."

"It was my idea, Herr Palmer."

"The bearer of such rotten news should at least call me Woods."

"Woods," she responded, handling the "w" with perfection. "I told him if he didn't get out of Switzerland, he was a dead man."

"And Urs always does what you tell him."

"Not often enough for his own good." She lifted her stein by the handle and clinked it with Palmer's. "To absent friends."

Palmer chuckled. "You're a cool young lady."

"You see," she went on more thoughtfully, her eyes fixed on Palmer's face amid the noisy background, "Urs isn't as secure at Bank Rup as the world imagines. He's the son, true enough. But the father is not senile. The kind of blackmail you were holding over Urs would have blown him out of the driver's seat almost overnight. You know Swiss fathers."

"It was not my intention to demolish Urs," Palmer confessed. "In fact, he's beneath contempt, in a slimy way. What I wanted from him was information."

"Another excellent reason for him to get out of Switzerland."

"I see." Palmer sipped his cool, heavy-bodied beer.

"Please don't think of me as an antagonist, Herr P—Woods. I have always been an admirer, never an opponent."

"Where did Urs go?"

"I can't tell you that."

They sat in silence, watching each other, the shouting and steam in the great room engulfing them without in any way altering their expressions or the guarded way they sat.

Palmer got to his feet. "Check. Mate, for all I know." He managed another smile. "Thanks for the beer."

Outside, although the night was warm, he shivered as he made his way back to the Hotel Basel. A cab was letting off a party of four. Upstairs in their suite, Eleanora was waiting. European women, Palmer thought. Deceptively casual. More manipulative than their American sisters, who hadn't yet learned how to camouflage what they were up to.

The cab started to leave. Palmer whistled and opened the door. "Take me to the airport and back?"

The cab moved swiftly along a four-lane highway guarded by high cyclone fencing on both sides. This thin finger of Switzerland prodded some twenty kilometers into France to reach the airport at Mulhouse.

Palmer talked to the few reservationists remaining on duty

this late in the evening. None was able to report a departure in the last hour or two, which led Palmer to believe that Urs had flown the coop much earlier. Except that he'd talked to him at six o'clock and made the date at the Rabbit Castle.

Palmer found an assistant manager of the airport who spoke fluent English. "We do have," he said, "quite a volume of general aviation." An assistant operations manager reported that a Learjet charter with one passenger had taken off an hour before.

Destination, Malta.

Back at the hotel, Palmer found Eleanora watching a television program in German. After they kissed, she clicked the program to French and continued listening. It seemed to be a documentary about the perils of building one's own home, what with uninterested architects, thieving contractors and careless workmen. In Switzerland? She shifted the program to the Italian channel and kept watching.

Palmer undressed and got in bed. Malta was obviously the jet's first touchdown, he thought, perhaps for refueling. Then on to... where? One of the Arab countries? The pilot wouldn't have had to file a flight plan beyond Malta. But once there he'd need to do a new one. Was it worth trying to call Malta airport?

Palmer yawned. The program was ending. Eleanora clicked off the set. "Woods," she said, "don't go to sleep yet. Elfi has given me an idea."

Palmer sat up in bed. "About what?"

"About what to do with my life."

He laughed out loud. "What a good friend to have."

"She does well with her translation bureau here. I think I might open one in Lugano." She paused, eyeing him. "It would require a loan from you."

Palmer said nothing. The idea had come to him so far out of the blue that he had no ready response. This was his second time tonight batting against female European pitchers.

"I thought—" He stopped. "Not that Lugano's a big city. But I thought you hated that whole urban nine-to-five life. Rush hour. Noise."

"*You* hate it."

"I don't *hate* it," he corrected her. "I would prefer to live without it. But..." Palmer surveyed her face. "I know. It can get boring on that mountain top."

"For you as for me." Eleanora got in bed beside him. "And,

after all, I can drive into Lugano quite handily each morning. It can't be more than a twenty-minute trip."

"In traffic."

She was silent. "What about you?" she asked then. "You're up to your ears in intrigue once again. By the time you're finished with Urs Rup he will be mincemeat."

"He's gone. Escaped." Palmer rolled over and reached for the remote control TV instrument. "Either I let it drop, or I shift into high gear. Knowing how much you longed to get back to solitude, it was an easy choice."

She took the control away from him and put it out of reach. "Woods, we must be frank with each other. Neither of us really wants a full-time vacation for the rest of our lives."

"I don't know." He twisted onto his back again, as if the sheets had grown too hot for him. "I don't know. You'd think at my age a man would know what he wants. There isn't that much time left to live, but here I am, not knowing how I want to live it."

45

Mary Lee Hunter lay quietly in her bed, eyes closed but wide awake. Curtiss had got up around midnight and, as far as she could tell, was standing out on the balcony of their living room, watching the London night. Did it often happen, she wondered, that lovers grew cold towards each other when a separation was in the offing?

That was what had been happening. The last time, in Paris, her flight had been too precipitous to notice this unhappy-making phenomenon. But now that she'd announced her departure tomorrow and got a ticket through the concierge at the hotel, a coolness began to separate her from Curtiss.

Why did she feel she was betraying him? Why did his unspoken attitude, the way he looked at her, what he failed to say more than the words he spoke, make her *feel* like a traitor? It wasn't as if she had masqueraded as a lady of leisure. She had business on Friday in New York and Boston. Curtiss knew it.

She had to be insane, trying to put together something lasting with a man who lived in another hemisphere.

On a different planet, to tell the truth. He hardly even thought as she did. That little speech of his at the wine bar had been meant to put Ben off the track. But Mary Lee could recognize that Curtiss really believed what he'd said. Certainly he'd delivered it with enough sincerity to worry Mary Lee about her own dedication to a career.

Why put all that time and energy and anguish into getting to the top of the totem pole, when the damned thing was full of termites?

But did he really believe it made no difference who ran things, the good guys or the bad guys? Even his friend and mentor, the renowned Palmer, didn't feel that way. Palmer recognized a difference between the sharp operators of capitalism and the agents of organized crime.

How could she contemplate devoting her life to the man she loved if he believed in something she knew to be wrong? The sex was good. But in between what would they talk about that didn't lead to a fight? Curtiss was too cynical. While she was... what? Would he call her naïve? Naïve or innocent or what?

Believing. That was probably the antonym. Mary Lee knew she still believed. A girl raised the way she had been could hardly have grown up otherwise. But the warmth and security of her family was based on a concept that Curtiss considered not too different from the way Ben's family operated.

She sighed and turned on her side, trying to see in the darkness where Curtiss had got to. It hardly mattered if he were right or wrong, did it? If her family and Ben's family were two sides of one coin? What mattered was that without belief, one had no life.

What had Curtiss said before they went to meet Ben? "When we get out of this, we'd better think of something marvelous to do with our lives."

Well, they were out of it, if you could believe Ben's promises of friendship. Now, what was their marvelous plan for a life together? If any?

The phone rang. Mary Lee's body flinched at the demanding noise. The double buzz started again but stopped in mid-ring. Curtiss had obviously picked it up in the other room, thinking she was asleep. Mary Lee lifted the phone by the bedside.

"Curtiss?" a man asked. "Can you talk?"

"Do you know what time it is in London?"

"I'm sorry," the man responded. "It couldn't wait."

"I don't have my scrambler," Curtiss told him.

"We don't need security on this call. They already know what I'm going to say."

"Who's they?"

"I just came from a meeting with Charley Oakburn. There were others there. It's not important who. The pre-meeting was the tipoff. Just Oakburn and your humble servant, William Fathead Elston, former Chief of Internal Security."

"Former?" Curtiss nearly yelped.

"There is some kind of conspiracy at UBCO which reached up from my own Mrs. Mulvey through Harry Kummel directly to the Executive Vice-President, Operations. Can you picture it, Curtiss? Charley Oakburn and the Mafia?"

"What?"

"When Miss Hunter reopened that stuff you dreamed up for Jet-Tech, Mulvey tried to get your dossier out of the files and— Anyway, I called it a conspiracy. It's not. It's an official thread woven into the fabric of UBCO. I mean, when you have Charley Oakburn protecting it, how secret can it be?"

"He's the mob's man at UBCO?"

"I'm afraid I lost my temper before I thought of asking a question that sensible," Elston replied. "As a matter of fact, you could say I was shouting. You could also say I quit."

"Bill!"

"Fifteen years guarding UBCO's innards from the enemy? Then I find him sitting in the catbird seat. That is not what I'd call a sterling testimonial to my abilities. So I quit."

"Who knows this?"

"Who cares? A new wind is blowing through the corridors of power. At next week's board meeting, when they nominate the new directors, a few old faces will remain for display purposes. And the new ones won't look like gangsters. But by the time the annual meeting's over and the proxies are counted, United Bank and Trust Company, NA, largest commercial bank in the world, will be a wholly-owned subsidiary of organized crime."

Curtiss was silent for a moment. Mary Lee could hear his

heightened breathing. "So will quite a few of UBCO's leading customers," he said then.

"What's that?"

"What're you going to do now, Bill?"

"I've already done it. Drop 23. I'm taking a vacation and not returning. Charley Oakburn seems to think he can find a new chief for my department, with Mrs. Mulvey as his assistant. He's quite right."

Quietly, Mary Lee replaced the phone and got out of bed. She found Curtiss's lightweight dressing gown and put it on. Then she padded on bare feet into the living room as he was finishing his conversation.

"Maybe so, Bill," he was saying. "I'm absolutely flattened. Thanks for calling." He hung up and refused to look at her.

"Curtiss."

"Shit." He got to his feet and went to the tray on which was a bowl of slowly melting ice cubes. He dropped some in a glass and added the dregs of two bottles of club soda. He watched the result fizz weakly, then began sipping it.

"Curtiss?"

He shrugged. "You heard. What more can I add?"

Mary Lee made a caught-in-the-act face. "You knew I was listening?"

He shrugged again, irritably. "Not important."

"It's bad, isn't it?"

"So bad I'm calling Palmer." He glanced at his watch.

"Curtiss?"

"Stop Curtissing me!" he yelled.

"Yeek."

"I'm sorry," he said in a disgusted one. "This was just what Julian warned us was happening."

"Curtiss." She stopped, made another face. "Sorry. Look, there was only one thing I didn't understand."

"Only one. Perfect."

"What's Drop 23?"

He stared at her for a long moment, then smiled weakly. "Christ, your mind scares me sometimes." He sat down and finished the last of his stale soda. "Drop 23 is a lockbox we keep for emergencies. It's normally empty. In fact, it hasn't been used for years now. But a drop's a drop. You know, a private, secure place you can leave something."

"In an UBCO safe deposit vault?"

He shook his head. "It's a neighborhood branch of Citibank,

our deadly rival." He glanced at his watch again. "The longer
I wait, the longer time they have to figure out what Bill
meant by Drop 23. Nobody in the home office knows, but a
few of us field reps do. When's your flight?"

"Ten-thirty tomorrow morning."

"Let's see if I can book the seat next to you."

46

The tall man guided the gray Fiat 127 onto the ferry boat at
Villa San Giovanni. Across the straits of Messina, Sicily lay in
darkness. A necklace of amber highway lights traced the
perimeter of this corner of the triangular island on which so
much bloody history had been made.

Still operating under the Ugo Pastore name, the tall man
had left Sabbia D'Oro only this afternoon, following lunch.
Don Gino had kept him by his side that long because the
changeover in fidelity was something about which Don Gino
had to reassure himself.

When the tall man had Don Gino in the sights of his deer
gun, the old man's guts a split-second away from exploding
into a cascade of blue and crimson, there had been what
amounted to a revelation.

The tall man was in no way religious. Like most Italian
men he viewed the church as a racket which preyed mainly
on women, but which enjoyed such immunity that it must be
given respect and lip service. So it was not a religious
revelation that had taken place.

It was perhaps more accurate to call it a sudden attack of
prudence. A vision had come to the tall man of Don B
besieged in his villa, surrounded by hired help, while Don
Gino relaxed amid his relatives and friends, his *paisani*,
infinitely more secure than the man who had ordered his
extinction. In that blinding flash of prudence, the tall man
had realized he was on the wrong side. And in a second flash,
which followed far faster than the eye could see, he had
returned the deer rifle to his side and announced his presence in Sabbia D'Oro on a mission of peace, not death.

It had taken some days before Don Gino could place full

credence in this startling change of allegiance. Not that such flipflops didn't happen, discouragingly often, within the honored society. There was no honor, only prudence. In his inside jacket pocket, the tall man had stowed the fruits of prudence, a packet of 100,000 lire notes that made a bulge three million thick over his heart. But Don Gino had delayed the tall man from setting forth on the last leg of his journey for a more practical reason than simply testing his new loyalty. Don Gino wanted to make sure his old comrade and trusted business partner, Don B, would be utterly helpless in his Sicilian isolation.

First the guillotined cook. Then the simple bribing of the guards. Finally the withdrawal of all the house servants under various threats. Now Don B sat alone, easy prey for the tall man.

"You know the layout of his villa?" Don Gino had asked so many times in the past few days. He and the tall man spoke English, for security's sake, and used American slang for faster communication.

"Every inch."

"He will hole up in the innermost chamber, like a whelk. I am told it can't be breached."

The tall man made a downward movement of his mouth, deprecating in a cautious way. He, too, was still feeling his way with his new employer. "Men made it," he stated flatly. "A man can unmake it."

Now, as he stood at the railing of the ferry and watched the shore of Sicily looming in the darkness, he ran over the layout of the villa near Palermo and realized that, in his eagerness to impress Don Gino, he had bitten off quite a mouthful.

No ordinary weapon would do. Why had he been so foolhardy as to leave his new employer with the idea that this would be easy? Thinking of Don Gino, a faint, reluctant smile curled one corner of the tall man's mouth. Little did he know who had actually killed his precious son in Paris. If he suspected that he had sent his son's killer to murder the man who had ordered the death, what would the old thief have thought? What wild tangle of revenge would crisscross his brain? But perhaps he was practical, as well as Calabrese.

Perhaps he would be able to slake his fiery thirst to revenge his son's death by reflecting that the same man had dispatched his hated enemy, Don B. Perhaps he was a philos-

opher, the sage of Sabbia D'Oro, and saw the terrible irony in
these deaths. Or perhaps, the tall man reflected, he was
already making plans to eliminate the killer of Don B simply
to stop his mouth.

The tall man shivered in the dark night. It was possible—
anything was possible with these old Ndraghetisti—that Don
Gino was using Don B as bait. The goat in the tiger trap.

The tall man was supposed to kill the goat. But then what?
He would know too much. He would be a tiger without a
friend on the pitiless landscape of Sicily and Calabria. Every
hand would be against him. He would die, if not at once,
then within days. Hours.

As the ferry boat rattled into its mooring, the tall man
looked back at Calabria. He was in a tight place. Perhaps he
should have killed Don Gino and taken his chance. Perhaps
his revelation of prudence had trapped him into a worse fate.
He was in for it, that was clear. He had no way of getting at
Don B in his impenetrable keep. But as soon as he did, his
life would be forfeit.

Not easy, being the cutting edge of Mafia vengeance. He
watched the lights of Reggio Calabria across the strait. They
twinkled like stars in the waves of heat coming off the waters
of the Mediterranean. How to kill Don B? How to escape
scot-free?

Suddenly the tall man grinned in the darkness. He slapped
the bulge of banknotes over his heart. He hopped into his
tiny car and stirred the engine to life. He gunned the motor
and rolled forward over metal ways onto the dock. He
glanced about him for signposts to Palermo. He had a few
hours of driving before him, but he would arrive at the villa
before dawn, surely.

And he would be *inside* the villa a moment later. The tall
man laughed like a boy. Why hadn't he realized before that
he possessed the supreme weapon: Don B's confidence. His
own victim would give him entry. His own victim would
make him welcome. That was how he would penetrate the
inner defense of the villa. The rest would be simple. A bit of
piano wire. *Finito*.

As for eluding those who intended to silence him, that was
still a problem. But the tall man had never believed for one
moment that he would ever enjoy a life free of problems.
One thing at a time was his motto.

47

Julian Sykes-Maulby, clinging to the ladder fastened into the inner wall of his Kinnerton Street house, watched Bennett Brown escape in the darkness below him. He pocketed the snub-nose Cobra .38 and calculated his chances.

Inside the gound floor flat everything lay in darkness. He had no idea if the kitchen, to which he would have access, would be occupied or empty. Ben would get to a telephone at one of the pubs along Kinnerton Street and dial 999. The whole thing would take under five minutes, after which the telephone operator at 999 would have to make contact with a higher-up.

The alert would then move through the Metropolitan Police with the speed of treacle on a snowy day, ending nowhere since it was not the regulation coppers who had responsibility for guarding Himself and the lovenest on Kinnerton Street.

Julian glanced at his watch and decided that in perhaps another five minutes some overly bright copper would twig and get on the blower to one of Himself's guards. That meant a total of fifteen minutes to sound alarm stations and begin swooping down on Kinnerton Street. If Ben called 999. There was always the possibility that in his haste to succor his father, Ben would let England down.

With or without Ben, Julian reckoned, Himself would surely have walked into the trap in under fifteen minutes. The worst, most scandalous, most potentially dangerous ransom heist in history would have sprung. Calculating the stakes, Dear God, what ransom could these fanatics not demand on a platter?

His eyes adjusted now to the dark, Sykes-Maulby eased open, inch by inch, the double-hung sash of the kitchen window. He paused to listen. Nothing. He breathed through his mouth, softly, as he crawled in over the ledge and moved on carpet slippers to the doorway that led into the parlor.

The floor plan of this flat was identical to his own on the

floor above. He was standing about where that silly sod upstairs had been standing when Ben had begun his fatal attack of coughing and Julian had fed the terrorist an overdose of champagne.

The Englishman grinned evilly in the darkness. He slid an inch past the doorway. A faint nightlight near the front door of the darkened reception room showed him Miranda Smith sitting in one armchair. A man in a well-cut dark lounge suit sat in the other. The gun in his hands was not a Cobra .38 but a far more destructive .9 mm Browning which for most criminal purposes had replaced the old Colt Army .45 as a close-in weapon of brutal destruction. Loaded with magnum rounds, the Browning could punch out the center of a man's body.

". . . possibly work," Miranda was chattering. "I'm alone here and will be. You're totally barking up the wrong tree."

In response, the man glanced at his wristwatch. He switched the Browning to the other hand, got up and peered out at the courtyard.

"If it's me you're after," Miranda went on in a voice that quavered slightly, but not too much, "it's another mistake. My husband and I are poor as churchmice."

Julian realized that her captor had yet to say anything. Miranda, suspecting the target of all this must be Himself, had as yet no confirmation of her fears. She was whistling entirely in the dark. She had no way of knowing what had happened to her friend and protector upstairs, but pretty much expected the worst.

The angles of fire were not right, Julian saw. On the other hand, if he could interpose himself between Miranda and the chap at the window, he had a fair chance in the subsequent shootout of getting his man and keeping Miranda punctureproof. The brouhaha would surely convince the rest of the terrorists that the trap had sprung prematurely and they must flee.

But there were terrifying holes in that line of thinking. For one thing he had no way of knowing how many more were outside or inside the house. Nor could he be sure how dedicated they were. If the answers to both were favorable, shooting it out with this man could only lead to ultimate defeat. The man would be dead. Perhaps Julian with him. But Miranda would still be a hostage and Himself would not yet have been warned.

So he'd somehow have to capture this bugger and hold him till an alarm could be sounded. Not bloody easy.

" . . . get up and stretch my legs?" Miranda was asking.

The man at the window whirled, automatic leveled at her. She settled back in the armchair.

"It's not easy with you so silent," she began again.

The man left the window and took up his post again in the chair facing Miranda. He had the same sharp, Mediterranean look as the other one. They were not brothers, Julian reflected, but they were kinsmen or tribesmen. Hard to tell.

He had begun looking at the fully-carpeted floor for a place he might safely place a foot without producing a squeak. He decided that the small Iranian rug he had bought in Tehran offered a bit of extra cushioning. Silently, the Cobra aimed at the back of the terrorist's neck, he took one step forward.

Miranda saw him. He was sure that slight flick of her eyes would give him away, but the gunman didn't stir. Holding his breath, Sykes-Maulby gave Miranda a series of palm-uplifted gestures along the lines of "keep it going."

"Can't imagine what you silly men have in mind," she instantly burst forth in a high, girlish voice. "The very idea of breaking in here like a burglar and hoping to scare a poor woman to death with your ugly gun. I don't know when I've seen anything quite as cowardly and comical at the same time. As if you could ever scare a woman like me with a gun. It's just not possible, you silly man," she rattled on as Julian took another step forward, any possible sound covered by her voice.

"And as for getting money out of it, you have absolutely come to the wrong country. There is no money in Britain, you clod. The whole world knows that. It's something anybody could have told you if you'd only had the sense to ask. We're dead broke."

The Englishman reversed the Cobra in his hand and hefted it. With its almost non-existent barrel, the short Colt left a lot to be desired as a club. He could barely hold onto it. He measured the distance between himself and the terrorist, particularly the hand in which he held the Browning .9 leveled at Miranda.

"But the funniest thing of all," she was chattering wildly, "is the way you repay us for centuries of helping you dismal sods with your own sordid lives, showing you how to use modern weapons and technology and educating you in cheating and chicanery and turning you from simpleminded Bedouin sheep-buggers to sophisticated cutthroats who—"

Frowning with concentration, Julian launched a kick that hit the man's gun-wrist and sent the heavy automatic clattering across the room.

"Hold it," he barked.

The man was on his feet in a crouch. He swiveled to look into the Cobra's muzzle. Still he said nothing.

"Mandy," the Englishman said. "Get rope or some ties. Belts. We have to truss this turkey for fifteen minutes in the oven."

She picked up the Browning. "Ugly thing." She went into the other room and returned with a handful of ties. "You took your sweet time, Jolly. It was not great fun."

She held the gun on the terrorist while Julian knotted his hands behind him. "The phone's cut," she said then. "How are we to—?"

"I'm going downstairs in a moment," he explained. "I will have a gun in each hand, quite like John Wayne. There will be the most ungodly racket you ever heard, dear girl."

"Jolly, they'll hurt you."

"Not before I rouse half of Belgravia with the noise."

48

"Did I wake you?" Curtiss asked. He was talking to Palmer on the telephone in the living room of the hotel suite. Mary Lee, anxiety-free, now that he was going back to the States with her, lay asleep in the bedroom.

"No," Palmer said. "I was sitting here with a map and a pocket calculator. Urs Rup flew the coop. Private jet. First stop, Malta. Then where?"

Curtiss sat without speaking for a moment, absorbing the news. "Look on the bright side, he can't handle buy and sell orders any more," he said finally. "We've broken the weak link."

"Hold it." Palmer left the phone, came back a moment later. "Eleanora's asleep in the bedroom, I closed the door." He chuckled. "Your lady asleep?"

"Like a log."

"While we agonize. What do you think?"

"Why look beyond Malta?" Curtiss asked. "It's got potential on its own."

"Um. No real government supervision of securities and exchange," Palmer was muttering to himself. "But he'd have to grease an immensity of palms before he could think of himself as home free." A long and expensive pause ensued. Normally Curtiss would have hurried along the conversation, but Palmer was paying for the suite at the Carlton. The silence continued for at least 50 pence worth.

It was the older man who finally spoke. "Why did you call me?"

"Bad news from Elston." Curtiss reported briefly, answered a few even briefer questions from Palmer and waited. A silence worth just under a pound ensued.

"Palmer? You still there?"

"Ah, shit," Palmer muttered. "Julian was right about UBCO after all. Have you told him?"

"Not yet."

"It's so frustrating!" Palmer burst out. "I can't get my feet out of the goddamned quagmire. Flypaper. We no sooner close down their Basel operation than they pop up right at the top of UBCO, thumbing their noses."

Curtiss cleared his throat. "I hope you don't take this wrong," he began, "but when did somebody elect you Chief White Knight? I mean, do you really care who runs Western civilization?"

"If you mean I ought to stop worrying about life, you can go—" He stopped himself with an effort. "Curtiss, you continue to amaze me," he went on in a calmer tone. "Do you really believe there is no difference between them and us? Do you really think it doesn't matter who runs our society?"

"You know how I feel," Curtiss responded in what even he could hear was a mulish tone of voice. "The people who care about such things are the people who already run the world. The rest of us couldn't care less."

Palmer fell into another of his costly delays. "I suppose," he said at length in what was for him a resigned voice, "it's a natural result of your consorting with cops and bad guys. It's your job to understand how criminals think. But that doesn't mean you lose the ability to tell them from the good guys."

"Oh, for Christ's sake."

Curtiss tried to sort out a polite way of telling a long-time friend he was full of shit. Then, "Palmer, nearly every criminal I've chased and caught for UBCO has been a good guy gone bad. He's been a treasurer or a cabinet minister or a military consultant or a chief of police or a senator or a corporation executive and even, once, the pastor of a Fifth Avenue congregation. You have the bloody, fucking nerve to tell me I should see a difference between the good guys and the bad guys?"

"But—"

"Somewhere in the world there *are* good guys," Curtiss rolled on recklessly. "Somewhere there are incorruptible men and women of principle. I know they're out there, Palmer, even though I've never met them. But I can tell you, none of them has anything to do with the world of business."

"Jesus!"

"The world of business is filled with enough hypocrisy to flood the Grand Canyon to the rim. Everybody lies. Everybody cheats. Everybody steals. And just because a few of them *also* murder doesn't put haloes over those who have yet to pull a trigger. Or pay for it. They will, Palmer. They will."

"Curtiss, you—"

"The fact that one sector of business doesn't murder is a recent event in history when you remember all the killing they paid for in the last century, all the strikebreaking violence, the frameups. When the need arises, all your good guys take off their white hats and revert to slaughter. And then you'll be sitting where I am now, absolutely unable to tell one player from another."

His pulse was hammering in his throat. He stopped talking and laid the telephone down on the end table while he took several long breaths. He could hear Palmer's voice squeaking from the phone. He picked it up.

"What?"

"Have you unloaded the last of it?"

"Don't know," Curtiss admitted.

"When did Elston say the next board meeting was?"

"Next week."

"It's always a Friday morning. Can you get into Drop 23 before that?"

"I'll be in Manhattan by noon tomorrow."

"You have a key?"

"Yes."

"See Elston first," Palmer said.

"He's off on vacation."

"Try his apartment."

"Waste of time," Curtiss demurred.

"Do what I say!" Palmer's voice crackled so loudly through the phone that Curtiss held it away from his ear.

"Why?"

"Because," Palmer said, "I'm worried about Bill."

In the silence that followed, Curtiss could hear gunshots in the distance. He looked up. Someone was shooting two different weapons, both loud. Now the ti-ti-ti of an M-10 sounded, stitching the night with nasty blips of sound. The original guns responded thunderously.

"Curtiss?"

"Somebody's having a shoot-out."

"What? In Belgravia?"

"Here come the cops," Curtiss announced, hearing the oo-wah-oo-wah of a police van. Somewhere a burglar alarm bell pealed forth. The heavy handgun explosions went on. The submachinegun stitched back.

"All hell breaking loose," Curtiss reported. He carried the phone to the window. Two white police Rovers with horizontal red and gold stripes careened around the corner from Sloane Street and roared off to the left.

"Somewhere east of here. Maybe Motcomb Street or Wilton Street."

"Curtiss. Julian lives on Kinnerton Street. You know it?"

"Just off Motcomb. I'll check him out. Look," Curtiss said, "about what I said before."

"No need to apologize."

"Apologize, hell. I want you to know I meant every word."

"Oh, I knew that," Palmer assured him. "Now get going."

They had already cordoned off Motcomb Street at both ends by parking police cars across the pavement. Curtiss pawed through his wallet and found an out-of-date press pass issued by the unlikely authority of the British Tourist Board,

something they give any travel writer who asks for it. Through
Louch, however, he had managed to get a police press pass
issued by the Paris prefecture. He flashed this at the bobby
guarding the entrance to Motcomb Street.

"Sorry, guv. Nobody."

Backtracking, Curtiss turned into Lowndes Street and entered
the Halkin Arcade between a print shop and the hotel. He
stayed in the shadow until he had almost reached the horsy
pub at the Kinnerton end. Police had already closed the
arcade behind him.

The M-10's ti-ti-ti sounded very close. The great hollow
boom of a gun reminded Curtiss of a Colt .45 automatic.
Police on foot dashed along Kinnerton Street. An inner
walkway ran through a housing project of low- and high-rise
buildings built around an underground parking garage. Curtiss
joined two plainclothesmen moving at a crouch towards the
sound of gunfire.

Up ahead someone blew a whistle. Small-arms fire opened
up, a barking chorus of .38's. The vicious whine-*thunk* of a
target rifle began to repeat in slow tempo. Shoot, eject,
shoot, eject, The marksman was taking his time.

Sudden silence. It persisted.

Two whistles now. Curtiss moved forward, still at a crouch.
Searchlights illuminated an entry into an inner courtyard. The
stench of cordite lay in waves, like greasy wisps of fog. He
walked into one, sniffed the tang of its odor, kept moving
until he was in clean air again. Then another layer of cordite
reek.

Men in uniform and plain clothes were converging on the
lane into the courtyard, Curtiss along with the rest of them.
He found two tall men standing over a body in a brocade
smoking jacket, its feet clothed in carpet slippers. Two other
men were escorting a young woman between them. They
appeared for a moment in a ground floor doorway and then
seemed to disappear into the basement of the house. Curtiss
drew near the body.

"Doctor!" one of the police called. "Doctor!"

A young man carrying a small bag ran in through the
courtyard entry. He knelt by the prostrate body, felt for its
pulse and then ripped open the brocaded right sleeve of the
smoking jacket. He started wrapping a tourniquet around the
forearm.

Curtiss knelt beside him, as if one of his medics. "Here,"

he said, holding one end of the tourniquet while the doctor
began applying pressure. "How's his pulse?"

The doctor looked up, frowned. "Better than one would
expect. Who the bloody hell are you?"

"An associate," Julian croaked. "Can you loosen that damned
thing a bit? It's hurting worse than the bullet."

PART SIX

·

The Siege of the Villa Margit

49

"*Padrone,*" the tall man whispered, "*sono io, Tonino.*"

Inside the villa, Don B heard the whisper and his heart seemed to leap toward his mouth like a trapped animal battering its way to freedom. *Dio mio, finalmente!* After all these days of waiting the tall man had arrived, bearing news of Don Gino's death.

Moving through the blacked-out darkness of his bedroom suite, Don B reached the six-inch-thick oak door to his dressing room. Bound in straps of vanadium steel painted black to resemble wrought iron, the door concealed two sheets of diamond-back steel sandwiched between its wooden façades.

As he stood there in the blacker night of his own castle keep, Don B could hear the tall man beyond the door, hear his breathing, hear it whistle faintly through his nostrils. Nervous, was he?

All the other sounds of the night came to Don B, the flutter of olive leaves shushing against each other in the breeze, the distant murmur of cicadas and, near at hand, the cli-click of some nightbird.

"Tonino?" he called.

"*Sì, padrone.* I am here with wonderful news."

Don B's forehead creased. The voice was that of the tall man. The words were his, too. But the force behind them was strangely urgent. Like most men in his profession, the tall man could discuss almost anything without raising his voice or betraying emotion. Death, life, good fortune, bad luck, he dealt with all of them as an equal. Was he not the dispenser of death and thus on an equal footing with avenging angels, holocausts of God and the brutal buffeting of misfortune? Was he not himself an act of nature? Had he ever before used the word "wonderful?"

"Tonino, tell me."

"*Apri la porte, padrone.*"

"It takes time," Don B countered. "To open this door takes three keys and two bolts. Meanwhile, give me your news, in the name of God."

He rattled one of the bolts, as if sliding it open. No words came from beyond the door. Don B could feel a beating begin in his throat, the hammering of his own blood through his veins as he contemplated the possibility that his own assassin stood outside this door.

How could this have happened? How much more could Don Gino have paid this mercenary? Or was it that the tall man knew Don Gino would be the ultimate winner? The throbbing in his throat seemed to fill his ears.

"Open up, *padrone*. You must hear how Don Gino died."

Deafening! The painful noise seemed to penetrate the very floor under Don B's feet, as if he were having some sort of stroke. He staggered against the door and stared up at the ceiling, from whence this vengeance of God seemed to radiate.

"*Padre mio!*" An immense voice filled his ears.

"*Padre mio.*" A monstrous bellow came from overhead, "*Sono io, tuo figlio Benedetto.*"

Don B's eyes seemed to swell in the darkness, first with religious fright, then with wonder. It was his son. The horrifying noise was a helicopter overhead. His son was speaking through a bullhorn.

"You know what to do," Bennett Brown's voice roared. "Do it at once."

Don B stood blinking, trying to remember. Yes! The escape hatch to the roof!

He scuttled through his bedroom suite to the bathroom, where a hank of rope hung down from the ceiling. He pulled down with all his might, hanging his small body from it like a clapper of a great bell. Amid creaking a steel ladder began to unfold from the ceiling. Don B scampered up it to a round steel plate hardly larger in diameter than the spaghetti bowl his dear wife Amelia once used for family dinners on Sunday. This hatch had never been meant for anyone but a person Don B's size.

He twisted two handles and pushed up. The steel plate squealed as it hinged back. Instantly the howl and flap of the copter was deafening. A down draft of wind drove dust into his face.

He squinted against it and climbed up the last rungs of the

ladder. His torso was now showing above the roofline. Off to one side he saw a flash of light. A projectile screamed past him and ripped away part of the copter's landing struts.

Ben was leaning over the edge, reaching for him. *"Presto, presto!"* Don B grasped his hand and was half pulled up into the tiny cockpit as the small helicopter started to rise into the night.

From below came the sound of a heavy-caliber gun. A slug blasted two holes the size of a grapefruit out of the copter's plastic bubble. As the little machine soared high into the moonlit night, the triangular perimeter walls of the villa's enclave dropped away. Suddenly the earth was far, far below.

The copter pressed forward at a speed that kept its tachometer needle on the red line. Don B stared at the night and the fields of Sicily below him. He felt sore, confused, disoriented.

"Belt yourself in, Pop," Bennett Brown yelled. "Then find me a map that slid off the seat. There. Give it to me."

The wind tore at his face through the openings the tall man had blasted in the plastic canopy. Don B's eyes began to tear. As he passed it to his son, he saw it was a map of Malta.

50

At JFK Airport, with nothing but carry-on baggage, Mary Lee Hunter and Curtiss got through customs fast. Curtiss called Bill Elston's home number before they got in a cab to town. "Not there," he told her. "Maybe he did take off on a vacation."

"You can try again from our hotel."

"Where have you got us?"

"I couldn't get the Waldorf. Besides, my would-be replacement, Dave Grissom, will be checking in there. So I'm in a double at the Summit. Will you do me the honor of being an illegal occupant?"

"Why illegal? I'll be Mr. Hunter."

She gazed earnestly at him for a long moment. The cab was racing along Grand Central Parkway past LaGuardia Airport. "Really?"

"Don't get any ideas," Curtiss growled. Then, in a really bad Bogart imitation: "You dames is all the shame."

Although there was still no answer from Elston's home, Curtiss took a cab uptown in that direction. Drop 23 was located only a few blocks from Elston's apartment on 75th Street between Lexington and Park. There was, in fact, a UBCO branch much closer, but that would have been too easy to fathom. Instead, Drop 23 was in the basement vault of the Citibank branch on 72nd Street and Third Avenue.

He had an hour or more until closing time. Curtiss asked to be dropped on 75th Street. The apartment building was old but well kept. A doorman-elevator operator sat in one corner of the small lobby, reading a tabloid newspaper.

"Mr. Elston, yes. Apartment 1A. He's in."

He ran Curtiss up one floor in the elevator. As Curtiss rang the bell of 1A, the elevator door clanged shut. Curtiss rang a few more times. Elston had probably left the building without the doorman knowing. But was that possible?

Curtiss let out a long, heavy sigh. He hated getting caught at this sort of work because it was so hard to explain his way out of it. There were three other apartment doors on this floor and at any moment an occupant could arrive or depart, spotting Curtiss at his nefarious worst.

He began by trying to loid the door with a credit card, but Bill had thrown a deadbolt which defeated Curtiss's most artistic wiggling of the stiff plastic. No. Wait. What seemed to be a deadbolt was something else, a second spring latch. It was retreating under his coaxing. Funny, Bill not bolting the door.

Once inside, Curtiss realized why. Whoever had left Bill Elston on his living room floor had exited without being able to throw the bolt from outside. Whoever had left must have carried with him a silenced .22. No. Wait. A pillow with part of its kapok filling blown out showed how the gun had been silenced. Such a caliber rarely sounded loud anyway; the pillow would have done the rest.

The entry wound was between Bill's eyes. There was no exit, since few .22 slugs have the power to travel through a human skull.

Curtiss sat down on a pale pink velour chair and stared across at Bill's body, lying on his back in a kind of sprawl, as if dropped there from high up. The corpse was icy, even in the heat of July. Curtiss shivered.

Palmer must have had a premonition. But, then, Bill Elston had been one of Palmer's protégés, like Curtiss, a fellow recruited from outside banking to handle an element of the business—security—that had little to do with banking itself. Elston had been older than Curtiss, more Palmer's age, but they'd both been protégés. Now Bill was dead because he'd done his job too well.

Christ, Curtiss thought, if nothing else would've, this murder had the power to bring Palmer back to the States on the double. He got to his feet and started for the phone, intending to call the police. At that moment the phone began to ring.

He stood there eyeing it, not sure what to do. Finally he picked it up but said nothing. "Hello?" a man demanded. "Bill, that you?"

"It's Curtiss."

"You made good time," Palmer responded. "Let me t—"

"Can't."

"What d'you m—?"

"Hard to explain," Curtiss interrupted a second time.

"You're not telling m—" This time Palmer cut himself off. "I'll be right there."

"From Basel? Forget it."

"I'm not in Basel. I'm at JFK. Flight just got in."

"There is a not-bad fish restaurant on Third Avenue, south of 72nd Street. Meet me at the bar."

"This is the most pointless, nasty kill I've ever run into," Palmer said. He needed a shave. There were leaden pouches under his eyes. He carried a battered leather attaché case and nothing else. He stared into his Scotch-on-the-rocks and shook his head. "Poor bastard never had a chance. What do you think? He wouldn't tell them where he'd hidden the stuff?"

"Except," Curtiss mused aloud, "once you kill a man you sort of cut down on the amount of information you might get out of him. And this was a very deliberate kill. Close up. Not the almost accidental shot of an excited guy who wasn't getting answers. The shot of a pro hit man fulfilling a contract. In the caliber of choice, by the way. The native hoods prefer a .22. In Europe they go for cannons like the Browning

.9, but here it's a matter of macho pride to use the tiniest caliber. Also, it's hard to hear in a noisy town like New York."

"Can you get into Drop 23?"

"We're sitting half a block from it."

It was easy to see that the downstairs vault guard, a pleasant black man with a cultured Barbados voice, wasn't at all pleased at allowing both men to examine Box 914 at their leisure in a private room. Curtiss's name and signature were on file. And he had a key. But the unshaven, elderly gent who looked like he'd been on the road for a week did not inspire confidence.

To make sure they were not interrupted once in the private room, Palmer wedged a chair back under the door knob. Curtiss sat in the only chair left. Palmer perched on the top of the desk.

Slowly, painstakingly, they went through the contents of Box 914, Curtiss examining each document, then handing it to Palmer, who placed them in three neat piles as he finished reading.

Half an hour passed without a word. At the end Palmer stood up and stretched his middle-aged bones. "Okay. In that pile to the left are the detective agency reports on meetings, tapped conversations, secret itineraries, the dummy corporations and safe deposit boxes. It's solid third-party evidence, particularly those phone-tap transcripts. In the second pile I have affidavits and other documentary proof: letters of incorporation, photostats of bank deposits, UBCO dossiers from Internal Security, those lists of interlocking directorates. But it's the third pile of stuff that fascinates me. Bill wouldn't have known what he was collecting. Some kind of sixth sense told him it was important."

"Those buy and sell orders," Curtiss said. "All we need is the originals out of Bank Rup. We can tie this whole bunch into the Bennett Brown thing. Gameplan, he calls it."

Palmer's head was shaking from side to side before he had finished speaking. "We'll never get anything out of Bank Rup. Or any other Swiss bank. Forget that angle. I'm gambling these are not duplicates. I think they're original orders executed here in Manhattan."

Curtiss's lips pursed in a silent whistle. "You mean Gameplan was being operated through two banks?"

"And probably through Brown's own brokerage as well. He

knew he'd have to spread exposure. But how could we dream he had people that high up in UBCO to help him?"

Without waiting for a reply, Palmer flipped open his beat-up brown leather attaché case. From it he removed two pairs of underwear shorts, a folded shirt, a rolled-up tie, some socks and a shaving kit. These he threw in the wastepaper basket. He then loaded the case with the contents of the box and snapped the lid shut.

"I'll take this to my hotel," he told Curtiss. "You turn the police loose. Did Bill have any relatives here?"

Curtiss shook his head. "A brother somewhere in the Midwest."

Palmer said nothing but continued to stare, empty-eyed, down at the attaché case. After a long moment he sighed. "Poor old guy." He was silent an even longer time, his face turned so that Curtiss couldn't see even his profile. "Poor old Bill," he said then.

"I keep asking myself," the younger man responded, "what could have been done to head this off? I mean, should I have said something to him on the phone? Even something as simple as 'watch yourself, Bill.' Anything."

Palmer's face was totally hidden now. When he spoke his voice had a strained, almost choked quality to it. "No," he said quietly, "nothing like that would've helped. The man was associated with me." He swung around and stared into Curtiss's face. "In case you didn't notice," Palmer said, "people around me get hurt."

Curtiss nodded somberly. "You remember that slug I took in Basel? That was on a mission you dreamed up. And last week in Paris?"

"If you were smart, you'd quit," the older man told him.

"You're some kind of hoodoo, huh?"

"Ask Eleanora some time."

"I sure as hell will," Curtiss assured him, "if I get out of this one alive." He picked up the safe deposit box. They returned it empty to the guard and left. Outside, the July heat seemed to bear down on them with an almost physical weight. Traffic moved up Third Avenue in a haze of fumes, radiating still more heat as it lurched sluggishly northward, as if in search of polar cold.

"Be careful with that stuff," Curtiss said as Palmer flagged a cab.

"Right. Oh. Lend me a ten?"

Smiling grimly, Curtiss handed over a ten-dollar bill to the man who had once controlled the largest bank in the world. He watched the cab carrying Palmer, in his slept-in clothes and unshaven face, disappear across 72nd Street. Curtiss started to hail a cab of his own, then realized Palmer had taken the last of his paper money.

Seething, as much from the July heat of Manhattan as the thoughtlessness of the rich, Curtiss walked back into the bank and stood there in the chilled air, trying to cool off.

Arrogant son of a bitch. "People around me get hurt." But stick around, anyway, bub. Borrow your last sawbuck and disappear, leaving you to make excuses to the cops for reporting a murder an hour late.

Chasing dragons again, the silly bastard. Because slaying the dragon was important to the rich who pretended they weren't dragons. Those very few rich who could fool themselves into thinking they were a different breed from beauties like Bennett Brown, his family and their associated clans.

Temper under control, Curtiss walked up to the armed guard. "Where's the police precinct for this area?"

The guard pointed south. "You go down to 67th Street and—"

"And why the hell do I keep stooging for him?" Curtiss demanded hotly.

"Huh?"

51

Holding onto the helicopter controls with one hand, Ben managed to shrug out of his aluminum-colored anorak. The blast of chill air from the two holes in the canopy ripped at his eyes. He balled up the anorak and stuffed it into the hole at eye level, but the one beneath his feet continued to shoot a gust up into the cramped cabin.

"Pop, belt in!" he shouted against the rotor noise.

Don B seemed to have grown smaller. The Savoia-Marchetti aircraft tilted slightly forward as it raced horizontally across the Sicilian plain, now beginning to round and swell in the moonlight as they flew over foothills. The old man's small body tilted forward with the posture of the helicopter. Relinquishing the controls, his son reached across Don B and cinched a safety harness across the old man's chest.

"That'll hold you."

Ben took the map from his father's hand and snapped on a small orangey-red nightlight. Agrigento was almost due south, between fifty and sixty miles. The copter's fuel tank showed full, but Ben knew from long experience in airports around the world that rented helicopters rarely had full tanks, whatever the guage showed. He had no experience with this tiny Savoia-Marchetti, but hoped that its fuel tank was adequate.

Still, even three-quarters full would be enough for the thirty-five minute flight to Agrigento. He would have to do the math in his head, dividing gallons into minutes while redlining the copter in excess of a hundred miles an hour. By the time he refueled in Agrigento, he would be able to estimate if the aircraft could hold enough fuel for a sea crossing.

Ben snapped on his radio. Very little traffic could be heard at this late hour, although a few intercontinental airliners, at altitudes of thirty-five thousand feet, were getting transient instructions as they passed through various ground-control zones. Ben could barely hear them over the beat of the rotors.

The undersized copter began to buck and weave as updrafts hit it. Off to the right, shimmering in the moonlight, the Lago di Piana lay like a giant teardrop. The route Ben had chosen led over almost uninhabited mountain terrain. The only town of any size would be Corleone, to the right.

At this altitude, however, mountains and lakes created updraft thermals, even at night. Ben tilted the copter up slightly at the nose and climbed to three thousand feet. Even so, in this moonlight, he could easily see the snakeline progress below of *Strada Statiale* 118. It would lead him directly, without the need of a compass, into Agrigento.

And the possibility of a trap. Just because it was late there was no guarantee that Don B's enemies slept. By now the man who had fired that immense slug at the copter would have raised an alarm across all of Western Sicily. Since the escape involved an aircraft, all airports would soon be alerted.

Ben found himself wondering how it worked in Sicily. In the States the mob controlled every major airport by means of its lock on trucking and freight handling. Nothing moved in or out without the *capo* knowing. No merchandise was stolen without his being tithed. Was it the same in the Mother Island? Ben turned to his father.

"How fast could they get word to the air—" He stopped.

The old man was asleep. He seemed to have slumped forward, hanging into the harness. Ben eased him back into a more comfortable position.

"*Dormi bene, papa.*" Ben's throat hurt from shouting over the rotor roar.

He pulled open the zipper of a small shoulder bag stuffed under his seat. From within, he pulled out a CB radio of the size that fits into automobile dashboards. One eye on the moonlit landscape, Ben clipped the radio into a power source and ran a wire lead to the copter's radio antenna.

The distance was too great, he knew. Yet from this height, ordinary CB radio sometimes carried hundreds of miles. He switched on the set. Its dials glowed in the dark. "Breaker Niner," Ben murmured into the hand microphone. "Breaker Niner. Do you copy?"

He switched slowly through several wavelength bands. Nothing. He switched off the radio. Coming in low over the town of Aragona, he saw that almost no lights shone in any house. His watch, still on London time, indicated eleven p.m., which was midnight here. *Superstrada* 189 below was empty of cars as it curved in from the east towards Agrigento.

Ben craned sideways, staring down through the canopy and the landing gear. Something well-lighted marked its position on the *superstrada*. He dropped lower and saw that an all-night filling station lay beneath him. By now they would have heard the beat of his rotors.

He sent the Savoia-Marchetti down at a rapid rate until its skids touched asphalt. It settled into a cockeyed position, listing hard to starboard. Ben shut down the engine and leaped onto the pavement. A man in greasy coveralls was watching him from a safe distance. Ben ducked under the aircraft. His right landing strut had been cut in half by a shot back in Palermo. It was a miracle it had taken even this gentle landing.

"*Benzina, c'è?*"

The filling station attendant seemed to rouse himself out of some sort of stupor. His glance shifted from Ben to the holes in the canopy, to the sleeping old man. He approached almost unwillingly. "*Quanti litri?*"

"*A pieno,*" Ben said.

The rotors came to a stop. Shrugging, the attendant yanked the hose out of a gasoline pump and carried it two yards in the direction of the copter. It fell short by another two yards. He disappeared for a moment, then returned with a twenty-liter plastic container. By filling and carrying it to the copter's fuel tank, he began fueling the aircraft. The place reeked of cheap gasoline.

Ben watched him for a moment, then checked his wristwatch. It had stopped at midnight. His mouth flattened in a hard line as he glanced around this oasis in a sleeping land. Should he ask if the man had coffee?

His glance reached a lighted public telephone booth. Ben stepped inside the cabin of the filling station. When the attendant's back was turned, Ben opened the cash drawer and removed a small brass *gettone*, used for public telephones. He pressed it into the slot and dialed 170.

It seemed to ring forever but, in fact, only as long as the attendant took to fill and empty two more plastic containers of gasoline. *"Sí?"* a male operator said over the phone. *"Che vuole?"*

Voglio chiamare a New York."

"Il prefisso e numero?"

Ben reeled off a telephone number. *"Qui paga?"* the operator demanded.

"Paga New York."

There ensued a long silence, filled with clicks and the astral bleeps of faroff galaxies. Ben watched the attendant's movements, never hurrying, never delaying, the routine of a man much used to manual work. *"Va bene,"* the operator said suddenly. *"Commincia."*

"Freddie?" Ben asked. "You know who you're talking to?"

"Wha'?" Alfred J. Marston, at six in the morning, was not at his best. "Uh, oh, yeah. Sure."

"Get the shit out of your ears, Freddie. Activate that trust fund."

"Now?"

"Now." Ben hung up immediately. The attendant had finished fueling the copter and was standing by the pump. Ben reached in his pocket for a fat wad of Italian money. *"Il vecchio,"* the attendant said, *"sta bene? O no?"* His head jerked in the direction of Don B, eyes closed, sleeping heavily in the co-pilot's seat.

"Sí, bene." Ben resisted the urge to thank the man. If he

committed the error of thanking someone for service—which no Sicilian ever did—he would immediately be identified as a polite American.

"*Ciao.*" He gunned the engine and the aircraft lifted up into the night like a bubble.

Once his eyes adjusted to the dark, Ben consulted his map. He had about seventy miles to another refueling at Ragusa, then a journey of similar length over water to Malta. Or he could make a beeline routing of about one hundred and ten miles, over water every inch of the way, not knowing if his fuel would last. But the trip would take a bit more than an hour. Copters carried at least an hour's worth of fuel, even a shrimp like this Savoia-Marchetti. Of course, redlining all the way meant using fuel inefficiently, but . . .

Lips moving, dark eyes concentrating first on his watch and then on the fuel gauge, Ben calculated his chances. The landing gear would surely not survive a touchdown at Ragusa. This late he could not count on any fuel being available except at the airport. He would have to try the over-water route.

"Breaker Niner," he said into the tiny CB radio. "Do you copy?"

He repeated his slow combing of the channels. ". . . and clear," he heard someone say in English. He turned up the volume.

"Say again."

"That's a four, good buddy," Urs Rup's voice came through. "Do you copy?"

A grin distorted Ben's small, careful mouth. Their strategy had paid off. Nobody but auto drivers used CB. Every enforcement agency on both sides of the law would be combing the normal aircraft channels. In this part of the world, using CB jargon in English would be as secure as Sanskrit.

"I'm hanging an ETA of one tenner."

"That's another four, big fella. Go for it."

Ben snapped off the radio. He sent the copter upward to three thousand feet. The moon cut a pale swath of light across the sea below. At this altitude he could watch the shimmer of rippling water. The lights of Licata were his last landfall, directly behind him now as he headed SSE on his compass.

Also behind him, but unseen now as the helicopter tilted forward and homed in, a DeHavilland Twin Otter banked sharply at five thousand feet as it crossed over the coastline at Agrigento. The high-wing monoplane provided perfect forward and downward vision, not only for its pilot but for the passenger, now equipped with an Ingram M-10 as well as a deer rifle.

52

From the 60th floor, one can watch the East and Hudson Rivers flow together at Battery Park. One can see New Jersey, Brooklyn and Staten Island. On a clear day aircraft can be observed taking off in the far reaches of Queens. Tugboats chuff past the Statue of Liberty. Cruise liners make their majestic progress in and out. Tiny helicopters bear sightseers and executives in a hurry. In short, one is standing high above Manhattan's financial district.

It was here that Mary Lee Hunter invited Curtiss and Palmer that morning. Her club occupied nearly half the 60th floor. She had become a member the year before when women were first allowed to join. Being based on the West Coast, she had used the club only three times in a year and never for the purpose to which she now put it.

Being so new a member it did not irritate her that, among the people eating breakfast at round tables in the dining room, most knew Palmer, not her. They would wave to him across the room or even come over to shake hands and chat for an instant.

He had picked up a ready-to-wear summer suit at Tripler and looked smoothly presentable again, which was more than she could say for Curtiss, who looked ill-at-ease. There was nothing wrong with his clothes; it was his attitude that Mary Lee found out of place. He seemed to have taken an instant dislike to something as inanimate as a piece of real estate on which a dining club was being operated.

"You're the only female here," he pointed out to her. "Are you sure you're a member?"

"There are four women members, the last I heard."

"Did they have to build you your own washroom?"

"Women come here as guests. There have always been female toilets." She put her hand on his. "Lay off."

Palmer, who was pretending to be absorbed in a manilla folder of typed material, now looked up. "It's the best dining club on Wall Street," he announced. "I'm grateful to be asked here, Mary Lee."

"Something special about your toast?" Curtiss persisted.

The older man shook his head. "The food is incidental in these places. It's being seen that counts."

"If I wanted good food," Mary Lee told Curtiss, "I'd stay away. But when my image needs burnishing, I invite two attractive men for breakfast and . . . bingo."

Curtiss stared at her with almost the same cold look that Palmer occasionally got. Mary Lee could now read him well enough to know that he was forming and rejecting hostile remarks, none of which got said. Instead he seemed to put on a lid and settle back in his chair. He had not yet touched either his toast or his coffee, as if to say: I am so much my own man that I'll starve to prove it.

"How did you make out with your brokers?" Palmer asked politely.

Mary Lee gave him a smile. He wasn't really interested, she knew, but he was a gentleman of the old school. Protocol demanded that if they were to spend most of this breakfast hearing out his problems, they had to give hers at least a token audition.

"I managed to crack Merrill Lynch's corporate heart. They finally stuck at 17 percent discount. But I did better in Boston. I got my 15. So now I'm going back to Merrill Lynch and offering to let them out of the deal." Her smile broadened. "That ought to bring them down two points in a hurry."

Palmer laughed appreciatively. "Any flak from your Number Two?"

"Grissom! A perfect doll. Spoke when he was spoken to. Pleasant, cooperative. He's either a very good actor or I've maligned him. Even his pal at UBCO was a doll. Name of Harry Kummel?"

"You met with Kummel?" Curtiss burst out. "Why?"

"He wanted me to try out a broker he likes a lot." Mary Lee's eyes glinted with malice.

"Don't tell me. Brown, Brown? That sadistic shit!"

She glanced around the room "Easy, Curtiss. He sounded innocent as a babe."

Palmer listened and said nothing. Curtiss's hand reached for his coffee but stopped short as he said: "That's because this thing is organized in compartments. Grissom's compartment is Jet-Tech. The UBCO people at your meeting only know about UBCO. They know nothing about killing Bill Elston. The man in *that* compartment only knows about murder. But he knows nothing about *why* Elston. If you had an aerial view of this conspiracy you'd see a conglomeration of compartments, all separate. Only one player dances along the edges in between. Only he has a map for the whole thing. And the last we know of him, according to Julian, is that he went off in the night because his father was in big trouble."

"We know he phoned in a police alert for Julian," Palmer said then.

"No skin off his nose." Curtiss reached for the coffee again. "Although I guess we have to be grateful for small favors."

"I think we have to assume," Palmer said, "that his Gameplan syndicate is in disarray. If it was his father's prestige that enabled him to put the combo together, it's now come unstuck."

"Especially since you blew his Swiss connection," Curtiss added.

Mary Lee listened to them restating the obvious and wondered why they were wasting time. It dawned on her that part of this performance was to impress her. Each had to be in true Alpha Male control of his environment. She could, dimly, understand why Curtiss would do this. They were still in a courtship stage when people put on their best performance. What was Palmer's reason? Reassertion of seniority rights? Male ram butting off intruders?

As long as she lived, Mary Lee decided, there would always be an area of male-female relations forever shrouded in primitive mists, forever mindless and wasteful of energy, forever silly, even ludicrous. She wasn't sure whether this was shameful or just endearing.

And now, she addressed the two men silently, as soon as you've hoofed up the earth and bellowed a bit and strutted, let's get to it. "All I could get out of Curtiss," she announced then, "is that Drop 23 is dynamite." Palmer nodded. "He said there's enough in there to blow UBCO sky-high." Palmer frowned. "Or at least blow the present management out of the saddle."

"Is that how you see it?" Palmer asked, turning to the younger man.

"You've not only got evidence of criminal association and criminal conspiracy, but you can tie it into a fresh murder. If that isn't headlines for a week, I don't know the New York press."

"You think going public with this is our best move?" Palmer eyed him sideways, then Mary Lee. "What do you think, Mary Lee?"

"I'm no banker, but—"

"Neither is Curtiss," Palmer interrupted. He made a small, exasperated letting-off-steam noise. "The trouble with young people," he went on in a cool voice, "is that they haven't lived long enough." He tried to smile but made a botch of it. "Neither of you have lived through a bank panic or even a run on an individual bank. You've *read* about such things. But you've never been part of the hysteria. People lining up to withdraw their life savings. Riots at the doors. Not enough in cash reserves. It's a nightmare. And in every case it's caused by bank customers who have lost faith in their bank."

Curtiss actually picked up his coffee, but still refused to sip it. "You think blowing the whistle on UBCO management would precipitate a panic?"

"There's no question of it," Palmer told him. "It spreads overnight to our correspondent banks all over the country, then to our major corporate debtors, then to the politicians who have to beg votes on the one hand and satisfy big contributors on the other. Before you know it, you've got chaos in every major financial center."

"Because one bank has a crooked management?"

"Take my word for it." Palmer looked around the room, where a few dozen people were finishing their breakfasts, and lowered his voice. "The effect on Wall Street, the effect on the Federal Reserve, on the Treasury Department in Washington, on banking departments in twenty states coast to coast . . ." His voice died away. "Of course the chief victim would be UBCO. It simply wouldn't recover."

"Come on," Curtiss muttered.

"What do you suppose a bank has to sell, Curtiss? Security and expertise. You want its people to be honest and know what they're doing. Everything else is window dressing. A customer wants the solid feel. Or he goes elsewhere."

Mary Lee was holding Curtiss's left hand now, but her

glance was on Palmer. Behind him, through the picture window, the almost horizontal morning sun bathed the double top of the world Trade Center with hot pink light.

"It's hard to believe," she said. "All that outstanding paper. All those billions in loans. A bank has to hang together if only to collect from its debtors."

"No law guarantees that." Palmer looked down at the curls of butter sitting in their saucer of crushed ice. He speared one curl with his knife and buttered a triangle of toast.

Curtiss's eyes followed this movement as if it had great significance. He watched a corner of the toast enter Palmer's mouth and get bitten off. He watched the faint play of muscles in Palmer's face as he chewed. The older man seemed aware of this scrutiny, but without any embarrassment.

"So," Curtiss said at last, "what's your idea? Sit on this stuff and let the bastards go scot-free?"

"Curtiss," Mary Lee objected.

"No, he's right. That's one option," Palmer admitted. "We have to reject it. A man died because he uncovered this conspiracy. None of us would dream of covering it up. But if exposure means chaos, what other options are open?"

Curtiss laughed unhappily. "I don't understand you. There are only two options. Use the material or suppress it."

"Mary Lee?" Palmer asked.

"Pass," she responded.

"Does that mean you have no opinion?"

"It means my opinion has zero weight. This is your show, you two."

"It's not mine," the younger man snapped. "I'm only here because I haven't figured out a way of turning my back on Palmer. The minute I do, I will."

"Woods!" a tall, gray-haired man called, striding towards their table. "Nobody told me you were back in town."

Palmer made introductions, all smiles. He and the man chatted briefly. As the visitor left, Palmer stopped smiling as he told Curtiss in a deadly cold tone: "You can walk away from me any time you feel like it. I already know you consider me on a par with the Bennett Brown team. So there's no need to hang about. You'll be free to pursue your destiny independent of UBCO and the corrupt, hypocritical business establishment."

Curtiss got to his feet. He let his napkin fall on his plate. "As for Drop 23," he told Palmer, "I'm the fellow who reported a killing to the police, so I expect several more interrogations before they're through with me. I don't claim to have a photographic memory. All I can do is tell them who had Drop 23 in his possession last." He started to leave the table.

"Sit down."

"Why?"

"Mary Lee?" Palmer begged. "Do something with him?"

"Why?" she asked. "He makes as much sense as you do. Meaning none. Oh," she went on, "I do appreciate the problem for the financial community and UBCO."

"And for one of its major stockholders," Curtiss muttered, "sitting at this table."

"But when you have a situation like this," she went on, "perhaps the only solution is to let it happen. Money aside, why does UBCO deserve to be propped up and cuddled back to health?" She squeezed Curtiss's hand. "Please sit down."

He did, without speaking. Palmer's eyes flashed around the room, as if checking to see that they were not becoming a spectacle for those breakfasting. "Money aside," he repeated on an almost venomous note of sarcasm, "some situations in life are irreversible. Losing that much money would be one. Another would be all the other banks dragged under by UBCO's collapse."

"Collapse," Curtiss growled. "What a delicate little flower. One cold snap and it's finished."

"The whole structure of the West is fragile," Palmer retorted in an insolent tone that suggested he was addressing a cretin. "We are all hanging by our fingernails and well you know it. Curtiss," he went on, trying to soften his tone somewhat, "you of all people should know how close the financial institutions are to terminal destruction. By insatiable credit policies we have inched our way so far out on the limb that any shock could snap it. And down we'd come."

Curtiss tried to hide his smile. "I love that 'we' business."

"All right." He appealed to Mary Lee. "Do I have to tell you how tenuous a hold Jet-Tech has on its corporate life? On any industry that depends on government bailouts, like the auto-makers and space manufacturers like Jet-Tech? Or industries that depend on government protection, like oil and steel and the airlines?"

Mary Lee put down half a croissant she had been nibbling at. "What a terrific meal this is turning out to be."

"You two don't seem to understand what we're up against," Palmer said. In the past minute his tone had shifted desperately from true bankerly insolence through fake fatherly warmth to where it was now: plain worry.

"You don't realize what's happened in the past twenty years. You're too young to have anything to compare it with."

"But you're going to explain it to the kids," Curtiss guessed.

An extremely acid remark nearly passed Palmer's lips, but he seemed to bite it back. He put a neutral look on his face and seemed to be watching the progress of a small helicopter that was circling the building they were in. As it crossed through one segment of the sky over lower Manhattan the sun flashed on its rotors and reflected a hot spark from a panel of glass.

"What we call the parliamentary democracies of the West," Palmer said then in an almost indifferent tone. "They exist on an unwritten covenant. Pay your taxes and the government will provide all the services you require. Safety from attack or crime. Clean streets. Old-age pensions. Even health care in some countries. That's been the covenant at the city, state and federal levels. But for at least the past twenty years, at the local level, no government has lived up to it."

"Especially city governments," Mary Lee put in. "Look at New York. Or L.A. Most of what the cities collect in taxes goes into welfare."

"Goes into two bottomless pits," Palmer corrected her, "called poverty and crime. Have you any idea how much more the anti-crime establishment costs each year? I don't just mean cop salaries or the cost of prisons. I mean the courts, the parole bureaucracies, the guard facilities and alarm systems and the tax billions we have to pay because Bennett Brown's families launder their cash through Switzerland to avoid paying tax. What city and county money is left over goes to keep the poor people alive. There is nothing left to fix streets or clean up the air or any of the other things we pay taxes for. *And* every year there is more crime and more poverty."

Curtiss picked up his coffee at long last and sipped it. "It's cold," he complained. Mary Lee flagged a waiter and ordered a fresh pot.

"So local governments line up at the federal spigot for money," Palmer went on after the waiter had left the table. "Most cities in the States would have gone bankrupt long ago but for a steady diet of federal money. In Washington, when they realize they are about to go as bankrupt as the local governments, what is their solution? Borrow."

"At ever-higher interest rates," Mary Lee suggested.

"Which they have to re-borrow to pay. If you include the hidden 'off-budget' part of the economy, every other dollar collected by income tax is immediately spent on debt servicing. About $220 billion a year. Not on building highways or making sure milk is pure or protecting us from Godless Communism, but on paying back interest so more money can be borrowed. Two hundred and twenty billion dollars."

"Nice," Curtiss responded. "That why inflation keeps cheapening money."

"And that's why government will do nothing to curb inflation." Palmer told him. "It wants to be able to pay off debts in ever-cheaper money."

"I can't stand it," Mary Lee burst out. "The two of you are like a pair of hi-fi stereo speakers, trying to enunciate more clearly the shape of impending doom. I really hate this."

It was Curtiss's turn to take her hand. "We don't have to worry. Palmer is going to ride to the rescue." He turned to the older man, but the waiter chose that moment to pour fresh cups of coffee all around. Curtiss sipped his.

"It's like one of those insane TV series, everybody sitting around drinking coffee while civilization crumbles." He glanced at both of them. "It's so comforting. Cream? Sugar?" He grinned at Palmer. "And then an elder of the tribe sets it all straight and you know life will be fine and let's brew another pot of coffee."

He sat back and looked from one to the other of them. "That lecture of yours," he told the older man, "that was vintage Palmer."

Palmer picked up his coffee, frowned at it and shoved it away from him. "It *is* like TV, a soap opera."

"You're the reason I stayed this long with UBCO," Curtiss told him. "You're even more of a realist than I am. So how come you don't see this one the way I do?"

"Maybe I can trace even better than you that fine line between two sets of thieves." Palmer smiled grimly. "Take a look at the UBCO board, if you want an example. Eddie Hagen, the chairman, is only where he is because he was my commanding officer in Sicily during the war. Made it to Major-General. Then he became the head of some big defense-industry firm and I put him on the board to back me up when I needed backing. Eddie's been on the take for as long as I've known him, even in Sicily. Your average general has no idea of what honesty is. He comes naturally to thievery because he's lived his whole life in a tiny cabal of thieves called the Army, or Navy or whatever. I don't call such a man dishonest since he never even knew what honesty might be. But Eddie's got shrewder as he's got older, which is more than you can say for Charley Oakburn. With each successive year he more and more resembles a male model who's wandered into the executive suite from some photography session next door. You expect him to lift that glass of cognac and give you a hearty twinkle. When you think that people like these are still alive and flourishing, while a first-rate mind like Bill Elston's is six feet under and no clue as to who put him there, you begin to understand why I turned my back on banking a long time ago."

"We have clues," Curtiss said quietly.

"Yes," Palmer agreed, "we think we know who paid for the hit. Can we prove it?"

"Not in the state we are now."

The older man frowned. "What state?"

"The state of being outside the power structure."

Palmer's tiny smile went almost unnoticed. "At the moment that structure is as porous as lace."

"Implying," Mary Lee spoke up, "that it can be penetrated."

Palmer was silent. Curtiss did a funny thing then. Under the table he moved his knee to give Mary Lee's thigh two slight pushes. "But only by one like you," she went on. "Only by—" Curtiss touched her thigh three times, less gently. She frowned and shut up.

"Only by me," Palmer finished for her. Curtiss sat back. He seemed to have got the response he wanted.

"Because I'm the one who's been programmed not to make use of all these handy modern excuses. You know, 'well, I did the best I could.' I'm not bragging. If anything, I'm complaining. It's no fun the way I was brought up."

"The do-or-die school," Curtiss suggested.

"That's only half the school name," Mary Lee put in.

The two men turned to look at her. "The name in full," she told them "is the do-or-die-but-if-you-have-to-die-at-least-take-some-of-the-bastards-with-you school."

Both men burst out laughing, but it was obvious to Curtiss

that the gesture was costing Palmer something. The older
man stopped laughing almost at once and when he did his
face fell into a morose look. Palmer's gaze followed another
circuit of the building by the helicopter. It then landed on a
waterfront pad below.

"If you had the ability to take some of them with you,"
Mary Lee said in the most matter-of-fact tone in the world, as
if wondering whether he might like more toast, "how would
you go about doing it?"

Palmer shook off the question. Then, sensing he was being
rude, he glanced back at her. "I don't know," he said.

"Oh," said Curtiss. "I do."

53

Compared to the tiny cockpit of a Savoia-Marchetti helicop-
ter, the cabin of the DeHavilland was roomy and fairly quiet.
One could converse without shouting, the tall man noticed.
He had not yet begun to be worried.

The fact that he had been able to race to the airport and
commandeer both a STOL plane and its pilot gave him the
feeling that, far from having failed, he was about to win.

He had not yet begun to think about how many people he
was dragging into what had been a simple contract between
one employer and one specialist. The damned pilot had
insisted on filing a flight plan, even though a false one, and
was charging the tall man twice his normal fee. After the
dispatch of Don B and his impetuous son, the pilot/owner of
the DeHavilland Twin Otter would be the night's third
casualty.

But what luck! Precisely the type of aircraft from which to
chase a slow-moving helicopter. If there had been only a jet
or prop-jet on the field at Palermo, the tall man would have
been defeated. But the Twin Otter could reduce its flying
speed to match the Savoia-Marchetti and then fly rings
around it. The tall man had used them in New Mexico,
handling illegals over the border.

He opened the breech of the deer gun and reloaded. He
knew, from what his pilot had told him, that the Savoia was

crippled already. Its speed was not affected, but its next landing would be its last.

From the way the son was holding to a three-thousand-foot altitude, it seemed to the tall man that he hadn't noticed his pursuer. "Now," he commanded the DeHavilland pilot. "Close in."

"How close?"

"Almost touch him. Then hold steady."

"*Mamma mia! Che cosa fa?*"

"What do you care?" the tall man asked. He took out the packet of 100,000-lira notes Don Gino had paid him. Holding the bundle in front of the pilot's face he riffled his thumbnail across the edge of the bills. "Almost touch him," he repeated.

The Twin Otter was hanging above and behind the copter, tracking it like a slow-moving owl tracks a mouse in the field. The pilot nudged his controls gingerly. The space between the aircraft shortened.

The tall man opened the window on the co-pilot's side. He braced the thick cylindrical silencer of the Ingram M-10 on the edge of the plane and sighted along its barrel. "Left," he ordered, "and forward. Pass him slowly."

"What do you think you're doing with that?"

The tall man showed all his even white teeth in a fierce grin. The pilot nudged his controls. Taking careful aim, the tall man let off a burst of five slugs. He was being cautious, the Ingram's firepower being more than a thousand rounds a minute.

Holes appeared in the engine mounting behind the Savoia's cockpit. From a distance of perhaps fifty yards, the tall man could see the son peer out of the plastic bubble. "Bastard sees me for the first time," the tall man crowed. "Look at that!"

Like a lead ball, the copter seemed to sink out of sight, plummeting downward, rotor churning loosely. The tall man peered over the edge. "Son of a bitch is skimming the water. Get down there."

"I can't skim it like that."

The tall man lifted the machine gun off its improvised perch and swung the barrel. Its tiny muzzle prodded the pilot's ribs. "Sure you can."

The DeHavilland banked sharply and lost four thousand feet as it executed a series of textbook right-angle turns. But it was still a thousand feet above the choppy Mediterranean

as it closed the gap behind the helicopter. The Savoia seemed
to skim the very wave tops. Its downdraft flattened the waves
and sent a line of ripples out ahead of its progress.

"Dive on him," the tall man commanded. He braced the
Ingram on the window again. "We're going to strafe. Come
right in and don't pull out till we're past."

The Otter's two engines whined angrily. The high-wing
plane seemed to leap forward and down as if kicked from
behind. It howled in on the slower-moving copter as if it
intended to ram it.

The machine gun was chattering. Spent shells shot out to
the right. In the bluish moonlight a line of white splashes
moved along the water behind the Savoia, bit into its tail
rotor, stitched across its spine.

Yanking back with all his force, the pilot pulled the
DeHavilland out of its dive. It angled skyward at a crazy
slant. The tall man held on, trying to catch a glimpse of the
copter, but the angle was wrong.

"Turn!" he shouted.

"Not yet."

"Turn!"

The pilot stared at his instrument board, then leveled off at
under a thousand feet and banked at a shallow angle. His face
was the color of *mozzarella*, the tall man noted. Later, it
would be even paler, would it not?

Now he could see the helicopter. Its nose was lifted slightly
and its speed seemed much reduced, but still it flew. Still it
skimmed over the waves like a dragonfly silhouetted in the
broad shimmering path cast by the moon. Its pilot had been
talking into a microphone. Now he put it away and seemed to
be holding some sort of pistol.

"How slow is he going?" the tall man demanded.

The pilot's lips were bloodless. "I d-don't know. S-sixty?"

"How slow can you fly beside him?"

"Not that slow."

"Did I ask that? How slow?"

"Ninety." The pilot's eyes flickered sideways in a sick look.
"Eighty."

"Do so. At once."

The tall man snicked the Ingram's magazine out of the
weapon and slid a new one into place. "Come in on the left
side."

The DeHavilland banked through more altitude-losing turns.

Now it was loafing across the moonlit waves at a height of about a hundred feet. The Savoia loomed ahead. Its engine was sputtering. Rags of smoke leaked from it. The tall man crouched by the open window and once more fitted the magazine outside the frame, steadying it as he took aim.

"Closer."

"Too dangerous. The wash from the rotor."

"Closer, you bastard."

The pilot touched his steering wheel. The Twin Otter was almost abreast of the copter now and less than fifty yards away but the tall man had realized by now that in the moonlight distances were deceiving.

"Closer!"

The tall man watched the copter pilot aiming some kind of weapon at him. There was a sunburst of magnesium fire and a star-shell arched through the night sky, missing the DeHavilland by a yard. No other weapon than a Very pistol? The tall man grinned.

Recklessly, his pilot swung to the right, wing tip only yards from the Savoia. The tall man could see Ben's face, blue-white, his coal black eyes burning in the up-from-under red of his dashboard lights. The pursuer squinted down the barrel of the machine gun and squeezed off a long, chattering burst.

The helicopter seemed to fly apart. The rotor broke into separate blades. Each one scythed through the night, spinning on its own axis. The plastic bubble flew into flickering pieces, curved like shards of an exploded light bulb.

The tall man glanced back at where the copter had been. He saw one body hurled sideways into the sea. One of the spinning rotor blades sawed through the DeHavilland's right wing. The plane groundlooped to the left in a sickening arc that sliced into the sea. And then under it.

For some time the surface of the Mediterranean lay calm under the merciless eye of the moon. Then bits and pieces bobbed to the surface, random blobs and shards that disturbed the perfect symmetry of the night. Some pieces had been men.

54

Within sight of the cricket grounds at Lord's, not far from the London mosque built for the faithful in Regent's Park, stands a kind of ziggurat of a building which the unworldly, who have never spent time in an American hospital, refer to as "the most expensive hospital in the world." Its stepped-back profile provides a series of even small floors, each with long terraces that give patients both a room and a view of the heavy rush hour traffic twice a day along Finchley Road, or in some rooms, a far glimpse of cricketers at play.

The man sitting in a wheelchair on his terrace, watching a bad game of cricket without having to pay for the privilege, wore both a bandaged arm and a leg in plaster. A beaten-up old pair of trench field glasses, brass showing through rubbed-away places in the leather, lay in his lap. Slowly, his eyes closed under the weight of the summer sun. He slept.

Miranda, who had been visiting him, stood up and started to tiptoe out of the hospital suite. Julian Sykes-Maulby's eyes opened at once. "Fleeing so soon?"

"Jolly, I can't stay. Officially I'm not even here." She smiled down at him in his wheelchair. "But I couldn't resist bringing you the news in person."

"No doubt about it?"

"The very next Honors List."

He puffed out his cheeks, as if in chagrin. "I suppose this knighthood signals the end of my, er, arrangement with our mutual friend."

"You pious fraud. Haven't you promoted and wangled for this? You can't possibly have the cheek to complain about it now it's done."

He gave her a somewhat nasty grin. "Have you any idea, dear girl, what the title means to me in a business way?"

She shook her head. "I'd rather not know. Jolly, you performed services above and beyond the call of duty. Let's leave it at that."

He had the good grace to look ashamed. "Yes, let's."

She bent over and kissed the top of his head. "Nap time."

Moving swiftly out of his suite and down a hall, she nodded pleasantly to the nurse who had brought her and was now escorting a man and a woman. It was a pity, Miranda thought as she left the hospital by a side entrance, that Jolly couldn't announce his knighthood now. He'd get *so* much better service from the nurses.

On second thoughts, she reminded herself, nurses probably had a thing for him, with or without a title.

The plump, dark-haired nurse who ushered in the next two visitors paused at the door to the terrace. "He's dozed off," she said to the man and woman. Of the hospital's patients, the vast majority came from the Arab states. They were here because they could afford it and because the mostly Israeli staff spoke Arabic.

"I have not," Julian Sykes-Maulby called. He swung his wheelchair around in a blur of movement. "Oh, you two!" His face lit up as he wheeled himself inside, past Mary Lee Hunter and Curtiss towards a white Formica sideboard with a built-in refrigerator. "Champers?" he asked, bringing out a bottle with the familiar orange label.

The nurse poured three tulip glasses, full for the visitors, but barely an inch for the patient. "I warned you," Julian chided her. "If you pour a meager tot, you drink the rest." He turned to Curtiss. "She hates brut," he remarked. The nurse poured herself half a glass, blushing.

"Confusion to the enemy," Sykes-Maulby said, raising his glass.

"Whoever they may be," Curtiss intoned piously. Everyone drank.

"Don't let him have more," the plump nurse said, her cheeks bright red as she left the room.

"That means we have to finish it ourselves," Mary Lee pointed out.

"You two look disgustingly fit."

Curtiss shrugged. "How are the wounds coming along?"

"Whell." Julian made a small explosion of the word. "I shan't play the violin again," he explained facetiously, moving his arm, "but I'll still be able to outrun your average pretty girl." He patted his leg plaster. "Those damned Browning .9's take away half a shinbone, so they do. Mine's all stainless steel and nylon."

"Julian," Mary Lee asked, "no one has ever told us the story. Was this more of Ben's doing?"

He shook his head. "Top secret stuff, my dear."

"Bullshit," Curtiss announced.

"It had nothing to do with Ben, I can tell you. Poor devil."

The three were silent. Mary Lee sat in a rather expensively upholstered guest armchair, Curtiss on the edge of the bed. "I've just come from California," she told the Englishman. "I've persuaded B. J. to stay with us either here or in Paris."

"Us, is it?" Julian gave Curtiss a ghastly fake grin, his long face and nose puckering like Punch's.

Curtiss ignored the remark. "B. J. is in her sixth month, carrying Bennett Brown's baby. We have some evidence that the father may be dead, but officially he's only missing. In any event, his will is particularly clear. His 'son' inherits everything."

"Dear me, these emotional Italians." Sykes-Maulby sat back in his wheelchair and massaged his knee. "I do recall that most of these *mafiosi*, when they die, are found to have no assets whatsoever. The estates will have been stripped to avoid inheritance tax and so on."

"That may be so here," Mary Lee said. "In which case, B. J. needs all the help we can give her."

"But, if he's alive . . ." Sykes-Maulby let the idea die away.

"And staying out of sight deliberately . . ." Curtiss's thought also faded off.

"Then we've got a hostage in the form of a baby," Mary Lee finished for both of them. "If Ben's alive, we'll flush him out sooner or later."

"Meanwhile," Curtiss added, "he was last seen heading in the direction of Malta."

"A very popular island, suddenly," Julian mused. "My former business associate, Urs Rup, is there. It's an intriguing place for a financial wallah with high cash flow and low morality. A man—the right kind of johnnie—could buy himself a crushing amount of clout among the local bankers, brokers, politicos, coppers, military. It's a country in a state of fantastic flux. And danger. The two things produce moods of derring-do in which the itch to line one's pockets overcomes one's natural timidity and prudence. Yes, Malta. Umm."

Once again the three of them sat in silence. A rather glum note seemed to have settled over their shoulders like a gray cloak. "Here, here," Sykes-Maulby said, clapping his hands. "Champers for all!"

Mary Lee poured her glass and Curtiss's. "Has news of the last UBCO board meeting reached you?" she asked then in a tentative tone of voice.

"I may have a gammy leg but I still run a rather first-rate intelligence service from this damned wheelchair."

"Then you know what happened," Curtiss began.

"But not how."

Curtiss gestured rapidly, a mixing motion as of a squirrel in a rotating cage. "We had the goods on the bastards," he told the Englishman, "including the part they played in Bennett's Gameplan. And there was complicity in a murder. I mean, it was a blackmailer's dream."

"So you blackmailed them?"

"Don't ever use that word with Palmer," Curtiss warned him. "That's precisely what he went into the board meeting and did. He's had the stuff sealed away in safe deposit boxes around town with instructions to his lawyers in case he should meet with foul play. So he's safe enough. Over the next six months until the annual meeting, there will be some resignations from the board for reasons of personal health or family considerations. Not too many. Four. The rest have been happy as hell to be allowed to play ball with Palmer. He'll fire them later, when they least expect it. Meanwhile, he walks a tightrope."

"But who's his chief executive officer?" Julian asked. "And how is it explained to the financial press?"

"That's the beauty of the deal. It doesn't need explaining. Major-General Edward R. Hagen, USA, Ret., is still board chairman but Palmer has his balls in such a vice that Hagen can't make a move unless Palmer lets him. Hagen has reconstituted the executive committee as a four-man team, himself, two more tame bears and he's about to announce that UBCO is thrilled to be relying once again on the services of its former chief executive, Woods Palmer, Jr. That simple."

"Hardly that."

Curtiss paused. "You would have loved it. Shootout at the O.K. Corral. Bodies all over the floor, particularly that bastard Charley Oakburn. Early retirement, they called it, but in his case, no pension."

"And who was handed over to the police?"

Curtiss glanced at Mary Lee. "What kind of talk is that? We're bankers, not cops. You would have been proud of

Palmer," he went on then. "He dangled that murder over each and every one of them, but privately. In the board room, it was all chillingly polite. Even Oakburn took his lumps like a little soldier."

"But surely he wasn't the—"

"No. A fella named Kummel. Apparently he ordered the hit from one of the families, the Luccheses. And then, the usual follow-up. Kummel should have known that when you call in a hit that way, you then have guilty knowledge. So his car crashed into a ramp support of the feed-in to the George Washington Bridge. He was going eighty at the time. The cops figure that something happened to the steering *and* the accelerator cable at about the same moment. That kind of precision is very professional and terribly expensive. It doesn't pay us back for the loss of Bill Elston, though." He lapsed into silence.

"And you called it all simple?" the older man asked.

"Blood simple."

"Blood simple," Julian echoed. Then he laughed silently. The Punch-like resemblance became almost too realistic. "So Woods has had to forsake his mountain eyrie after all. Eleanora won't like it."

"She's already closed the place," Mary Lee said, "and taken a temporary flat in Lugano."

"But surely Woods will want her by his side in Manhattan?"

Mary Lee sipped her champagne slowly. "It's not that kind of relationship, Julian," she said then. "It's fluid. Changing. Eleanora's starting up a business of her own, a translation bureau. Palmer's staking her to it. For the next few months they'll both be too busy, anyway. And then . . ." She sat back in the armchair and smiled very slightly.

"My word." Sykes-Maulby wheeled his chair over to the sideboard and poured himself another inch of champagne. "The world *is* changing. Here's to it, then." He lifted his glass. "What about you two?"

"What about us?" Mary Lee fended him off.

Immediately, Julian seemed to retreat behind a wall of British tergiversation. "That is . . . you know . . . one feels a certain sense of . . . but of course it's none of my . . . and in any event . . . well, there it is."

Curtiss cracked a broad grin. "Absolutely," he agreed. "We're going to be as forthcoming as that explanation you didn't give us about how you copped the arm and leg."

"But I told you, old boy. Top secret."

The younger man turned to Mary Lee. "You satisfied with that?"

"I haven't bought 'top secret' as an excuse since the days of Richard M. Nixon." She patted the arms of her chair. "But it can't hurt if I tell you we're on leaves of absence, Curtiss and I."

"Really?" Sykes-Maulby's eyes sparkled maliciously. "How American. Have the old cake and eat it too."

He wheeled himself to the side of the bed opposite where Curtiss was sitting and, before anyone could offer to help, had boosted himself expertly onto the bed and under the sheets. He lay there, propped halfway up. "So old Woods is back in the saddle. Nose to the grindstone sort of thing. How he must hate it."

"I didn't have that big a job convincing him," Curtiss recalled. "Not after I found another word for blackmail."

"Every man his price. In the case of those Mafia puppets at the helm of UBCO, the price is silence . . . and no punishment whatsoever. Not a hard deal to accept. In Palmer's case he's protecting all his UBCO shares from turning into toilet tissue. Still . . ." He shook his head. "Palmer is balmy on the subject of staying *out* of the ratrace. But here he is, King Rat."

"Again," Curtiss added.

"Yes," Julian said in a doubtful tone. "There's that. But one mustn't probe too deeply into the whys and wherefores of an old friend one's about to do business with."

"Again," Curtiss added.

A flicker of irritation crossed the Englishman's face. "If I detect a pejorative note, Curtiss, why did you aid and abet his takeover—or is it a takeback?—of UBCO?"

"I owed him one," Curtiss explained. "He was badly conflicted over this. It's hard to watch a thing like that. Business is not the real world for a lot of us. The way you make a living is not supposed to eat up your life. Well, it does, especially for your generation. So I sort of nudged him back on the rails and he did the rest of it quite neatly. Coldbloodedly."

"Is that your philosophy as well?" Julian asked Mary Lee.

"I have always been scared stiff of Palmer," Mary Lee confessed. "He's always seemed like one of those, uh, Tokomak machines. You know?"

"Not bloody likely."

"They build up this plasma of ionized particles," she explained. "The idea is to shape it into a container for a controlled nuclear fusion that produces energy. The way the sun does."

"Ah."

"In one form its got this Tokomak name, from the Russians. I have always seen Palmer as plasma without a safe container. He's always seemed dangerous to me. So have you."

A look almost of pride suffused the Englishman's face. "Really? How flattering. But you think UBCO will be the proper container for Mr. Plasma?"

"You tell me," she countered.

"We old birds," Sykes-Maulby began. Then he stopped and his eyes unfocused, staring out the window at a cricket pitch he couldn't see from this angle. "We old birds were trained in a different school from you young'uns. I quite understand Woods, wanting to stay away from it but when it goes wrong, unable to keep from grabbing control. I mean, look at me. If I told you this gammy leg and arm had not a damned thing to do with making money. If I told you I behaved like an absolute idiot in a Wild West shootout with some johnnies I couldn't even see. If I told you I get nothing out of this except hospital bills. I mean . . . I mean . . . you'd think me the bloodiest fool in England."

"Nothing?" Curtiss asked.

An odd look came over Julian's face. "Well . . ." He stopped and made pursey movements with his lips as if tasting something like a quince. "The old *quid pro quo* some day, perhaps," he suggested airily. "Somewhere. Somehow."

Curtiss nodded complacently. He let a moment of silence pass. "If he's alive," he said then, "Ben may try to get through to you. B. J., Mary Lee and I would love to know if that happens."

"Will you be here in London?"

"Here or at the Cité Odiot, rue Washington, Paris."

"I mean do you have a place to stay here?"

"We're in a service flat. People on extended leave have to watch their expenses."

Julian pointed to the drawer of his bedside table. "There are keys to my Kinnerton Street place. I won't be back in it for at least a month. It would be a tremendous help to know friends were using it."

Curtiss slid open the drawer. "No gumshoes flatfooting around?"

"I promise you the coppers have lost interest in it."

The younger man pocketed the keys. "Very decent of you."

Sykes-Maulby gestured. "English-Speaking Union, all that rot." He looked at Mary Lee. "And I promise when Ben calls, I'll get word to you."

"When he calls?"

"Did I say that? I'm afraid I'm an incurable optimist. *If* he calls, then." The older man settled back on his pillows. "All that champers," he said in a soft voice, "has made one quite torpid."

His eyelids lowered. Curtiss eased off the bed and tipped his head in the direction of the door. He and Mary Lee left the room. Beyond it lay an anteroom where the usual patient, someone of at least the rank of sheik, would install his bodyservant. In this area they crossed paths with the Israeli nurse, who nodded pleasantly as the young couple left.

She stood in the doorway of Julian's room. Seeing him asleep, she decided not to tell him yet that his Malta call had come through.

55

North of the main island of Malta lie two more, all together making the country called Malta. One island, Comino, is hardly more than a speck of land which, nevertheless, is the source of the spice cumin. The big island, Malta, with its deep harbors and pink chalk landscape, is largely a sterile land on which it is hard to grow much vegetation. But on Gozo, the last of the three, nature has been less forbidding. Crops flourish. Cattle graze. Grapes are cultivated for wine. Gozo's beaches, tiny fingernail parings of sand lying beneath pink limestone cliffs, are secluded.

It is an island of rather luxurious private villas. The Villa Margit, for example, stands on a headland at the northeast point of Gozo, not far from Ramla Bay and the town of Marsalforn. Although the Gameplan consortium bought the place, Urs Rup named it after his wife, and his mistress. From its carefully traditional—almost Palladian—windows the villa looks northward some eighty miles to Punta Religione on the south coast of Sicily.

Visitors to Villa Margit can take a rambling walk along the rocky shore to the original, authentic, unique Cave of Calypso, one of many to be found throughout the Mediterranean. Further inland, but still only a few minutes by car, lie the monumental megaliths and cyclopean ruins of Ggantija, relict of the Bronze Age.

But Villa Margit rarely has visitors. Supplies are occasionally ferried across the eighty-mile strait from Sicily in a small boat captained by its owner, Athanasios Zigouras. He calls his boat *Madonna Gioiosa*, after his native town on the Ionic coast of Calabria for, despite his Greek name, Athanasios is a first cousin of Don B.

The *Madonna Gioiosa* is a fishing boat, shielded at the prow by a small cuddy cabin and overpowered by a V-6 engine stripped from an old Pontiac.

Athanasios unloads at the beachside dock belonging to Villa Margit. It does not occur to him to wonder why the occasional occupants of Villa Margit send all the way to Sicily for supplies, rather than buy them in Victoria, Gozo's main town. It would even be possible to have them delivered by boat from Valetta or Marfa on the main island. But, perhaps, thinks Athanasios, what I bring them from Italy is fresher, tastier. Who knows the vagaries of the rich? Especially the rich under Don B's protective hand.

This time a lovely blond woman with glorious breasts barely hidden behind tiny bikini cups came down seven flights of stairs cut into the beige-pink limestone to bid Athanasios goodbye.

"You will remember to mail these," Margit urged the captain. She placed a plastic bag containing letters in Athanasios' hands.

"Most certainly, *bellissima donna*."

"In the Syracuse post office."

"Most certainly." Athanasios fiddled with the painter rope, knowing he had to untie and move off, but wanting to watch the play of her nearly naked body as she made slight, meaningless movements so close to him. "The gentleman is better?" he asked. "Last week he seemed quite weak."

"Yes, much better," Margit told him. "The blood was, as you know, from superficial wounds. But he needs much rest before he leaves us. He owes you a great debt of gratitude."

"It was nothing. When I saw the star-burst in the sky, I knew someone was in trouble."

Margit nodded gravely. She had worn a thin robe over her bikini but the unwavering regard of the captain's eyes was beginning to unnerve her. *"Buon viaggio, capitano,"* she said, handing him a separate envelope. "The gentleman asked me to give you this."

She turned and left, Athanasios' fierce gaze following the jut and waggle of her buttocks as she strode off the dock and began mounting the first flight of seven.

Then he looked down at the envelope. He knew it would be a reward. Therefore a treat. He liked to prolong treats. He untied the *Madonna Gioiosa* and switched on the engine. Shifting into reverse, he backed away from the dock in a neat half circle, then put the drive-shaft into forward gear and fed more gas to the V-6 engine.

A powerful snoring sound echoed back from the chalky cliffs as the boat lifted her bow and sped northward through the Mediterranean. Only then, casting a casual eye on his compass, did Athanasios Zigouras open the envelope. A broad grin split his swarthy face as he counted the 10,000-lira notes. There were ten of them.

As a living, saving drowning men was far more lucrative than smuggling heroin, the usual work of the *Madonna Gioiosa*.

At the top of the cliff stairs, Margit stopped to catch her breath. She was too young to let even seven flights wind her this way, she thought. This next month would be a good time in which to diet down a few kilos. The villa was more like a clinic these days, anyway.

She had very little else to keep her occupied except her two patients. Urs, shivering as if with the ague, was detoxifying in the master bedroom. He had sniffed his last line of white, shot his last skag, or so he swore. Margit noted that he had made no promises about pot.

Her other patient, until the sea yielded his almost lifeless body up to her last week, had only been a voice on the satellite-relay. He lay in deep depression. There was nothing physically wrong with him that a night of clinging to a styrofoam float couldn't account for. But his listless manner, lifeless gaze, poor appetite, inability to respond except in rare monosyllables, all convinced Margit that she had two mental cases on her hands.

Her high-heeled wooden clogs clattered across the marble sweep of terrace that led from the cliff stairs to the villa's grand living room, presenting three windowed walls to the sea. Urs, unshaven and grubby with sweat, lounged in the darkest corner of the room, playing with the television set and getting nowhere.

In a chaise-longue across the room, so sunk into the upholstery that she almost failed to see his long, skinny frame, lay Bennett Brown. The pink pages of the *Financial Times* whispered between his dry fingers. His big, black eyes flickered sideways, as if reading down a column of type, but Margit had noticed that he never seemed to reach the end of such reading. Often he would let the newspaper or magazine fall, but his eyes would continue to flicker across the fabric of his jeans, or the parquetry of the floor, as if reading it for news of the outside world.

"The sailor's gone," Margit told Urs. "I don't think he understands who he picked up, but with the Italians one never knows. Let's not use him again."

Urs had difficulty responding. His teeth began to chatter. Tears sprang up in his eyes. He sniffed mightily and tried to pull himself together.

"Because," he said, as if having paused in the middle of a sentence, "if he ever finds out he saved the Crown Prince's life, he'll t-tell the whole world. The next thing we'll have is a hostile invasion f-force that makes Anzio B-Beach look like a p-picnic."

"An amphibious landing might be a welcome change." She eyed Ben across the immense room. "Has he said much this morning?"

"N-nothing," Urs stammered as a spasm suddenly shook him. "Goddamn this cold t-turkey!"

"Time for another Librium." She got to her feet.

"In ruins," Ben croaked suddenly.

Both Swiss turned to stare at him. "The whole Gameplan in ruins," he told them in a voice so choked that it sounded like an old man's.

Urs struggled to his feet and limped across the room. "D-don't forget, Benny," he encouraged him, "the p-plan may be ruined. But—" He dropped to his knees by the chaise-longue and took both Ben's hands in his. "Are y-you listening to me, Benny?"

There was no response. The big, dark eyes rolled listlessly in Bennett Brown's head. They seemed opaque, leading nowhere.

"The p-plan is gone," Urs Rup assured him, "but, baby, we have the s-securities."

A shock wave of tremors seemed to buffet the young banker. He settled back against the leg of the chaise-longue and concentrated on living through the spasm. Then he took a long breath. "We have the stocks, Benny," he said more calmly. "Every certificate of ownership is ours. That's clout, baby. They have to treat us with respect."

Something stirred behind the ripe-olive irises in Ben's eyes. He pushed the newspaper aside. "He was dead already," he announced in a ragged voice. "Dead when I strapped him in."

But Urs seemed to have fallen asleep. "What do you mean?" Margit asked.

Ben gazed up at her with such a pitiful look that she went to him. "My father," he explained and burst into tears. Margit sat beside him and rocked him back and forth for a long time. Tears poured down his face. Lying on the floor, Urs snored and wept and snored in his sleep.

Orphans of the storm. Margit's pretty mouth quirked upward at one end in a tight smile. At last count something like thirty billion Swiss francs' worth of securities were hidden away throughout the world and coded into the Villa Margit computer. Only these two helpless waifs knew the access codes.

It was hard, Margit realized, to feel sorry for these two. Both had brought it on themselves, Urs with his drug-taking, Ben with an excess of misplaced filial devotion. Of the two, she preferred Ben, but he had never been her lover. Perhaps because he had never been.

Also, to her mind, Ben seemed to be coming out of his trouble more quickly. There was more backbone to him than to Urs, whose life resembled that of a sea slug, alternately comatose or shaking with ague. If one were unfortunate enough to have to rely on one or the other, relying on Ben was a gamble. Relying on Urs was simply not possible.

The telephone rang. She took her arms away from Ben and

handed him back his newspaper, which he continued reading. "Hello?"

"Darling girl," Julian Sykes-Maulby began. "How is Sick Bay?"

"How are you, may one ask?"

"Mending. Any problems?"

Margit quickly described the two young men's condition. "But we're supplied for a long stay," she concluded. "The boat brought enough food for a month." She paused. "One thing. The sailor did ask about Ben. And I did give him the reward. Now I'm not so sure it was right."

There was a longish pause at the London end of the conversation. Then: "You may have less time there than you expect, sweet one. It's fatuous to assume Don Gino won't, in the fullness of time, learn that Ben is still alive and thus in dire need of killing."

"Possibly."

"Meanwhile, you're doing those two no good letting them mend on their own. What Urs needs is medical treatment. As for Ben, perhaps a spot of psychologizing might be the ticket. But you certainly can't just sit there, hoping for the best. Whereas here in London I can get them the absolute tops in medical care."

And keep my hands on the access numbers, Margit added silently. "You may be right, darling," she said at length. "You usually are."

"Ah, the voice of sweet reason, agreeing with me, as always. When can I expect you?"

"Soon. Urs really can't travel."

On the northeast corner of Malta, dawn hits early. Margit awoke under the pressure of sunlight flaring through chinks in her bedroom draperies. In her dream she had been on a magnificent ocean-going yacht which Julian owned. The two of them were making their way around the world, stopping at exotic and charming ports of call.

For a moment, her eyes still closed, Margit brooded over the fact that she was as much a prisoner as her two charges. Then she realized that the beat of marine engines in her dream was a reality. She pushed aside a corner of the heavy damask curtain and saw what looked like a 60-foot motor yacht moving slowly into anchorage off the Villa Margit dock. At the prow two men in jeans and tee-shirts stood poised to

drop the heavy anchor. In the open stern near the entryway
to the cabin, five more men were lowering an inflated rubber
boat with an outboard engine on it. All five were carrying
guns in holsters.

Margit jumped out of bed, pulled on her clothes and raced
for Urs's bedroom. "Wake up, please!"

His lank blond hair, matted with sweat, hung down over
his face like seaweed. He stared at her. *"Was gibt?"* He fell
asleep again in the middle of a yawn.

She ran into Ben's room. "Up! Up! They're here."

His black eyes opened wide. "Gino's men?" He was halfway out of bed. "Can Urs get—?"

"No. We have to leave him."

"I can't—"

"We must," she cut in. "They don't want him anyway."

It wasn't until later that she remembered. At first there
was too much to do, dressing Ben, getting him to curl up in
the luggage trunk of the little white Renault 5-TS and silently
coasting away from the Villa Margit without starting the
engine. Behind her, Margit could hear gunfire.

Surely Urs was asleep? Surely he had no gun to return fire.
The invaders must simply be trying to force a bloodless
surrender. She turned the key and jump-started the Renault
half a mile down the hill from the villa. Ben lay completely
hidden from view inside the closed trunk.

The roads through Gozo were twisting, surrounded by
luxuriant tropical trees and vines. Margit had no idea what
kind of surveillance she was under, if any. This only made her
more fearful. A rural crossroads with a single gasoline pump
stirred visions in her of Don Gino spies hiding everywhere.

The pale white car ghosted into the ferry landing at the
village of Mgarr and braked to a halt in front of a seedy
hotel-cum-bar. No ferry stood at the dock. Margit glanced at
the dashboard clock and saw that it lacked ten minutes of
seven a.m. "Ben? Is there enough air?"

"More or less. Why the pause?"

"Ferry's not in."

She could see it in the distance across the channel that
separated the main island from Mgarr. It had just left the
Malta landing with a few cars and a few early-morning people
on their way to work in Gozo.

Overhead a helicopter hovered above the channel. It was
not one of the government machines, neither police nor

military. Margit's heart began to thump. She tried to work out how she might invade the Villa Margit. Arriving by sea was foolish. Opening fire as one climbed the stairs to the villa was childish.

As the ferry drew nearer, a flat, bargelike craft with wire cable handrail around it, Margit could see a knot of men at the bow. Behind them stood a white pickup truck, empty. The men were unarmed, or so it seemed at this distance, but there was a similarity of size and age that made Margit think they were the real invasion force.

"Ben, I'm leaving the car for a while. Be cool."

"You, too."

She moved the 5-TS, using its body as a shield, until she was behind the hotel building. The ferry bumped gently into its mooring. Margit watched six or seven men jump into the back of the pickup, while two others got into the truck's cab. The instant the ferry barrier dropped there was a blat of dark exhaust smoke and a fearful roar as the pickup shot forward onto the dock and disappeared along the road to the Villa Margit, leaving a thick plume of dust behind it.

There had to be radio contact, she told herself. The people who had come from the sea and this load in the truck had to be coordinated from the copter overhead. She got back behind the wheel of the Renault and watched the empty ferry standing in its dock. "Ben?"

"I haven't left."

"When I yell, brace yourself."

Margit's glance moved back and forth between the ferry, the helicopter and her rear-view mirror. She saw the ferrymaster light a cigarette. He seemed in no hurry to recross the channel and, in any event, he had no customers at this hour. Time passed. A tiny bead of perspiration rolled down between Margit's neatly shaped eyebrows and ended at the slightly upturned tip of her short nose. She dabbed it off with a wisp of handkerchief.

The ferrymaster flicked his cigarette into the water. Margit started the overpowered 5-TS engine. The ferrymaster cast off one line. Margit watched the copter overhead moving northeast to take up a new position over the Villa Margit.

The ferrymaster slipped off the second hawser. He moved forward to the control box. Margit saw his hand reach for the throttle of the engine. She shifted into first gear and tramped on the accelerator of the Renault.

The tiny white car shot forward with an eager howl. The ferry was starting to move away from the dock. Margit shifted into second. The speedometer showed she was doing thirty kilometers an hour already. She floored the gas pedal and the car leaped over a five-foot gap of water.

The front wheels, churning with power, bit into the wooden deck of the ferry and hauled the car forward to safety. The ferrymaster glanced at her in surprise. He started to yell at her, then got a look at her face.

"*Carina mia*," he called. "You like taking chances?"

Margit shrugged prettily. "I have to be at the airport to meet my dear father," she told him.

"You'll be there in half an hour."

It was then, her mind occupied with making the first flight out to London, that Margit remembered the most important thing. In leaving Urs behind she had made the conscious triage necessary in emergencies. The weak are left behind. And it was true, as she had told Ben, that Don Gino's men had little interest in Urs.

Except that, in his drug-battered head, lay the same access codes as in Ben's.

56

Summer was nearly over. The crowds of August had deserted the Côte d'Azur beaches. With September arrived the maroon and black Citroën 2CV6 "Charleston" painted in huge looping Art Deco circles with silver trim. Curtiss had bought it used when he shut up the Cité Odiot apartment.

He and the two women had come slowly down the beautiful center of France, down the valleys of the Dordogne and the Lot into Perigord, then Nîmes and Arles and Avignon.

Curtiss had gone back to travel writing. The baby inside B. J. was nine months old. The weather was cool and sunny.

They had found a small apartment with a view of the harbor at St. Jean Cap Ferrat in a hotel called Les Tourterelles. Although it had a pool—kept quite clean by French standards—the weather was a bit too cool for swimming. They drove up into the hills, watched them blow glass at Biot, make perfume in Grasse. They attended a wild *vernissage* of an American painter named Steve Carpenter in a village perched high above the coast called Rocquebrune. More of an open block party, the *vernissage* went on all day and all evening with wine and food. No paintings were left unsold.

It was dusk now. The three of them strolled slowly along the chichi harborfront of the port at St. Jean. Curtiss was reminiscing about the way it had been before the town had enlarged and prettified it. They moved at a leisurely pace out of deference to B. J., who had not grown bigger during the last few months, but carried her child lower and, if anything, more awkwardly.

"I absolutely refuse," she said then, coming to a halt where they could watch the rose sky of sunset darken beyond the Voile D'Or hotel.

"It takes no time at all," Mary Lee argued. "And at least you know the sex of your child."

"I'll know it soon enough."

The incontrovertible wisdom of this silenced them all. Finally, B. J. broke it with a question in a small voice. "Are we looking in the direction of Malta?"

"More or less," Curtiss indicated the direction. "But you've got Corisca and Sardinia and Sicily in the way. B. J., let me tell you something."

"Curtiss," Mary Lee began on a warning note.

"She's a big girl now," he responded. "We have to stop pretending Ben may still be alive. This was a man who gave his life to save his father's. You understand what family meant to him. Such a man is not going to keep hidden when his son is about to be born."

"Such a man," Mary Lee added, "is perfectly capable of having had the three of us under surveillance all this time. There are compelling reasons why he has to stay hidden, but don't think he can't keep tabs."

"Who cares?" B. J. asked then.

Curtiss frowned at her. "Be sensible, B. J."

"I meant it, people. In me you see a lady perfectly capable of handling the fact that the no-good, lying psychopath who sired this infant will not be around to fuck up its life. Oh, my, yes, can I handle that?"

She nodded gravely and began massaging the lower part of her back. Mary Lee moved behind her and continued the massage. "You're forgetting the money," Curtiss told B. J. "If he's dead, there is a lot of loot that goes to you and your child."

"Who cares?" B. J. repeated. "Did any of us hurt for money this summer? Lower. There. Harder. Oh, yes. To the right. Yes! *Yes!*"

Mary Lee burst out laughing. "People will think..." She shook her head, but kept up the massage. "You see," she went on then, "this is that dark male world I warned you about, B. J. Curtiss understands that world. In that world men kill each other for money. They murder themselves for money. And for the kind of nestegg Ben would have left you, men would wipe out whole countries and races."

"Nobody listens to me," B. J. complained. "When I say 'who cares?' it's a matter of utter indifference to me. It's the will-o-the-wisp the two of us were chasing all those years, Mary Lee. And it always leads down a rat-hole."

"Money?"

"Not the kind of money Ben was sitting on," B. J. told her. "It was driving him insane. The decisions. The gut-eating necessity to guess right. And in the process he died for it. Do you remember how he was when we met him?"

Mary Lee nodded. "Much nicer."

"Much poorer. I have a theory. In his family he was supposed to go straight. He was to be a professor or something. But you can't fight genes." She stared at a Bermuda ketch tacking in out of the east. The mainsail dropped and a lone figure began wrapping it around the boom. The ketch moved on under engine power, edging slowly into its berth.

"Here I am, spoiling a perfect sunset," B. J. mused. "I really wanted that painting I nearly bought."

"What would we do with it?" Mary Lee wanted to know. "We're gypsies."

"Not after this one is born," B. J. reminded her. "And I can't keep sponging off you at the Cité Odiot."

"You stay as long as you want," Curtiss said. "You and Junior."

"It's just big enough for the two of you." B. J. hesitated. "Just before I left the States for Paris somebody named Freddie Marston called me to ask where I wanted the check sent. 'What check?' I asked him. He gave me some mumbo-jumbo about a trust fund that automatically activated. So where should he send the check? I told him—" She gave a hoot. "I told him how to roll them up and where to put them. Now I'll have to give him a real address."

They began strolling again, rounded the near end of the port and climbed up the slight hill onto the main street of town. At the Civet Niçoise bar on the corner they chose one of the empty outdoor tables. Curtiss and Mary Lee ordered Pernod and B. J. took an orange soda. The light was dying in the sky. Across the street a bus loaded passengers for nearby towns between Cap Ferrat and Nice.

One of the passengers, a slight young man in a pale sports shirt, failed to board the bus. Instead he stood at the railing of the belvedere, looking out at the harbor as the bus pulled away. Not for the first time this summer, Curtiss found himself wondering if, as Mary Lee had suggested, the three of them had been under surveillance. There had been someone else in Nîmes and for several days along the roads south of Mâcon there had been a pale green Peugeot behind them now and then. Even here, a young man somewhat like this one had wandered the crooked up-and-down bricked pathways of Rocquebrune. It would never have done to use the same man all the time. But perhaps Ben's organization was pinched for personnel.

Curtiss turned his glance from the young man to Mary Lee, who had seen the whole thing. Neither of them spoke now.

B. J. pointed in a southerly direction. "That way?" she asked.

"Hm?"

"That way to Malta?"

Curtiss nodded. They sipped their drinks and the scent of orange and anise mingled in the soft evening air. Silence. The closing of shop shutters. Another bus arrived. A few people got on. The bus left. The young man in the pale shirt was sitting on a bench across the way, near where the flower woman set up shop each morning.

Silence.

57

At eleven thousand feet, dawn breaks fast over the Sangre de Cristo range. An orange rim burns the bowl of indigo black to the east. Suddenly the sun explodes the sky into fierce azure from east to west.

In the solarium cube at Snowfire, the tall, thin young man came awake at once, his deep black eyes squinting as he glanced at his wristwatch. He rolled off his bunk and made for the semi-dark of the terminal room. It was six a.m. in New Mexico but financial markets in most European cities were already teeming with action.

Bennett Brown seated himself at one of the keyboards and prepared to play his kind of music. He had arrived late the previous night after taking three airlines and using two copter connections to disguise his trail from London. No one, not Margit, not Julian, not Freddie Marston, knew where he was.

By the time they did he would be gone. It was the start of a new existence for Ben, the theme of which would be "hit and run."

This morning it would take no more than half an hour to search and override access codes in Frankfurt, Milan, London and New York. Once changed, only he—alone in the world— could get at the Gameplan securities. Then he would be off again, moving in and out of the shadows. If he needed help, he would use the few men he had personally trained, not the treacherous support seconded to him by other families of organized crime.

His mistake, he reminded himself as he punched in the Gameplan access program and watched it unfold on his video, had been to rely on people whose motives were their own, not his.

From now on, he would stay on the move. He needed only a few minutes now and then at some computer terminal somewhere in the world to continue his work. From such a

terminal he could reach out to the Gameplan portfolio
add, subtract, shift to his heart's content.

Staring at the access codes on the video, he decided on
simple conversion formula. Divide each nine-bit into three
sets. Transpose one for three or two for one, and so forth. His
fingers tapped out the override commands.

Rank by rank, the shining green numbers began their
dance. They broke apart, recombined. Inched upwards. As a
music lover hears Bach, Ben watched the sheer physical
prodigiousness of the patterns. Bigger, his own pride demanded.

He switched them to a display projector that covered the
rear wall with his new access codes writ large. His! The
global hoard of Gameplan was his alone.

He knew he was cut off from more cash. Not important.
What he had was enough. The leverage was powerful in a
game where leverage was all. Leverage and now, as a lone
wolf, secrecy. How could he lose?

Repressing a grin of triumph, Ben switched the computer
to an alternate memory module that contained the Kondratiev
program. Instantly the rear wall of the terminal room was
covered with the joy and sorrow of the past two centuries.
The ups and downs glittered like the ragged fangs of some
fabulous dragon. Prosperity followed depression in great jolting
shock waves of 50 to 60 years each.

Bennett Brown sat back with some satisfaction and watched
the wave of the 1980s reform and crash. This time he allowed
himself a smile. It was a lonely act of triumph and he knew it.
His father dead, his wife deliberately kept in ignorance,
Urs . . . dead, perhaps? But he had learned by his one mistake. This time he would go it alone, slipping in and out of
deserted offices by night, using his most trusted people
sparingly if at all.

He might not surface for a long time, but it would be in a
triumph the whole world would be forced to admit. He had
no idea how old his son would be by the time he was able to
hold him in his arms. Not long, he hoped. A year. Two? Not
long.

This time he would do it all by himself. And he would do it
right.